CW00521904

NO OPTION

A JACKSON SHAW NOVEL

Acknowledgement

Firstly, I would like to thank my wife Zoe for all her support while I was writing this.

Secondly, I would like to thank Louis and Dave, who were my Guinea pigs for this project. Their input has been priceless in keeping me focussed on finishing it. It has been a journey of discovery for me, and very satisfying from a personal perspective. Lastly, I would like to thank you for taking the time to read this. I set out just to see if I could write something worth reading.

I hope that you will share my enthusiasm as you follow this journey.

First paperback edition January 2022

Book design by Darren Frazer
Front cover image by Zachary DeBottis
Back cover image by Karolina Grabowska

ISBN 979-8-4048-5934-8 (paperback)

Chapter 1

Ultimatum

Jackson opened his eyes and everything was black. Panic set in immediately. "Am I blind? " He thought. He reached out to feel his surroundings. Suddenly his fingers felt something solid in front of his face. He reached out to the side, and again a hard surface met him with a stubborn unyielding resistance.

"Oh my God!" he screamed, as the realisation hit him. He was in a box. Suddenly, the air became hot and he was struggling to breathe. The panic began to take hold of him, he thrashed wildly at the surface in front of him, but it was not going to budge.

"Help….Is there anybody there?" He screamed at the top of his lungs. The hoarseness in his throat was beginning to burn like acid. His breaths became frantic. As if the box was answering him, it began to rock from side to side, faster and faster. Then out of nowhere, he dropped and stopped abruptly.

He woke in the same panic. He focused in front of him. He was in a seat. His senses returned to him as the plane jolted and bucked in the obvious turbulence. Relief washed over him as the realisation of his nightmare ending brought his heart rate back under control.

Jackson looked around him. Had anyone seen him? Thankfully, nobody was taking any notice of him. The two seats next to him were vacant, which was a relief. Jackson's claustrophobia developed when he was a child. When he was at school, some kids in his class locked him into a small cupboard just for kicks. From that moment, it became his only true fear.

He landed at San Diego International Airport. He had travelled to LAX, and then took a hop to San Diego. Customs and baggage was a mere formality. It was early evening and the lights outside gave the palm trees a yellow glow. The Mid-June heat gave the air a muggy feel. He hailed a taxi with little effort, as the airport was uncharacteristically quiet for this time of the year. He had booked this trip at the last minute. It was going to help him switch off and decide what to do with the rest of his life.

As the taxi trundled through the streets, Jackson zoned out. His was mind racing through the events of the last few months. Back in the UK, Jackson was a promising Detective Sergeant in the Metropolitan Police. He had joined up after leaving the Army for a new challenge. He found that he adjusted to life as a civilian very easily, although he did miss the camaraderie that the Army instilled in him. He rose through the ranks in the police force quickly. He had a knack for being able to see things others did not. Almost like a sixth sense. He could look at a scene and the clues just seem to appear in front of him. Everything was rosy. Until it wasn't!

During his last case, he was investigating a child sex ring. Four men from Belarus were shipping young girls to the UK, forcing them into prostitution in order to pay off their debts. During one interview session, Jackson had been questioning a man named Pulev on the whereabouts of the safe house that they were holding the new arrivals.

The smirk on Pulev's face as he answered every question with "No comment" snapped something inside Jackson's head. He sprang from his chair, grabbing Pulev by the throat. Lifting him up off his chair, Jackson slammed him against the wall. Instantly the red mist descended on him. He rained blow after blow into Pulev's face. The bones in

Pulev's nose became so broken that his nose took on a fluid like state. When Jackson had regained his composure, he was staring at a mangled mess of a face, and a Chief Superintendent glaring at him.

The disciplinary was brief. Resign or be prosecuted, so he resigned and kissed goodbye to his career. So here he was, trying to make sense of his future options. Danny would know what to do. He always did.

The taxi pulled up outside a terracotta bungalow on Windsor Drive. Box hedges lined the front garden, which surrounded a cherry tree standing proudly as centrepiece to this dated but inviting property. It wasn't the largest place he had seen, but it was well maintained. Danny was meticulous in his presentation of anything he owned.

After paying the extortionate taxi fare, Jackson dragged his heavy bag up to the door and rang the ornate bell. It was a sculptured cherub holding the buzzer aloft. Immediately the bass boom of a dog filled the void. As the door opened, Jackson felt the full force on his chest, sending him sprawling onto the lawn. Max was a Golden Retriever, big, hairy and adored Jackson. Although he only saw him once a year, Max instantly knew him, subsequently covering him with wet, slimy affection.

A deep booming voice erupted from the doorway. "Max! Leave him alone for God's sake!"

Danny Hughes was a big man. Standing at six feet and three inches, he filled the doorway easily. His muscular frame and Germanic blonde hair and blue eyes made him a firm favourite with the ladies. He was ruggedly handsome, but had a steely stare that could intimidate even the hardest soldier. Danny was Jackson's Sergeant in the Parachute Regiment that they both served. Always firm, but fair, he and Jackson became firm friends instantly. At 5'11", Jackson was a lot smaller than Danny was, but his wiry stature disguised his immense strength.

The grin spreading across Danny's face widened. "Well, Shaw! You gonna just stand there like a muppet?".

They embraced, as only guys who have been through life or death situations together can. Down the cramped hallway to the left was a decent sized living room. Large cream corner sofa hugged the edges that faced a 60-inch TV and a fireplace loaded with pictures and ornaments. Bright and airy it had a warm but efficient feel. They passed by this and entered the kitchen. It was enormous. Large Island in its centre housed the cooker top with hanging copper pans from steel frame. The large split oven took up most of the far wall. Jackson took a seat at a vast dining table. Although there was only Danny and his wife, Cathy living there, Danny always liked to be able to accommodate everyone.

"Brew?" Danny said, "Or beer?"

Jackson rolled his eyes. "Beer, definitely."

"How was your flight?"

"Flights," Jackson corrected, "yeah, they were ok, surprisingly quiet. Sorry for just landing on you, I know it was short notice, but I just had to get away!"

Danny just smiled at him. "Mi Casa, Su Casa, amigo! So, what's been happening? Why the urge to come Stateside?"

Jackson massaged his temples; the journey had drained the energy out of him and he felt 100 years old. "Just let things get to me, my temper. You know how it is."

Danny shook his head and smiled. "Oh yes I know that one. You really need to wind that in mate!"

"I know, but I can't change just like that."

Danny handed him a cold bottle, the condensation immediately clouding the clear glass. Jackson rubbed the moisture off and wiped it across his forehead. He felt like he was lost. Hoping something or someone would spark him into gear.

He spent the next hour telling Danny everything that had happened to him in the last year, it made for a grim narrative. Lost his job, threatened with prison, lost his wife and his daughter will not speak to him.

"Jeez mate, that's quite a list!"

"Yeah tell me about it, hence I am here Brother!"

Danny looked at him with a worried expression. "You ain't thinking of doing anything stupid are you?"

Jackson looked up from his clasped hands. "Nah...I'm not that bad yet."

"Well you know where the spare room is. Go and sort your shit out and we can have some food. Cath's back from the store in an hour."

Jackson's voice croaked with emotion. "Thanks mate!" For the first time in a few months, he actually felt positive.

The spare room was more than adequate. Decent size double bed centred the room. The room was a light purple and it had an air of a female's touch about it. Soft, silky pillows on the bed and a white dresser sat under a big picture window. It used to be Sonia's room, and they had kept it this way when she visited. Sonia was their only child after two miscarriages, so Danny doted on her. She was 32 years old and Danny still treated her as if she was 10. She was very bright and had a great education, passing her exams with straight A's. She became an intern at the Home Office and given a role as a PA to the UK's Embassy in Bogota, Colombia. Danny could not have been more proud of her, and made sure everyone knew how successful she was at every opportunity.

Jackson stripped his clothes off and went into the small en-suite bathroom. He stopped at the mirror to look at himself. He looked drawn and grey. His hair was a mess and the dark rings under his eyes gave him a truly ghoulish image.

He turned the shower onto its hottest setting and stepped in. The water burned his skin, but he barely noticed it. His mind began racing back to past events, then came back to his dream. I must be losing it, he thought to himself. After 20 minutes, he washed and got out. Once he was dry, he dressed in clean jeans and a T-Shirt and looked at himself in the dresser's mirror. He looked better.

As he returned to the kitchen, the aroma of pasta sauce hit him like a hammer. He had not realised how hungry he was until now. Standing at the stove was Cathy. She was a lot smaller than Danny by nearly a foot. She was still very pretty even at 54. She had retained her elfish good looks. Piercing brown eyes and smooth complexion made her look 20 years younger. She was very petite, but behind her tiny frame lurked a powerful woman. She certainly kept Danny in check. 'His Little Viper' he liked to call her.

She turned as Jackson entered the room. Her smile was infectious and he returned the smile without thinking.

She glided over to hug him. "It's great to see you." The hug seemed to be extra firm this time.

"I take it he's told you then?"

"Yes he did," she said, biting her lip like a coy child, "I hope you don't mind, Danny didn't want me putting my foot in it!"

He chuckled. "Of course not Cath, I have no dignity left anyway."

"Well come and sit down. Food will be ready soon."

The three of them spent the evening chatting. Wine flowed and they all went to bed drunk and happy. They filled the next three days with trips to the beach, drinks in the evenings and a lot of talking. By the time he went to bed on the third night, Jackson was feeling more like his old self. The constant scowl he seemed to adopt lately, replaced by a serine, contentment. He was actually happy.

The next morning, he showered and dressed early. He was wearing white shorts and a sleeveless black running top. He decided the best way to fully get back to his old self was to adopt the routine that had been his life for years, he'd run. He left the property and tagged the house in his GPS maps app on his old, but reliable mobile phone. Last thing he wanted to do was get lost. He set off at a reasonable pace, taking in the surroundings as he travelled. Immediately the lactic acid built up in his legs. He had not run like this for a while, so he knew it would take a little time to regain his form. After about 20 minutes, his heart rate regulated with his breathing, and he started to feel a lot better. He ran for another hour, circling back to the house. When he came into the hallway Danny was standing transfixed on the wall. Jackson looked at what had caught Danny's attention. It was 6" by 4" photograph of Sonia when she was 8 years old. Jackson was about to say how cute she was, and how quickly she had grown up, but something seemed wrong. Danny's expression was not one of pride or love. It was pain.

"What's wrong mate?"

"They've taken her!" Danny said.

Jackson took a moment to process what his friend had just said. "Taken who?"

"Sonia...they've got my little girl Jax!"

"Whoa! Slow down, who's taken her and where?"

Danny turned to him and the anger building in his expression was evident. "I got a call 10 minutes ago saying that they have my little girl. I have to stay by the phone for further instructions. But if I call the police she's dead!"

Jackson put a gentle arm around Danny's shoulder and guided him to the living room. "Does Cath know?"

Danny put his head in his hands and sobbed uncontrollably. The emotion was beginning to take hold of him.

Jackson shook him to bring him round, "Does Cath know? Have you told her?"

Danny lifted his head, the tears evident in his eyes. "How can I? It will crush her"

"You have to tell her mate. Better she knows now, than later"

Danny put his head back in his hands. In a muffled whisper, he said "OK".

They sat in silence, lost in thought. A high-pitched tone shattered the silence. Ascending to a trill then returning to its original tone. Danny leapt off his sofa and rushed into the hallway.

"Hello?" he said. Danny stood listening for what seemed like an eternity. Jackson assumed these were the instructions he was being given. Just as abruptly as it started, the call ended. Danny just stood there looking at the handset in his hand.

Jackson looked at Danny impatiently. "Well, what did they say?"

Danny returned the handset to its cradle. "They are saying Sonia has taken something that belongs to a very powerful man in Colombia. They want it back in four days or they are going to kill her!"

"Did they say what it was mate?"

"No, apparently they are going to send instruction by text from Sonia's phone along with proof of life. But they also said I can't tell anyone. Cathy included!"

Jackson looked pensive. Thoughts were rattling through his mind. How can we get out of this? What can we do to find her? If we give these people what they want, will they not just kill them all anyway? Every question he thought of came to the same conclusion. We have to find her in four days.

Jackson turned back to Danny. "Do you have any hardware here?"

Danny, as if prodded with electricity, sparked into life. "I certainly do mate."

Since leaving the Parachute Regiment 13 years ago, Danny had moved to the US in search of a new chapter in his life. Trouble was the only thing he was good at was soldiering. Like Jackson, Danny hailed from Newcastle-Upon-Tyne, growing up in the tough streets of Benwell, an area of depressing poverty and crime. This gave the two men an understanding of the criminal mind and the lengths they will go to, to get what they want. Danny became involved with a group of ex Delta, the U.S. equivalent of the UK's famous SAS. They recruited him into their security firm, offering protection for business executives, and foreign dignitaries.

Jackson followed Danny to his garage. The door to the garage opened to reveal a space so vast, that it would have been as big as the flat Jackson rented when he was 20.

Inside there were two cars, an ACE Winnebago along with a full workbench. Danny walked over to the workbench. On the wall next to it was a 4-foot square hanging rack complete with tools for every job you could think of hanging from its green face. Danny pushed the frame in the top right corner. An audible click followed and the frame moved out an inch. Danny pulled the frame open like a door. As it swung open, it revealed what looked like a safe. Next to the safe was an electronic keypad. Danny punched in a six-digit number that Jackson saw. Even though Danny was quick to enter it, Jackson's gift of seeing everything kicked in.

787167

The safe door clicked and the whirr of a motor started. The door slowly opened to reveal four shelves. On the top shelf were four M4 Assault rifles, lightweight, accurate and reliable. Below that shelf were two Stoeger M3500 tactical shotguns. The third shelf housed an array of side arms, ranging from SIG Sauer P226s to Beretta M9s. The last shelf housed ammunition boxes, Flashbang grenades, a pair of NVG goggles as well as two Motorola DP4400 tactical throat mikes.

Danny stood back and let Jackson in.

"Is that enough?"

Jackson looked like a child in a sweet shop. "Hell, yeah mate."

Danny closed the safe door, and then the tool rack covering. They returned to the house and sat facing each other at the dining table. Danny sat staring at his phone; he looked like he was willing it to come to life.

"She will be OK mate." Jackson said, trying to sound convincing, but failing miserably.

Danny's phone buzzed. Immediately he snatched it up. Jackson could see his thumb scrolling wildly. Then it stopped. Danny was transfixed on the screen.

Jackson interrupted the pause, "What have they said mate?"

"They want us to go to London. There's a PO Box in Waterloo Station. Apparently, there's an envelope addressed to a Chris Tanner. He's a journalist for The Guardian Newspaper."

"What's in the envelope?"

"Dunno mate! But they want us to break in, steal the envelope and return it unopened to an address in Bogota."

"What's the address?"

Danny shrugged his shoulders. "They say they will tell us where to take the envelope once we have it and are in Colombia."

Jackson slammed his fist down on the table almost causing Danny to drop the phone. "Damn it Danny! "You do know they are going to kill her, and possibly us too the moment we hand that envelope over. You do know that don't you?"

Danny slumped in his chair. "Yes mate. I'm not stupid!"

"OK then focus on the things we can control. Have they given you proof that she's even alive?"

Danny's thumbs went back into action. When they stopped, he turned the screen to face Jackson.

The image of Sonia made Jackson's face redden with anger. Seated on a wooden chair and dressed in, what used to be a white shirt, and a grey skirt. Her shirt, soiled with dirt and blood, ripped down to her lacy white bra beneath. A red cloth tied tight across her mouth. Her blonde hair matted with mud, and blood. Her face was dirty and smeared with her blood. Red swollen patches made her face look out of shape. Clearly, she had taken a beating. Her arms, bound at the elbows and her feet tied to the chair legs. Her hands, placed on her thighs showing her bloodied fingers, obviously been tortured first. The anger in Jackson welled, and his knuckles whitened and he balled them into to shaking fists.

"These fuckers are going to die! Send me that picture; there might be something we can see that might let us know where she is!"

Danny's brow furrowed. "I can't mate. What if they are monitoring my phone?"

Jackson thought this was unlikely, but Danny was not the person to push at this moment. "Ok why not create an email with it attached but don't send it. Save it as a draft and give me the log in details. That way we can communicate without anyone intercepting it."

Danny's face lit up. "That's genius Bruv."

After a while, and a lot of swearing, Danny finally set up the email and passed the information to Jackson. Jackson

13

opened the email and clicked on the attached image. He then saved it to his phone and closed the APP down.

"What are you going to tell Cathy?"

"I dunno mate. She knows when I am lying. She has radar I can't defeat."

Jackson thought for a moment. "Ok this is the plan. We are going on a hunting trip. I have never been while I've been here and it will get my head sorted. That way we can take the hardware too."

"Again you are a genius."

"Well let's save the praise until she's back home and safe."

Danny looked pensive. "Where are we going to start?"

"Well we need to get in country first of all."

Danny thought for a moment. "I could call in a favour from my Delta guys."

"Can you trust them?"

"Yeah, we got each other out of some holes in the last ten years. They are good guys."

Jackson nodded. "Well go set it up and I'll see what I can figure out from this picture."

When Danny had left the room, Jackson opened the image again, focusing on the room and the things around Sonia. It looked like a barn. The floor looked like it was dirt and not concrete, which looked like a farmyard style. Behind Sonia were two boxes with letters stencilled on them. Unfortunately, the focus was not good and Jackson could not really make out what they were. Looked like a J an M and an E, but it could have been INS, or LNF. Frustration washed over Jackson again. Keep it together son he thought to himself. You are no good to them if you are unfocused.

His attention kept moving back to Sonia. Something was troubling him about the picture. He put it down and rubbed his eyes. Suddenly he felt tired again. When he had composed himself, he picked the phone back up. Once again, his focus returned to Sonia. She was Danny's image, blonde hair, blue eyes and tall for a woman. She was slim, but athletic. Danny had taught her from a child to defend herself. She learned Krav Maga, Israeli Special Forces martial arts, from the age of 10. Therefore, she was no push over. I bet she gave a few of them some bruises he thought. He looked at her hands again, the telltale signs on her knuckles from impact, meant someone took a few from her. Sonia was looking at her hands in the picture. Was she inspecting the damage? Then Jacksons focus moved to her fingers. Bloodied and dirty. Her hands placed on her thighs, but with her left hand, she was showing two of her fingers, whereas her left hand, all five were in view. Was that what she was looking at? Was it a two and a five? Alternatively, was it twenty-five? Suddenly it dawned on him what he was looking at. He leapt off the chair and rushed into the back office, where Danny was finishing sending something from his computer.

"Is she just Daddy's girl or what?"

Danny looked perplexed. "What the hell are you on about mate?"

"Here…look!"

Danny still looked vacant. "What am I looking at?"

"Her hands…I was sitting wondering why she wasn't blindfolded, but they clearly fucked up or don't expect her to be coming home, but look at her eyes. She's looking at her hands, so we would too."

Danny's face lit up. "Twenty-five?"

"Exactly!" Jackson said excitedly.

"Twenty-five what though, address?"

Jackson stopped. In his excitement, he had forgotten about the letters. "Do a search for these possible letters in Google maps. See if anything clicks"

He relayed the possible combinations to Danny as he powered up his map software. Firstly, he typed LNF and drew a blank. Next up, came INS. This took him to a site to register immigration papers. They both quickly dismissed this one too. Next up, came JME. Bingo! It listed Juan Martinez Exporting as the only company in Colombia with those initials. Listed in Suan

Danny looked at Jackson excitedly. "Got to be, right?"

"It looks right to me too. Look at the address, Suan. Just off the E25. You taught her well Brother."

"Ok, I'll get some background on this Juan Martinez fella. With a bit of luck we may have a few options up our sleeve. And we have an ace up our sleeve."

Jackson looked puzzled. "What ace is that?"

"You my friend, they don't know about you!"

The two men grinned at each other. Now they had a plan. Now they were going to show these people that they are not the guys to mess with. Now these bastards were going to die!

Chapter 2

Day One

Jackson convinced Cathy that their pending hunting trip was going to be the best way to release his problem. She was suspicious, but saw the look in Jackson's eyes. He was determined again, and that was better than the lost look she saw when he first arrived.

They would not need their weapons. Danny had arranged with his former security commander John Milton, to have all the equipment they would need sent via his connections to Isla Fuerte, just off the Colombian coast. From there they were going to fast boat it to the Columbian coast. Jackson and Danny took a separate flight to Mexico first. Once inside the terminal, Jackson paid for a locker and stashed his passport. He then wired £1000 into a wireless account. This account, accessible at most websites, and used if they needed emergency funds. They had chartered a small aircraft to take them to the island to meet John at a grass landing strip on the island.

The journey was uncomfortable and cramped, but at least they were getting closer to their goal. As they stepped off the small plane, a black Range Rover approached them. The doors opened and five serious looking men stepped out. All five looked military and tough as they come. They all were dressed in green jungle fatigues and wore Kevlar body armour. Each man carried an M4 assault rifle strapped to a chest harness. Jackson looked questioningly at Danny.

Danny merely shrugged. "Guess he's brought help"

As they approached the men, one of them broke ranks and came to meet them. He was a solid looking man. Tall and lean but muscled. His buzz cropped hair, tanned face and mirrored sunglasses gave him the quintessential American look. Even more so as his smile spread across his face revealing a set of perfect pearly white teeth.

"Danny boy!" Milton said, with a deep southern drawl, "Nice of you to join the party!"

Danny stepped up to him and they shook hands. The mutual respect was evident to Jackson. This was obviously Danny's contact.

Danny nodded towards the men behind Milton. "You brought the guys too?"

"You couldn't stop them when they heard my friend. We gotcha back on this one, Buddy!"

Danny nodded to the men, who in tandem nodded back in unison. Tight group thought Jackson. Danny turned to face Jackson. "Jax, this is Lieutenant Colonel John Milton, Delta Six commander, retired of course."

Jackson smiled and offered his hand. "Jackson....but you can call me Jax." They shook and Milton's grin returned.

"Hey, heard a hell of a lot about you from this big lump. If half of what he says about you is true, then we're lucky to have you in on this one!"

Jackson could not tell if that was sarcasm or not, so he let it slide. Jackson was not as tolerant of Americans as Danny was. He found them loud and fake, gauged by the few he had actually met. Maybe these guys were different. Either way, they were willing to put themselves in harm's way to help them, so they cannot be all that bad he told himself.

"Go and say hi to the guys, they are dying to see you again Dan"

Jackson winced. Danny hated anyone calling him Dan. He always said, 'My Mam gave me two more letters for a reason, use them.'

Danny went over to the men leaving Jackson and Milton behind. As soon as Danny was out of earshot, Milton turned to Jackson. "We got the intel on this Martinez guy. He is one serious motherfucker dude. This guy controls the cocaine and weapons distribution for the whole of the South West U.S. He's got military backing and has killed more people than smallpox!"

"Have you told Danny this?"

"Hell, no dude! Don't want panic clouding his judgement do we?"

Jackson nodded in agreement. "OK, we keep shtum and deal with it when he finds out."

Milton lifted his thumb in the air. "Shtum it is buddy." Milton handed Jackson a folder. "In here are the photographs of Martinez and his family. I will keep the Intel with me for now. But study them and let Danny see them when you know he's calm."

Danny returned a few minutes later. He looked at Jackson. "The guys are going ahead on the plane and set up recon on Martinez's headquarters. We will follow with the gear and hook up once we've established who's who in this game."

"OK, let's get going."

The rest of the Delta team boarded the plane and once it refuelled, they took off. At the same time Danny, Jackson and Milton got into the Range Rover and set off to meet the boat. The trip lasted only a few minutes, but the scenery was breath taking. Jackson made a promise to himself to take a holiday when this was finished. See the world in all its glory.

When they arrived at the coast, they parked in an old weathered white wooden lock up garage and got out. Moored at a makeshift jetty there was a sleek looking speedboat. The long sweeping curves and black and red paint reminded Jackson of the Batmobile.

Milton saw Jackson's expression and put his hand on his shoulder. "This baby has stealth capability. It can run in silent mode and outrun any gunboat in even our fleet. Plus we have some cool toys on board too!"

Jackson nodded his impressed appraisal. These guys clear get an 'A' for tech.

Milton gave Jackson's shoulder a firm squeeze. "The gear's all aboard guys, time to get this show on the road. Clock's ticking fast so let's get going."

The three men boarded the vessel. Danny and Jackson stowed their bags. At the helm was another one of Milton's crew. He was most definitely Hispanic. He was smaller than the other men he had seen so far. With his slicked back jet-black hair, and pencil thin moustache, he looked like a young Gomez Addams from the 'Addams Family' film he watched with his daughter Ellie.

"This is Marco, Jax. Best helmsman in the business."

Jackson waved and Marco returned the wave as he fired the engines up. The growl pierced the silence and hurt Jackson's ears.

Milton gave Marco the thumbs up and said in his best Captain Kirk voice. "Full speed ahead Scotty."

Marco replied in the worst Scottish accent Jackson had ever heard "Aye, Captain!"

After two or three revs, Marco pushed the throttle lever forward and they lurched away. The journey was about as turbulent as physically possible, but their progress was fast. In no time at all, they approached the Colombian coast. Night was drawing in and the lights on the shore twinkled like stars.

Marco shut the boat down and came back to join the others. "Right it's slow and silent from here on. There is a cove about two klicks to the left. We'll put ashore there and hide this baby in the cave on the left."

They edged towards a dark section of the coastline. Twenty agonising minutes later, they were ashore and the boat, safely netted up, and stashed out of sight. Milton pulled a radio from his pack, turned it on and gave two squelch pulls on the transmitter. A few seconds' later two squelches were returned. A pair of headlights emerged from the black curtain of night. They stopped at the edge of the water in front of the new arrivals. The headlights belonged to a rusty wagon. It looked like it was about to fall apart and it was only the rust holding it together. It was a red Bedford flat bed with a brown covered cargo area. Faded stencilled writing on the doors and the cover were barely visible. The engine rattled and popped as the truck idled. It was a wreck.

Jackson frowned at Milton. "It doesn't look very efficient mate."

Milton smiled tiredly at him. "It doesn't have to be efficient. It just has to blend."

After they had loaded the wagon, and climbed into its cargo hold, they pulled away. The roads were mainly dirt tracks with big holes scattered all across their surface. The going was tough on the Bedford's suspension and Jackson's neck. He was sure he would get whiplash at this rate, but tried to get his head down. The army mantra was, 'always sleep when you can, because you may not get another opportunity.' Mercifully, they reached Sincelejo in good time and joined the E25. It was a metallized road and the going was smoother.

Apart from stops for refuelling from the Jerry Cans they brought with them, they made great progress. They bypassed San Jacinto to avoid the tollbooths, but still made the outskirts of Suan in just less than three hours. When the truck finally stopped and the tail dropped, the men climbed out. Stiff joints, from the cramped space they had occupied for hours, popped and cracked, as they were finally able to stretch out.

Jackson looked around him. The moon cast its silvery glow over his surroundings. They were in what looked like a small farmyard. A dilapidated 2-storey building sat at the end of a dirt-turning circle with a small barn to its left. Opposite the house was a sturdy looking gateway to the road and trees encircled the whole place. This was a perfect place to stay out of sight.

Jackson started to unload the truck as Danny and Milton went into the house. A thickset man joined him to help. He looked older than the rest. His receding grey hair cut short, as they all seemed to be. His dark tanned skin had a weathered leather appearance. This guy clearly spent his life outdoors. Jackson noticed his heavily scarred and calloused hands as he picked up the boxes, perhaps he was a rancher.

"Hi, I'm Henry. But most guys call me Hal"

Jackson could not really work out where they got Hal from Henry, but chose not to ask. He could never understand the American nicknames they gave each other.

He extended his hand to shake, his embarrassment showed when he realised Hal's hands were full.

"Sorry mate. I'm Jackson, but you can call me Jax"

Seeing Jackson's embarrassment, Hal immediate put the boxes down, and with a huge grin, shook Jacksons hand vigorously. "Hey, no sweat buddy, it's great to have you on board".

Jackson liked him instantly. Maybe he was wrong about them. Maybe they were not all the same. Whatever, he thought. I like this one anyway.

Danny and Milton returned, followed by another member of the team. He was younger than the rest he had seen so far, but he was massive. Built like a bodybuilder, his heavily tattooed arms were almost the size of Jackson's thighs. His head was clean-shaven and his long black goatee beard stretched down to his chest. He had a permanent scowl, which made him look sinister.

"Jax, this is Sergeant Brad Taylor. He is our chief tactician and recon specialist. He knows what he's doing and I trust him unequivocally, so you should too!"

Jackson nodded to him and Taylor returned the mutual gesture.

"Now, Brad has put two of our guys in some trees overlooking Martinez's compound. They have been there for a few hours and say there are many trucks coming in and out. They have seen many heavily armed men patrolling the area, so whatever is in there, it is valuable. Could be a bargaining tool, if we strike out in the search for Sonia."

Jackson looked at Danny, whose face fell at the thought of not finding his daughter. He put his hand of the big man's shoulder. "We will get her back mate. I promise you." He turned to look into Danny's eyes, "Or we'll die trying!"

Danny forced a weak smile and nodded softly. "Love you Brother."

Milton let this interruption pass, but immediately returned to his briefing. "Brad thinks that there are no buildings that look anything like the one Danny described to me, so we think they are holding her elsewhere. But he has offered an alternative to wasting days searching for her."

Danny was about to explode at this, but Jackson held him back.

Milton raised his hand in protest. "Hear me out Dan."

Jackson winced again. Do not push him, he thought, friend or not he will have you.

"What Brad is proposing is this. He has something we want, right?"

Everyone nodded.

"He wants something in return; that we all know won't save her, right? So this is the plan. Brad tells me that Martinez is not here, he is currently in Costa Rica, which is bad news. However Brad says Chuck has just told him that Martinez's son Ramon is there however!"

Jackson could see everyone's expression change as the plan became clearer.

"What Brad proposes is this," Milton continued, "We snatch Ramon. We trade him for Sonia. When we get Sonia safe, we come back and kill them all!"

Milton left his gaze on Danny and Jackson, who looked at each other for a brief moment. Both men had had the same thought.

Jackson was the first to speak. "There's obviously someone else involved in this. We need to expose, whoever this is before we kill Martinez"

Danny nodded in agreement. "Whoever they are, they are going down too."

Milton looked at Taylor and both men nodded in agreement. "OK agreed. Once we have Sonia safe, we get what's in that envelope and bury everyone."

Danny then spoke up again. "My brother-in-law works in London for the post office. He is going to get the box opened to intercept the envelope. When he has it, he will bring it to us so we don't waste time in the UK. He's going to open it first and take a picture. Jax and I have an email set up so it can't be intercepted. We should know by tomorrow night at the latest who we are dealing with."

With that, the five men moved the equipment into the house. The house was old and shabby. It had a small, grey hallway that led to a tiny living room. The dust was so thick in the air that it caught their throats as they breathed. A small table stood in one corner with two very tired looking chairs either side of it. Dreary brown 2-seater sofa sat in the middle. All of its padding had sunken from years of people's backsides. Holes were visible all over it; obviously heavy smokers once owned this place. On the opposite wall was a fireplace. Cobwebs had formed a theatre style curtain over its opening.

The team had taped blackout film over the windows, so the gloom was contained. The final wall housed a curtained doorway, through which led to a kitchen. Basic kitchen, with a large 6-seater dining table pushed against the wall. It looked sturdier than the house itself. A wood stove and sink with two cupboards were the only things making this room a kitchen.

On the table stood a pack radio, its huge antennae rose from its top and a hand held paddle mic curled from it. Seated on front of it was another member of the team. He was average in build, but the veins in his arms suggest that he was strong. His sand hair had a wave that a surfer would love. His complexion was mottled and he had a scar running from behind his ear to the right side of his mouth.

Danny pulled Jackson out of earshot. "That's Simpson; he's our comms guy, a real whiz kid on any form of communications or audio surveillance."

Danny cupped his hand to Jackson's ear. "Just don't mention his face."

Jackson looked at him curiously. "IED mate?"

Danny gave Jackson a sombre look and nodded.

An IED or Improvised Explosive Devices was the weapons of choice for insurgents during the coalition's occupation of Iraq and Afghanistan. They claimed the lives and legs of many a soldier on patrol during this time, and were a soldier's biggest fear.

Jackson nodded, he understood, probably more so than others. During one tour in Iraq, he was part of a six man recce team just outside of Basra. Tasked with clearing out a nearby compound, Intel sources indicated that there were insurgents holed up inside and needed neutralising. They had cleared 80% of the structures when Jackson entered an outbuilding. Just as he was about to cross the threshold of the door, he lost his footing. He fell sideways just as the device ignited. The blast threw him over luckily missing his legs. Had he not slipped the he would have been dead for sure. After that moment, his perception heightened beyond his comprehension. He still to this day believed that it was the impact on his head that prompted this sixth sense he seemed to have.

A voice from the radio brought Jackson back to the present day.

"Tango one? This is Charlie six over!"

Simpson put the mic to his lips. "Charlie six, go ahead."

"Voodoo 2 is still static, but looks like he's going to be mobile soon, over!"

"Roger that Charlie six, wait one".

Simpson turned to Milton . "Looks like he's going to be on the move soon sir. Do we follow and intercept?"

Milton looked at Danny. "Negative, I'll get Hal to follow. Find out where he goes. Maybe we can take him when there are less X-Rays watching him"

"Roger that, Sir," Simpson acknowledged, "Charlie six, this is Tango one over"

"Go ahead Tango one."

"Charlie one says stay put. Charlie four will shadow Voodoo 2 over."

"Roger that Tango one, Charlie six out."

Milton gave Hal the thumbs up. Hal grabbed his pack and weapon and left the house. The dull rumble of the truck's diesel engine sparked to life and then faded away into the night.

Danny looked at Milton and asked, "OK Boss, what's the plan. Where do you want us?"

Milton shrugged. "For now all we can do is gather Intel. Just sit tight for now, get your packs and weapons ready for the go when I give it."

Danny and Jackson nodded in unison and left the room to reclaim their equipment.

While Danny assembled the Comms equipment and did the safety checks of all their grenades, Jackson stripped and checked all the weapons. This was second nature to them. An important task that will save your life, their CO had instilled in them. They did not need forcing to do it.

"They seem a tight crew. Wound a bit tight, but I have to say they are efficient. They've got their game on quickly on this one mate"

Danny nodded. He too, clearly impressed by how quickly they had their Intel and plan of action in place.

"Yeah Milton is definitely an act now think later guy, but Taylor is the plan man. He is the best tactician I've seen mate"

They spent the next few hours in agonising inactivity. Danny spent them pacing in and out of the kitchen in the vain hope that a breakthrough would come. However, nothing did.

"Get some shut eye Danny," Milton ordered, "You are no good to her if you are out on your feet. I promise I will wake you if we learn anything remotely helpful. That goes for all of you."

Danny joined Jackson and Taylor upstairs in one of the two tiny bedrooms. There were no beds, so they unrolled their bedrolls and bunked down on the hard wooden floor. When Jackson woke, the room was empty. He got up and padded to the bathroom. In the brown foggy mirror stood the same haggard face, he had seen four days ago. At least now, he had a reason to be tired. He washed up and went down to the kitchen. When he entered the room, everyone had gathered round the radio.

"What's the word then?" He said. Collectively they all turned to look at him, "Sorry am I interrupting?"

Danny beckoned him over. "We've just had word that Ramon is back at the compound. Looks like he's supervising the delivery of whatever is in that compound himself. He has been in and out five times this morning. It could be our best chance to grab him."

On the table next to the radio was a map of the surrounding area. As Jackson nestled into the group, he could see their position marked on the map. Also marked was the compound. From the compound came three lines ending at various points on the map. Two of the lines had the number 2 written at their destinations.

"Do we know what these destinations are?"

Milton nodded. "Yeah we do. They are grassed airstrips. Obviously they are flying the shipments from these locations."

"They are rotating fields by the looks of it Jax." Danny said.

"Ok what's our plan?" Jackson asked.

Taylor turned the map so he had control of it, pointing at the one marker without a two.

"Ok well we think this one will be next. If they follow their previous protocol then it will consist of four vehicles. Lead vehicle is a black Buick Enclave SUV, it's usually 4 up inside. We'll call that Foxtrot 1. Next up is the Ford Transit panel van, which must house the product. That's Foxtrot 2 and that's two up inside. Then we have a red Toyota Hilux. This is Ramon's transport. We'll call this Foxtrot Voodoo again two up including Ramon. Lastly, there's a silver Mercedes Benz sedan. Again that's four up inside"

Taylor returned the map so the others could see more clearly.

"Now that means we are looking at potentially twelve X-Rays including Voodoo two." Jackson pointed out.

Taylor looked irritated. "Yep." Clearly not used to interruptions during his briefings.

"Now," he continued, giving Jackson a look that said 'pay attention,' "I think we should hit them when they are loading. Hal says that even Ramon gets his hands full of boxes and they only have four guys watching the perimeter."

Taylor paused to make sure that had sunk in. "That means during loading we take out the armed guards. Then we drop the ones closest to their weapons. We send two guys behind the plane and take out the top guards, then the pilot and his co-pilot."

Again, he paused for effect. Jackson hated the theatrical way these guys did things, but it was their show and they were helping him to help Danny.

Taylor continued. "Now once their numbers are halved, I predict they will surrender. If they don't, then obviously we will drop everyone except the principle. But it would be nice to leave one alive to relay our message to Martinez. Once we've snatched Ramon, we'll RV back here and return to the boat, where we will hold him offshore while the rest of us establish communications with Martinez. I hope that Danny's Brother-in law will have the goods by then. Any questions?"

Jackson wanted to wait, but just could not resist. "What if they deviate and go somewhere else?"

Taylor nodded as if he was waiting for that one. "Well then we go to plan B. We hit them in transit and hope he doesn't get nailed in the crossfire"

They all nodded in agreement. Milton stood back from the table and announced. "OK you heard the man, let's get our shit together, and remember, stay frosty out there guys. This is an unsanctioned op and we are most definitely in hostile territory. We have no friendlies here and our Exfil may become compromised, so stay sharp. Simpson is going to remain here on Comms; we will scoop Chuck and

Hawkins on the way past the compound. OK Saddle up guys!"

On that command, they all gathered their equipment, and began doing their final checks. Once they were all happy, they filed out and onto the truck once more. The excitement hit Jackson as they pulled away. It had been a while since he had seen any combat. He just hoped he did not let anyone down.

After a while, they came to a stop. Everyone checked their throat mikes were working and called out their call signs as they went. Jackson was Charlie eight. From now on, only call signs used over the net. Their lines were secure, but you just never know, so due diligence was the key. They had moved the truck into a small copse of trees out of sight of the main road. If the convoy passed them then it would be hard to spot, but suddenly the red wagon seemed very conspicuous to Jackson.

After about half an hour, the airwaves burst into life.

"Tango one, this Charlie five over?"

Charlie five was Chuck. Danny had told him that both chuck and Hawkins, who was Charlie six, were ex Delta Sniper team.

"Charlie five, this is Tango one, go ahead." Simpson replied.

"Tango one, be advised all Foxtrots being loaded and are 'bout to go mobile, Confirm?"

"Charlie five, that's a Roger. Prepare to move out to pick-up point 'A' if they going right or 'B' if going left. Acknowledge?"

"Tango One that's an affirmative."

Milton leaned forward, and they all huddled together. "Ok guys! This is a fly by wire op. We will have to be on our toes in case we get any variables in the plan. Keep sharp and good luck guys."

Once again, the airways burst into life. "Tango one, Tango one. This is Charlie six, be advised plan 'A', I repeat plan 'A'. Acknowledge?"

"Charlie six, that's an affirmative. Move out to point A, over."

"Charlie six Roger that. Charlie six is en-route."

"Charlie five is en-route."

Chapter 3

The Snatch

The truck manoeuvred to the pickup point just as Chuck and Hawkins emerged from the trees, quickly jumping into the cab with Hal. Hal put his foot down and within a few minutes, they were within sight of the convoy. Jackson's adrenaline levels were beginning to spike. The section of the mission that gave soldiers the most fear was the waiting. Once the action began, he usually went into soldier mode. Everything was instinctive. You do not think about it, you just do it, but here right before the event, this is the point of maximum fear.

After about forty minutes, they came to a stop. Chuck and Hawkins jumped out. As soon as the door shut, Hal was on the move again. Fifteen minutes later, they stopped again. This time they all got out. Once Jackson's eyes had adjusted to the light, he took in his surroundings. They were on a dirt track with a gate at the end. Either side of them, dense trees hugged the track, holding the warmth and humidity in like a blanket. Milton took out his compass and did a quick 360 turn to get his bearings.

"OK guys gather round," Taylor said as they huddled up, "Jackson, you are with me right side. Danny, you are with the boss on the left, watch your six and the guy next to you. We will hit the clearing either side of the plane according to Hal's descriptions. Anyone to the right of the plane, are ours. Anyone to the left are yours boss."

Milton nodded. "OK you heard the man, move out."

With that, both pairs separated.

Jackson followed Taylor closely. He moved surprisingly stealthily for such a big guy. Jackson kept systematically checking behind them for signs that they were being followed, they were not.

When they reached the edge of the treeline, the view opened up to an area of grass about the size of a football field wide, but very long. Reminded Jackson of the golf courses he had tried to play on while being dragged around by Danny. Jackson hated golf, but Danny loved it. In front of them, the plane was directly opposite. The transit had backed up to the side of the plane with the other vehicles fanned out facing away with Ramon's Hilux in the centre.

As predicted, four armed guards stood in the four corners of the area. They were scanning the trees, but generally looked bored. They had clearly been doing this regularly for a while now and were not as aware as they should be. Jackson and Taylor spread out. Jackson took the area nearest the plane, while Taylor concentrated on the vehicle area. They both knew that Danny and Milton would be doing the same. This way they would not cross targets, which made for an efficient killing ground.

The men helping fill the plane had formed a human chain from the panel van.

Now it was a case of patience. Let the targets relax and think that there is no immediate threat to their task.

The airwaves came to life again.

"Charlie one, this is Charlie five, I have X-Ray 1 locked, over"

No sooner had Chuck finished, when Hawkins came onto the air. "Charlie one, this is Charlie six, I have X-Ray 2 locked, over."

Milton was ready to act. "This is Charlie one, all call signs stand by for my command. Charlies five and six, as soon as your primary X-Rays move behind the plane, drop them on my go, Confirm?"

"Charlie five aye"

"Charlie six aye"

Jackson had selected his target, meticulously following his every move, anticipating where to take the shot, in relation to his movement speed, also to make sure Ramon was not in the firing line. He imagined all the guys doing the same.

The two guards behind the plane turned about face, slowly walking towards each other. The time to strike was near.

"All call signs this is Charlie one, Stand by. Stand by!"

As soon as the two guards moved out of sight from the men loading, the call came out.

"All call signs this is Charlie one, Stand by. Stand by. GO! GO! GO!"

Instantly the two men behind the plane dropped, as if someone had turned them off mid stride. The wounds in their heads were catastrophic. Death was instantaneous.

Gunfire erupted as soon as the bodies dropped. The two other armed men stitched with bullet holes and crumpled onto their sides. Jackson froze. Not through fear. His target had stopped, frozen to the spot right in front of Ramon.

"SHIT!" Jackson shouted as he looked for another target. As soon as he found one, he opened fire dropping the next man in line. Danny must have dropped his target too, because now there were six bodies on the floor.

The pilot and co-pilot had bolted for the cockpit in an attempt to escape. They both dropped in unison. Chuck and Hawkins were good. Unfortunately in the moment's hesitation, Ramon and Jackson's initial target, made a dash for the Hilux. On cue all the team burst from the tree line, concentrating fire on the remaining henchmen still standing. Two were behind the Mercedes now with handguns ready and returning fire. Danny and Milton split further to give the enemy more choices to make. Jackson and Taylor did the same.

Jackson was up and running. "I'm going after Ramon!"

Taylor merely nodded and started putting rounds down as cover. The two men at the SUV instantly ducked behind for cover, as bullet holes stitched the side of their vehicle, the glass erupting and showering the cowering men.

Jackson saw that Ramon and his guard had made it it to the Hilux and had dived inside. Immediately it sparked to life and lurched away.

Jackson veered towards the speeding Ramon.

"Voodoo two is getting away!" His breathing had become more rapid.

He dropped to one knee to make himself stable as the Hilux sped away from him, putting rounds as low as he could, to avoid hitting Ramon. His attempt to hit the tyres was fruitless as the Hilux ploughed through the gate between the trees and disappeared. Jackson was immediately up and running after it. The gunfight was still raging behind him, but he paid it no mind. He had one mission now. Stop Ramon at all costs.

The gunfire behind him stopped as he reached the mangled gate, leaping it mid stride. Debris from the Hilux's shattered front grille lay scattered like metallic confetti. Jackson made it to the first bend at full speed. As he rounded the corner, the Hilux came into view. It had stopped. Fearing a trap, Jackson moved sideways into cover with his weapon raised to cover the cab.

As Jackson tried to get his breathing under control, the airwaves erupted again.

"Charlie one, this is Charlie four. I have Voodoo 2 turkey wrapped. What's your Status?"

"Charlie four, this is Charlie one, stay put. I'm coming to you"

"Charlie one, Roger that".

Jackson's heart leapt. "Way to go Hal!"

He was about to run to meet him, when he paused. "Charlie four, this is Charlie eight. I am at your six and approaching." Jackson did not want to get shot because he had not identified himself first. Besides, the guard may still be at large. "Charlie four, what's the status of the other X-Ray over?"

Hal immediately responded. "Oh he's down. He's most definitely down Buddy!"

As Jackson drew near to the stricken Hilux, he became aware of Hal's meaning. The Hilux had clearly slewed off the track and into the nearby trees. As he rounded the hood, he saw bullet tracks running up the bonnet to the windshield. The windshield had caved inwards. The cause of this devastation was the branch that had not only impaled the windshield, but had completely removed the driver's head. The cab splattered with blood and tissue. This was a massive impact.

Jackson walked over to where Hal was standing. On the floor by Hal's feet lay Ramon. He wore black chinos with a matching black shirt and waistcoat. He was lying in the foetal position, with his arms tethered behind his back with Plasticuffs, and subsequently tethered to his ankles by more bindings. He looked like a Christmas Turkey, prepped for the oven. Jackson grinned at Hal.

He patted Hal on the shoulder. "Nice going mate."

Hal smiled warmly back. "I decided to stand to when the shooting started. Good job I did. When this fucker came at me, I just fired." Hal looked down at Ramon. "Good job this one wasn't driving. I was lucky I guess," he looked slightly ashamed, "he was out of it when I got to him, so gave him a sedative. It should keep him quiet for a bit. I nearly fucked the op though Jax."

Jackson gave his shoulder a gentle squeeze. "Your secret's safe with me mate." He grinned as Hal returned the squeeze.

A few moments later Danny, Milton and Taylor rounded the bend. They inspected the stricken Hilux. They all winced as they discovered the macabre vista inside the cab.

"Fucker never knew what hit him." Taylor said.

Jackson just nodded knowingly. He turned to Danny as he approached him. "How did it go back there, mate?"

Danny just ignored the question and barged past. He was striding straight to Ramon. As he got there, he grabbed Ramon by his bindings and with one movement, lifted him straight up.

"Where is she?" Danny screamed. "Where is my little girl you bastard?"

Ramon said nothing, because he couldn't, he was unconscious.

Hal guided Danny's arms down, slowly setting Ramon back onto the floor. "He's out cold buddy. I had to give him a shot so I could secure him. He will come to in half an hour or so. Chill my friend. He'll talk. I guarantee that"

Over the radio, Chuck came to life. "Charlie one this is Charlie five. Area is secure and charges set. 30 minutes till lights up, over"

"Charlie five roger that, you and six make you way to the pick-up point and we will be there soon, Charlie one out"

Two squelches returned, signalling message received and understood.

Milton turned to his men. "Ok mount up. Let's put some distance between us and here, back to base for the debriefing." He looked accusingly at Jackson. "Fall out!"

Jackson could feel his temper rising. He knew Milton was going to blame him for letting Ramon get away.

They all climbed into the wagon dragging Ramon onto the floor at the team's feet. After picking up Chuck and Hawkins, they set off back to base. The journey back was silent. As the adrenaline levels decrease, the exhaustion sets in, but Jackson could feel something else. Slight cold looks were coming his way. He felt like an outsider again.

When they arrived at the farmhouse, they got out and formed together at the side of the truck. Milton came close. "OK Guys let's get him secured and the gear squared away," again he looked at Jackson, "inside in an hour for debriefing. Move out!"

Danny and Taylor hauled Ramon into the farmhouse followed by Milton. Jackson and the rest of the team stowed the equipment into the outbuilding securely. Jackson went upstairs to gather his thoughts and wash up. Once again, he felt 100 years old.

Jackson entered the kitchen to find everyone gathered around the table. Milton and Taylor stood at the head. They all turned to look at Jackson as one.

Milton scowled at Jackson. "What the fuck happened out there soldier? You let the primary target not only reach the vehicle, but then leave the zone!"

Jackson could feel the heat of anger burning into him. He wanted to march over and drop this cocky fucker. Who the fuck does he think he's talking to?

Jackson took a second to calm down. "I couldn't take the first shot. My guy was standing in front of him." Jackson thumbed to the other room where they had stashed Ramon. "So by the time I'd slotted guy number two, those two had bolted!"

Milton looked at the rest of the guys as if to say, do you believe this?

"OK but when they got into the vehicle and moved off, you still couldn't neutralise them. I thought you were good.

Danny here said you were the best soldier he had served with, so far I ain't seen shit!"

Jackson's anger rose again. "Listen mate. I don't work for you, I-"

Before Jackson could say any more, Hal interrupted. "Hey guys what gives?"

Everyone stopped looking at Jackson and looked at Hal. "The mission was a success, right?" He looked around the room. "Right?" he repeated. They all nodded.

Hal continued. "Nobody got hurt right? We got the sumbitch right? Well that's a job well done in my book."

Hal pointed at Jackson and gave him a look like a father protecting his child. "This guy ain't served for years, but still stepped up and put himself in harm's way. How 'bout we cut him some slack? Eh guys?"

Milton seemed to thaw. He stepped up to Jackson and extended his hand in peace. Jackson took it, but secretly wanted to deck him.

"Just be more careful next time eh?" Milton grinned, his white teeth exaggerating the false smile. "Especially if I'm standing next to you."

Jackson nodded and then nodded at Hal. He liked Hal. He reckoned he would become friends with Hal, if they lived that long!

As if to change the mood, Taylor said. "Ok now that sleeping beauty in there is awake why don't we see what he knows?"

Danny launched off the seat towards the door. Taylor stopped him with a huge arm across the doorway. "Erm not you buddy!"

Danny tried to push him away but then found himself restrained by the others, Jackson included.

"What the fuck man?" Danny screamed, "That's my Daughter they've got. Not any of yours. It should be me that interrogates him, not you!" Danny's rage was boiling.

Jackson turned Danny's face to look at his eyes. "We get that mate. I would love to let you tear his fucking head off, but where will that get us? Eh?" Danny tried to force his head away, but Jackson was stronger, stronger than all of them were.

"We need to give him hope mate" Jackson continued, "He has to think that we'll hand him back to Daddy in return for Sonia and they will walk away alive," he shook Danny's face as if to make his point more intense, "that's not going to happen if you half kill him or worse"

Danny's resistance softened, as what Jackson said made sense. Taylor removed his thick arm and added. "Don't worry Danny. He'll talk, trust me!"

With a wink and a sinister smirk, Taylor left the room, followed by Milton. As they left, Milton turned to the room and said. "Hal get some chow going, save some for us. Think we're gonna need it!" He grinned then he was gone.

Jackson turned to Danny, who was calm, but definitely like a coiled spring. Hal saw this and stepped up to Jackson. "How 'bout you and him go get some firewood and I'll get some chow going?"

Jackson smiled, great idea Hal, yet again. Danny held his hands up in mock surrender.

Jackson grinned and slapped Danny's shoulders before roughly massaging them. "OK, big guy, let's go. I will chop you carry. Don't want you armed with anything other than some twigs do we?"

Jackson guided Danny past the living room where Ramon was lying on the small table. He resisted the temptation to stop and watch. He would have loved nothing more, than to watch the man being tortured, but Danny was not in the right frame of mind to be there.

His mind returned to Pulev's interrogation. How he had let his anger get the better of him. He could only imagine how Danny must be feeling right now.

Once outside Jackson turned to Danny and said. "I'm sorry I sided with them mate, but the guys were right. Your judgement was clouded. Mine too. Let's just see what they get. If they strike out? Then fuck 'em. We'll batter the fucker till he blabs. Deal?"

Danny looked back at the house and then back to Jackson, his eyes dark with malice.

"Deal."

Chapter 4

The Package

It took Danny and Jackson a good three quarters of an hour to collect the wood. Once they returned the kitchen had gone from a military briefing room to an actual kitchen. Simpson was peeling potatoes while Chuck and Hawkins were busy cutting up four skinned Rabbits.

Hal took the wood and got the fire going. "Won't be the best meal you've had, but beats MRE's any day."

MRE or Meals Ready to Eat, were field rations that you either, ate cold straight from nondescript silver foil pouches they came in. or attempted to heat them up in the vain hope that they would taste better. They did not. They were dreary and tasteless, and the running joke within all military personnel, no matter where they were from.

Watching Chuck and Hawkins dismember the Rabbits, Jackson studied the two men. He had not really seen much of them since arriving here. Chuck was the image of what Jackson would describe as a 'Jock'. He had an athletic build with a blond flat top haircut. His pointed nose and slightly large mouth, gave him a resemblance to the actor Gary Busey. He looked American.

Hawkins on the other hand, had almost an olive skinned Eastern European look. With his aquiline nose and thin small mouth, his almost black eyes and hair gave him a sinister look. Unlike most of the rest of the team, Hawkins was tall and gangly. It seemed to Jackson, that Chuck and Hawkins were two opposite sides of the same soldier. They worked well together, but neither looked complete without the other there.

Danny broke Jackson's thoughts. "It's quiet in there," he said, nodding towards the living room, "they haven't killed him yet have they?"

Chuck looked up and shook his head. "Naw, they're just letting him stew for a while. They are gonna teach him to surf soon!"

Chuck looked at Hawkins and they both hi fived each other.

Jackson knew what that meant. Waterboarding is an interrogation technique that although frowned upon, was widely adopted as a seriously efficient and severe way to extract information from even the toughest subject. It involved laying the subject in an inverted position with either, a cloth towel or hessian bag covering the eyes, nose and mouth. Water poured in the general vicinity of the mouth. The cloth restricts the natural flow of air, giving the subject the experience of drowning, without submerging them. Natural fear and an in-built survival mechanism cause the subject to gag. The whole experience can break the hardest of men and women.

Suddenly a commotion erupted from the next room. Lots of muffled shouting followed by what sounded like a scuffle. Then it was silent. Less than a minute later, it began again. By the time it went silent for the last time, the team had not only eaten, but cleaned up. They had been going at it for an hour and a half.

Milton returned to the kitchen drying his hands. He was soaked and looked physically exhausted. "Simpson, keep an eye on our guest, he's all washed up!" Chuckling to himself at his joke, Milton took Simpsons seat at the table. "OK Hal what've we got?"

Hal opened the oven, and took a metal pot out and placed it in the centre of the table. When he lifted the lid, Milton smiled. Taylor joined him at the table. They ate in silence. Jackson could see Danny's impatience mounting. He gave

Danny the universal signal to calm down as Danny's frown deepened.

When both men had finished, Hal took away the dirty plates and cleared the table.

Danny could clearly wait no longer. "Well?"

Milton wiped his mouth with the towel. "She's being held on a little island off the coast of Cartagena. It turns out that Daddy has a small fortress there."

Danny looked pensive. "So what are we thinking? Go and get her?"

Milton nodded. "That works for us." Then he pointed at Jackson. "But as your esteemed colleague over there pointed out, there is obviously a higher power involved that we need to stop." He let that pause sink home before returning his gaze to Jackson. "So! Jax? What do you think we do?"

Jackson looked down at his hands. They were shaking. He was not sure if it was the pressure of having to come up with a plan, or the anger at the condescension, with which Milton was addressing him. Either way the tremors were evident. Get a grip Jax, he thought to himself. He looked up and then he was calm.

"Well I am all for snatching her back, but we run the risk of them offing her before we can get to her, even if we are stealthy. I can imagine it's going to be heavily manned and armed, not to mention surveillance and alarms to the military."

He looked at every one of them as he continued. "Don't forget that in two days Danny needs to be at the airport with an envelope in his hand, his Brother –in –Law is bringing it to him personally. If he's not there, she's dead regardless. Martinez may trade for Ramon, but whoever is pulling the strings stateside, won't give two fucks about him." Jackson nodded to the other room.

Milton looked puzzled at him. "OK Wise guy! What do you suggest?"

"Let me get in there alone. Be on standby in case I need the cavalry. I get her out and off the island. Then we trade Ramon for the top boy."

Taylor let out a belly laugh. "You gotta be kiddin' man!" He was shook his head theatrically. "You think on today's performance, we're gonna let you go in there an' fuck this up? FOR-GET-IT!"

Jackson fixed him with a steely glare that caught Taylor off guard. "I know you think you are hot shit, and I'm just the fucking Limey who fucked up, but, I see things you guys don't. I know how to be mobile and silent. I am invisible when I want to be. I could sneak up behind you and the first time you knew I was there, would be when the blood is oozing down your fat fucking neck!"

Taylor lunged at Jackson. "Why you little-"

He did not finish the sentence. Faster than anyone could register, Jackson had reached forward and straight chopped Taylor in the throat. Everybody was stunned, including Danny. He had seen Jackson's skills before, but never at such speed.

Taylor slumped back down coughing and spluttering, his face turning purple as he fought to breathe. The rest of the team jumped up to grab Jackson.

Milton halted them with a wave of his hand. "OK Guys let's all calm down here. We are all on the same side here."

Taylor regained his breath but was still very purple. Snorting through his nose, he glared at Jackson, reminding him of a Bull just before it charges.

Milton looked at Danny. "This is your call my friend. I personally think it's suicidal. But if you want to go with this fool's plan then I'm at your disposal." He looked around the room. "We all are, right fellas?"

Nods were forthcoming from all but Taylor who was still brooding at Jackson.

Milton stooped to look into Taylors eyes. "Sergeant? I asked you a question"

Without taking his eyes off Jackson, Taylor nodded.

"OK then. Are you sure he has the skills to pull this off Dan?"

Danny nodded. "Jax is like every book you read about assassins. We did a three day escape and evasion exercise where Jax was the quarry. By the end of the third day, not only had we not caught him, but also we found out he had been in our hunting party all along. Nobody saw him, but he took pictures of the back of each man in the exercise. That is thirty-five confirmed kills he chose not to make. So yes I know he can do it!"

Taylor huffed at this. "Well let's hope he performs better than today. Or we may all be dead."

Jackson conceded this. He knew himself, that he had to sharpen up, or Sonia was dead.

Milton gave everyone time to calm down, especially Taylor before announcing. "OK then we better get going. Get that piece of shit to the boat and get 'Bruce Lee' here to his destiny with death."

They all rose and began to collect everything. Leaving no trace that they were ever there. Even footprints and tyre tracks heavily disguised. As the wagon trundled out of the gate for the last time, they failed to notice the motorcycle that had slipped in behind them.

They made steady progress, deliberately driving at the speed limit so as not to draw any unwanted attention. Jackson used the time to study Ramon. He was a thickset man, overweight rather than muscular. He did not look at all like the son of a powerful criminal. In fact, he looked more like an accountant or a banker. He was only young but looked a lot older. His face was round and he sported a thick black moustache. His dark waved hair was matted and unkempt, but Jackson knew this was the result of a serious waterboarding.

On his right hand was a gold ring. It was a gilded square with Diamonds encrusted around its perimeter. In the centre was an embossed motif that looked like a bulls horns. Two Rubies sat where the Bull's eyes would be. It looked expensive, but also vaguely familiar to Jackson. I have seen that ring before, he mused.

The wagon juddered to a halt as they reached the alcove. As they jumped out, the sun was beginning to descend into the ocean. The sky had taken on a dark look. What was once bright blue, gradually being smothered by a blanket of dark storm clouds. This would make it interesting Jackson thought.

Once they had stowed the equipment alongside their prisoner, they hid the wagon in a small dry ravine. Not completely hidden, but these types of vehicles were abandoned every day. Hal had disabled the engine. It was just yet another victim to old age.

When Hal stepped over the embankment to return to the boat, Jackson turned to give him a hand onto the boat, which was by now starting to rock quite vigorously as the currents increased with the pending storm. "Take care there Hal," Jackson chuckled, "this bronco's a buckin'" He put on his best Southern drawl as he grinned at Hal.

Hal responded in an exaggerated accent too. "Y'all going to 'Bama Son?"

Jackson was about to reply, but something caught his eye.

Hal noticed Jackson's mood change and the direction he was looking. "What's wrong Jax?" Hal said worriedly, "whatcha' lookin' at?"

Jackson did an about face and headed over to his pack. After a couple of minutes rummaging, he returned with his NVG Night Goggles. Immediately firing them up and putting them to his eyes. The green glow he peered through turned pitch-blackness into a surreal green daylight. Jackson scanned the horizon but found nothing. Was he seeing things? His senses rarely let him down, but he felt sure he had seen something, a glint of glass or metal perhaps. He was just about to give up when saw movement further up the bank. Sure enough, there it was. A silhouette.

It was moving back up the hill away from them. Every few metres it would stop, then turn to face them lifting what Jackson could only assume were binoculars. Shit! He thought to himself.

"We're blown fellas!" He yelled. "let's get the hell out of here!"

Danny was the first up to join him. "What you on about? No one knows we are here mate."

Jackson handed Danny his NVG unit, pointing up where he had seen the figure. "Up there near the ridge. We got company."

Danny put the unit to his eyes and tried to work out where Jackson was looking. Left and right he moved, but saw nothing. "There's nothing there mate!"

Jackson snatched the unit off him. "Give it here ya blind tosser." He looked to where he had seen the figure, but there was no sign. "He was there, I'm telling you!" he protested, "you know me, I rarely mistake what I see."

Danny had to admit, his friend was seldom wrong in cases like these. "So we'd better get out of Dodge then eh?"

They went over to where Milton and Marco were discussing their direction.

"Jax has seen a spotter on the shore. He reckons we are blown. Better hightail out before his mates arrive?"

Milton looked puzzled. "How could they know we were here? How could they know where we would be?"

Jackson had thought the very same thing. They had been so careful not to stand out on the way there and back. During the op, they encountered nobody, so nobody could have seen them. How could someone follow them all the way here?

Milton turned to Marco. "Get us out of here Scotty. Warp factor six, please." Marco nodded and fired the engines to life. As they pulled away, Jackson returned his gaze to the bank. It was hard to focus as the boat lurched and dipped, but he could have sworn that the figure was back. The element of surprise may have just been lost!

Once they were away from the shore, they slowed the boat down to stealth mode. They each took up defensive positions all the way around the boat. Each man had NVG head gear on and stood to. The feeling of space is lost when you look at the ocean though Night Vision Goggles. It is almost impossible to gauge distance.

About 20 minutes into their journey, Simpson shouted out. "Ship on the horizon! Heading this way, and fast sir."

Milton moved up next to Simpson, looking at the arc area he was observing. Jackson followed the line of sight. Sure enough, in the distance was a vessel. They could not tell how big it was, but it was closing rapidly.

"How in God's name have they locked on to us?" Milton rasped the frustration evident in his voice, "get us out of here Marco. Fuck the stealth, top speed son."

Marco threw the throttle forward all the way and the boat rose out of its watery bed and tore away from its pursuers. Milton came back to where Ramon was tethered then looked at Jackson. "Jax! On me!" He began dragging Ramon below deck.

Jackson followed helping guide Ramon to a seat.

Ramon sat there defiantly. "You might as well turn me loose. We might let you all live!" A smirk of contentment grew across his face.

He spat at Milton. "My people will not stop till you are all dead. Give me back to them while you still can. My father will kill all of you, and not just you! He will kill your wives, girlfriends, children and your children's children!"

Milton caught him full in the face with the back of his hand, instantly drawing blood from Ramon's nose. He turned to Jackson and whispered. "You think he's bugged?"

Jackson thought about it for a while. "He might have one inside him, but be hard to tell without a scanner." No sooner had the words left his mouth that something dawned on him…The ring.

Jackson rushed over to Ramon and flipped him onto his front, grabbing at the ring on Ramon's right hand. Almost as if he knew what Jackson was doing, Ramon balled his hand into a tight fist. "Give me a hand here Milton!" he barked. Milton saw what Jackson was trying to do and put his weight on to Ramon's wrist as Jackson tried to prise his fingers apart.

From up on deck a shout went up. "Helicopter inbound Sir!" It was Taylor. "ETA 8 minutes to contact!"

Milton drew his knife. "Hold him still!" The exertions and the heat of combat had taken his breath away. "I'll cut his hand off!" Ramon bucked and kicked like a Rodeo Horse as the realisation hit him that these guys were willing to dismember him. Suddenly, as if in a state of submission he relaxed his hand. Jackson swivelled the ring off, ran up onto the deck and with all the strength he could muster, threw the ring out into the black arms of the ocean.

Jackson pointed forwards. "Hard about! Marco!"

Marco looked at him puzzled.

Milton emerged from below deck. "You heard the man! Hard about!"

Marco began a sharp turn, "Aye sir!"

They were now heading at ninety degrees to their original course.

"Stealth mode now Scotty." Milton said, looking at Jackson. "God I hope you are right, because we are sitting ducks here if you ain't boy!"

Jackson nodded. He too hoped he was right. Two fuck ups and they would probably kill him themselves.

They took up defensive shooting positions facing the incoming threat. Only Simpson and Marco faced the direction they were travelling in. Their weapons would struggle to defeat a helicopter if it was military, but it was all they had. What Jackson would give for a 'Gimpy' right now. A 'Gimpy' was the affectionate name the British Army called the' General Purpose Machine Gun', it was a 7.62mm belt fed machine gun that was supremely accurate, even at high rates of fire, as well as being reliable. It would give the helicopter a big headache.

However, the chasing aircraft did not deviate from its course. Instead, it seemed to stop and hover. Then like a dog looking for its ball, it started to circle around its surrounding area. Clearly, the signal from the ring was there. Jackson let out a long breath, as did the rest of the team.

Milton came over to him and put a hand on his shoulder, his grin had returned. "Outstanding work soldier, that's evened the score."

Jackson sensed that this was about as close to an 'all is forgiven' comment that he was ever going to get out of Milton, so he just nodded and walked back towards his seat on the boat.

He was packing his NVG set into his pack when a huge hand grabbed him and spun him around. He came face to face with an angry looking Taylor. He looked incensed. Jackson was preparing for the impending fight when Taylor suddenly grinned at him, clasping him in the hardest 'Bear Hug' imaginable. When Taylor released him, Jackson stared at him puzzled.

"You saved our asses back there Buddy!" he said, "and you saved mine"

Jackson still looked puzzled. "I don't follow."

Taylor looked down embarrassed. "I was the one who searched Ramon. I should have checked his ring out, I fucked up"

Jackson tried not to gloat, but he also felt his pain. No soldier wants to admit he made a mistake, especially one that nearly cost them all.

"Hey, don't sweat it," Jackson said patting Taylor on the shoulder, "we are all human. But we learn from our faults yeah?"

Taylors smile returned. "You got it Buddy!" He extended his hand to Jackson who took it and they shook firmly. Ceasefire established.

Using the cover of darkness, they slipped into a ravine to the East of Cartagena and hid in a small culvert entrance. Danny was going to go ashore with Simpson. Danny and Simpson were going to the Airport to meet Danny's Brother-in-Law. He was arriving at the Rafael Nunez Airport at 8.30am and Danny and Simpson wanted to get there in plenty of time to put a full surveillance on the people milling around. They figured Martinez would have the airports watched for his arrival and wanted to identify them before breaking cover.

On the boat, they were unpacking and assembling the one piece of kit that they had not used yet, a drone. This compact miniature aircraft was fitted with live footage digital cameras that could capture from distances of over 1000 feet. Unfortunately this close to an international airport, they would have to fly it to the island as close to the sea as possible to avoid any radar. Once they got within 100 yards of the target, they would take her up high and watch from there. They would be static enough to avoid the civil radars and unheard from the ground.

Once they had assembled the drone, Marco fired it up. With the remote pack on the table, he started the drone's tiny propellers. It sounded like a wasp, a big, big wasp Jackson thought.

"It's a bit loud mate!" he said loudly over the noise.

Marco just smiled at him. "Yeah? Well listen to this!"

With a touch of a button, the whine stopped, but the propellers continued to turn.

Jackson smiled at him. "Smooth and silent. Just like me." The two men exchanged a knowing smile.

"Okay," said Marco, "let's go take a look at Jabba's Palace." Using a joystick and a toggle paddle, the small craft lifted silently off the deck. Instantly the split cameras came to life on a large screen in front of Marco. Split into four quadrants, top two quadrants were fore and aft. The bottom two, angled down at the area below the drone. The thermal imagery was not grainy or frosted at all. It was immaculate. Once again, Jackson gave them an 'A' for tech.

Marco expertly manoeuvred the drone through the entrance to the ocean, skirting around the Isla Grande and onto the target. About 100 yards from the little island the drone suddenly rose, gaining height rapidly. Marco flipped a few switches and the drone seemed to come to a stable hover over the target. Marco brought one camera angle to the front so it filled the whole screen, save for three tiny versions of the other views in the bottom left corner. The thermal image that filled the screen was flawless, even from the height the drone clearly was maintaining.

Marco proceeded to move the camera around the target slowly, taking stills as it turned. Jackson marvelled at skill and speed in which Marco worked. He understood the reasoning behind Marco's approach, not to expose the drone any longer than necessary. Once Marco was satisfied he had the island mapped, he brought the drone down, quickly doing a lower sweep of the island using both cameras this time. This time when he was satisfied, he brought the drone back out to sea. Dropped it back down and guided it back to the boat.

"Ok Scotty," Milton said, "what we got?"

"Bringing it up on the ship's briefing room now Sir."

They moved below deck. Marco remained up top on stag in case anyone took an interest in them. Milton used a remote control to drop a big 50" screen, which immediately glowed into life. Once in place, Milton connected the drone's unit to it via the USB port and the screen changed to show the images Jackson had seen earlier. Using the unit to navigate through the images, the island became clearer.

It was not that big. It consisted of a small wooded area next to a small cliff edge to its northern curve. A little beach followed round its clockwise 3 o'clock position that merged to a wooden jetty where Martinez clearly moored his boat. At its 6 o'clock and 9 o'clock faces, were sharp rocks that created a natural reef and wave break to the island.

There were four buildings in its centre. One looked like a vast house complete with huge terrace, swimming pool area and sculptured garden. To the right of the house was what looked like a barn, it could be the one Jackson saw in the picture, but there was no telling. To the left were two smaller buildings. One looked as though it could be a guardhouse or or small barracks. The last building overlooked the South and Westerly cliffs, a watchtower.

Jackson broke the silence. "Zoom onto the wooded area."

Milton rewound the footage and paused at the point Jackson indicated. Using the toggle switch, he increased the magnification.

Jackson saw it straight away. "Pan left a touch"

Milton nudged the toggle left. Jackson went to the screen and pointed at a spot where the small cliff formed a 'V'. "There! You see that? You know what that is?"

Everyone looked blankly at the screen and then at Jackson. Danny broke the impasse. "What are we looking at mate?" Everyone muttered their agreement.

Jackson rolled his eyes. "That my friends, is my way in. Islands like this have to pump their wastewater into the ocean. No sewage works on these things. That there…" he pointed at it again, "…is the waste pipe for the Island"

He waited a few minutes, holding their attention until his idea hit home. They all started to mutter amongst themselves.

"Do we have any scuba gear on board?"

Milton went to the back panel of the room and gave it a shove. The wall swivelled to expose a narrow storage area. Oxygen tanks, wet and dry suits hung from the wall. In addition, masks, flippers and harpoons adorned the space.

Jackson grinned. "Perfect! I need you to get me close enough to swim to that spot. I may need two guys to help me get through the filter grate." He had their attention now. "Once I'm in, I will move to the internal manhole that's closest to the woods. Then I will get into the barn and hopefully she'll still be there. Just be ready to give me back up if it all goes tits up!"

Danny was the first to see the problems with this. "OK mate how are you going to know where you'll be coming out? You could walk straight into a hostile area and then….well, it will be game over!"

Jackson smiled at his friend, and then returned to the image in front of him. He pointed to a space in the trees about halfway in. "You see that? Well that is a blockage junction. That will have either a short drop or a ladder access to the pipe in case they block up during storms. There are four of them along this path"

He moved his finger and Milton followed him with the toggle. Another three areas came into view, two in the woods and two in a straight line from there to the house.

"There may even be one in the house or basement if it has one"

Danny pointed to the house. "Why not go into the house from there then?"

"Too risky!" Jackson replied," I could walk in on lots of hostiles that I can't see. With the one in the woods, Marco could act as spotter and let me know when it's safe to emerge."

Taylor nodded his approval. "Sounds workable, but still doesn't say how in hell you gonna break her out, even if you do find her?"

Jackson nodded, it was a fair point, and one he had been rolling around in his head too. "I'm afraid I'm going to have to wing it from there. If it looks like I'm going to strike out I always have plan 'B'."

Taylor looked puzzled. "And what is plan 'B'?"

Jackson merely shrugged. "I get myself captured and they may take me to her"

The room suddenly was loud with noise; everyone was talking over each other, clearly not happy with that idea.

Danny shouted over the top of them. "Are you insane, Jax?"

Jackson shook his head. "Not at all, I reckon this guy's ego will compel him to show me how smart he is, and just how safe they are from me. That'll be their mistake!"

Milton looked at Jackson approvingly. "You got balls. I'll give you that, Jax!"

Taylor and the others nodded their agreement to that sentiment. Jackson felt a little embarrassed, not to mention afraid. Plan 'B' sounded like a long shot even to him. Mind you, so was plan 'A'.

Danny's mobile phone buzzed. Danny scooped it up and looked at it. After reading it twice over, he handed the phone to Jackson. Jackson looked at the message; it was from Paul, Cathy's Brother.

Jackson had met Paul Douglas a few times before. He had Cathy's build and was a shorter man. Straight laced, he wasn't as fiery as his sister was, but was no coward either. He went up in Jackson's estimation, when he agreed to bring the envelope himself. Took balls, he thought.

The message said:

Check email.

Jackson then closed the message down. Behind it, another window was open, it was the email he and Danny had created to talk covertly.

In front of him was an unsent email reading:

Hi Danny

PO Box opened. I got the letter and steamed it open.

Just looks like an invoice to me.

Dunno what you make of it. I've attached a shot of it below.

But means nowt to me. Will bring it with me.

Bout to get my connecting flight.

See you in a few.

P

Jackson looked at the bottom of the email. There was a little icon of a paperclip with a filename next to it. Jackson touched the paperclip, and the screen opened up to a photograph. Sure enough, Paul was right. It did look like an invoice from JM Exporting to a company called Trident Holdings. It stated that a delivery to Dryden was arriving on June 30th at 04.00, which was 12 days away.

Jackson looked blankly at it then looked up at Danny. "Any ideas mate?"

Danny rubbed his chin. "Nope, not a clue Bruv."

Jackson downloaded the image to his own phone after shutting Danny's down. He then gave it to Milton who in turn took a copy. Once Milton cast to the screen, they all looked at the invoice.

Milton turned to Danny and Simpson. "Better get going guys. Simpson, I'll keep you informed using the usual secure channels. We will try to get some answers before you leave there"

Simpson nodded. "OK, Boss. Ok Danny, let's boogie." With that both men left the cabin.

Once they had left, Milton returned to the rest of the team. "OK guys, Priority one, get Jackson to the DOP. Chuck? I want you on this Trident Holdings problem ASAP. Someone's pissing in our pond and I want to know who these fucking traitors are."

Chuck went to his pack and got out a laptop and a small case. "On it boss."

He set it down on the table and attached a small lead from the laptop to the box. It fired into life. The top sprang open and a motor began to whir. A small fin shaped antennae opened up. Once it had reached its limit, the motor stopped. Then another one started. The fins suddenly spread out to form a satellite dish.

Chuck saw Jackson's interest. "Sat-Com, I can hack into any encrypted site with this baby, untraceable and more powerful than its size says."

Jackson nodded his approval. These guys had all the toys, a lot more than you'd expect for a private security firm. They looked more like Government or National Security to him.

Suddenly Jackson felt the weight of betrayal forming on his shoulders. What was Danny keeping from him? What was he into, why would Sonia even intercept this document? She was a PA for God's sake. She should be taking memos or booking flights. All this seemed straight from a spy novel.

Jackson decided that he would keep anything he found to himself. He was sure these guys were on the good guy's side, but did they have another agenda? Suddenly the speed in which they got everything in play made sense.

For years, the American government and the CIA had this running game of deception. The CIA claiming it had no troops involved in overseas drug wars. The Government stringently denied sanctioning such operations. Jackson could see the hint of cover up going on here. Were these guys investigating, or helping cover it up? Either way it was on a need to know basis from now on. He wished Danny were here, so he could get the truth out of him, but with Danny out of the picture, he could concentrate on what he had to do.

He had been standing there lost in his thoughts so long; he had not noticed Taylor move behind him until a big hand landed on his shoulder, making him jump and spin round.

Taylor stopped his momentum with a strong grip. "Whoa there partner. Didn't mean to make you jump Buddy. Milton wants to know what you need to make this trip work, and when do you want to do it?"

Jackson regained his composure. "I want to get in as soon as possible. See, if I can get in there during the day, I can hide up in the woods. Will give me a good eight to ten hours of daylight to observe and assess. I can see if they bring food to the barn or not. I can monitor the guard's rotation patterns as well as a head count."

Taylor nodded. "OK that seems fair. What about equipment?"

Jackson paused to debate on how he would be best equipped, light and nimble or heavy powerful. He sided with the former.

"I'm going in there light. I need to be able to move fast and quietly. So, I'll take the suppressed SIG, some extra clips, my KA-BAR and the NVGs."

A KA-BAR was a seven-inch combat knife, it was comfortable in any close quarter's situation, but best of all, it was silent.

"You want any rations?"

Jackson shook his head. "Nah mate, just a waterproof knapsack to keep the Sig and the ammo in. Don't want a stoppage do we?"

He winked at Taylor, who gave him the thumbs up and went off to gather the gear.

Marco set off and guided them to a small rocky formation about 100 yards off the island. From here, he could successfully conceal the boat from view. Jackson, Chuck and Milton were all in their wet gear. Small tanks attached to minimalist breathing apparatus, designed for short spells under medium depth water. Jackson hoped they would not need any more than this. From the Island behind them, they would look like a diving charter.

All three men entered the water and dropped as deep as the light would allow. They swam confidently until they reached the opening to the waste pipe. It was about three feet wide and had a thick rusted metal grille, hinged on one side with a padlock at the other. Chuck attacked the lock with a pair of bolt cutters. It was hard going, as the lock was sturdy, but after a few minutes, the padlock dropped softly to the sea floor and the grille glided open.

Once Jackson was inside, Chuck pushed a temporary stopper into the grille to prevent it swinging open in low tide and giving the intrusion away. Jackson took off his fins and handed them to Milton through the bars, replacing them with hi-grip underwater shoes. He checked his pack firmly secured to his back and his knife, safely strapped to his thigh. They had also gave Jackson a spare set of breathing apparatus to stow in the pipe, just in case they could get off the island the same way they got in.

Jackson gave them a thumbs up and set off into the pipe. After only a few metres, it became too dark to see, so he dropped his NVG goggles and forged ahead. In front of him, the pipe slowly rose and within a few metres, he emerged from the water. He continued for a few more metres before checking the air. He could breathe, but it was incredibly hot and the smell was oppressive. A dank mixture of stagnant water mixed with human waste made him gag and retch.

I need to get out of this he thought. His claustrophobia was beginning to take hold. Little waves of panic washed over him as he pressed on into the pipe. The slime attached to the pipe made the going slow. His gloved hands and hi-grip shoes struggled to get purchase. It felt like he was crawling along a reverse travellator, often scrambling and getting nowhere.

Eventually, after what seemed an eternity he reached a break in the view. He was at the first junction. He rose up to find a metal set of rungs set into the concrete upwards pipe. He lifted his goggles and climbed to the top. Blocking the top was another grille, he checked the sides for locks or alarm sensors, there were neither. Jackson gave the grille a gentle push to gauge its weight. It was heavy but manageable.

He decided to go back down and bypass this one, because he knew the next one offered more cover as it was deep into the trees. So once more, he descended into the dark and ploughed on in a green hazed nightmare. Eventually, exhausted, he reached the second junction. Again, he climbed to the top. The light was not as bright here, obviously because of the tree cover. He reached the grille and did the same checks, no locks and no alarms.

Jackson went back down. Removing the breathing apparatus and the spare units, he tied them off to the bottom rung of the ladder, via a small bungie cord. This way he could get them on and be away from the hole quickly, in case they had company.

Once he was satisfied they were not going to clank around and draw attention, he returned to the grille. Placing his hands firmly on the bars, he slowly began to push. The noise that hit him was deafening. The high-pitched metallic whine of the rusted hinges seemed to resonate throughout the pipe. He immediately stopped. Holding it in position, he waited. If someone had heard it, then he would quickly have company. He prepared himself to drop if necessary. Nobody came.

Jackson had to make a decision now, fast or slow. He knew that if he got it open fast, he could clear the area quickly, but risked increasing the noise. However if slowly had not been heard so far, then likelihood was it would not now. He opted for the latter.

Again, he began the agonising push, and again his ears filled with high-pitched shriek of protesting hinges. Mercifully, after a couple of inches, the hinges gave up their protests and conformed. Jackson used this stroke of luck to get the grille opened quickly. He emerged into a small clearing about six feet square. He decided to close the grille, which did not seem as loud out in the open.

Jackson took his compass out and got his bearings, the house was due south of his position, so he went west into the trees. He stopped a short way in, turning to face the clearing and made himself as small as possible. He had to know if the suspected his intrusion or not before he pressed on. As he studied the surroundings, he noticed the small pathway that seemed to connect the house to the access grilles. He made a mental note to get deeper into the trees. If they did patrol this, he did not want to stumble into company.

After thirty minutes observation, he was satisfied he was ok to continue. He pushed west through thick foliage, the spiny bushes that hugged the forest floor dropped his progress to a crawl. The only thing in his favour was, no guard was going to be this deep into the wooded area.

Once he was satisfied he was far enough away from the pathway, he changed direction and inched slowly south towards the house. The previous night's storm had presented him with plenty of water, collected on the palm leaves. He had brought water, but any extra was always welcome, so he drank at every opportunity. There was no bigger enemy to the soldier than dehydration.

After an hour of razor sharp thorns and ankle twisting vines, he reached the tree line. He lay down, collected his thoughts, and got his breathing under control. He was exhausted, but exhilarated at the same time.

Jackson took a small pair of digital binoculars out of his pack and surveyed the vista in front of him. He had emerged facing the pool area in front of the main house. Stone steps rose up to a large swimming pool with scattered blue and red sun loungers, currently unoccupied, however three guards stood looking out, they looked bored. Jackson imagined that no guests would be present without Martinez being there, so other than domestic staff; he did not expect to encounter any other civilians.

Beyond the pool area was another set of raised steps to what looked like a paved sun terrace. White tables and chairs were dotted around, reminding Jackson of the package holidays he, Sarah and Ellie took, when they were still a functioning family. All that changed the moment he snapped and beat Pulev almost to death. The long hours he spent at work, coupled with the mood swings and night terrors he developed because of the horrendous pressures that detective work placed on you, made his marriage slowly erode. His daughter naturally took Sarah's side, so by the time the inevitable divorce filed, he was a stranger in his own home.

Jackson snapped himself out of his dark thoughts. Concentrate, he thought to himself, focus on the now! Standing in all its splendour in front of the terrace stood the house. It was magnificent. All white and glass, it gleamed proudly in the sunshine. It was enormous, clearly the drug business paid well, because this must be worth a fortune, he thought. Two white stone pillars offered splendour to a heavily ornate rear entrance. The huge, solid wood, white door decorated with sculptured black iron bulls. They were in different poses, and all faced into a centrepiece of a Matador, complete with cape and Muleta.

There were four huge windows facing the pool area. Above these, a white balustrade encircled a balcony and a smaller roofed addition, obviously the master suite. To the right stood, what Jackson had originally thought was a barn. It was in fact a gardener's storage garage, also painted white and simply constructed with a single door.

To the left was another white stone building. It was a large building, probably as big as Danny's house. It was two storeys with small windows and a flat roof. A balustrade ran the full length of the roofed area. Two armed guards paced lazily around its edges.

The door facing him opened and two men emerged, one armed with an AK 47, the other, carrying a box. They walked towards the house but stopped before they got there. Turning left, they proceeded down the side of the house. They stopped halfway, and the armed man squatted down. When he stood, he had opened a steel door encased into the ground. Both men descended into what Jackson assumed must be a basement. Was that where they were keeping her? He would bet it was.

To the left of the guardhouse was a watchtower. It was slightly behind the guardhouse by about 100 metres. It looked sturdy and stood about fifty feet high. Access via a long ladder was on its underside. From where Jackson was looking, he could see the unmistakably barrel of a Russian DShK .50 Cal machine gun. A formidable weapon that fired a 12.7mm x 108mm round, initially designed as an anti-aircraft weapon, it became popular as an all-purpose heavy machine gun. It would stop most lightly armoured vehicles or boats.

Jackson assumed there would be another two covering the south and east of the rocky coastline. This would mean that an approach to the south of the island would be out of the question. He could only assume that Martinez considered the small forest un-penetrable and figured any incursions would be from the south, another mistake.

Jackson watched the guards circle around the house. They changed personnel every two hours, meaning there was a window of five minutes where the pool area was clear. This was Jackson's opportunity to get across the open ground. He had toyed with the idea of circling around to the garage, but that would mean losing sight of the guardhouse. He needed to be able to react if they changed sequences.

The light was fading as dusk approached. The exterior lights flickered to life and the whole area was awash with amber rays of intersecting light. This was going to make crossing the open ground extremely hazardous. Jackson needed a way to get between the house and guardhouse in one motion, because it would leave him seriously exposed, if anyone inside the house were looking out. He decided he might need help.

"Charlie one, this is Charlie eight, over." Jackson waited, never taking his eyes off the house.

"Charlie eight, go ahead!"

"Charlie one. I have eyeball on possible location of our package, acknowledge?"

"Charlie eight, Roger that! What's your plan of approach?"

"Charlie one, I need to cross open ground, so will attempt once the house is tucked up in bed. Only trouble is, I have roof lights flooding my ground ahead. Any way we can disable them temporarily, so I can make access? "

"Charlie eight, wait out, will find you a solution."

Jackson sighed. He hated waiting for anything. "Charlie one, roger that. Charlie eight out and standing by!"

About fifteen minutes later, the airwaves burst into life again. "Charlie eight, this is Charlie one, over?"

Thank god for that, Jackson said to himself. "Charlie one, this is Charlie eight, go ahead"

"Charlie eight, be advised, Scotty has done a drone sweep of the island and your house and has come up with some good news and bad, over."

"Ok hit me with the bad news Charlie one."

"Scotty says, not only is the open ground illuminated, but there are six thermal imaging cameras in that area alone, acknowledge?"

Jackson felt his heart sink. He had not factored in the fact that they might have better surveillance equipment than the usual compounds of this type. This means even if he could disable the lights, then he would still stand out like torch as his body heat gave him away. Instinctively, he moved deeper into the trees.

He regained his composure. "Great! That's just great! What's the good news, Charlie one?"

"Well Scotty reckons there's a control box circuit breaker housed in a unit about fifty metres to the right of the garage. He says these islands use external boxes to safeguard the house from electrical storms. If you can get to it, he will drop you some equipment to knock it out temporarily. That way you can go from there in darkness."

Jackson's mood soared. "Charlie one that's affirmative, making way round to location. Oh and tell Scotty first beers on me….genius! Charlie eight out!"

Jackson withdrew further into the woods and made his way around to the side where the garage was. Marco was right. Sitting almost at the treeline was a metal box standing all on its own. It reminded him of the telephone terminals at the end of the streets where he grew up. Engineers would park up in front of them, fiddling inside their open doors.

Jackson moved and positioned himself behind the unit. He could kitten crawl up to it unseen.

"Charlie one, this is Charlie eight. I am in position in trees next to the unit over?"

"Charlie eight, drone is inbound. Package attached, confirm?"

"Roger that!"

About ten minutes later a dark shape appeared in front of him. Dropping down and coming to a stop on the floor about two feet away from him. Jackson crawled up to the drone and unhooked the small pouch tied to it. He gave a thumb's up to one of the cameras and immediately the drone lifted off the ground and silently skulked away into the almost black sky.

Chapter 5

Extraction

Jackson opened the pouch and inspected the contents. It consisted of four crocodile clipped bypass leads, a small pair of wire snips, some plastic cable ties and what looked like a pager with four terminals to it. Two on its left and two on it right. On its front, it had a small front flap that opened up to reveal an LCD display and keypad.

"Charlie one, this is Charlie eight. I have the gifts and am standing by, over?"

"Charlie eight, this is Charlie seven. I will walk you through it, acknowledge?"

Jackson knew Marco was smart, but he had doubts about his own ability with this kind of delicate work. He was a soldier, not an electronics expert.

"Ok, Charlie eight confirmed, making way to the unit now!"

He crawled the few yards to the unit. It stood about four feet square. It had a panel held on by four large screws.

"Charlie seven, I am at the unit, awaiting instructions"

"Charlie eight, be advised, I am bringing the drone back to you, to get eyes on."

"Charlie seven, roger that"

Suddenly the drone dropped down and hovered next to him. "Ok," said Marco, "remove the screws bottom first."

Jackson took his knife from its scabbard and began unscrewing the locking screws. They moved easily, were not very long, soon he had them all out, and let the panel fall into his hands, shuffling back to lay it on the ground. The drone moved in front of him, a small pencil light ignited in front of it and began scanning the contents of the unit. Jackson waited, feeling very exposed.

"Charlie eight, here's what I want you to do. From the two boxes to your left are two brown wires, you see them?"

Jackson followed the drones light. "Roger that Scotty."

He tried to sound confident, but was genuinely nervous.

"Right, I need you to strip about an inch off each shroud about five inches from its source"

Jackson took the snips, and positioned them over the rubber shroud. His hands were shaking badly. He took a moment to compose himself. Gently he squeezed until the jaws bit into the rubber, then he rotated them to complete the first cut. After a while, he had both wires stripped and exposed.

"Charlie seven, brown wires stripped, what now?"

"You are doing great Charlie eight. Now, there are two red wires running from the exact opposite box to the brown one. I want you to do the same to the red wires. But be careful, these ones pack the punch, so steady as she goes!"

Great, Jackson thought; could you not have kept that shit to yourself, pal? Nervously, Jackson repeated the process on the red wires.

"All wires ready to go, Scotty!" he said, relieved that he had not fried himself in the process.

"Good job. Now plug the bypass wire's into the small pulse unit, but don't switch it on yet"

Jackson did so and confirmed this to Marco.

"Almost there, Buddy. Now, with the unit facing you with the flap opening right to left, take the top left bypass wire and attach it to the top brown wire. Then the bottom left wire to the bottom brown wire. Repeat the opposite with the red wires. Once you have all four wires securely bypassed, cable tie them to prevent them slipping off."

When Jackson had all wires secured, he gave his throat mic's PTT button two presses.

Marco understood this and continued, "Now open the flap and press the red button to power up the unit. Tap the up button till you get to set interrupt entry point, click ok and enter the time you want it to interrupt the power. Then scroll down to restore point, repeat with the time you want it to restore. Remember the longer the power is out, the more chance someone will come and investigate."

Jackson gave two presses. Now all he had to do was work out what time he was going to make his move. It was almost 22.30. Ideally, he would like as many of the people in the house and guardhouse tucked up in bed, and the ones awake to be tired. He set the interrupt for 03.00, restoring at 03.05.

That gave him 5 minutes to get to the trapdoor and get inside before the lights returned. After that, he was just going to have to take his chances and hope for the best. He returned the panel to its position and screwed it in place before returning to his original viewpoint. Now he waited.

He did all of his equipment checks. He was not carrying much, but he still needed everything in working order. He could not shake the nagging doubt that had been eating at him. He felt like a pawn in a game that he was not in control of. Someone was lying. Question was, who? He pushed these thoughts to the back of his mind. Concentration on the task in front of him was priority number one.

Jackson checked his G-Shock watch, careful not to allow the dial glow to be visible. 02.45. The guards seemed to be regular with their shift changes and route. A second trip made with a box to the trapdoor about 23.50, giving Jackson the impression that this was the end of shift check. Whoever, or whatever down there secured there for the night. He had not seen anyone come up who had not gone in while he was watching. Jackson was hopeful that there were no guards down there, or if there were, they had been there all day. They would be tired and probably sick of their lives. Hope for the best, but plan for the worst.

Timelines were tight, so Jackson called his plan in. At 03.00, he hoped that the power would drop. Once the countdown started, Marco was going to give Jackson a countdown as the minutes passed. Once he reached thirty seconds remaining, he would have to abort if he had not reached and entered the trapdoor. Jackson checked his watch again, 5 minutes to go. Jackson went through his mental preparation. Control his breathing then control his emotions. He planted himself into the ground, like an Olympic sprinter awaiting the pistol's retort.

Jackson positioned his NVG goggles ready to drop them as soon as darkness consumed the light; he needed to have all the advantages he could get. Ideally, he would have had about three days on target, to get a full appraisal of the constraints of his surroundings, but time restraints would not allow such luxuries. Therefore, he would have to rely on his training and his instincts.

Marco burst to life in his ear. "Charlie eight, ten seconds to lights out, nine, eight, seven, six, five, four, three.....stand by...stand by..."

Then the lights went out. Jackson was up immediately, dropping his goggles over his eyes to illuminate his way. He ran straight to the first cover, which was the stone rise to the pool area. He paused there to take in the scene. He could hear voices off to his left, orders issued. The two guards in front of him had already turned their respective corners and were out of sight. Jackson took advantage and sprinted up across the poolside and up the terrace steps.

Suddenly the large wooden door burst open. A large figure exited the house and it looked like it was struggling with something in its hand. A torch beam ignited and began to sweep across the terrace. Jackson darted to his left. He took refuge behind a metal table and chairs as the beam swept in his direction. He removed the night sight in case the beam hit him, last thing he needed was being blinded.

"One minute down." Marco said.

More voices broke the darkness as two more bodies emerged from the doorway. The beam passed over Jackson's head and concentrated its dance on the trees he had just vacated and then it travelled to Jackson's right coming to a stop at the power unit. The beam stopped on the unit before extinguishing. Jackson took his opportunity and sprinted silently to the corner of the house. With his night sight back in place, he made it around the corner, instantly checking the floor for the trap door.

About five yards in from the corner, he found it. It was a double steel access door. The kind you would find outside an old British pub. Access to a basement or cellar Jackson thought. Martinez obviously has his provisions delivered into here.

Jackson gave the door a gentle pull. It moved without resistance, it was clearly unlocked. He opened it enough to get a look inside; a steep staircase went down about ten feet. There was no movement from the bottom. Whoever was down there was either shocked or waiting. Wasting no more time, Jackson entered the Basement, gently closing the door behind him. As he made his way down the steps, he placed each foot down edge first, then bringing the rest of the foot down. Mercifully, the steps were metal and gave no sound away.

"Two minutes down."

Jackson drew his knife as he reached the last few steps. In front of him, the passage turned to his right, he turkey peeked around the corner. It opened up to a cellar. Four large columns rose from the floor holding the ceiling up. He could see boxes in one corner of the vast cellar. Two long tables ran down its north and south walls, more boxes filled their surfaces.

On the opposite wall to where Jackson stood was a metal door. This must lead to the house. The only thing missing was Sonia. Jackson rounded the corner and carefully crept into the room. He secured the KA-Bar and drew the SIG. It was fitted with a Trident Suppressor. It would not be silent; the working mechanism still made a loud noise, and the escaping gasses would be audible, but as the name suggests, a suppressor does just that, it suppresses the retort.

Jackson made it to the first column, and peeked around it. There was nobody there. Then he heard it. A shuffling sound followed by a metallic rattle. Somebody was down here with him. Jackson stopped and opened his mouth to reduce his own breathing masking the sound. There it was again. He pinpointed it coming from behind the column in the opposite corner. He circled left to the corner and slowly made his way so he was parallel to the column.

As he peered around the column, he saw her. Sat with her back against the concrete pillar, her hands chained to a ring tether set into the floor in front of her. She was frantically moving her head left and right, clearly aware that someone was there.

He desperately wanted to rush over to her, but mistakes like that get you killed. Instead, he softly stepped around, checking his blind sides.

"Three minutes down. Get a move on buddy"

With this Jackson moved over to Sonia. "Son, it's me, Jax!"

Sonia jumped at the sudden voice by her side. She let out a short gasp, clearly disorientated.

"Sonia, calm down. It's me, Jackson. I'm here to get you out of here!"

"Jax!" she said loudly.

Jackson put a finger to her lips. "Ssshhhh! We need to keep quiet. We don't have much time. Can you stand?"

Sonia rose, little unsteady at first but she was up. Jackson looked at her bindings. Her wrists clasped together by a set of metal cuffs in a figure of eight. There was a padlock on her right side and a hinge to her left. In the centre was a loop leading to a chain. The chain was about five feet long and sturdy; it led to the tethering ring secured into the floor.

He tried the padlock but it was a strong heavy-duty one. He could pick it but it would take time. He removed his pack and set it down on the mud-covered floor, clearly the one from the photograph.

"How did you find me?" Sonia whispered.

Jackson replied softly. "Your picture, I got your message loud and clear."

Jackson took his entry kit out and started to work on the lock. The noise was loud in his ears, but he had no choice. Soon time would be against them, and they still had to get out of the cellar. If the lights went up early, they would have to fight their way out.

After a few seconds if gently probing, Jackson found the tumblers. He use the top tool to create the fulcrum and rotated the barrel. With a click, the padlock sprang open. Quickly releasing Sonia, he grabbed her by the wrist.

He guided her towards the steps. "Do you trust me?"

"What?"

"Do you trust me?"

Sonia put her hand in Jackson's and whispered. "Of course"

They had made it to the steps. "There are steps here Son; I'm going to go up. Stay here till I get you OK?"

Sonia nodded even though it was pitch black. "OK, Jax!"

Jackson was about to push on the door, when he heard voices outside. Carefully he raised the door a crack. Two guards were standing with their backs to him. This just got serious.

"Four minutes down Charlie eight. Get your ass outta there buddy!"

No time for finesse now, Jackson thought. He drew the SIG and returned to Sonia. "Put your hand on my shoulder and follow me!"

Using his head as a ram, Jackson burst from the door with his weapon at the ready. As the two guards started to spin towards the noise, Jackson shot them both in quick succession. They fell without a noise as Jackson grabbed Sonia and sprinted for the treeline, no time for stealth now. Distance was the key.

"Thirty seconds, move your ass!" Marco had the drone in play now.

Shouts went up behind them, followed by gunfire, but Jackson ploughed on.

"Twenty seconds Charlie eight. Almost there!"

Jackson felt the impact and searing pain in his left shoulder as he fell forward dragging Sonia with him. Scrabbling to get hold of her, he stumbled to his feet. The trees were only a few metres away.

Shots rang out, and Jackson could hear the rounds thumping into the ground next him. Two feet from the trees he felt Sonia go down, at that moment, the lights returned, temporarily blinding him.

He lifted his night sight, turned and saw Sonia lying face down. He instantly grabbed her by the arm and dragged her into the trees as more rounds smacked around him.

"Marco!" Protocol was out the window now and urgency was the key. "Trauma kit needed at Infil site, over?"

"Roger that Buddy en route."

Jackson pulled Sonia to her feet, she was dazed and unsteady on her feet. They stumbled into the scrub and put as much distance between themselves and the pursuing guards. After about ten agonising minutes, the sound of the pursuers became faint. Jackson stopped and using his Maglite, checked Sonia's injuries. She had taken a round to her side, luckily it was a through and through. He ripped the sleeve off her shirt and plugged the holes. It would not stop much, but it was better than nothing.

"Hold the pressure on and we will get you out of here!" His breathing was rapid and the pain in his shoulder was burning.

Once he had her steady on her feet, they pressed on. Eventually they emerged next to the entrance to the pipe.

"Marco, we're here, where's my pack?"

Marco's answer was immediate, a bag about the size of a bag of sugar dropped into the clearing. Jackson ran and scooped it up; he was aware of voices getting louder. His throat gasping for liquid. "Need a diversion guys!"

A light ignited as Marco navigated the drone into the trees heading in a perpendicular direction to their position, purposely making as much noise as he could. The shouting became more excited as the guards bought the ruse.

Jackson quickly opened the pack of Traumafix clotting powder. He covered both wounds, and then applied the waterproof dressings. It would not hold for long under water, but might just stop the excess blood loss. He would deal with his once they were clear.

"Are you ok to run?"

Sonia nodded and they set off towards to grille. Jackson opened it quickly, ignoring the noise, and they dropped into the pipe.

He untied the breathing apparatus and secured Sonia's before putting his own on.

"Going for a little swim girl"

He got a thumb's up in return and they crawled through the slime towards the water. They stopped just before the first junction, to make sure nobody was waiting for them. The coast was clear so they pressed on to the end. Jackson removed the stopper and pushed the grille open and they pushed off away from the island. Jackson could feel his muscles beginning to tighten up. He was losing blood and his oxygen was limited. The extra effort to keep moving was rapidly depleting his tank. They needed to surface to get their bearings in the dark.

As soon as they broke the water, they were aware of lights scanning the water around them. Jackson used his night sight to see the rock formation he wanted. They submerged and pushed on towards the boat. Sonia was in front of him now and pulling away.

He could feel the energy leaving him quickly, and when he surfaced, again he had lost sight of her. Desperate to find her he submerged again, his breaths became laboured as the oxygen level dropped. He could feel himself losing consciousness.

As if the ocean came to life, a hand grabbed his mask, ripping it off and replacing it with another one. He instantly took a full lung full of oxygen. His head cleared quickly and he realised Sonia had come back for him. Reinvigorated they pushed on towards the rocks, surfacing only when they were safely amongst them. They reached the boat, their bodies hoisted out of the water by strong arms. Jackson could feel his head becoming heavy then he blacked out.

Chapter 6

Traitor

When Jackson came to he was no longer on the boat, he was in bed. It took him a while to focus, he still felt groggy and heavy headed. As he tried to move the pain in his shoulder seared through him like a hot poker. Oh yes, he thought, I was shot. He tried to sit up but found he could not, not because of his injury, but because his right wrist was handcuffed to the bed.

He lay there trying to remember the events leading up to the boat. Did they catch him? No, he remembered Sonia lifted into the boat, then him, then nothing. Panic started to creep in. Where was he? Who cuffed him to the bed?

He was in a small private room. There was a small cabinet and a large window to his left. The sun bleaching through the blinds told him it was daytime. To his right was a door with a closed curtained window. The room looked like a hospital room, but he could not be certain. On the wall in front of him, a small dated looking clock told him it was 12.30.

About half an hour later, the door opened and a petite female entered. She wore the white uniform of a hospital, but Jackson could not see any emblem.

"Nurse?"

The nurse looked up from her charts and gave him a tired smile. She was in her early twenties by Jackson's reckoning. Her long brown hair was tied up into a loose ponytail and covered with light blue nurses cap. Her eyes were dark brown and with her tanned skin, she looked Latino.

"Where am I?" he asked. Trying to sit up again.

The nurse gently pushed him back onto the bed. "You must rest sir."

Her accent was definitely a mix of Spanish with a slight American twang.

"Where am I?" he asked again.

She looked at him with a frown. This time she came closer and leaned into him. "You are in the Hospital de las Californias in Mexicali. Do you not remember why you are here?"

He rubbed his eyes, and then looked up at her. "I got shot, but can't remember why!"

She came closer still shaping up to whisper in his ear, he could see her nametag and it read Catalina. Catalina cupped her hand and whispered into his ear, "You were brought in by two men, who said you were a drug courier."

She moved away and Jackson could tell the she was not buying that. "We have been told to treat you," she continued, "but under no circumstances are we to let you leave!"

Jackson could feel the anger building, what was this shit? Who is setting me up here? He looked at Catalina and beckoned her closer. "Were the men Mexican?" he asked, already knowing the answer.

Catalina shook her head, "No Senor, they were white. They looked like policemen." Of course they did! Jackson fumed.

"Can you describe them to me?"

Catalina nodded. "They were big men. One was very tall with no hair and a long beard!"

Jackson nodded, Taylor! "And the other?"

He was expecting her to describe Milton. He knew there was something wrong. The anger was boiling inside him to.

Catalina tried to calm him down with a hand on his arm. "The other one was even taller he looked like a model you see in the magazines, except he was big!"

Jackson looked at her dumbstruck. "Blonde hair?"

Catalina simply nodded. Jackson felt as though hit by a wrecking ball. Surely not, surely Danny hadn't double-crossed him. They were brothers! Jackson felt nausea wave over him.

He had to think quickly. "Listen Catalina, you have to help me." He fixed her with a serious stare. "If I stay here, they are going to kill me. You have to believe me, I am no drug courier." His eyes pleading with her. "But the guys who are coming to get me are, and they are very angry with me for spoiling their day. If they take me, then I am a dead man. You have to get me out of here!"

Catalina shook her head, clearly conflicted. "I cannot Senor, I was told not to let you leave. If they are who you say they are, they will kill me for helping you."

That is a fair one, Jackson thought, change tactics. "Listen to me, these people will kill a lot of people if I don't stop them, including women and children on both sides of the border." He could see Catalina's battle within. "I will protect you!" he said, "do you have children, Catalina?"

Catalina shook her head, "No Senor, but I have a little brother that I look after since our Mama died!"

Jackson knew this was his chance. "Well I have a little girl and I want to see her grow up without the threat of drugs and people who would harm them." He let that sink in for a few moments before continuing his pitch. "If I can get you both over the border and safe, would you help me?" He could see the draw of a new life bringing her round.

She nodded slowly. "OK, Senor what do you want me to do?"

Jackson smiled at her. "My name is Jackson, but you can call me Jax." He looked at her warmly. "Thank you Catalina"

Catalina went to the curtained window and peeked out. Then she turned to Jackson. "What do you want me to do?"

Jackson thought for a moment, looking down at his restraints. "Don't suppose they left you a key to these?" he said more in hope than expectation.

"No Senor Jax." she said embarrassed.

Jackson just smiled at her. "OK, how about a large paperclip?"

Catalina looked blankly at him, and then her comprehension hit, she beamed and reached for her charts. Flicking the pages shut, she removed a sturdy looking paperclip and handed it to him.

Jackson used his teeth and his left hand to open the clip up so it resembled a capital 'T'. He inserted the tip of the stem into the mechanism ratchet of the cuffs. After a little jiggling and a lot of concentration, the teeth holding the cuff in place clicked once, and then released the rest of the shackle. Jackson rubbed his sore wrist and sat up. Instantly the pain in his shoulder gripped him. Catalina noticed his pain and handed him a small paper cup of water and some tablets. He swallowed them and with a nod.

"My clothes?"

Catalina pointed to the cabinet next to him. Inside, neatly folded, was a pair of blue jeans, a yellow T-Shirt and a pair of Timberland boots, along with underwear. Jackson quickly stripped his hospital gown off; oblivious to the fact he was naked, until he saw Catalina's face flush. She was embarrassed, but she did not look away, he thought. Was she checking him out?

He put those thoughts out of his head. He dressed and went to the window. Looking through the blinds, he could see there was a flat roof about four feet below. He went to the other window and peered out. Sitting on a chair with his back to him, sat overweight man. He could tell by the bulge in his jacket that he was armed, clearly a guard.

He turned back to Catalina, "Can I get out of this window?"

She nodded at him and produced a key. It slotted into a small lock at the bottom of the window's runner. Once released, the window slid open, leaving him just enough room through which to crawl.

Before going through he took Catalina's hand. "When I've gone out, lock this behind me. Then leave the room." He looked out and saw a small group of bushes near the outer gate. He pointed at them and said, "I will meet you there, please trust me, I will get you out of here!"

She nodded and he went through and turned to face her. "Thank you, Catalina. Thank you."

He waved and headed across the roof. At the edge, he saw he was directly above the ambulance bay. He swung his legs over, ignoring the pain, and dropped onto the roof of an ambulance, before sliding off and racing into cover.

From his vantage point, Jackson could see the main entrance and the ambulance bays. To the left was a barrier-controlled car park. After what seemed like an eternity, Jackson saw Catalina leave the hospital and head towards the car park. She got into a battered and rusted light blue Renault 4. It reminded Jackson of the French movies Sarah used to make him endure when they were dating. It was a heap of junk, but it was his way out.

She swung the car out of the car park and headed to the exit in front of him. Jackson was expecting her to carry on past him without stopping. He would not have blamed her she surely knew the kind of people she was crossing by helping him, but to his astonishment, she stopped and swung the passenger door open. Without hesitation, he dove into the car and hunkered down. As soon as his door shut, Catalina sped away.

Her driving was erratic and her speed was slowly creeping up. "Calm down," Jackson said calmly, "they don't know I'm gone yet. Plus they will search the hospital first, but if you get stopped by the police or worse, we are both finished"

Jackson could see her hands relax slightly on the steering wheel as her speed dropped.

"Good," he said, "now where is your Brother?"

Catalina turned to him realising that she had to make a decision. He could see the conflict in her eyes.

"You know they will put two and two together, and work out pretty quickly that you helped me, so we have to move fast!"

Catalina nodded slowly, the realisation of her decision finally hitting home.

"He's in school at the edge of the old town."

Jackson pondered for a minute. "How old is he?"

She looked at him quizzically, "He's eleven next month"

Jackson could see a problem arising here getting a minor into the USA would be tricky without a valid passport, or letter of release. He thought about how the school would react to them taking him out too.

"Is this going to be a problem, Catalina?" he asked, "Are the school just going to let you take him out without a good reason?"

Catalina nodded vigorously, "Si, Senor Benito often goes to a special camp around this time. He is different to other children. He doesn't speak very well and the volunteers in the camp work with him to bring him along"

Jackson had the one burning question rattling around in his head. "Will he kick off if we take him away to a strange place?"

Catalina looked puzzled, "What you mean kick off? I don't understand."

Jackson smiled sometimes he forgot where he was. "Will he kick off, get upset or angry and be a problem?"

Catalina shook her head, a sad expression creeping across her face. "No, Senor Jax. I tell him stories at night when he has bad dreams. I tell him one day we will leave this place, go somewhere nice, where people smile at you."

Catalina seemed to drift off into her own word. "I tell him his nightmares will be over and he can be a normal little boy again. This lights his face up again so no, he will not be upset!"

Jackson could see the pain in her face. "What happened to you and him? How come you ended up his only guardian?" He wondered if he had gone too far. "If it's too painful it's OK. I didn't mean to cause offence."

She smiled at him softly. "It's OK." She drifted off again but continued. "When Benito was five we lived in Guerro, very poor. Criminals owned everyone. We all worked for them even at school age. My Papa was Policia. He was a good man. One day we came home from school and there were men in our house.

"Benito and me, hid underneath the floor in our special place. They had a gun to my Mama's head while they were beating Papa with bats. They were shouting at him, telling him that if he didn't drive for them then they would kill Mama."

Jackson could see tears welling up in her eyes; he knew what was coming next.

"My Papa was a good man," She repeated, "he refused to be a criminal. Then the men held Papa down while the others took Mama over and over and over. When they finished they shot them both. We hid until it was dark and ran. We hid in a big lorry and ended up here. Benito never spoke properly after that, so I became his Mama and we lived in trailers near the hills. I put Benito into school and got a job helping in the Hospital. I have been here ever since."

Jackson knew a lot about the atrocities suffered by the poor in the slums of Mexico. The brutality was widely publicised and he sympathised with her entirely.

"I will get you away from here, I promise!"

He put his hand on her shoulder and they looked at each other softly, probably longer than Jackson thought normal. Get a grip Jax, he thought, she is younger than Ellie.

They drove in silence for another thirty minutes when she eventually pulled up outside a mesh fenced off building. It was white and blue with painted jigsaw pieces on its walls. The sign outside read; 'Centro de Atencion al Niño Autista de Mexicali'. Autistic school, Jackson thought, makes sense.

Catalina got out and leaned back into the car. "I had better go in first, Benito doesn't react well to strangers, especially men"

Jackson nodded. He could understand that. Strangers had scarred the poor boy; it was only natural that he does not trust people. While Catalina went inside, Jackson sat thinking. How is he going to get out of Mexico without a passport? He certainly did not enter Mexico legally. There was no record of him entering, so the British Embassy was out, besides he would never get two Mexican nationals through without lots of questions.

Thousands of migrants took the drastic step to cross the Rio Grande on foot and risk the border forces as well as the corrupt human traffickers. This may be their only chance to get into the states. He had a visa to be in the US, but Catalina and Benito did not.

The sight of Catalina pulling a hesitant little boy towards him broke his thoughts. He was a very thin boy, not very tall for his age, Jackson thought. His eyes looked huge compared to his thin features. He reminded him of the Anime characters in the cartoons Ellie used to watch on Saturday morning. He had on a bright blue T-Shirt with a white jigsaw piece printed on the front and black shorts. They were about two sizes too big for him. His sandaled feet covered in dirt.

Catalina opened the rear door and Benito was about to jump in when he stopped. Frozen in fear, he was staring at Jackson, the terror evident in his expression. Catalina shook him out of his stupor shouting at him in high speed Spanish. Reluctantly Benito got in, but stayed as far away from Jackson as was physically possible.

"I am sorry," she said quietly, "he's not been the same since that day."

Jackson waved it away, "Hey! Don't worry about it, I don't blame him for not trusting men like me. I have done bad things too, but I am no threat to either of you. You saved me, so I am going to save you."

He smiled his most convincing smile hoping she believed him. He had his doubts that even he could pull this off. "You need to gather anything you can carry and nothing more. We are going to have to get across without the car."

They travelled a few miles towards the hills and entered small gathering of about twenty metal trailers, rusted and covered in a thick layer of orange dust, arranged in a loose circle like the minutes on a watch, with a small rudimentary children's playground assembled in the community's centre. Catalina stopped outside the two o'clock position.

"This is it."

They exited the car, Benito clinging to Catalina's side unwilling to release her. They entered the trailer and the smell of dust and heat hit him like a wave. No openable windows meant there was no fresh air in this place and it was stiflingly hot. There was a basic cooking and washing area with a bottle gas stove. A small table sat in the middle but it was full of clothes, obviously ready to wash. There was no washing machine, so Jackson could only imagine Catalina visited a laundrette in the city. There was only one bed at the very end, which they must share.

Catalina got busy grabbing a few clothes and stuffed them into two backpacks. She picked up a small battered teddy bear. It was brown and most of the fir around its old ears had worn down to the thread. It was missing an eye, but looked loved.

"Have you got any money?" Jackson asked hopefully, not really expecting a positive answer looking at his surroundings.

Catalina went to the cupboard above the sink and pulled out a jar. She opened it and tipped it onto the bed. There was just short of 1000 pesos, about £35. Not going to get us far he thought, not going to buy our passage out of here. OK plan 'B' he thought.

"Have you got a phone?"

Catalina nodded and dug into her bag, pulling out an old Samsung S3 mini. The screen was cracked and scratched but it powered up first time.

"Internet?"

She just laughed sarcastically at him, which he took for a no.

"I need an internet café or access somehow; do you know where we can go?"

Catalina again brightened up, "Si, Senor Jax, we use a café a few blocks down. It's not so good and not very fast, but it works!"

Once they had all their things together, Catalina drove them to a dingy looking café. It was small with two old and weathered sets of tables and chairs outside. The varnish had peeled off them years ago from the searing heat of the sun. The window had grime frosting it so it was almost opaque.

Inside there were two similar tables leading to a small counter. Various drinks taps and spirit optics adorned the mirrored wall behind the counter. Along its right hand wall were four booths, each containing an ancient looking PC and tiny monitor. Catalina went up to the counter and lifted a small bell from the side of the till on top.

She gave it a little jiggle, eventually greeted by a toothless smile. The old woman that greeted her must have been ninety. Her lined face adorned facial hair even he would be proud of, all shrouded by a flowery headscarf. They exchanged pleasantries as well as money.

Catalina led them to the furthest booth away from the door. She fired it up and waited while the cursor spun around for what seemed like an eternity. The Windows 95 logo staring defiantly at him, almost taunting him as it waited to finish its laborious process. Eventually it was awake. Catalina clicked Internet Explorer open and changed the language to English.

Jackson loaded Google maps up and slowly trawled the coastline for what he needed. Eventually he found it. It was a small group of fishing shacks near to Vista Azul. He asked for Catalina's phone and registered it to his account. He then downloaded his account details to it, this way he could use the phone to buy things without leaving a trail. He then bought three tickets to the Channel Islands National Park tour and had them sent to the phone.

They left the café and filled the car with diesel. He drove from there on. He knew where he was going and what he was going to do. They drove to Tijuana and visited a local Western Union where he wired himself cash. They bought bottles of water, a box of snickers bars, a 5-gallon empty fuel can and short hose, a set of waterproof coats and buoyancy jackets each.

He also bought a cheap inflatable dinghy and paddles along with a child's bucket and spade. He discarded the dinghy but kept the sturdy looking plastic oars. They loaded the car and drove down the coastal route to Vista Azul, pulling off the main road at a junction before the town. The dirt track wound down towards the coast.

After half a mile, they came to a gate with a sign on it. The sign had a crude outline of a fishing boat and fish. Jackson moved the car alongside a stone wall, that ran behind a small hillock. He parked there as it was out of sight from the road and anyone behind the wall.

Jackson told them to stay put, while he had a look beyond the gate. He slipped over the gate and keeping low crossed the field to its far wall. He lifted up slowly and peered over. To his left was a small rundown shack. It was rotten and sinking on one side, there were various nets and buoys hanging from its rear. In front of the house was a small path that led to a basic wooden jetty. Tied to it was a small boat with a little wheel house and an outboard motor attached to the rear. Tied only at the front and was ambling side to side in the soft tide.

Jackson smiled to himself; this would be perfect, big enough to take them all, small enough to row away. He slipped back, and returned to the car. He opened the car's rear door and removed the fuel container and hose.

Catalina looked puzzled as she unpacked the supplies as Jackson syphoned the remaining fuel from car.

"We are going to wait here until it's dark," he said seeing her puzzled look. "Then we are going to take the small fishing boat that's just beyond the other side of the field."

Catalina looked worried. "We are going to steal?" she said, clearly unhappy at this new turn of events.

"No," Jackson said with a smile, "we are going to trade." Again, Catalina looked puzzled until it must have dawned on her what exactly they had to trade with.

"The car?" she said looking longingly at her only prized possession.

"I will get you a better one when we are safely stateside, I promise."

She seemed happy with that and nodded excitedly. "I will write him a note with the keys!"

Jackson was beginning to like her more and more.

When it was dark, they collected their provisions and struggled over the gate and field. Jackson scaled the wall and Catalina passed him the supplies over. She then helped Benito over, before climbing over herself. It was dark and the trail down to the sea was rocky. They had to go slow to be as quiet as possible, but the ground underfoot was treacherous.

Benito struggled to keep his feet and cried out a couple of times as he lost his footing. Mercifully, the trail levelled out as it split. Jackson went right towards the jetty. Catalina however took the left fork towards the house. Jackson began to load the provisions he had into the boat. He glanced at Catalina hoping she would hurry up. Discovery was going to be a big problem if the owner was armed. To his horror, he saw Catalina knock on the door.

"No!" he screamed, but it was too late, the door had opened.

Jackson could not see whoever was at the door, but they were talking for what seemed like an age. Catalina kept pointing at the boat and then to the ridge where the car was. After another ten minutes, she turned and headed back towards him. As she approached him, she saw the anguish on his face and smiled.

"I have made the trade."

Jackson still looked troubled. "The note would have Done!".

Catalina shook her head, "If we had just taken it, he would have raised the alarm that it had been taken. I told him Benito needed specialist help and we were taking him to the USA to get treatment!" she smiled at him innocently, "he said he could buy another two with the money that the car would fetch, and said the engine is full"

Jackson breathed a sigh of relief; things just seemed to be opening up ahead of them. However, in his experience, that was just the moment they went wrong.

Chapter 7

The Escape

They finished filling the boat and Jackson untied it. He turned the fuel intake valve and gave the starter cord a pull. The engine spluttered but died. He tried again, but had the same result. After four more attempts, the engine coughed to life. The noise was deafening in the still of the night.

Navigation was going to be the biggest problem, without visual aids he was likely to go round in circles. The wheelhouse contained just that, a wheel. There was a compass and a throttle control. In front of the wheel were two dials, one for speed, the other was a clock, which was clearly broken.

Jackson looked at the compass then at the house. He tried to visualise the map he had seen on the computer screen. They were facing west directly away from the house. He figured he would head dead west for half an hour before heading north and hope that he would come across land before he actually hit it.

He did final checks and securely seated his passengers.

"I am going to try to get us over the border area, I might miss my destination, but I will do my best"

Catalina jumped up and began rummaging into her pack. She produced a folded map. "The fisherman gave me this!" she said proudly.

Jackson opened the map. It showed the west coast in detail including the borderline and the surrounding islands. There were lines and numbers starting from their position to the borderline and then on to their destination. Jackson studied it carefully under the boat's dim wheelhouse light.

"Way to go old man!"

The numbers were degrees, speed and minutes. The old man had plotted him a course out of Dodge. He looked back towards the house and saw a figure standing at the doorway. He gave him a wave. The figure waved back.

Jackson set the phone up and pushed the throttle forward. He had to follow the compass at 300 degrees north-west at eight knots, for 45 minutes and then head due north, for another hour and a half at the same speed to reach the border His destination was another hour or two beyond the border. Jackson had toyed with going faster, but the old man must know these waters better than he did.

The sea was calm and the swells light. It took him a few minutes to get the steering under control, the wheel was not as responsive as he would have liked, but in the end, he got the hang of it. Catalina brought him some water and a chocolate bar. He had not noticed his hunger until he took a bite. As he stared out into the blackness, his thoughts wandered to Danny.

Danny was his best friend they had put their lives in each other's hands on more occasions than Jackson could count. Why had he betrayed him? It just did not make sense. What about Sonia? Was she innocent in all this or was it a big charade? Had Jackson's arrival cause them to change their plans at the last minute?

He thought back to the hostility he received from both Milton and Taylor. Danny had not really backed him up except when it suited him. He tried to remember the invoice that Paul had brought. Where was the shipment going? What was the name of the recipient? His usual infallible memory seemed to be very hazy lately.

The waters were beginning to get choppy and the boat rocked and swayed in the deepening swells. Jackson's attention returned to the task at hand, as they came upon the first turn. The waves increased their intensity as he guided the small boat around to a northerly direction. They travelled unmolested for an hour and a half, fatigue starting to build in Jackson's arms and legs. Water and chocolate were no longer helping and he was beginning to drift.

Something caught his attention ahead and snapped him wide-awake, lights! They were in the sky and looked like searchlights to him.

Helicopter, he thought, must be. Had they popped up on the radar of someone? They were only small. However, would give off a trail, especially at the speed they were travelling. Jackson ran to the engine and shut it off. He marked the direction and time on the phone.

Extinguishing the wheelhouse light, and dragging the supplies with them, they lay down into the rolls of netting covering themselves as much as they could. After a few minutes, the boat was awash with light as the searchlight honed in on them. Jackson was aware of the downdraught of the rotors lifting the netting off them. He wrapped his fingers into the holes trying desperately to keep them in check.

The light stopped on them for what seemed an eternity, then just as quickly as it arrived, it left. The thump of the rotors slowly receded and Jackson risked a look. The aircraft was heading away from them fast, maybe they got a more urgent call, he hoped. He told Catalina to stay out of sight for now while he went to see where they had drifted.

They were now facing the wrong way. He decided to fire the engine again to correct their direction. He gave the starter a tug, nothing. He tried repeatedly, still nothing. They were now adrift with no way to know how far they had drifted. They would never paddle the rest of the way.

Anger and a little panic set in. This was a long shot plan and he should never have dragged this woman and her vulnerable little boy into harm's way. His temper boiled and he gave the toggle a violent tug. The engine spluttered to life and ticked away, they were back in business.

He turned the boat to face north once again. He reckoned that they needed another half an hour past the border, before they needed to be careful. The islands would be nearby and he now had no idea how far off course they were. The helicopter did not return so Jackson relaxed slightly. The blue glow of dawn was beginning to grow to his right, a good sign that he was heading north.

He checked the fisherman's map again. In about ten minutes, he had to make a turn in a 50 degrees northeast direction. If he had not drifted too far, then the Channel Islands should be directly in front of them. If not then they could hit the mainland, which would definitely alert the coast guard. Jackson made the turn in faith and hope.

As the dawn broke, the horizon became distinguishable now. A landmass loomed in front of them, but there was no way to identify there they truly were. As they got closer, the light increased and they could see some natural caves, so he headed towards those. They would take refuge there until they could work out where they were.

Daylight was beginning to descend on them, which was good for navigation, but would leave them hopelessly exposed. Jackson made a decision to go for it; he could always talk his way out of it if they found themselves approached.

He left the cave into the light. The cloud cover cast a gloomy veil over them; there was definitely rain in the air that might come to their aid. Jackson skirted around the the island they had encountered first looking for tell-tale signs that could identify it using the fisherman's map.

After a couple of laps around the island mass they'd taken refuge in, Jackson could see they were at the third of the group of three closest to the mainland. The one he wanted was the middle of the three.

He had fished here with Danny about five years ago and knew they ran hiking and fishing tours here regularly. He slowed the boat down and set off for Santa Rosa Island. As they approached, he found what he was looking for, a small shale beach surrounded by a rock shroud. To the left of the beach was a tight trail leading up into the main stretch of the hiking trail.

He aimed the boat at a slight angle to the shore, to make sure he got as much of the boat broadside as possible. They crunched into the shale; the speed was low so the hull integrity was intact. Once the boat could go no further, it pitched sideways giving them a shallower exit. They climbed off into the shallow warm water as Jackson unloaded the water and provisions.

He gave the bucket and spade to Catalina. "Let him play for an hour, I'll be back."

He left them there and headed through the gap to the trail. The walk was steep but easily manageable. It slightly spiralled up through long grass and gorse. As it levelled off, he could see a few families exploring the views from this stunning island. Perfect he thought.

He walked along the trail until he came to the landing Jetty. It was a wooden structure with two tour craft tethered to it. There was a tour 'A' board placed at the head of the jetty. As Jackson approached it, a young woman in matching green shirt and skirt approached him carrying a clipboard.

"Are with the tour, sir?"

Jackson pulled his phone out and showed her his tickets. She looked at the names and perused her list.

"Ah yes party of three? We don't actually have you down as boarded?" she said looking around him for the rest of them.

He smiled his best-embarrassed smile. "We missed the boat, my fault, had to use my charm to get here ourselves, I was just checking we hadn't missed the boat back too."

She beamed a fake smile at him, "No not at all, sir. We set sail at 16.50 back to the mainland, or you can take the 10.30 one to the left, to Santa Cruz if you missed it."

He waved his thanks and returned the way he came.

When he returned to the beach, Catalina and Benito were gone. Panic gripped him, were they discovered? They did not know the story he had just invented and the border patrol would arrest them as illegals immediately.

He called out, but there was no reply. He ran to the water to look into the boat, nothing there either. He was about to turn and head back when he saw them. They were washing the bucket out next to the rocks. Catalina waved at him and they came happily back to him. The smile on Benito's face was priceless he thought.

"He's not had this much fun before" she said "Thank you Senor"

Jackson rubbed the boys hair expecting him to flinch, but he did not, instead he hugged Jackson's legs. Jackson bent down and looked into the boy's eye smiling. "Nearly there little man."

While Benito played in the sand, Jackson relayed his plan to Catalina.

They were going to pretend that she was his stepdaughter and they were here for a holiday, once they were on the mainland, they would try to blend in and he would get them to a motel to lie low, while he worked out what to do next. She did not seem convinced that it would work, but agreed to go along. Benito seemed to warm to Jackson, so hopefully he would not be a problem.

They hid there for a couple of hours before heading back to the jetty. The same tour guide welcomed them. She gave him her fake smile again and welcomed them aboard. With the stragglers finally rounded up, they set off towards the mainland. Jackson hoped that this part would be a formality, unless they found the boat.

They landed at the marina and disembarked without any problems. Jackson finally relaxed. He had no passport, but that was ok for now. He was on a holiday visa, which would run out in a few days anyway, so getting home was the last thing on his mind right now. First thing he needed was money, then food, then transport and accommodation.

After a few attempts he finally located a Western Union on the other side of a golf course, which claimed to 'cash pay checks without hassle', where he withdrew more funds. Across the street from the Western Union was a mobile phone repair shop and small pizzeria.

He took them into the pizzeria and sat them at a narrow booth near the back. He bought two large Pizzas, potato wedges and three large fizzy drinks. He ate a couple of slices, which brought him to life again. He was motivated now and did not want Catalina and Benito to slow him down. He needed to sort stuff out before moving on to his next move.

"I need to check a few things out; stay here and I'll be back soon." He handed her $100, "Get him anything he wants, but do not leave here, OK?"

She looked at him worriedly, but nodded. He could tell she was uneasy about being alone in a strange country with no ID, but he could not help her right now. Speed was of the essence now. He left the pizzeria and headed right.

He entered the mobile phone shop. It was a small repair store, but did have a number of prepaid phones for sale. These would be perfect as they were untraceable. He bought two and programmed each phone's number into both handsets as well as a tracking App, then returned to the pizzeria.

Catalina was still where he had left her. He handed her a phone and plugged the charger into one of the booth's customer USB charging ports.

"This number," he said, scrolling the screen, "is mine, if you have to move, or you are in any danger ring me, I will come for you, Ok?"

She looked even more worried now.

"Look," he said, trying to give her his best reassuring smile, "if for any reason you are detained by police, then you tell them I kidnapped you and forced you here at gunpoint. Then you claim asylum. Tell them that Juan Martinez thinks you helped me and will kill you if you return to Mexico. They will have to investigate it fully. That will buy me time to get to you."

He left her even more worried than before, but he could not help that just now. He needed information and he needed to find out just where Danny fits into all this. He just could not believe that his best friend would double cross him like that. There must be more to this, he told himself, more in hope than expectation.

This time he went left. About two blocks away he found an internet café hidden in a back street. It was small but clean, and the equipment looked up to date compared to the last on he had frequented. He paid for an hour and a strong black coffee and sat down at a terminal.

He typed in the email address he and Danny had shared, it was risky but he needed to get any shred of information he could. Once he logged on, the email showed two drafts pending. The first draft was the last email Paul had sent before bringing the envelope to them. He opened it and downloaded the image. He would transfer that to his phone via Bluetooth later.

The next email was from Danny, and this one took his breath away. It read:-

Jax

I heard about your escape, so if you are reading this, well-done brother.

Believe me I had no idea they were planning this and I had no choice but to play along. I didn't want you involved, but they told me I had to use you. They were going to kill my little girl, Jax. I have included an attachment with some information that will help you, password is my old local back home. I have also placed some toys for you if you make it stateside. Unfortunately, they are watching me every second, so I am no help to you. But I can be your comms. I know you probably don't trust me, but when you see what I have sent you, then you will know I got you.

D

Jackson opened the attachment. It was a PDF file with a password protection. He decided to download both files and look at them in private. These places had little to no security. He was relieved that Danny had not deliberately double-crossed him, but was still angry that he had not let him in on it.

He closed the email down, and spent the next 45 minutes setting up internet on his phone and checking out ads for cars for sale. He found one not too far away. It was a 1990 Datsun Cherry. It looked like a wreck, but with one alleged 'careful owner' and a $300 price tag, it was ideal. Jackson left and hailed the first cab he came across and gave the driver the address.

He pulled up outside a pink 'L' shaped bungalow underneath electric pylons. I was clean looking but old. It had a neat square lawn and six tall conifers shielding the drive from the neighbours. On the driveway was the car. It looked in better shape than the picture did it credit. It was red with a black plastic vinyl roof that had faded to grey over years of sunlight. There were a few rust patches but other than that, it looked in reasonable condition.

He opened the slatted screen door and knocked on the main door. Nobody answered so he knocked again. He then heard all manner of locks and chains rattling before the flimsy metal door squeaked open.

Behind it stood a frail woman, she was thin and her skin was almost transparent. She wore a light blue knitted cardigan and a long flowery skirt. Her thick glasses gave her brown eyes a fishbowl like appearance.

"Can I help you?" she croaked, her voice barely audible.

"Yes Ma'am." He said in his best American accent. It would not fool anyone, but he assumed she was most likely deaf anyway. "I have come to look at the car for sale." He continued, flashing the same type of smile Milton had given him.

"Oh yes!" she beamed, "It was my son's car, but he has bought a new one and it has been cluttering up my driveway for years. No one has been here to see it before. I don't see my son much these days. I don't see anyone!" Her sad eyes trailed down into her own thoughts.

Jackson wanted to hurry it along but felt a pang of guilt. He had a very similar relationship with his mother when his dad passed away. Now he felt the guilt that this old lady's son should be feeling right now.

"Can I start her up?" he said, breaking her trance and making her jump.

Confusion flooded her face until the realisation of whom he was and why he was there returned to her.

"Oh yes of course, I'll get the key, it's here somewhere"

She retreated inside and after what appeared to be a ten-minute search; she returned with a key and handed it to him. The door opened with a creak. It was sweltering inside and the fake leather seats were unbearably hot. He tried the key in the ignition, but it refused to fire. He tried again and this time it coughed to life. It rattled as he applied the gas, but it sounded ok other than that. It only had a quarter of a tank of gas, but it would do.

He shut it down and returned to the old woman.

"It's perfect for what I need, I'll take it"

Her eyes seemed to sparkle at the thought of being able to tell her son she had done well.

"What's your name my dear?" he asked kindly.

She smiled at him, "I'm Mabel and I'm nearly ninety you know?"

He counted out the $300 and handed it to her. Then he counted out another $100 and put his fingers to his lips.

"Well, don't tell your son, but this is your commission for being the best sales lady I've seen today Mabel."

He grinned at her and passed her the extra money, giving her a soft polite kiss on the cheek. He backed the car off the driveway and with a soft peep of the horn and a gentle wave, set off back to the pizzeria.

After he had filled up with gas and parked the car, he entered the pizzeria. There was no sign of them. He checked his phone, nothing. He began frantically checking the restrooms and the food areas, again found nothing. He left and stood outside looking in all directions, trying to think of where they would have gone. Beyond the phone shop, was a small mall, so he decided to try there. As he walked, he dialled her number. It rang five times before offering him the opportunity to leave a message.

After the beep he shouted. "Catalina, where are you? I came back for you but you were gone. Phone me please, let me know where you are!"

He headed into the mall. It only had a handful of cosmetic, hair salons and a department store. He entered the department store and headed to the children's section. He found Benito playing in the middle of a multi-coloured children's play area. It had brightly coloured soft play animals and cubes on which to bounce. Sitting on a plastic bench seat was Catalina. She was staring into space and did not even see Jackson approach her.

She jumped as he put his hand on her shoulder.

"I thought I told you to ring me if you had to move?" he said angrily.

Catalina looked down at her feet, like a scolded child, and he immediately felt guilty.

"I'm sorry; I just worry about you, that's all."

He pointed at Benito, who was jumping from one cube to another, with an enormous smile on his face.

"He's having fun."

She smiled and nodded. "I am sorry we scared you. There was a policeman. He came in and started looking at everybody. I got so scared so we left and we ran into here!"

Jackson nodded. "It's OK. Police officers do that here; they look for anyone they think they are after. They don't know who you are so relax. Anyway it's time we got out of here; we have a lot to do!"

Before leaving, Jackson bought them all a couple of pairs of jeans, some T-Shirts and underwear, alongside a green canvas hold all. They packed the car and left town.

Chapter 8

The plan

They drove out of town and booked into a cheap motel near Panorama Heights. It was a modern motel with a clam shaped pool. They booked two rooms and he paid for Wi-Fi in both. The receptionist asked for ID but after showing her his wound on his shoulder, she believed his story about losing everything to a mugger.

The rooms were small. They each had two large single beds with light blue quilt covers. The floors had a laminated covering. There was a table with a TV and a mirror at one end and a hard wooden chair. There were framed pictures of canyons and birds on the flower patterned walls. They each had a small bathroom with a shower, toilet and sink. Not a lot of room, but it would do for one night.

Jackson put his bag on the chair and sat on the bed. It felt like ages since he last slept and he could feel exhaustion setting in. He pulled out his phone and fired up the Wi-Fi code. He then opened the PDF file. The password prompt flashed up and he had to remember what Danny's email had said.

His password was his local pub back home. Now did he mean Aldershot where they were they stationed? Or did he mean his local pub in Newcastle? He tried 'The Kings Arms' but got nothing. He tried it with capitals, without capitals with numbers in place of letters, still nothing. Next, he tried 'Fox & Hounds' Danny's favourite drinking place back home.

Instantly the PDF opened. It was another letter, this time it was longer and more detailed. It read:-

'Jackson

If you are reading this, then you are back in the game. I am under close scrutiny so I have prepared this file to help you stop these bastards! First let me explain how we've come to this. Before you arrived, I got a message from Milton, saying Sonia was working for the CIA. He said she'd been recruited by them to spy on the communications floating back and forwards from Colombia and the US. They think they have a rotten apple within the organisation who is arranging the transportation and the distribution of narcotics on the US side of the border.

Sonia was copying files from a target source in the Colombian ministry that she'd befriended. The CIA had selected him and used Sonia to get to his personal files. He wasn't much of a drinker, so she used to get him drunk and steal files while he slept. She apparently supplied the CIA with countless factories and players, including Martinez. Unfortunately one of those files contained the name of the head contact in the US. This CIA operative has been tipping Martinez off about the hits on his factories. Every time our guys got there, there was nothing to destroy, but the shipments kept coming.'

Jackson rubbed his eyes, how did he let his daughter get involved with this? He continued reading.

'Then one night, he must have pretended to be drunk, and when she left, he'd followed her. She ran from him but knew they'd get to her, so she posted an envelope to England. That's right, the invoice you saw. So when they tortured her she gave it up straight away. What she didn't say was that the communication she had seen between the CIA guy and

Martinez detailing times, figures and names was different,
she'd taken pictures on her phone and mailed the sim card
to a different address.

That's when Milton and Taylor rang me. They told me
what Sonia was doing and I had to stop her sending the file
to London. That's when I knew they were obviously working
for whoever this guy is and I led them straight to her. They
had Martinez snatch her and make it look like a kidnapping.
I was supposed to get her to hand it over for her release, but
I was too late. I was told to go to London and get it back, but
then you told me you were coming. I had to tell them, I'm
sorry. I didn't want you to get involved, but they insisted.
Said it would make their story more credible.

They had been tasked with killing the leak and Sonia too.
But then while we were planning getting her out, Milton told
me that the plan had changed. If you got her out, they would
let her go and only kill the leak, but only if I let you get
locked away in a Mexican jail or worse.

Jackson felt the knife firmly sticking in his back. He
could not decide whether to pity his friend or whether he
was going to kill him, but he read on.

Now I know by now you probably want me dead, and I
don't blame you. I would feel exactly the same. But I have a
plan to stop them all and get our lives back….all of us!
I have buried half of my safe contents in a location only
you and I know. With it I have given you a file with the list
of names that I know so far along with images. I wish I
could help you brother, but if I leave here, I would only lead
them to you. Then we'd all be dead right?
The stash is where we used to hide Max's ball when we
went into the hills.

106

Good luck my friend and I hope one day you can forgive me, or at least understand why I did what I did.

I will always be your friend

D

Jackson stared at the screen in a daze. He was torn. Did he just walk away and say 'fuck him'? It was tempting, after all Danny had dropped him neck deep in the shit and left him to paddle on his own. However, he still had a fierce loyalty towards his former officer.

The vision of Milton's false smile flashed into his head, and the anger returned. There was no way he was going to let that smug prick win again. He was going to take them all down.

The location was a hunter's lodge overlooking Lake Hodges. He and Danny used to go there fishing and use the lodge to stash their beer. They had had good times in the wilderness. In the morning, he would start the first leg of his revenge. They were going to pay for fucking with his friends, and more so for fucking with him.

He opened the invoice image and stared at it, hoping something jumped out at him. Again, Trident Holdings meant nothing to him, but whatever was coming in was going to be delivered to them at 04.00 hours on 30th of June in Dryden, wherever that was, and he would be there to make trouble.

He opened Google Maps on his phone and searched for Dryden. It was a small town just off the Mexican border in south Texas. He studied the terrain around it looking for areas that would be suitable to land a small plane or drop packages. He found a small airport about 8 km from Dryden. That had to be it. No one would think twice about a plane landing at an airport, and if they had the workers in their pockets, then they had the perfect cover.

He had six days to retrieve his supplies, get to Dryden and recce the area. First, he needed a shower, and then he needed to sleep.

They left early the next morning. Highway 15 was free flowing and they made good progress and made the lake in a couple of hours. He parked the car off the main road and led them to a small picnic area, where he left them with some sandwiches and potato chips that he had bought on the way. He then headed off towards the lodge.

After about an hour, he came across the clearing in the trees. The lodge stood in the centre of the clearing. It was about ten feet by six and made of fallen logs. It had a moss and mud roof and a metal flue pipe protruding from its right hand apex. Jackson stayed in the trees and circled around to its front, looking for signs that anyone was waiting for him to show himself.

He observed it for half an hour more before moving to its blind spot. There was a small woodpile against the wall and Jackson could see that there was a second smaller pile next to it. This pile shaped into a rudimentary triangle, two of its points were level with the wall, but the third pointed at ninety degrees. On top of the piles, there were ten randomly placed stones.

Jackson stood with his back to the triangle and measured out ten paces, he stopped at a nasty looking thorn bush. It had 2-inch long thorns coving ninety percent of its branches and looked impenetrable. "Thanks mate." He muttered to himself.

Jackson carefully slipped his hand into the bush, but to his joy, it moved easily. He studied its base. Someone had cut the base away and tethered it to the neighbouring bush with twine. He undid the twine, ignoring the multiple thorn pricks, until he could move the bush backwards.

The cleared area had two pieces of brown rope sticking out from the ground about four feet apart. Jackson pulled on the ropes and a wooden lip lifted and came away. Jackson moved it to one side and it revealed a small pit. Inside the pit was a long green army issue holdall. He lifted it out and set it beside him, opening the zipper.

Inside was an M4 assault rifle, the tactical shotgun, the Sig Sauer P226 9mm handgun as well as plenty of ammunition. He checked the side pockets and discovered the NVG goggles, binoculars, three fragment grenades and two flashbang grenades. However, most important of all, he found a plastic wallet containing a document file and his passport that they had stashed at the airport along with cash.

He zipped the bag up and returned the scene to the way he had left it, taking care to hide as many of his tracks as possible, before returned to the picnic area. They spent an hour there to keep the family outing look going, before returning to the road. They drove for seven hours solid; Jackson could feel the fatigue setting in, so decided to stop in Benson and refuel and paid for two rooms at a nearby motel.

With the bags safely out of the car and into his room, he opened the hold all and took out his cash and the folder. He opened the white plastic clip binder and removed the papers. He spread them out on the bed.

There were ten photographs, six of which he had already seen. Pictures of Martinez, Ramon and another man identified only as Phillipe. The next four photographs showed a plane. It looked like a Cessna 172 single prop light aircraft. Three men were in the process of unloading plastic wrapped bundles from its hold.

One man was clearly visible in all of the pictures. He was in his mid to late fifties, stocky with grey hair and a grey neatly trimmed beard. He was clearly in charge of the unloading. One of the photographs was a close up of his face. He had piercing blue eyes that held an inner menace, like the deathly stare of a shark. He had a shoulder holster that sported two Browning .45 automatics.

The other two men looked like hired help. They wore jeans and t-shirts, but did not have the air of importance. The background looked like an airstrip, which Jackson was convinced was the small airport he had seen on the map. He put them to one side and looked at the sheets of paper.

One had a set of co-ordinates on followed by 'Step four'. They read 30.0469, -102.1392. He put the co-ordinates into his maps; it directed him to a dilapidated truck stop halfway between the airstrip and Dryden itself. He bookmarked it and took a screen shot in case he had no signal there.

The next paper had a Company letterhead for Trident Holdings in El Paso. It gave him the address for the head office on Kingsway drive. Stapled to it was a company registry printout. Established in 2001 and its owner was a John Yorke. It claimed to be a haulage company offering next day and long haul deliveries.

The next printout was an Interpol rap sheet for a Jimmy Fallon. Jackson looked at the mugshot that stared back at him. Those dead eyes were unmistakeable. It was the same man he had seen in the pictures, only without the beard, but those eyes he would recognise anywhere.

According to his rap sheet, he was from Dundalk, County Louth, Ireland. He was a prominent officer in the Provisional IRA. He had a string of convictions from attempted murder, extortion and kidnapping to drugs offences.

Wanted in connection to two car bombings in County Armagh and considered extremely dangerous. He was an enforcer for the splinter group 'Green Ghost'. A terrorist organisation reported to have targeted loyalist members in New York. There was currently a joint investigation involving Interpol and the FBI. Chief Investigator was a

Special Agent Joanne Phillips and Frank Chambers from Interpol in Manchester.

There was currently a RICO investigation into Martinez and Joanne Phillips was Special Agent in charge of that too. He read lists and lists of dates, times and places, which he assumed were links between Fallon, Martinez and this John Yorke. Jackson finally felt as though he was getting somewhere.

The last sheet was a directive from an Intelligence officer named Mark Rourke, instructing Special Agent Phillips to follow all operations through Rourke's office. This last one interested Jackson the most. Rourke's name was ringed with a red pen and a big question mark written next to it. At the bottom was a handwritten addition.

Check him out!!! Possible mole??? Maybe Dirty??? Mentioned Private Contractors!!!

He wondered if this idea was what Sonia was puzzling about, either way it was his link to how Milton was involved, now he just had to put the pieces together.

Next, he checked all the weapons were clean and free of obstructions. Danny had supplied him with ten clips of ammunition for M4 and the same for the Sig. There was a box of 200 buckshot 12 gauge shells for the Stoeger. He repacked everything and planned his next leg of the journey. Once he had Catalina secured here, he would travel to Sanderson and book into a motel there. He would move onto the target. He would check out the coordinates first then find a decent Lying-Up Point where he can observe the airstrip and whoever comes into play. Then he would bring them down.

He knocked on Catalina's door and she opened it dressed in just a towel, her hair was wet and she looked beautiful. He stood at the door transfixed on her. She looked at him and he could see her cheeks flush.

"Are you coming in?" she asked coyly.

He seemed unable to speak; it was as if he had been jabbed with the local anaesthetic they used at his local dentist. His mouth moved, but his words seemed to stall.

He entered and sat at the chair. The TV was on and some cartoon that Jackson had never seen before was flashing on the screen. Benito was fast asleep on the other bed. He obviously crashed out once they got there. He regained his composure and watched her as she slinked into the bathroom. She left the door ajar and Jackson could see her in the mirror as she let the towel slip. Her body was a beautiful brown vision. Her pert breasts and natural curves flowed like poetry. He felt bad for looking, but he could not stop. She was younger than his daughter, but a million miles away from her.

Catalina bent down to dry her legs and caught sight of him in the mirror. He immediately looked away in shame; he would never felt this way about someone so young for years. When she emerged from the bathroom, she had dressed in a short-cropped white t-shirt and a very short pink pair of shorts.

When she looked at him, he felt his face flush, the guilt written all over it.

"I'm sorry. I didn't mean to stare!"

She smiled warmly at him and glided over to him slowly bending down to face him. He braced himself for the inevitable slap that was coming his way, but instead she softly cupped his face and kissed him on the lips. She held it there a little longer than he was expecting.

"I like the way you look at me. Most men I know look only for sex. You are kind too."

He flushed again. "You are younger than my daughter; I shouldn't have looked at you like that!"

She gave him a cute little chuckle. "Am I old enough to be a mother?"

He nodded feeling even more embarrassed.

"Then I am old enough to be a lover!"

She took his hand and kissed it lovingly. He held it there wanting her so much, but he knew he had to concentrate of the threat to them both.

He stood, held her face and looked into her eyes. "Listen Catalina, I have to leave you here. Where I am heading, I cannot take you. The people I am after will use you against me and I need to be focussed on them."

He could see tears beginning to well in her eyes.

"You won't come back. You will leave us just like the rest of them!"

He shook her to bring her back looking at him. "I will be back, I promise you. I will take care of you and keep you safe; you just have to trust me." He gave her an intense look, "You do trust me, don't you?"

Catalina nodded, her face was a shroud of sadness that tore him deep to see.

He kissed her forehead. "I will find a way for you to be with me, if that's what you really want? I will take you away from all the bad people and let you live a happy life! But for now I need you to stay here safe, so I don't have to worry about you."

He fished into his pack and pulled out the money Danny had left him. There was over $5000, so he split it into two bundles and handed one to Catalina. She looked at it as if it was radioactive.

Reading her mind, he put his hand in hers. Her skin felt soft and warm. She curled her fingers around his.

"This is just so you and Benito can eat and drink while I'm away, but if I message you to run, or you haven't heard from me in two days, then use it to get out of town. There is a bus. It comes through here to El Paso. Use the money and go there. I will meet you there"

He squeezed her hand. "Do you understand what I'm saying Cat?"

She nodded still squeezing his hand after he had relaxed his.

"My Mama used to call me Cat. Nobody has called me it since."

Jackson felt guilty again. He seemed to put his foot in it lately.

"I'm sorry, it just came out. I had no idea it was a painful name to call you."

She smiled softly. "It's OK. She called me it because the loved me, so you can call me it too."

She leaned forward and kissed him. This time it was deeper. He tried to resist, but he just could not. They kissed passionately and he could feel it becoming more.

He pulled away gently and looked deep into her beautiful brown eyes. "Hold that thought. I will be back, I swear."

He left her and returned to his room. His mind was racing. This was an unexpected turn, which could cloud his judgment. He tried unsuccessfully to sleep, but she flooded into his mind as soon as he closed his eyes. He lay there staring at the ceiling when he heard a soft knock on his door.

He immediately grabbed the Sig and looked through the door's peephole. Catalina was standing at his door. He quickly stashed the weapon and opened the door. She had the towel wrapped around her again. As soon as the door closed, she let the towel drop. She was naked and beautiful.

"I don't want to wait." she said.

Then she wrapped her arms around his neck and lifted herself up to kiss him. He responded instantly. He wanted her so much. Any feeling of guilt or doubt ebbed away like the tide. They made love fast and intense. The desire consumed them both and took over completely. Afterwards she lay across him, her heart pounding against his chest.

He softly stroked her face as she lay. He could happily stay here forever. He had not been this content in years.

"You are beautiful," he said gazing down at her face with a smile, "I didn't think you'd be interested in an old man like me."

Catalina propped herself up on her elbows with her hands under her chin.

"Age means nothing to me. Many men try to take me, but they don't look at me like you do. I would be happy with one night here, than a lifetime of false men."

They made love again. This time it was slow. They took their time and explored every inch of each other. Locked together in rhythmic poetry as she straddled him and slowly rocking in time together. Her skin tasted sweet and she responded to his lips as he kissed her breasts. When they finally climaxed together, it was deep and fulfilling. Afterwards they slept a short while wrapped together.

Eventually Catalina slipped out of bed and wrapped the towel back around her. She turned to look at him. "I will remember this night always," she said softly, "I will pray for you Jax. I will pray you come back to me."

He smiled at her and watched her leave his room. His smile faded once she had gone. He did not think he would see her again. He did not rate his chances against all these unknown entities he was facing. He could just run away with her, but he would be leaving a man in the field, and that is something you just do not do!

The next morning he left early and travelled straight to a Motel outside Sanderson. The journey was uneventful but Jackson had a strange feeling. He had had the same feeling about four days ago, a feeling of being watched. He shook it off and booked into the motel for five days.

He then drove down towards Dryden. He passed the airstrip and slowed to take a quick look. It was set up as an intersected 'X'. The area around it was flat shrub land, with very little in the way of cover until it reached a set of tree lined hills. There was a small access road, gated off with a wire fence skirting around its perimeter. There were no structures of any sort except a galvanised steel trailer. Jackson assumed it doubled up as the office.

He pressed on. The building he was looking for was on his right about 6 km from the airstrip. Why had she chosen this spot? He asked himself. Very risky to direct me here, being so close to the airstrip. He came across a run-down double fronted building. The faded signage of 'Burt's Diner' still adorned its fascia. It had clearly not been open for a number of years. The weeds and scrub almost covered the main doors and the windows had so much grime on them they were completely opaque.

He pulled around the back and parked out of sight from the road. The back yard was as overgrown as the front. There was an oil and water tower to the side, which would have supplied the place with its heating and water supply. Power lines channelled out to a small generator housed in a steel grille lean to at the back.

Jackson opened the glove compartment and took out the Sig Sauer, pulled the slide back slightly to check the round in the chamber was sitting properly. He had seen first-hand, the devastating injuries that a fouled round could make of a man's face when it misfired. He pulled the hammer back fully and applied the safety before tucking it into his rear waistband. He put two spare clips into his pocket.

He approached the rear door from the side being careful to stand on the scattered areas of grass. Leaving as few traces of his presence was vital in case they used this place for any kind of staging point. He stood with his back flat to the wall to the right of the steel framed door. He gave the handle a gentle pull. Nothing annoyed him more than wasting valuable time defeating a lock that was already open. It gave way slightly before the hasp caught the latch inside. He returned it to its place and waited. If anyone had heard him, then someone would no doubt investigate.

After five minutes, he was happy that nobody was waiting for him inside, if there was, then the enemy were disciplined and he would have to take the chance. He gave the door a bigger pull. This time the hasp rocked enough for him to prise it open. He swung it open flattening himself back against the wall, awaiting the rounds flying at where he was standing. They never came.

Convinced he was alone here, he entered the diner. This entrance led to what was the kitchen area. The stainless steel sink and tables remained thick with a grey carpet of dust. The cooker and utensils were long gone. Through the kitchen to the far wall he came across double doors leading into the dining area. Jackson was about to push through when he noticed that one of the push plates had a small clean area, like it had been opened recently.

He drew his weapon and removed the safety. Crouching low to make himself as small a target as possible he pushed through. In front of him, was a small bar area where the till would have been and a tiled floor area where the booths used to be lined. Jackson quickly moved behind the counter. Nobody moved on him. He risked a look around the dark wood bar. Happy that he was alone, he stood up and looked around the dining area.

There were remnants of the tables and booth coverings but it was a shell. The black and white checked vinyl floor was covered in old leaves and and dirt. A few old letters left strewn here and there. Jackson picked up a few, but they were just they dying epitaph of a failing business. The dull glow from the brown windows gave the place a sepia appearance.

At the far corner of the dining area, were the rest rooms and an office door. It was slightly ajar, and Jackson could see there was a table in there but at an odd angle. He entered the office. The table was missing a leg, which had been broken off and was protruding from one of the drywall panels. The boss's last act of defiance or rage perhaps?

The drawers were still intact so he checked them all, empty. He thought back to what the message had said, fourth step. There were no steps here, the building was single storey and there were only two steps up into it. He checked the restrooms, but they offered nothing too. He was about to leave when he noticed a small scuffing on one of the toilet seats. He looked up at the polystyrene ceiling tiles directly above the toilet, one tile sitting on its aluminium frame at an unusual angle. He put the Sig back into his waistband and stood on the seat. Reaching up he lifted the tile enough to get his hand inside. He felt around its edges until he came across a small key, devoid of dust or cobwebs, so its secretion was recent.

Jackson spent the next hour searching for a lock that the key would fit. He found nothing. He decided that this was a wild goose chase. He was never going to know what the key was for, so he decided to leave it. He was almost through the door when something caught his eye. Against the left hand wall was a shelving unit not unlike the others scattered around the kitchens walls. This one was different. It was standing slightly off the wall, and there was a definite hand mark on its edge, somebody had moved it recently.

Jackson pulled the shelves away from the wall. They revealed a small door with a padlock on its front. Jackson pulled the key out and tried it into the lock, it sprung open with little effort. Jackson drew his weapon and pulled the door open. It led to a short set of steps that went down into some sort of basement.

On the wall was a set of ring clips that supported a torch. He took it and covering its front turned it on. The pink glow of his hand meant the batteries still worked. This meant it had been put here recently too. Standard alkaline cell

118

batteries eventually leaked their contents after periods on inactivity, so this was a recent addition to the wall.

Letting only a little of the light through he descended the eight wooden, encased steps, into a tiny storage basement. It was about six feet square and was completely empty. He did a complete 360 of the room. There were no panels on the walls, nor were there and doors or loose bricks. He stood staring at the way out. Think…think, he thought to himself, what am I missing here?

He could feel the dejection setting in. He started to walk back up the stairs when they creaked loudly as he got halfway up. Jackson stopped and backtracked. No squeak when he went back down, however as soon as he went forward back up them, sure enough the squeak returned. He returned to the bottom and went up one-step at a time. At the fourth step, the squeak returned.

"Of course!" he shouted to himself, "what a dickhead!"

He leaned into the step and pushed on it, it did not move. Then he pushed on the vertical filler between steps four and five. Bingo! The panel flipped back slightly. He pulled it completely away. Inside was a small brown envelope, a hand written name on its front face, it read:-

Special Agent Joanne Phillips

Jackson opened the letter. All it contained was an SD card from a mobile phone. This must be the evidence Sonia had found. Was she working with the FBI too, a double agent, so to speak? It looked to Jackson that there was more to Sonia than he first thought. Maybe Danny had not trained her after all. She seemed to have government training.

Jackson rolled the envelope up and put it in his pocket. He initially thought about ringing his find in, but he stopped himself. I trusted people before and got burned. This was his insurance. Not just for him, but for Cat and Benito too. This was his bargaining chip to a new start.

He left the Diner and sat in his car contemplating his next move. He would love to get a look at what was on that card before the FBI got their hands on it. He had time on his side. He just needed a computer and a card reader. Nearest one to him was El Paso, so he set off to El Paso.

He made El Paso in just over three and a half hours and after finding gas and food, he located an electrical store, where he bought a power pack charger for his phone and a USB SD card reader.

The gaming café was on the outskirts of town. It was quite modern and clean. It served hot and cold drinks as well as snacks and magazines. He paid for an hour and settled in front of yet another computer. He hated computers. His understanding of them had only really manifested itself in the last few years of the police force, but he never trusted them.

He plugged the reader into the PC and downloaded the driver to it. He inserted the card and waited while the agonisingly slow hourglass spun. Eventually the window opened and he was instructed to browse files.

He opened the folder and was presented with a PDF file and 4 image files. He clicked on the PDF file first. It was password protected. He tried the password that Danny had given him earlier, but it was having none of it. He copied it to his phone and then set about the image files.

The first image showed a middle-aged balding man standing outside a white warehouse. He was medium height, but looked like he had enjoyed life's fruits. The paunch around his waist caused his blue checked shirt to bulge revealing a pasty white stomach bursting over his Dark blue Chinos. He was talking on a mobile phone. The white shutters behind him carried the large red letters T, R and I that Jackson assumed were the first letters of the word 'Trident' and the man was John Yorke.

The next image again showed the same man only this time it was at night. Outside a bar or club, Jackson surmised from the exterior. 'John' was shaking hands with another man while passing him a thick yellow envelope, this one Jackson did recognise, John Milton.

The third image showed the car park at Langley, Virginia, Headquarters of the CIA. Jackson recognised it from the many films he had seen. He zoomed into the centre of the grassed area. Standing in a black suit was John again, only this time he had a name badge on a lanyard that Jackson could not read. He was talking with a young slim woman about the same height as him. She had long dark hair tied back in a loose ponytail. She looked pale and serious in her black trouser suit and white shirt.

Jackson studied the two photographs. They were definitely the same man. Was he an executive and CIA? He suddenly saw the picture opening up in front of him. Sonia was clearly working for the FBI. John must be the mole in the CIA. He thought back to what the note he had read had actually said.

Check him out!!! Possible mole??? Maybe Dirty??? Mentioned Private Contractors!!!

This man, John Yorke and Mark Rourke are the same person. Then he remembered the directive to the Special Agent in charge of the FBI. Filter all operations through his office. "She got you, you motherfucker!" He said under his breath.

He then opened the fourth image. In front of him was a scene straight from a western he had once seen. Instead of Clint Eastwood and company, sitting around a large wooded banquet table was Martinez. He was at the head of the table with Yorke at his left. Sat next to Yorke were Milton and Fallon. To Martinez's right and with their backs to the camera was another man and next to him was the unmistakeable bulk of Taylor.

Rage built up in Jacksons head. He knew they were untrustworthy, but he had just helped the enemy pull off a cover up. He hated being used. His determination grew with his anger. He copied the images to his phone and shut the card down. He found a post office where he bought an envelope, a book of stamps and a pen. He wrote an address on the front and placed all the stamps on the front. Then he mailed it. It was safe.

Messing with the mail was a federal offence. The card now as hidden as he could get it. He now had two aces up his sleeve and payback was going to be sweet!

Chapter 9

Collaboration

Jackson returned to his car and set off back to his motel. He had done enough for today. The next part was going to take careful planning. Again, as before, he could not shake the feeling that someone was following him. He drove for an hour checking the vehicles behind him. During this time, only three vehicles had maintained his direction. He started to watch for cars joining the route and the speeds at which they were trailing him. He decided to take them on a tour of the area, see who came with him.

Instead of turning off Highway 10 and turning onto Route 285 to Sanderson, he kept going on towards Sheffield. One car left his tail, leaving two. Both cars were black SUVs, and kept a good distance behind him. After about an hour, he turned off again, up the 190. Both cars turned with him, so he floored it. The engine protested but obliged. As he rounded a bend, he saw a sharp left turn onto a dirt road. He took it at full speed. The plucky Datsun fishtailed, but made the turn, kicking up a huge cloud of dust.

He immediately spotted a small dirt road to his left and darted down it, just as the SUVs had slowed and taken the first turn. He had not fooled them at all, so at the next junction he retraced his direction. The Datsun was old, but it performed admirably in keeping his distance from his pursuers.

He spotted a small break in a stone wall about 30 yards from the roadside. He was safely enough around the bend so they would not spot him. He took the turn at high speed again slightly clipping the stone as he ploughed through the opening.

No sooner had he cleared the hole, he turned swiftly bringing the Datsun broadside to the wall. He was out of the car in an instant, weapon drawn and using the car to shield himself. He opened his mouth to regulate his breathing and listened. A few seconds later, he heard the deep throaty growl of the two SUVs as they tore past his position. It would not take them long before they realised they had been duped and would return.

He quickly returned to the car, backed up and sped out of the hole, back the way he had just come. When he reached the highway, he backtracked to the 285 and headed to Sanderson. These events troubled him greatly. Who were these people and how the hell had they found him?

He drove at a sedate pace, constantly checking his rear mirror in case his shadows returned, but they never appeared. They were not Milton's vehicles he knew that. Milton was a battering ram. He had very little finesse. Jackson was sure that they would have killed him, rather than follow him. Whoever this was had a plan for him that required him alive. It occurred to him that they might have been tailing him for a while. Just how long had they been on to him?

He took his phone out and checked his signal. He had one bar, which was not great, but it would be enough. He clicked on the only contact he had, Catalina. He clicked on the little envelope icon and began typing, while trying to keep the Datsun straight.

'I am ok. Is everything ok there? X'

Had they followed his Western Union trail? He doubted it. His withdrawals were too random to make any directional predictions. They couldn't trace the mobile phone as he bought what is commonly known as 'Burner Phones' because of their anonymous nature, there is nothing linking a name to the account.

Then it hit him. Internet cafés! He had searched on them. He had pretty much laid his plan out on it by researching. Only a government agency would have the manpower and resources to scan the internet for buzz words and phrases.

He checked his phone ringtone was loud. He had had no reply to his message and was beginning to fear the worst. As he came to the on ramps, he had a decision to make. Did he bale on his plan, and scoop Catalina and the boy up and run? Alternatively, did he remain vigilant and continue with his plan? He chose the latter.

His phone beeped loudly, startling him out of his thoughts. He looked at the screen, it read:-

'I am OK. But I'm scared too. Please come back soon I don't like it here.'

He knew this would be a problem, but he could not protect them and complete his mission. It had to be this way. He replied.

'I will only be gone a couple of days longer. Sit tight and I will call you later today. Make sure your phone is charged and somewhere safe and hidden. If I don't call you by 11 pm, then take Benito and head to El Paso as we discussed. I know this is hard, but I need you to be strong for me. Can you do that? X'

It was cold and callous, but he needed her to remain focussed. Last thing he needed was the distraction of her, while he was on the most dangerous leg of his plan.

Instead of pulling up in front of his motel room, he decided to park behind the office building and walk around the back of the block and enter his row from the opposite side. Happy that the coast was clear, he unlocked his room and entered.

His thoughts began to retrace the events of the last few hours. How long had they known about him? Did they know about this place? He could not afford to be sloppy. Up to now, he had broken no laws except a few minor traffic

125

violations. However, if he was caught with all these weapons and this amount of cash, they could hold him for days.

He decided to hide the bag. The Motel sat with its back to a small rocky range of low undulating hills. There were sporadic clumps of trees and shrubs, that gave the sand coloured hills a dark green mottle. He had noticed as he had walked around the back of the office, that there was a large water storage site nestled between two gently sloping sides.

He went into the bathroom. It was an old style motel bathroom. The décor was basic. The white sink, toilet and bath, transformed over time to a dull cream colour. The sink was orange around the plughole by the hard water that carried traces of the desert conditions. The bath was an old plastic one with so many scratches that it had become a crosshatch pattern. It had a lift out front panel that housed the plumbing. Jackson lifted the panel off, and secreted the Sig there before returning the panel.

He protected the ammunition by wrapping the towels around them and loading the holdall. The light was fading fast outside and the terrain would be treacherous underfoot, but he still had the torch from the diner to aid his plan.

Within an hour it had become dark enough for him to conceal himself from view, but light enough to move without the torch. He switched out the light and stood for another ten minutes scanning the area through the window, looking for anything out of place.

He picked up the bag and slipped out into the night. The ground was undulating badly. It reminded Jackson of the dry Wadis of the Afghanistan bushlands. They had patrolled a lot at night, supporting British Special Forces intelligence gathering missions.

He made slow progress but eventually found the water station. A large tower rose majestically from the floor and loomed over surrounding area. A steel ladder hugged its side, leading to a small platform that ran along its circumference. A small wooden hut stood alone next to what looked like four water treatment tanks. The pipework ran in maze of twists and turns through several junction points.

Jackson peered through the window of the hut to make sure it was unmanned. Happy that he was alone, he tried the door, firmly locked. He gave up on this option, as he did not want to alert anyone to his being there. He searched around the hut for anything he could use to hide such a big bag. All he found was a length of rope and a few empty wooden crates. He dropped the bag behind the hut and made towards the tower.

Dust had settled on the rungs and coated them, making the ladder very slippery. He made it to the top and stepped up onto the walkway. It seemed to follow all the way round to the back of the tower. Jackson followed it all the way to the back, happy that he was out of sight from the houses in front. He switched the torch on. From the back of the tower, there was an intersection of pipes running down and heading towards the treatment area. Where the pipes entered the tower was a boxed in pressure gauge housing. Jackson lifted the lid and peered inside. 'This is perfect,' he muttered to himself.

He returned to the hut and collected the bag, the rope and a small splinter of wood from the empty boxes, dropping the bag at the base of the ladder. He tied the handles of the bag to one end of the rope and proceeded to climb up again. Using the railings as support, he hoisted the bag up carefully. He did not want to make any excess noise and draw attention of any late night dog walkers.

Once successfully hoisted, he carried the bag and the rope to the box. It fit perfectly. He then placed the splinter so that the lid held it in place. If anyone opened the lid, the splinter would fall to the ground, his tell-tale sign that he was compromised.

He pulled out his phone and clicked on Catalina's contact details. This time he clicked on the little green handset. After a small pause, the purr of the dialling tone filled his ears. After six rings, eventually someone picked up.

"Hello?" her voice sounded calm, "Jax? Is that you?"

"I'm here, are you OK?"

"Yes," she said, "your friend is here. He said he was going to look after us until you returned."

Jackson felt his blood run cold. Who was it? Feds? Milton? Martinez?

"Put them on the phone Cat."

He could hear a muffled conversation as Catalina's finger must have covered the microphone hole. Then there was a lot of rustling and a man's voice burst over the earpiece.

"Well, great to finally make your acquaintance Mr Shaw!" The Irish accent was unmistakeable, Fallon!

"What do you want?"

"You've been a busy little bee my boy haven't ye? I have to say springing the girl alone was impressive. Oh yes they told me all about your heroics. I did think it would be too much for you, but my friends faith in you was well justified 'A tell ye!"

Jackson's blood was boiling now. "Get to the point, Fallon!"

"Now, now Jax, be nice. I'm being nice. The little lady here might find out how nice I can be if you like? Oh by the way, you will have to tell me how, for the love of the Almighty and all the Apostles, did you manage to escape Mexico with these two in tow. That would be a tale I'd pay to hear!" The chuckle in his voice had a seriously sinister undertone.

"What is it you want Jimmy?" Jackson tried to keep his voice neutral.

"Miss Sonia has been a naughty girl, hasn't she Jax? Well in the end, she talked. They always do. I know about the distraction of the letter to London. I know that her dad reached out to you, and I also know she directed you to the item I want. That my son... is what I want!"

Jackson pictured the card sitting in a post office sorting house.

"What if I don't have it?"

"Then that's unfortunate for you. But most of all very unfortunate for the wee missy here!" The threat in his voice was very real.

"I don't have it, but I can get it back. I just need a couple of days." Jackson did not think he would get it but it was worth a try.

"You've got twenty four hours, son. After that, you will only be able to imagine how many pieces these two are going to end up in. Think I will start with the boy. Wouldn't want his 'Mammy' to miss that would we?"

"I'll get it, just don't hurt her."

Fallon's sarcastic laugh buzzed in his ear. "Sentimental old sod. I'll be in touch with where to bring the item and collect your woman."

The line went dead and Jackson stood there transfixed on the blank screen. He could not intercept the mail. By the time he returned to El Paso, the letter would have gone. He was going to have to bluff his way out of this one. He thought about the next part of his plan, but it looked like he would have to ditch it. Catalina was his mission now.

He returned to the motel room and unlocked the door. He went in and locked the door. He stood with his head against the wooden door. His mind was racing. How was he going to bluff his way around this? He knew what was on the card. Then he had an idea. He did not need that exact card. All he needed to do was get back to El Paso, buy a similar SD card and copy the files from his phone on to it. "Jackson you are a genius" he said happily to himself.

"Not quite, Mr Shaw!"

The bedside lamp illuminated as Jackson span around. He came face to face with Joanne Phillips. She was sitting on the bed and she was pointing her service issue Glock 17 at him. She was dressed in the same trouser suit he had seen in the picture. Her cheekbones were angular, giving her a hard expression. She was not unattractive and her almost black eyes gave her a mystical look. Her pale skin showed little exposure to the sun, clearly she was a career woman.

"I'll have the gun, Mr Shaw!"

Jackson lifted his shirt slowly at did a 360 degree turn to show her he was unarmed. "I'm not packing!"

Joanne relaxed her weapon hand but still kept it trained on his midriff. She waved him towards the chair against the wall.

"Take a seat Mr Shaw. We need to have a chat, you and me, a seriously long one too!"

Jackson sat down, cursing himself for being so blasé about the way he had gone about things. He was usually so very astute, but he had allowed himself to become sloppy and careless.

She broke his thoughts. "We will deal with the aiding of a foreign national to enter the United States illegally and the reckless endangerment of my fellow agents, with your little 'Smokey and the Bandit' stunt back there, later. But right now I think you know why I am here?"

Jackson nodded. "You want the card?"

Joanne gave him an exhausted smile and said with condescension that teachers used with children who test their patience.

"Yes Mr Shaw... I want the card!"

Jackson dropped his head in despair. "Well lady, you are going to have to stand in line!"

She looked at him puzzled, "What do you mean, stand in line?"

Jackson shook his head in exasperation. "I know who you are and I know who you are investigating. Clearly, you know who I am and who I am after. So you also know who I helped get here, and that I helped your source escape. But you still haven't heard from her have you?"

She eyed him suspiciously, before lowering the weapon. "Go on?"

Jackson proceeded to fill her in on the double cross, the link between Martinez, Milton and Yorke. He left out the fact that Yorke was in fact Rourke and that he had copied the files to his phone. She was obviously one of the good guys, but he'd been wrong before.

"So do you think Yorke has Sonia?"

Jackson nodded sadly. "Yeah I'd say so and they've tortured her enough to crack her."

Joanne looked at him sceptically. "And just how would you know that, Mr Shaw?"

Jackson smirked at her. "Jax or Jackson please. You say Mr Shaw and I expect to see my old English teacher. Jax please"

Joanne rolled her eyes at him, "OK Jax," she said sarcastically spreading the word out, "go on?"

He filled her in on the conversation he had just had with Fallon. Joanne's face grew more and more ashen as the reality of the situation hit her.

"So you see," he interrupted her train of thought, "You both want the same thing from me, but only I know where it is. You want Yorke, but you also need to find your mole. I want Fallon and Milton. The way I see it, we need each other. You help me get Catalina and Benito back and help them settle here, and then I'll help you get your man or men."

They sat staring at each other for what seemed like an eternity. She seemed to be weighing up the implications of allowing a foreign national to conduct a covert unauthorised operation on US soil and be complicit in the proceedings. It would ruin her if it went wrong. Finally, she seemed to have come to a decision.

"So what is your plan?"

He laid out his idea, still keeping the fact he had copies of the SD contents to himself. When he had finished she seemed convinced that it was feasible.

"OK, so what do you want from me?"

Jackson thought a moment. He finally had resources to call upon that he did not have before. He clasped his hands together and looked at her seriously.

"I will need a signal trace on a mobile phone. I put a tracking app on Catalina's phone, but I have limited coverage. I need you to get into the app and find where they are holding her. Then I need you to look the other way while I get her back. If you have done your homework on me then you will know I am more than capable. Just be my back up for Catalina if it goes tits up."

Joanne looked conflicted again but nodded nonetheless.

"Anything else?"

Jackson leaned closer. "Yes, once she's safely out of danger I want you to place her in protective custody and get her a new identity. You have witness protection programs don't you? "

Joanne nodded at him. "Yes we do. I can pull some strings especially now she can identify Fallon." She gave him a long hard look, "You do realise what this means though don't you?"

Jackson's eyes dropped and his head lulled against his hands. He nodded softly, "I'll never see her again right?"

Joanne looked almost sympathetically at him. "That's right. Once you hand her over to us, you cannot have any contact with either of them. You won't know where she is"

Jackson sighed in resignation, "OK so be it."

"Why do you care so much about this girl?" Joanne added, "you hardly know her, but you are risking your life to save her. It's a big commitment?"

Jackson fixed her with a steely stare. "She risked everything to help me and I've put her in danger so many times and she's stayed by my side. I owe it to her and I promised her that I'd give her a good life. I keep my promises."

He seemed to look into space, "Except one."

Joanne stood up and looked at him puzzled. "What one was that?"

Jackson looked up at her and said sadly. "To be with her."

Joanne headed towards the door, she turned to him before opening it. "Stay put. I need to make some calls, then we have to get going" with that she left.

Once she was gone, Jackson retrieved the Sig and stashed it back into his waistband. He needed his weapons but did not want to give them away just yet. The least she knew the better.

When Joanne returned to the room, she seemed invigorated.

"We are on. I have sanctioned your involvement in our investigation as an advisor only. The operation to retrieve your dependants is going down as a reconnaissance operation. Your involvement has not been logged in as an armed one. As far as my boss knows you are here."

She looked almost pleased with herself. Jackson thought about it for a moment. Where were the problems going to come from? What could go wrong with this? Then it hit him.

"Who have you involved in this so far?"

Joanne was obviously irritated by his question. "Just my director and my team, why what's wrong?"

Jackson debated on whether to mention the CIA link or not, but he really had no choice.

"Sonia said that you were liaising with the CIA regarding all your movements?"

Joanne could seemed to see where this was going. "I know what you are saying Jackson, but no is your answer. There's no way I was letting those assholes anywhere near my investigation. For all I know they are in on it."

Jackson smiled. 'If you only knew the half-of-it love' he mused. "Good, the fewer people that know what we are doing the safer both women are."

Joanne shrugged it off in an 'I'm not stupid' manner. "So, what do you need from me to pull this off once we locate her?"

"Firstly, I will need weapons, ideally quiet ones. Then, perhaps night optics and some sort of communications. It would be nice to have a few spotters to be on location, to give me the heads up on potential threats on my blind spots."

Joanne nodded writing down what he had asked for on a small black notepad. "What about body armour?"

Jackson shook his head. "Would just slow me down and I need to be mobile and silent if possible. A combat knife would be good."

Joanne looked at him seriously. "I'm doing all the giving here. When do I get the presents to open?"

'It's a fair point' he thought. "OK, I will give you this much. Whoever is involved in this conspiracy is most likely getting ready for the next shipment. I know where and I know when. Once I get what I need, I will gift wrap the lot of them for you, including one big surprise."

He winked at her but she did not look convinced.

There was a knock on the door and Joanne opened it. There was a man standing there. He looked the FBI type. Solid but not bulky, short black hair and was wearing the FBI staple uniform. Black terrain boots, black canvas pants and dark blue jacket with a yellow 'FBI' emblazoned on his chest. Jackson would bet his life there was a huge one on the back too.

"Excuse me Ma'am" he said in a nasally pinched accent that had a slight New York twang to it. When Joanne nodded, he continued. "We have a fix on your transmitter, looks like its heading through New Mexico at this moment. They are still mobile though. What are your orders, Ma'am?"

Joanne turned to Jackson. "It's your call. You really wanna do this?"

Jackson just looked at her incredulously. "I have to. It's all or nothing now."

She turned back to the guy in the doorway. "OK Mike, saddle up the crew. Get them ready to follow in five minutes."

Mike nodded and was about to leave when Joanne put the notebook in his hand. "Get this man what he needs, and that means everything."

As Mike went to leave again she grabbed his arm. Mike stopped and looked at her.

"Oh, and Mike? Keep this between you and me OK?" she looked at him sternly.

Mike looked at the paper in front of him. "Yes Ma'am." Then he was gone.

They left the room. In the car park in front of his room stood the two SUV's he had given the slip earlier. They were still covered in dust from their off road pursuit. Jackson waved at the driver of the nearest one, but in return, he got the middle finger.

"Touchy, aren't they?" he said as he passed Joanne.

"You're lucky he didn't shoot you." she retorted holding the door open to the back seat of the black Crown Vic in front of him.

They drove in silence for over an hour. They were sandwiched between the two SUV's travelling at a decent pace. Their driver was getting instructions and directions over his earpiece as he drove. Mike was in the passenger seat. Joanne sat next to Jackson looking out at the scenery as it skipped by.

Jackson could not stand the silence any longer. "So, when did you get on to me?"

Joanne turned to face him. "We followed Mr Hughes at first. We thought he was the one that would lead us to whomever Sonia had implicated. But he only went to one location."

Jackson smiled and shook his head in mock defeat. "The woods?" He already knew the answer.

Joanne smirked at him. "Yes Jackson, the woods!"

"So when I showed up and went to the very same spot, I walked right into the trap, eh?"

She chuckled at his vulnerability. "You got it!"

He thought for a moment. "So if you've been following me all this time, why didn't you just lift me when I got the SD card, or even when I looked at it?"

It was her turn to look embarrassed this time. "We lost you,"

Jackson let out a sarcastic laugh. "Ha, Where?"

She shook her head, clearly uncomfortable at admitting she was fallible.

"We put a tracker on your car while it was outside the Motel in Benson. Only when you left in the morning, it had fallen off. We returned to continue surveillance and the car was gone, but the tracker was still there!"

This time Jackson's laugh was genuine. "I had a feeling I'd been watched, just couldn't shake it off!" he said. "So don't worry, we all get sloppy at times."

They drove on for another half an hour when Joanne's radio burst into life. A female voice broke the silence, "Ma'am?"

"Go ahead Ruth."

"Ma'am, the signal has stopped moving. We have the general co-ordinates, sending them to you now Ma'am."

"Thank you Ruth. Have our teams move into the area but keep your distance. I want a full tactical team on standby and drone units up in the air, get me pictures and live feed and patch them to my tablet. "

"Yes Ma'am."

Joanne fired up her iPad and turned to Jackson. "Well Mr Shaw, it's your show. However, I have tactical command. If I feel you are endangering any of my team un-necessarily, I won't hesitate in pulling the plug, are we on the same page here?"

Jackson resented the tone, but understood where she was coming from. She was putting her career and the lives of her team in harm's way without proper authorisation; it was not lost on him. He put his hands up in mock surrender.

"I get it; no one is going to get hurt, except me maybe." He fixed her with a steely stare. "But if I die, then so does your lead, might want to think about that." He knew it was a cheap shot, but he needed all the edge he could get.

She looked at him coldly, "I am well aware that you have me over a barrel Mr Shaw, but know this. If you get any of my team killed through you actions, then I'll shoot you myself and face the consequences later, capisce?"

He nodded. "Yeah I got it."

Joanne returned to her tablet and logged into her mainframe access. Several messages appeared, but she honed straight into the one from Agent Ruth Clayton, entitled 'Co-ordinates'.

Jackson watched as she copied the link to a new file and dropped it onto a map icon on here desktop. It took her to an area in North East area of Las Cruces. The map then zoomed in automatically. A top down view of a crossroad intersection between Peachtree Hills Road and Jornada Road zoomed into view. Joanne clicked on another tab, and a satellite view filled the screen.

Joanne could see Jackson straining to see, so she turned the screen and leaned into him slightly. He caught the faint aroma of her perfume and shampoo. She smelled good. He could see a small two building complex surrounded by a concrete wall. There was a large building at the front and a smaller one to the rear. Both structures were slightly off centre, giving room for what looked like a generator and utilities unit. There was only one entrance to the complex via the main road. He could see bushes and shrubs around the back and two sides that might provide cover. The live imagery would give him a better idea.

The light was beginning to cast its welcoming blanket to his right as they approached El Paso. They pulled into a truck stop halfway between El Paso and Las Cruces. There were five black SUVs already parked up side by side when they pulled in. They saddled up next to them and they all exited the vehicles. This must be the team, Jackson thought. He counted at least thirty members of her team; they were all in body armour and armed with H&K MP5SD submachine guns. They were a 5.56mm lightweight assault weapon that was a firm favourite of the SAS back in the UK. It was particularly capable in smaller spaces thanks to its small footprint. The SD version was fitted with a built in suppressor. Make the rifle longer and a little less accurate, but in the right hands, was still a formidable weapon.

Joanne left him and gathered her team together. She spread a map of the area on the hood of the Vic and they all gathered round. Jackson moved in to get a better look. An arm pushed across him blocking his pathway. It belonged to the disgruntled driver he had obviously still pissed off. He was a thickset man with short-cropped curly blonde hair. His complexion mottled from severe acne when he was young and his ginger looking goatee beard gave him a gipsy appearance. He was about an inch taller than Jackson was.

Jackson growled menacingly. "Move your arm big fella!"

The man stood firm, glaring at him. Jackson could tell he meant him harm.

"Max!" Joanne shouted, clearly seeing where this encounter was going, "Let him through!"

However, Max was not listening. He pushed his weight harder against Jackson's chest.

"Max!" Joanne repeated, only this time her voice was louder. Jackson looked into Max's eyes. "Last warning son, move it!"

Max just stood smirking at him, "Make me."

Jackson moved like lightening. In one smooth motion, he grabbed Max's thumb, twisting it towards him, while at the same time reversing the direction of his shoulders. The result sent Max's elbow into a reverse lock. Jackson then pushed his whole body weight down on the already strained elbow joint. Max's legs buckled as his body was forced to travel with the momentum or risk the elbow snapping. Max's other hand instinctively came up to support his elbow as he was forced to his knees. With both of Max's hands busy, Jackson used his left hand to grip Max's throat either side of his 'Adam's Apple'. Max started to choke, his face began to turn a deep shade of purple as the airwaves were slowly being crushed.

Joanne screamed at him. "Jax... Let him go or this mission's over! I shit you not!"

Jackson looked up at Joanne then released Max. Max fell to the floor gasping for breath, unsure what to touch first, his throbbing elbow, or his crushed larynx. Jackson left him floundering on the floor and pushed past the bodies in front of them. They parted without protest, their faces clearly shocked at the intensity of the violence they had just witnessed. Jackson did not mind that, he liked it when people underestimated him. It gave him the edge.

Joanne eyed him with a mixture of anger and mutual respect.

"When you are quite finished beating your help up, maybe we can concentrate on the task at hand, yes?"

Jackson raised a hand in apology to her. "OK, chief. I'm all ears."

Max re-joined them sheepishly. He made no eye contact with anyone. His ego clearly had taken a bashing.

"Right, listen up people," she said, getting into business mode. "This operation is a purely support role only!" she paused to let that sink in before continuing. "This is Jackson, for all those who don't already know."

She looked at Max with a fierce stare. "Jackson is conducting the extraction of two civilians alone. We will provide Comms and Intel and will provide armed support only if needed. Jackson is a trained soldier and is more than capable."

Again, she looked at Max. He seemed to relax knowing that Jackson was not just some shmuck who just handed his ass to him.

"We will provide cover and real time sit reps of the situation in front of him. We follow his lead and his requests. Once he's inside the compound buildings, we will move in to help the extraction and deal with any potential visitors!"

She pointed at an area on the map behind the complex.

"This area here, there are a few storage containers. They should give enough elevation for Mitch and Andy to get eyes on the rear and sides."

She turned to Jackson, "These two are part of our sniper detail and will be your cover to the rear."

Jackson nodded to them. They returned the nod. They were both similar in stature, though Jackson could not truly tell any of them apart with all the body armour and headgear.

Joanne turned to a wiry looking guy at her right hand side. He was the only one not in full tactical gear. He wore a blue shirt and black canvas cargo pants. He had dark wavy hair and a set of round silver framed glasses that were perched halfway down his nose. 'Tech Guy' Jackson thought.

"Karl, I want you and Phelps to head there now with Mitch and Andy. Get the drone up and give us live feed. Remember, this is a remote location, so keep it high and use mag lens, we don't want to spook them. They have to believe that they are just waiting."

Karl gave her a thumb's up and departed with Mitch and Andy, alongside a female agent. They loaded into one of the SUVs and glided out of the carpark.

Returning to the map, Joanne started to indicate the area to the front of the complex.

"Unfortunately the cover to the front is only bush and very low trees, plus there's a road running across our path, so Mike, Pete!" she looked at another two men, "you two will have to make do with covering our exit."

She looked around at the rest of them. "Team one; you guys are left. Team two; I want you to take the right. Ruth; you Perkins and I will set up HQ in that park area. We will liaise from there and it will be our RZ once we have the packages clear…..any questions?"

Max raised his hand.

"Yes Max?" Joanne said irritably.

"Sorry Ma'am, but what's the plan? How are we supposed to deploy with no executive orders?"

He turned to Jackson. "No offence Buddy, but what exactly are you planning to do? Kill them all by yourself?"

It was a fair point, Jackson thought.

He looked at Max then pointed at the area where the generator was.

"The way I see it, this is their only major blind spot. They will have at least one guard posted there, but the area up to it is thick scrub. I will get close to the wall and as soon as the rear snipers see an opportunity, I will neutralise them. I'll take the rear building first, then the front, but from the rear."

He looked at the rest of them. "I will keep in touch all the way. All I may need from you is to storm the place if it goes south!"

Max looked at him sceptically. "You're very sure of yourself ain't you pal?"

Jackson just smiled and turned to Joanne. "My kit?"

Joanne nodded and addressed the teams. "OK guys, you know where to be, mount up and good luck".

They dispersed and left one SUV and the Vic there.

Joanne led Jackson to the back of the remaining SUV. The back was open. Inside was a full communications set up. Video feedback monitors, High frequency encrypted radio network, as well as a satellite network port.

Jackson nodded his approval. "Nice set up."

She just smiled and hauled a bag out, dropping it at Jackson's feet. "I think that should be suitable for the job."

Jackson unzipped the bag and opened it up. Inside was a H&K MP5SD with three spare clips, also there was a small foldable crossbow. It was shorter than the ones Jackson had seen in the past, but it would be perfect for covert entry. Next out of the bag, came a Glock 17 with a Nuprol suppressor. It was not the best but if it came down to shooting, then stealth would be out of the window anyway. He pulled out a pair of NVG goggles, a matt black Ka-Bar knife and scabbard alongside spare magazines for the Glock and a black Tactical vest and uniform.

He handed the vest back to Joanne without looking at her. "No armour, it will just get in my way!"

She pushed it back towards him defiantly. "This one is non-negotiable Jackson. It's supremely lightweight. Probably won't stop you getting some sort of injury, but will save your life. Just try it on, at least."

He knew he was not going to win. He slipped the vest over his head. She adjusted the strapping to get it as tight to his chest as possible. He was shocked at how flexible and light it was.

"You win, I can't argue with this now can I?"

He stripped down to his shorts. He could feel eyes watching him as he disrobed. He looked up to see both Joanne and Ruth watching him in mock appraisal.

Joanne gave him an approving nod. "You're in good shape for your age Mr Shaw." She looked at Ruth and they gave each other a knowing look before they turned, "Not bad at all!" they said in unison and headed inside the SUV.

Jackson chuckled to himself. He was beginning to like Joanne more; in fact, he was beginning to like the USA more and more.

He dressed in the black combat canvases and replaced the vest. He filled the magazine slots with the spare ammunition and bolts for the crossbow. He strapped on the Glock and clipped the crossbow to his side, before attaching the drop cord for the MP5 to his chest. He carried the rest to the SUV and climbed inside. They then headed out into a mission that he had not planned for, but may just define his whole life.

Chapter 10

The take down

They pulled up at the Park area and got out. The sun was high in the sky and the heat became oppressive. Black was the last colour he wanted to be wearing, but needs must. They fired up the equipment in the back, and after a few checks, they were ready to rock.

Ruth sat at the communications station while Joanne sat behind her next to the monitors; they were only showing white noise. Joanne swivelled around so she was facing the same way Ruth was.

"OK Ruth, let's have a Comms check."

Ruth nodded. " All call signs. Comms check and sit reps please."

"Eagle One check, we're in position. Have eyes on back of compound. Have three X-Rays including one at Jax's entry point. All look relaxed, over!"

"Roger that, Eagle One."

"Eagle Two Check. We're in position. Gate is open and can see two vehicles. Can't see if there are any guards this side, but all seems calm over."

"Roger that, Eagle Two.".

The two side teams checked in too. That just left Karl.

"Birdseye Check. Drone is primed and ready for launch on your command."

Ruth turned to Joanne for approval, she nodded and Ruth returned to her radio. "That's a Roger Birdseye; you have a go to deploy."

There was a short pause. "Copy that!"

The screens in front of Joanne stopped their black and white visual dance and were replaced with crystal clear images of the area as the drone rose. It climbed a long way before it moved off. Jackson doubted it was as high tech as Milton's was, but the imagery was good.

After a few minutes, the camera panned down on top of the compound. Jackson could see the three guards that Mitch and Andy were tracking. They looked bored. Two of them stood together chatting. They did not seem to be taking much notice of the outer areas. The guard at his entry point was even worse. He had sat with his back to the generator, and looked like he was asleep. His weapon was leaned up against the wall in front of him, totally out of arms reach.

The camera panned to the centre. There was a Land Rover parked between the two buildings facing out. The front of the compound came into view. There were actually three vehicles parked out front on what looked like a gravel driveway, two dark sedans and a grey Panel van.

There were also three guards patrolling the front. They looked more switched on to Jackson. They were making choreographed sweeps, so they were always facing in each direction as they overlapped. They obviously saw the front gate as the biggest danger area.

"Can they do a sweep of the area directly behind the generator?" Jackson asked.

Ruth clicked the send button. "Birdseye, can we view the area outside the compound, concentrate on the approach to the generator first over?"

The camera stopped hovering and started to move. The screen filled with the wall and the bush around it.

Jackson leaned closer to the screen. "Can I talk to him?"

Joanne nodded to Ruth.

"Birdseye, Jax needs more information, and he is going to navigate for you, over?"

"Copy that, go ahead Jax"

Jackson looked closer at the screen. "Can we pan out and look for a secluded entry point in that area, preferably one with no line of sight to the wall?"

Karl moved the camera up and out, "Copy that!"

Jackson pointed at a small hillock about 100 yards from the compound's corner.

"There. That is where I need to be. Birdseye, hold there then move back at ninety degrees from that spot."

The camera slowly floated backwards and out, revealing a road with a dirt track branching out towards the hillock.

"That's perfect thank you

He turned to Joanne, "Can your snipers take out the roof lights at the back?"

Joanne could see what Jackson was thinking, "Of course, just give us the nod and we'll turn out the lights."

They spent the next few hours making sweeps of the compound, looking for signs of movement or changes in personnel, apart from the guards moving outside, very little happened.

Suddenly Karl came on the radio. "Be advised we have movement."

The camera had panned into the centre area where the Land Rover sat. A door had opened from the back of the main building. One man emerged; he was dragging a woman and a little boy along, followed by another man. They looked like a line of elephants, trunks attached to tails. Jackson knew instantly it was Catalina and Benito. His heart soared; at least they were still alive. Then as the camera angle changed, he could finally see the lead man's face. It was Fallon.

They entered the rear building and disappeared. About twenty minutes later, Fallon came out and returned to the main building alone.

"Keep Karl on that building," he shouted, "If they move, I want to know where and who with!"

Both Joanne and Ruth seemed surprised by this sudden emotion.

There was very little activity and as the sun started to descend once more, it was time to put the game on.

Jackson packed the rest of his equipment and left the park to the south. There was a small gathering of houses in front of him, so he avoided getting too close. Skirting through a patch of scrubland he stopped regularly to make sure there were no spotters around. Often organisations like these would employ children and young adults to hang around the surrounding area and call in any strangers.

He pushed through a small treeline and came out at the back of a small farmhouse. Keeping low the the fence that ran around the edge of the unkempt garden. The light was fading fast and darkness had almost completely wrapped its arms around the area. There were little in the way of streetlights, the glow from nearby houses providing what little light there was. Jackson made it to the road and crossed it quickly.

Suddenly a shaft of light washed over him. He dived for a low shrub bed in-between two buildings and lay as still as possible. He risked a quick look. There was a man standing at the corner of a low wall. Jackson was not concerned about the man, but he was concerned about what the man was looking at, a dog.

It was big and looked like a German Shepherd, with the colouring of a Doberman. This was bad news for Jackson. The dog would inevitably pick up his scent soon and then there would be drama. Jackson tried to slide his body backwards, pushing his body into the shrub without moving it too much and giving himself away.

As if sensing his movement, the dog stopped sniffing at the ground around him and looked up. Its ears instantly pricked up and its nose went into overdrive. Jackson knew that if he hung around too long, the dog would inevitably come over and investigate. The dog began to edge towards him, its owner unwilling to deviate from his planned route, tried in vain to dissuade his furry friend from its task. The owner relented and followed the dog.

Jackson pulled his knife, he did not want to kill a dog, and he loved animals more than people, but this was getting serious. The dog was about three feet from the shrubbery when something shot out from his left and ran into the garden next to him. The dog immediately gave up on his investigation as his need to catch whatever quarry had exposed itself took priority. Again, its owner reluctantly followed. Jackson used the opportunity to move out and away. He pushed on through the scrubland until he reached the dirt road. The hillock was directly in front of him.

Out of the glow of the houses, the surrounding area was pitch-black. Jackson engaged his night sights and used the green hue to navigate to the treeline at the hillocks summit. Below him was a small hedgerow that ran parallel with the compounds wall, it would give him perfect cover to approach the wall. He could see the guard behind the generator; he had stood up and was leaning against the wall smoking.

Jackson slipped out of the trees and headed down towards the hedgerow. Keeping low, he skirted along until the wall and the guard were five yards in front of him. The lights of the compound illuminated the dead ground between him and the wall. Jackson removed the night sight to maintain his natural night vision. The guard put down his weapon and reached into his pocket, pulling out a leather tobacco pouch. He turned his back to Jackson leaned back against the wall. This was Jackson's opportunity.

Slipping out silently from the hedgerow, Jackson made up the ground to the wall in seconds, unsheathing his knife as he moved.

In one smooth motion, he reached up, and grabbed the man around the mouth and pulled him back over the wall. In the same motion, he pushed the tip of the knife into the man's neck below his jawbone. Using momentum and his own bodyweight, he brought the man to the floor, the guard's attempts to free himself softened as the life drained out if him. Jackson dragged his lifeless body through the hedgerow and set him down behind it, before slipping back over the wall.

The generator and utilities hub was about six feet wide and protected in a caged outhouse. Through the pipework, Jackson could see the two guards standing together. They looked bored, not switched on. To Jackson's right, Jackson could see the panel van. A guard appeared behind it, his weapon was poised down at his waist as he scanned the area in front of him. He walked to the wall to Jackson's immediate right, stopped, scanned the area, then did an about face and returned where he had emerged from.

Jackson held his position. Checking with his G-Shock, the timing of the guard's circuit was consistent. That gave him a window of one and a half minutes to drop the two guards, and cover the distance to the rear building. Jackson used this time to formulate a plan.

"Base, this is Jax. Stand down on the lights until I say. Can Eagle one see the front guard as he enters my field?"

"Jax?" came a voice over Jackson's earpiece, "This is Eagle one, I have eyes on your X-Ray, what do you need?"

Jackson knew that engaging the enemy was Joanne's last resort.

"I just need one of you to cover him in case he gets alerted. I am going to take out the two X-Rays on my twelve once he's out of sight, but it may go noisy quickly!"

"Roger that Jax, Mitch has him; I will deal with the lights, over!" Jackson gave him two clicks in response.

Jackson positioned himself to the left of the generator. This gave him a good field of vision and gave him cover from the front guard. He checked the MP5's breech to ensure there was a round there and seated properly. A 'dead man's click' would spell death.

A 'dead man's click' was the noise the chamber made when the firing pin entered the chamber, only to stop at the springs end. That click would send a cold wave of fear through even the hardened soldier.

He removed the safety and brought the weapon to his shoulder. He looked to his right; the guard was at the wall and had turned around, only this time he seemed to glance in his direction. He shouted something, Jackson did not understand. Jackson pushed a thumb in the air. The guard shook his head and carried on his route. The sweat was beginning to soak Jackson's brow. As soon as the front guard had disappeared behind the front building, Jackson stepped out, weapon raised.

He double tapped the guard furthest away from him. The rounds hit him once in the chest and once in the throat. He crumpled like a puppet with the strings cut. The closest guard spun to look at his fallen comrade. His shock made him pause before turning to face Jackson, while raising his AK47. He never made the turn. Jackson put two rounds into his chest and he pivoted backwards with a thump.

Instantly, Jackson was running. He reached the small building and flattened his back against its farthest wall from the front. Turkey peeking around the corner, he prepared for the front guards to descend on the scene, but there was just silence.

"Eagle One. Sit rep?"

"This is Eagle One, X-Ray is unaware, I repeat, X-Ray is unaware, over."

Jackson dragged the two fallen men into a small courtyard, and then returned to the small building, shimmying along the wall to the rear entrance of the building. The sandstone wall gave way to a thick set of double wooden doors. A large padlock held a thick metal chain between the two loops of each door.

"Shit," he said under his breath, "should have asked of an entry kit!"

Jackson returned to the corner. He moved along the wall and came to a small window overlooking the courtyard. If anyone looked out, then they would surely see the two bodies. Jackson kept as flat as possible and peered around the window frame. Inside looked like a stable. There were eight pens in two rows of four. At the very end was a small door and a set of double doors set back to its left.

Jackson moved to the next corner. He could see the Range Rover and the rear door to the large building. The Range Rover was empty, so he put himself between it and the rear door.

Along the small building was the door, through which he had seen Fallon push Catalina. He softly tried the handle. The door opened a fraction. Jackson moved the MP5 to his back and drew the Glock. With his back against the wall, Jackson opened the door and peered around its frame.

There was a set of high ceiling lights, whose bulbs were so low, that the orange glow they filled the stable with barely helped. Jackson checked the first pen it was empty. There were the remnants of livestock on the floor, and by the looks of the manure, horses called this place home.

There was straw still scattered on the floor, which was starting to rot in the heat, the smell was oppressive. Jackson used the natural cover to look directly in front of his pen. It was empty too. The coral gates were wide open revealing a space identical to the one he was in.

Jackson carefully went to the wall adjacent to the next pen, lifted himself up onto the support beam and peered over the side. The next pen was full of various forms of machinery. There were two lawnmowers, a petrol powered edge strimmer as well as a quad bike and a motorcycle. At the far edge was a metal tin with nuts and bolts, as well as a fuel canister.

Jackson slipped over the side into this new pen. He ducked down behind the quadbike and eased himself to the next wall. He looked at the closed gate in the pen opposite, but there was no movement behind it to suggest anyone was awake. In fact, the whole place was eerily quiet. Jackson repeated the process for the next pen. It was empty, so he slipped over and into it.

At the next wall, he heard a noise, a small shuffling, barely audible but enough to tell him something of someone was in the next pen. He lifted himself up as he had before. As his eyes cleared the wooden divide, he saw a man's head. He was side on to him, and looked as if he was asleep. He was in his sixties and was bald except for a feint ring of grey hair at the very bottom of his hairline. He had a shoulder holster on his right hand side. Jackson lifted up further and looked into the pen.

On the floor tied to the chair the man was sitting at was Catalina. She was lying in the foetal position with Benito curled up into her. They were both asleep too and tied via a length of rope that wound around the legs of the chair, Benito tied to her.

Jackson lowered himself back into his pen. He holstered the Glock and unclipped the crossbow. It folded out from the centre and clipped into place. Jackson drew it back and locked the release tab. He loaded a bolt and using one hand, lifted himself back up. He was about to slip over the wall, when the man opened his eyes.

His head spun around to look directly at Jackson. He went for the pistol at his side as Jackson released the bolt. The bolt struck him in the side of the face, tearing a deep channel through his cheek. Falling backwards, the guard's gun went flying across the floor. Instantly Jackson dived over the wall, drawing his knife as he went. He landed on top the man and tried to grab his neck.

Catalina woke with a gasp as the two men grappled. As she repelled away from the scene of violence, her tethers pulled the vacated chair over and on top of the two men. Jackson's grip loosened by the falling chair and he lost his hold on the knife, sending it skittling across the floor.

The guard was getting to his feet frantically searching for his weapon, blood pouring from the horrific wound on his face. Jackson launched at him again, this time he tucked his chin down into his chest and using his head as a ram, drove into the man's chin lifting him up and off his feet. They landed against the far wall, this time Jackson managed to clamp his arm around the man's neck, despite being slippery with the man's blood, he managed to get a firm grip. Holding this right fist and pulling backwards with all his strength, he clamped down hard on the man's throat, arms flailing at his face in a vain effort to dislodge his grip. Jackson was unfazed as he lifted up and bent his body backwards, putting all his weight on the gripped neck. A sudden pop and the guard's flailing stopped and the man went limp in Jackson's arms, he was dead.

"Head's up Jax, you got company." Mitch erupted in his ear, "Get yer ass out of there."

Jackson pulled himself clear of the dead guard and stood up. Catalina was staring at his, the sheer terror welding her to the spot.

"Cat. It's me, Jax," he screamed at her, "we have to go, can you walk?"

She nodded as Jackson retrieved his knife and cut her bonds. He brought the rifle forward and aimed at the door he had just come through, expecting it to burst open any second, it did not.

"Eagle One, sit rep mate?"

"You got two assholes covering the door and two new assholes flanking your six, copy?"

"Fallon?" Jackson asked, already knowing the answer.

"You got it buddy."

Jackson acknowledged with a tired affirmative.

Jackson turned to Catalina, "We may have to shoot our way out of here" he said giving her a serious look handing her the Glock pointing at the double doors, "If I go down shoot anyone who comes through those doors!" Catalina nodded, pointing the gun at the double doors, shaking wildly.

"Eagle One, sit rep?" he asked again, "Assholes one and two are holding at your door. Assholes three and four look like they are coming in on your six."

Jackson dragged the lawnmowers to the door he came in by and wedged them up against it. He then pulled Catalina and a terrified Benito into the middle pen with quadbike in.

"Get behind that and stay there!"

She complied without question, dragging Benito with her. Running to the opposite pen, he lifted himself up and onto the wall, giving him an elevated angle to both doors.

Something caught his eye down to his right, a pair of shackled hands. Glancing down while trying to hold his aim on the double doors, his jaw dropped, it was Sonia.

"Jackson Shaw. Is that you in there my boy?" the Irish accent instantly recognisable, "You've got balls son, I'll give ye that, son!"

Jackson was silent at first, then turn to Sonia. "Can you stand?"

Sonia lifted her feet and shuffled forward, bracing herself against the wooden wall, lifted herself up. She was unsteady on her feet.

"You're good Jax. Didn't figure you'd find us here, but you see, now that you have, I don't need you all. If you come out now, I'll let the others go. Then you and I can go find my card."

Jackson's earpiece burst into life. "Jax, this is Max!"

"Go ahead Max."

"You got four more X-Rays coming from our side, and unless we do something you are all done!"

Jackson thought it was a weird thing to say, then he realised, it was not for his ears, but for Joanne's. Would she let them suffer just to save her own ass and more important to her, her career? Jackson had been subservient to bureaucracy for all of his adult life, from his early military career from the tender age of sixteen, to his police career. There was always someone telling him how he should and should not act.

The single door creaked as the force of someone pushed against it. They were coming in. Jackson turned the weapon to face the new threat and let two rounds fly. They smacked into the framework, sending splinters flying in all directions. This seemed to deter whoever was attempting to gain access from that door. The mowers were doing their job nicely. He opened the pen Sonia was in and released her from her ropes.

"You still remember how to shoot?"

"Of course, Dad took me to the woods every other weekend. I ain't forgotten."

Jackson rushed over to Catalina and took the Glock from her.

"Keep out of sight," he said, holding her shoulders tightly to make sure he had her attention, "we are all getting out of here, Ok?"

Catalina nodded. She looked like a frightened child. He looked down at Benito. The kid looked traumatised. He had a vacant stare that focussed on nothing at all. He wondered if the poor little boy would ever get over this. He felt the burning fingers of guilt grip him. This was his fault. He brought them here and used them to escape; now they have suffered a worse ordeal than they ever had before.

He looked back up at Catalina. "I am so sorry Cat. I never meant for you to get involved like this. I guess I didn't think this through at all."

Sonia stepped up behind him and gently pulled him away out of earshot of the two frightened Mexicans.

"We have to get out of here. We can't take them all Jax. What are we going to do? We are trapped in here!"

Jackson knew all of this. He needed to split their strength, but that just was not going to happen without help. 'Come on Joanne, get off the fence' he thought to himself.

"Jackson!" Fallon shouted again, "You've got five minutes to come out quietly or I'm going to have to kill the Chicos, oh yes, and the snitch too!"

Jackson looked at Sonia she was starting to shake. He put his hand on hers.

"We are not going to die here. I promise you."

Jackson climbed up onto the wall and looked at his surroundings. What could he use to his advantage, the quad bike and motorcycle? Even if he could get the things started, they would need the doors open to drive out. That would mean letting Fallon and his goons get inside, too risky. They could never smash through the doors with the quad; it did not have enough weight to break through. He would kill for some explosives right now. Then it hit him.

"Fallon!" He shouted, "I want you assurances that you will let these three go. They have nothing to do with this now. Only I know where the card is and where it is heading.

You kill them and I'll put one through my own head and you can all get fucked!"

He looked at Sonia, who was staring at him in amazement.

"What the hell are doing Jax?"

Jackson just smiled at her. "Buying us some time Son. He's got to unlock the gate to get in right?"

Sonia nodded. Jackson looked over at the tin with the nuts and bolts in and grinned.

"Ok, well we let him get the gate open and we fry his ass!"

Sonia followed his gaze with a puzzled look. "What do you have in mind?"

Jackson pointed at the single door. "Just keep those guys out and leave Fallon to me."

"Ok Mr Shaw, but you have only five minutes to surrender or we will make sure you remember how they die!"

Jackson grabbed the tin and the fuel canister and shook it, it sounded about half full. 'That will do nicely' he thought to himself. He wheeled the motorcycle to the double doors, checked its tank, there was fuel in it, enough for what he needed. He stuffed some of the straw into the tank and laid the bike down with its tank facing the door.

Somebody tried the single door again. This time Sonia let the rounds fly into the frame. As before, the would-be intruders retreated. Sonia pushed the mowers tight up against the door.

Jackson poured fuel into the tin, covering the nuts and bolts with the accelerant. He unloaded a clip of 5.56mm rounds from the MP5 magazine into the tin. Jackson replaced the lid and laid it onto the block of the motorcycle, wedging it to the manifold so it would not move.

He then checked the dead man's pockets. He knew he had what he was looking for; he could smell it on him. Sure enough in his right hand pocket was a petrol Zippo style lighter. He gave it a test and it worked perfectly.

"Ok, guys," he said to them quietly, "I am going to let them get the chain off and as soon as they open the doors, I'm going to set this baby off. I need you to get behind me and be ready to run, OK?"

They nodded in unison.

Jackson took the canister and poured a trail from the pen to the bike, making sure he covered the bike, and more importantly, the straw. He then laid the canister next to the tin. Once he was satisfied that his IED was set up correctly he called out to Fallon.

"OK Fallon. Open the doors and as soon as I see they are safe, I'll surrender!"

The doors started to rattle as someone fumbled with the lock. Jackson could hear metallic rhythm of the chain as it unthreaded from the door loops.

"Get ready guys."

Sonia gave his shoulder a squeeze while grabbing Catalina's hand. Catalina then pulled Benito into her, bracing to move.

The click of the handle brought Jackson's attention to the front. As the door opened slightly, he paused. He wanted them to relax.

He then lit the fuel. The flames danced high, and took off in the direction of the bike. Once they reached the bike, the straw ignited. The door then opened and standing in the opening was Fallon and three others. He looked at the flames and his mouth dropped. There was an almighty 'crump' as the tank and the tin released the pressure built up inside. The homemade claymore unleashed its metallic payload.

The explosion filled the doorway with flames and the lethal shrapnel held within the tin. Fallon instinctively dived to his right as the blast sent searing hot metal ripping through the men standing in front of him. The impact of the shrapnel tore the flesh off their bodies as they pierced clothing, skin and bone. The shockwave lifted the men off their feet, propelling them several feet backwards.

Fallon had escaped the main force of the blast, but several shards of metal had embedded into his calf and shin, sending a grimace of pain through across his face.

"Go! Go! Go!" Jackson screamed, as he yanked Sonia into motion.

He let go of Sonia's hand and brought the weapon up. They ran at the inferno in front of them. Jackson leapt over the burning bike and aimed at the men in front of them. No one was moving, but then gunfire erupted to his left. He dropped to one knee and returned fire. The gunmen dispersed and dived for cover.

Jackson noticed Fallon scrabbling on all fours in front of him. He took aim. He was going to kill this man. He was about to pull the trigger when he was knocked sideways by a flying body. It was Catalina still clinging on to Benito. Jackson abandoned his revenge and hustled them towards the near wall. Sonia finally emerged from the flames and landed in a heap on the ground.

Jackson hoisted Catalina and Benito up and over the wall as large pair of hands grabbed them from the other side. Max stood up and pulled the two frightened figures down and into cover.

Sonia was just getting to her feet, when Fallon pounced on her, grabbing her by the waist and slamming her back onto the floor. Jackson heard her scream as she tried to release Fallon's grip. Fallon hoisted the stunned Sonia up and in front of him, using her body as a shield while holding his pistol to her head.

Jackson skirted to his left and Fallon mirrored his movements, keeping Sonia between himself and Jackson. Only now, he had put himself between Jackson and the rest of his men. They could no longer fire without hitting him, Impasse.

Jackson tried to judge whether he could get the rifle up and shoot Fallon before he got a shot off. He gave up on that idea. Any movement would alert Fallon to his intentions. Fallon gave Jackson a ghoulish grin.

"Looks like we got a Mexican stand-off, don't we Jax my boy?"

Jackson tried to raise the weapon slowly, but Fallon dug the barrel of his Smith & Wesson .357 into her temple.

"Ah-Ah-Ah. Don't even think about it," Fallon taunted, "I'll splatter her shit all over you!"

Jackson suddenly remembered something, He touched the mic transmitter.

"Come on Fallon let her go, why don't you and I sort this out like real men. Surely you don't need to hide behind a woman?"

Fallon snorted in defiance. "Yeah right like I'm going to drop my guard. Tell you what, put the gun down and I'll make it quick!"

Jackson thought a moment longer. "You are threatening to kill an American citizen on American soil. Surely lethal force is permitted in this case?"

Fallon looked at him puzzled. Jackson could see the cogs turning in his head as the statement rattled around. Suddenly Fallon's expression changed to panic as the round slammed into his right shoulder, sending him flying against the concrete wall of the stables.

Sonia was up and running immediately as the rounds from the guards returned. Jackson returned fire, covering Sonia's path. They both made it to the wall and clambered over it. Max helped Sonia into cover with Jackson backing into them, still sending rounds towards the wall.

They kept low running out to the scrubland and dropping down behind cover.

"Eagle Two, we have vehicles leaving the compound at high speed. Looks like big man has gone Rabbit, Over?"

Joanne's voice rattled over the net. "Let them go. Return to base and get out of here. Remember we're not supposed to be here."

All teams acknowledged and Max led them out of the scrub, with the backdrop of a burning building casting a amber floodlight over their progress.

Chapter 11

The Trade

When they got back to the park Joanne was standing waiting for them. Jackson could tell by her posture that she was not happy. Fuck her, he thought, I do not care, I don't work for her.

She stormed up to him and put her face right in front of his.

"What the fuck was that?"

He could see the fury burning in her eyes.

"How the fuck am I gonna explain that to my boss? Huh? I mean a foreign national playing 'Die Hard' on the streets of America, and I help you do it. It was supposed to be discreet, covert. What the fuck was 'Covert' about that?"

Jackson looked straight at her, fixing her with a steely stare.

"I got them out, none of your team got hurt and I managed to retrieve your asset on the ground at the same time. I'd say that was a job well done. With the exception of a moment when a federal agent stopped an American citizen from being killed by a foreign national, no FBI rounds were fired!"

He barged past her and dropped his kit at the back of the command vehicle.

Joanne marched after him, clearly miffed at having just been cut up by him.

"That's not the point Jackson and you know it!" she countered, "I still have to account for my actions here!"

Jackson looked at her calmly. "Just tell them you had a tip off that a foreign embassy worker had been snatched, and working in conjunction with the family, you managed to co-ordinate her release. You take the Kudos and we stay eternally grateful to the FBI for the efficient and professional way Special Agent Phillips handled the whole thing!"

He flashed her his American smile and began to strip the tactical gear off.

Joanne walked away as Sonia, Catalina and Benito came over to him. Catalina wrapped her arms around him and sobbed. Jackson held her tenderly. He realised just how young she was. This was more than most people of her age had been through. He forgot he was used to this kind of life, how could he sustain a relationship like this?

Sonia broke the moment. "So what happens now?"

Letting Catalina go, he stepped back and looked at the huddle of federal agents in the process of debriefing and no doubt getting their stories straight.

"I think now we need to box clever."

Sonia looked at him quizzically, "What do you mean Jax?"

He looked at Catalina. "Firstly we need to get these two into protection, get them into witness protection and safe. Then we need to cut the surveillance of your 'old man' and then I hold up my end of the bargain."

"What bargain is that?" Sonia asked suspiciously.

"I located the Data Card you so cleverly hid. They want it." He pointed at the huddle. "I hid it, but copied it. One file was pass-worded, but I managed to look at the other parts."

Sonia looked troubled.

"I pass-worded it so it couldn't be read or deleted, I only briefly looked at it. I had to run before they caught me. It was the only way I could think of saving my life."

Jackson looked at her. "So even you don't know what's exactly on this file?"

She shook her head." All I saw was a set of names and figures. It looked like an accounts ledger but I didn't get chance to look closely. All I know is that a Mr Yorke was paid a lot of money for services rendered and it had something to do with someone in the CIA."

Jackson looked at her quizzically. "I thought Fallon said you had talked? He told me you had told him everything you knew and he needed me to get the card for him."

Sonia's face darkened as she looked at Joanne. "The only person who knew that I'd sent a decoy to London and the real thing to Dryden was her."

Jackson nodded. It all made sense to him now. "Don't be too hard on her Son, she's one of the good guys, I can tell. She's been liaising with the CIA under the directive of a Mark Rourke. She's been ordered by her Deputy Director to channel all correspondence through his office. I'm betting that this Rourke is linked with Yorke and Martinez, but I think we need to keep this all between you and me for now. I don't know who to trust, and the less we give them the more they need to keep us alive."

Sonia nodded. "Yeah sounds fair to me, you don't think my Dad is involved in this do you Jax?"

Jackson paused for a few moments. "I have to admit, I did at first Son. I mean he did help them stitch me up, and if it wasn't for Cat, I'd be languishing in a Mexican jail, so yes I did think so."

He put his hand on Sonia's shoulder gently. "But I know why he did what he did. He did it to save you, and I would have done the same, so don't beat him up too badly OK?"

Sonia looked at the ground sadly, as the tears started to build. "I am so sorry Jax. None of this was your responsibility, and we all dragged you into it."

Jackson shook her shoulder, bringing her eyes back on him. "Hey, I love you all. I would do it all again if it gets you both out of the hole you are in, so stop that shit and let's focus on the plan, we need to get your Dad clear and then bury the lot of them. But first of all I need to get Catalina and Benito safe and I need your help."

Sonia's resolve returned and she wiped her wet eyes. "Anything you need Jax, I'm in all the way."

They hugged briefly and turned towards the agents.

"Just follow my lead." Jackson said winking at Sonia. She winked back.

As they all approached the agents, Joanne turned around to look at him. Jackson could still see the anger in her hard eyes but ignored it.

"Well, Mr Shaw."

He was obvious off the first name team and back on the shit list.

"Where's my evidence?" she continued coldly.

"There are still a few things I need first Agent Phillips." He said equally emotionless, two can play at this game.

"Special Agent Phillips to you Mr Shaw!"

Clearly she was irked at the obvious and deliberate disrespect. Jackson shrugged it off.

"Whatever. Firstly I need to get Catalina and Benito safe, and I don't entirely trust your security's integrity, so this is how it's going to play out."

Joanne did not let him continue; instead, she marched up to him and glared into his eyes.

"Just one god damned minute. We had a deal. We get them out and you give me what I want. I will vouch for every one of my team. Our integrity is without question and don't you fucking forget it mister!"

Jackson stepped back. He did not like being crowded and resisted the temptation to punch her. His renowned temper was boiling and he needed to stay in control.

"I'm not saying you or any of these guys are dirty, but Fallon knew about the London decoy. He also knew I was going after the evidence. The only people who knew I was going after it was Danny and you Special Agent Philips!"

He paused to let that sink in before continuing. "So the operation to observe me and follow me to the evidence was set up by your department and channelled through the CIA? Yes?"

She nodded but remained silent. Jackson could see the conflict in her eyes now. Jackson moved closer again lowering his voice.

"Now I reckon you are on the level Joanne, but I need you to be completely clear that what we talk about here stays between you and me."

He filled her in on his suspicions about Rourke's office and the leaking of the information to Fallon. Joanne's jaw tightened with every revelation.

Jackson pointed to her team. "Now we can play this out for their benefit, so it looks like I am blackmailing you."

"Which you are!"

He nodded. It was a fair point.

"Anyway," he continued, "I am going to make a few demands, but know this, they are not up for debate. My ultimatum still stands. But if you give me what I want, I will help you bring these guys down."

"Doesn't seem like I have a choice now, do I?" she said sarcastically.

Jackson chuckled and shrugged. "OK, you wanna do this for the cameras then?" he said pointing at the team.

"What the fuck do you want Mr Shaw!" she bellowed.

It was a bit over the top Jackson thought, but it was a good start.

"I want a car. Then Sonia is going to drive Catalina and the boy to a location only she knows. Once I know they are safe and none of you know where they are, I want to get

Danny out and safely with me. Only then will I take you to the card. Fuck with me and the deal's off!"

Joanne poked him with a stiff finger. "You cross me in any way Shaw, and I will personally see to it that you never see daylight again. You feel me Jackson?"

Jackson gave her an appreciative nod. She was actually quite attractive when she was angry.

Jackson put his hand out. "Deal." he said and they shook.

Jackson returned to Sonia, handing her the keys to his Datsun.

"Take these, when they get you a car, take it to my Motel. There is a red Datsun parked outside room 118. Take it and head to somewhere only you and your Dad know. Leave the Fed's car there, but stash the keys. There is a planter hanging from the overhang. Put the keys in there."

He handed her a phone. "Take this, I've memorised the number so I will call you on this phone once it's safe to come out. Do not speak first. If either your Dad or I don't say the code-word which is Ellie May, then drop the phone and get the hell out of there."

He looked at her with a serious stare. "This is important Son. You got it?"

Sonia nodded. "Yeah, I got it. Ellie May."

Jackson turned to Catalina. "Listen Cat. I need you to go with Sonia."

She was about to object, but he cut her off.

"I need to know you are safe, and Sonia is the only person I can trust right now, so please do this for me, eh?"

Catalina nodded sadly. She had been through a lot, but she was tougher than she looked. Jackson hugged her tightly.

"I will come and get you when it's all over, I promise. Then I will get you and Benito somewhere you can have a life."

Catalina pulled away and looked at him with pleading eyes. "With you?" Jackson smiled. "I hope so, Cat. I hope so."

When the car arrived, Sonia got into the driver's seat with Catalina and Benito in the back. Jackson leaned into the open window.

"The Motel is tagged on the maps. Do not hang around there. When you get back on the road, do a few odd turns and double back on yourself a few times. Check your mirrors. If any car stays with you, then you have a tail. If you do, then head to the nearest cop and tell him to contact Joanne. Then stay there till we come for you."

He handed her the rest of the cash he had left.

"Take this to get food and supplies. Now get going."

Sonia spun the car around and headed away. Jackson had a feeling that he may not see any of them again.

He did not hear Joanne come behind him as he stared out at the space they had just vacated. He jumped when she spoke.

"So what now Jackson?"

He snapped out of his daze.

"Now I need Danny."

"Ah yes, Mr Hughes."

"And just how does he fit into this?"

Jackson ignored the sarcasm.

"I have fought alongside him more times than I care to remember. I trust him in a fight and I want him by my side on this."

Joanne rolled her eyes. "OK, this is your show, but my warning to you, applies to him too."

Jackson nodded. "He wouldn't have it any other way, love."

They loaded into the vehicles and headed out to San Diego. Jackson slept most of the way. He had not realised how tired he was until the adrenaline levels had bottomed out. His instructors taught him, 'Sleep when you can'.

When he woke, they were heading into the city. They took the Kumeyaay Highway and pulled onto a retail park a few blocks away. Joanne turned to Jackson and fixed him with a hard look,

"How do you wanna play this? I need to know how you intend to neutralise a team of ex U.S. Special Forces on your own."

Jackson gave her a sarcastic laugh. He was on his own here again, typical American bureaucracy at its best.

"Neutralise? I'm gonna kill the motherfuckers!" he replied menacingly.

Joanne looked startled at this sudden change in Jackson's demeanour.

"Jackson, I can't have you running around wasting people at will. The rescue was different, but these guys are respected former servicemen. The press would have a ball with it."

Jackson shook his head. He was growing tired of the entire ass saving mentality he encountered here. What happened to doing the right thing because it was just that, the right thing? These guys were traitors, they helped criminals kill thousands of Americans with the drugs they import. They are the enemy as far as he was concerned.

"Put it this way, Joanne"

He turned to look at her straight.

"They are members of an illegal operation by the CIA on U.S. soil. They are responsible for the deaths of thousands of people that you took an oath to protect, from all enemies, both foreign," he paused for effect, "And domestic! Plus, they will declare they were never there, so by that rationale neither was I!"

Joanne nodded her appreciation for what was actually a valid point.

"What do you need from us?" she asked.

"All the kit I had before, except the MP5. I need complete concealment this time. These guys are good, so I need stealth over firepower, but I could do with some sort of sedative. If I can disable them, I will, but Milton and Taylor? If they are there, then they go to sleep for good!"

Joanne looked at him, clearly debating on whether to try to talk him out of this, but one look at his face must have told her enough. This was personal now.

"OK, I can get you some Midazolam syringes. They will knock the person out in about ten seconds, but won't last more than half an hour without a top up."

Jackson smiled. "That's more than enough time."

"So when do I get what I want?" Joanne asked him.

Jackson knew this was coming. "Once I get Danny clear and we are safely out of the way, then I will tell you where to find the evidence."

They ate and topped up their fluids while they waited for the syringes. The midday sun had started to give way to the darkening veil of evening. Jackson needed darkness again. He did not need back up. If he failed here, then he would be dead.

Night came quickly to this part of America. The black sky filled with storm clouds and within minutes, the heavens opened and the deluge began. The rain came at them like a power shower. It was fast and heavy, but surprisingly warm for the time of night.

This was a good ally to Jackson's plan. Not only would the heavy drumming of the raindrops on the foliage mask his movements, but also the rain would make visibility lower. The light from the rain reflecting on the green light of the night goggles, that they would be inevitably be wearing, would break his silhouette up a little.

About 02.30, with the rain at its most intense, Jackson set off. He knew where he was going and cut through gardens and back alleys, keeping off the main roads. When came up to the street behind Danny's, he ducked between two houses until he hit a stone wall. He lifted himself over the wall and dropped into a small waste ground in between Danny's back garden and the house whose garden he had just left. There was a small area of tightly grouped trees, so he slipped into them and looked around. So far, there was no sign of anyone.

Jackson dropped his night sights and regulated his breathing. He sat as still as he could looking for any sign. He was about to move out when something caught his eye. On the other side of the waste ground to where he sat was an identical patch of trees. The leaves on these trees were rounded and short. They shined with the coating of water that the rain had covered them with, except for one patch.

About eight feet up from the floor, and right of centre was a mass that did not match the rest of the tree. The leaves were pointed and dull. They did not move in the breeze like the ones around them, all pointing to one thing, a 'Ghillie Suit'. A 'Ghillie Suit' was a covering that snipers used to hide in dense foliage and long grasses. It blended in to its surroundings and to the untrained eye rendered the sniper invisible.

He slipped backwards and over the wall behind him. It led to a garden with low cut conifers against the wall. He passed through them and, keeping low, skirted along its length until he was directly behind the trees that his prey occupied, silently slipping back over the wall.

Slowing his movements down, like a cat stalking a bird. He placed one hand onto the branch in front of him, and using the wall as leverage, slowly pulled himself up onto it. Inch by agonising inch, Jackson drew closer and closer, stopping every few minutes to allow the disruption he was making to the treeline dissipate.

After ten agonising minutes, he drew up to eyelevel with the figure. It had to be Hawkins; his thin frame was unmistakeable, even bulked out by the camouflage.

Jackson pulled himself up as high as the branches would allow, and with his KA-Bar in his mouth, pounced on Hawkins. Using all the strength he could muster, he wrapped his arm around Hawkins's neck and squeezed hard. Hawkins immediately fought to get Jackson off, bucking like a wild rodeo stallion. Jackson held with all his might.

Using his free arm, he slipped his hand into the side pocket of his combat pants and retrieved the pipette. Flicking off the top, it exposed a short needle, which Jackson plunged into Hawkins's neck. Hawkins flailed wildly as he realised what was happening, but as the chemical took effect, his efforts slowly lessened.

A few seconds later, Hawkins had gone limp. Jackson removed a set of Plasticuffs and a gag and bound Hawkins securely. He dragged his limp frame down from the tree and stowed it against the wall.

He returned to Hawkins's position and looked through the scope from his M110 long-range rifle. The M110 SASS was a formidable weapon, highly accurate a firm favourite of the military sniper. He scanned the field of vision that Hawkins was covering.

He could see the back of Danny's house including the garden and rear garage door. Nobody would have been able to leave without Hawkins seeing. Jackson panned left and right slowly. To his right he could see into the neighbour's garden. There was a large wooden summerhouse with a small, decked area in front. The lawn was square and not very well maintained. Maybe the neighbours were bad gardeners, which he doubted, Americans loved their gardens, they were the small victories they achieved in suburban life. The other explanation was they were not there.

Jackson concentrated on the shed for a few minutes. He was about to pan left again when a boot emerged from the side of the summerhouse. It looked like whoever was there was lying in a prone position, scooped up next to the side fence covering the side of the property. Jackson left the hide as he found it and climbed out of the tree. Confident that the waste ground was clear from view, he crossed the open ground quickly. The rain had intensified and the already softened ground was becoming increasingly slippery underfoot.

He made it to the neighbour's back wall and squatted down, shimmying along it until positioned diagonally away from the lurking figure. He slipped over the wall silently, and tiptoed to a low stone built wall, that had was sectioned off to house a barbecue and outdoor kitchen. The three-foot wall gave him ample cover from which to observe.

Beside the summerhouse lay a figure. It was not chuck. He would have been covering the front of the house from an elevated position. The figure was continuously looking through a single lensed night sight on a tripod poking through the fence into Danny's garden.

The rain was drumming a solid rhythmic pattern on the summerhouse roof. Occasionally the guttering would fail in its task of guiding the water to the drain and would douse the lying figure with water. He must be sick of his life, he thought. He was about thirty feet from him, and through the green haze of his night sight; he could see that there was nobody with him. He could shoot him from here, but with the wind and rain, a suppressed round may drift and give his position away.

Jackson emerged from behind his cover and crept forward. About halfway to his right were a set of wheeled trash bins. Jackson made it behind them effortlessly. He had not done this kind of stealth work for a long time, and had doubted he would be as sharp as he was, but those fears we quickly dispelled, he still had it.

He closed in on his target and timing would be everything. The wind was picking up and there looked like there would be a possibility of thunder and maybe lightening too. He did not want to be illuminated mid stride. These guys are switched on and would react rapidly to any potential threat.

As if on call, the thunder arrived. It was mild at first, barely audible over the staccato rhythm of the rain on the summerhouse roof, but gradually it was increasing its deep throaty rumble.

The figure must have developed a touch of cramp, because he took his eye off the sight and looked back at his legs, stretching his calves in the process. The scars on his face we as clear as day from Jackson's position, it was Simpson. Jackson thought he heard Simpson say something quietly to himself. Was he checking in? If so then they would know that Hawkins was unresponsive and go on alert. He had to move fast.

He took off from his position like an Olympic sprinter and covered the ground in a second, lifting his whole body into the air as he approached Simpson.

Almost instinctively, Simpson looked back, sensing imminent danger and attempted to rise. He was too late. All of Jackson's weight slammed down onto him, pinning him to the floor and driving all the breath from his lungs. Pushing his knee into Simpson's back, Jackson hooked an arm around his neck, cupping his right hand with his left in a classic chokehold.

Simpson was stronger than he had expected. Simpson tried to get his fingers in between Jackson's arm and his neck to relieve the pressure, but Jackson held firm, squeezing with just enough pressure so as not to kill him, after all he didn't know if these guys even knew why Milton had them spying on their colleague. He would give them the benefit of the doubt. The FBI could scoop them up and take them out of the equation later.

Simpson finally passed out. Jackson released him and checked his pulse. He was out but alive. Wasting no time, he stuck the sedative into his neck and bound him the same way as Hawkins. The summerhouse was open so he dragged him into it and closed the door, locking it with the chain that was hanging from the handle.

Two down. Now he had to clear the other side. Trouble was He did not know just what was waiting for him on the other side of the house. He had to be careful. If Chuck got a line on him, he would kill Jackson without thinking. Hawkins was one thing. Chuck? Well he was another story altogether!

Chapter 12

Teammates

Jackson went back out of the garden the same way he got in. He did not want to risk crossing Danny's garden in case they had viewpoint of it. He circled round the waste ground and came out at the side of the alley to the left of the back of the house. Turkey peeking around the corner, he saw a vehicle parked up close to Danny's sidewall.

It was a utilities van with 'Mitchell's Drainage' stencilled on the back doors. Jackson dropped down and pressed his body into the puddles. Kitten crawling, he crawled under the van and listened. The engine was off, but he could not hear anyone inside for the rain on the vans metal roof.

By now, its illuminating sibling, lightning, had joined the thunder. The flashes were about four seconds from the thunder and about a ten-second interval.

He rolled sideways so he could see the van's driver side mirror and waited. The thunder roared its call, four seconds later the place was lit up like Time's Square. Framed in the mirror in full view was Hal. Jackson certainly did not want to kill Hal. He was the one member of the team that Jackson thought had a bit of moral fibre. He liked Hal.

Jackson rolled to the opposite side and waited. The lightning revealed that the passenger side was clear. He drew himself clear of the van and hunkered down, drawing the Glock. He stretched his fingers around the handle and gently pulled, that catch gave slightly. It was unlocked. Using the thunder to mask his movements he flung the van door open and jumped inside, pressing the Glock against a startled Hal's temple.

Hal looked at Jackson with a mixture of fear and shame in his eyes.

"Jackson! Don't kill me please!"

Jackson could see his fear was genuine. He gave Hal a hard look.

"I could believe it of the others, but I thought you were different Hal?"

He could see Hal's face drop, the shame washing over it like a tidal wave.

"I'm not a part of this Jax."

"You are here Hal. You are effectively keeping my best friend under house arrest; of course you are part of this!"

The anger was beginning to boil out of control. He pressed the muzzle harder against Hal's head forcing it backwards.

"I swear to you Jax, I was told we were protecting him, but when I saw Hawkins with the rifle I knew that was a lie."

"But yet you are still here!" Jackson said sarcastically, "you could have walked away."

Hal shook his head. "No, Jax, I can't."

Jackson looked at him puzzled.

"They will kill my son if I don't do this. He's all I got in the world, now my Maggie's gone Jax."

"Well Hal you are going to help me, or I swear to God I am going to kill you. I have very little to lose, and you know I am more than capable."

Hal nodded, Jackson knew Hal was a good guy, but now was not the time to make mistakes. He had to follow his plan to the letter.

"This is how it's going to go down. You are going to give me the information I want. I am going to tie you to the van, then take care of the others. If you sit quietly, you will live. If not…"he gave Hal a sideways nod, meaning you know the rest.

"Anything you need Jax. I had no part in anything that they did to you. Milton told me you'd been caught, and we were guarding Danny."

Jackson nodded, he believed Hal. He was a good judge of people and Hal just did not seem the mercenary type.

"I need to know who is here watching Danny and where are they?"

Hal nodded. "Well Simpson is on the other side of the house watching the garden and the front drive. Hawkins is behind us in the trees somewhere, and Chuck is in the house directly across from the front door."

"What about the others?" Jackson asked.

Hal just shook his head. "As far as I know they are in Mexico finalising what Milton said were travel arrangements, but we weren't involved in that side. We never are!"

Jackson could see a pattern forming here. Milton, Taylor and Marco are the contacts, the rest of them were on a need to know basis, in other words 'Grunts'.

"OK Hal. I'm going to tie you up, you attempt to warn anyone, and I will return and finish the job the way I had originally planned. You understand?"

Hal nodded furiously. "You'll get no trouble from me Jax. But if Milton finds out I helped you, then he will go after my Shaun."

Jackson took the gun away from Hal's head and gently placed his hand on his shoulder. "Don't worry I'll make it look like I did to you what I did to the others so far."

Hal's eyes widened. "The others?" he asked.

Jackson gave him a menacing grin and nodded. "Simpson and Hawkins are out of the game, just Chucky boy to deal with."

Hal looked worried, His voice trembling again. "They're dead?"

Jackson fixed his gaze on him. "They should be, but I guess I'm going soft. They're alive, and so will you be if you are being straight with me, Hal"

"As an arrow, Jax. Straight as an arrow!"

Jackson cable tied Hal's hands to the steering wheel and took the keys with him; he did not want them to have any transport away from the scene. He stood behind the van debating his next move. The thunder and lightning were beginning to ease off and even the rain did not seem as heavy. His noise cover would soon go. He made his mind up, take out Chuck and then he can take his time with Danny.

He decided to backtrack and come at Chuck's position from the rear. He figured Chuck would not be expecting him so his rear flank would have some rudimentary tripwire or a motion sensor. Jackson would have to tread carefully this time. The weather outside would not help him once he was inside, it might even give him away. To the trained eyes and ears of a sniper, the littlest change in noise, shadows or even air pressure, can alert a trained sense to react. He needed patience with this one.

He moved through gardens and hedgerows until he came to the right house. The rear garden was more like a yard. It was all paved off with small potted plants dotted about, nowhere to hide. He looked to the side of the house and there was a walkway about three feet wide, linking the front to the rear. That would do nicely.

The rear of the house shaped like a squashed capital 'T'. The stem of the 'T' was a small extension that doubled up as a double-doored conservatory. Jackson figured that Chuck would no doubt have the back doors rigged to alert him if anyone made entry that way and probably did the same with the windows, but he reckoned upstairs would probably be relatively clear.

He scaled the fence and once he was over the side, drew the Glock and stood to. He waited five minutes covering both approaches until he was satisfied that he had made it this far undetected.

Keeping as close to the wall as possible, he skirted around the back, making sure to stay below and window lines, until he came to the conservatory. It was a brick based structure with a reinforced clear Perspex roof. It would take his weight but not for a long period. Using the framework and the brick base for support, he hoisted himself up and onto the roof. He could not hear any noise, but it would stand out more inside than his side.

Jackson pulled himself up and carefully made it to the window in front of him. There were no drapes or blinds and he could see that it was some form of office. In the centre of the room facing away from him, sat a table with a very old looking monitor sat facing him. A keyboard and mouse kept it company alongside a small photo frame and a penholder. The left wall had a long bookcase filled to the brim with paperbacks and reference books. Obviously an academic's house, but where was the owner?

Drawing the KA-Bar, he inserted it between the sill and the window frame, searching for the latch that looped over the catch. Eventually he found what he was looking for, and after a little careful play, he managed to unhook it. He lifted the window slowly in case it made any loud noises, but it merely swished as it rose on well-maintained runners. He made entry quickly and closed the window behind him, remembering to replace the catch. He did not doubt that Chuck would have checked that all the windows, locking them securely. A loose catch would definitely give the game away.

Quickly dropping behind the desk, he waited. Patience wins the day in operations like these. Little noises often discarded if not followed by another. Satisfied that he had made it this far, Jackson moved to the door, slowly turning the handle, drawing the door into his body, while using it as a shield. It would not stop a high powered round, but might take enough velocity out of it to save catastrophic injuries.

He eased his body around the door and entered a long upstairs landing that went in a horseshoe shape around a central staircase. The front bedrooms were on the left half of the 'U' and he was on the right, not ideal, but you deal with situations as they unfold. One door directly in front of him was slightly ajar, but the next one closed. That would be the one Chuck was in. He would not want any light emitting behind him to give his silhouette away.

Jackson silently navigated his way around the landing, stopping every few steps and opening his mouth to control his breathing noises in his head. He passed the closed door and went to the slightly open one first. He eased the door open a fraction and peered inside. It was a bedroom with a bed in the centre, too small for a double but bigger than a single. 'Guest bedroom?' he thought. Only on the bed was a lump of black cloth and a rifle.

"Shit!" He cursed, realising his error.

No sooner had he gotten the words out of his mouth, Chuck barrelled into him, knocking the Glock out of his hand, sending it skittling across the floor and under the bed. It was like a blow from an NFL blocker; the impact lifted Jackson off his feet and sent him slamming into the wall. He could feel the vessels in his nose burst and the warm blood was already pouring down his throat.

"Out of practice are we, pretty boy?"

Chuck sneered as he rained blows into Jackson's kidneys. Jackson slumped as felt the strength leaving his legs. If he went down now he was finished.

Using the wall as leverage, he thrust himself off, tipping his head backwards and catching Chuck full in the face. Chuck instantly grabbed his injured cheek, releasing his grip on Jackson, giving him time to spin around and launch a brutal kick to Chuck's groin. Chuck's knees buckled, but instead of going down, he launched at Jackson again, wrapping his big arms around him in a bear hug and squeezed. 'This guy's strong.' Jackson thought as he struggled to breathe with the blood in his nose and throat. The strength was beginning to ebb away and his arms were pinned to his sides. He could feel himself beginning to black out.

He fumbled around his leg for the knife, dropping his knees slightly to help ease it out. Chuck must have sensed that Jackson was failing, because he loosened his grip to get better purchase. Jackson used this opportunity to manipulate the blade upwards as Chuck pulled him in even harder this time. The blade entered Chuck's abdomen and buried deep. Chuck's expression changed from fury to shock in the blink of an eye. He released his arms and clasped his hands on the wound that was gaping.

Jackson seized the moment to thrust the knife deep into Chuck's neck, the blood cascading over his fingers like a waterfall. As he eased Chuck's fading body to the floor, he looked into his pleading eyes.

"I'm sorry mate," he whispered, "but you brought this on yourself."

Chuck's eyes glazed then fixed on a spot somewhere in space, he was dead!

Jackson drew his sidearm checked the other bedroom but there were no other threats upstairs. With his weapon still drawn, he slowly eased down the stairs to the ground floor. The house was in darkness. Straight from the stairs was a dining room that lead to a wide kitchen both were clear. He then moved down a dark hallway and emerged into an 'L' shaped lounge with a large sofa and coffee table taking up most of the floor space.

Beyond the sofa tied and gagged, he found the homeowners. They were in their late seventies and both had one thing in common, they had both been shot in the head. The unmistakeable metallic odour of their blood hit him like a shovel. Jackson felt his anger rage; he wished he had discovered them first. He would have made sure Chuck suffered.

Once he had secured the house, Jackson left the house the way he had entered. It was not that he did not trust Hal; it was just that he did not trust the rest of his team to keep Hal completely in the loop. They obviously did not let him into their circle. Milton and the others may still turn up.

He returned to the van and Hal, still tethered to the steering wheel. He looked uncomfortable and distressed. He jumped when Jackson opened his door.

"OK, Hal this is what's going to happen. Just sit tight a little while longer. I need to secure Danny before I come and get you. The last thing either of us wants is for him to shoot you when he sees you yeah?"

Hal nodded vigorously.

"OK, so sit tight and we will come back for you."

He left Hal there and returned to Danny's garden via the alley. He knew this route was secure, as Simpson and Hawkins were out of the game, if anyone had been observing then he wouldn't have gotten this far.

He flattened his back to the back wall and edged to the back door. A quick glance around the frame told Jackson that the kitchen was in darkness. Using the tip of the knife, he gave the glass a few light taps, then waited. After a few minutes he repeated the action, this time a faint glow filled the kitchen, someone had opened the door to the kitchen.

Jackson pulled the Glock and aimed at the frame as the sound of keys in the lock rattled loudly. The door slowly opened but no one emerged. Jackson took a few steps backwards and moved outwards, maintaining his aim of the doorway.

Danny stood there with a confused look. "Jax?" he said, the surprise in his voice evident, "You can't be here mate, they got eyes all over me. If they see you they will kill Sonia and us too!"

Jackson pushed Danny inside and closed the door, all the while maintaining his aim on Danny's midriff.

"Is there anyone here I should know about Danny?"

Danny protested. "What the fuck Jax?"

"Just answer the question Danny, I aint got time to fuck about, so make it quick!"

Danny nodded in resignation. "No mate, there's no one here! I've not been able to go anywhere for days. They still have my little girl Jax."

Jackson could see the conflict in his eyes, but also saw the man he trusted. There was no way Danny would lie to him right now. He lowered the gun.

"Where's Cathy?"

Danny gave Jackson a 'calm down' motion with his hands.

"She's gone to her mother's cottage in Berwick. There's no way anyone will find her."

Jackson was sceptical. "What did you tell her?"

Danny looked embarrassed. He clearly knew his face told it all.

"I had to tell her everything Jax. You know me, I can't hide stuff from her, she always sees right through me. But if they think I've crossed them, then they might go after her."

Jackson put a hand on Danny's shoulder. "Don't worry about the goon squad out there, they are all down, but I do need your help."

Danny brightened up. "Anything mate, what can I do?"

Jackson told him about Chuck and the rest of the team, he told Danny about his neighbours too.

Danny sat down slowly. "Oh God, I got them killed. Mr Watson was a nice guy, a little cuckoo but his heart was in the right place. I can't believe they shot them!"

"They are sick bastards Danny. You should know, you were part of that team. What have you got yourself, and the rest of us for that matter into?"

Danny looked at him like a scorned child. "I knew Milton was highly connected with the CIA. We did do a few recce missions that the U.S. military were not able to do, but nothing that was illegal. You know me Jax, I'm as straight as a die and I would never get involved with drugs."

"But you knew Sonia was working with the Feds though didn't you? You know she'd put herself in danger and you still said nothing. Even when we were going to snatch her, you knew there was more to this than I was privy to, and still you let me walk into the shit alone."

Danny looked like he was about to burst into tears. "I know mate. I wanted to tell you when we were outside the farmhouse, but I knew if they got wind that you knew, then they would just take you out. They had nothing to lose while I was onside, but then I knew you could pull it off. I was going to meet Paul myself and warn you once you had Sonia out of there, but Simpson came with me. He watched me like a hawk, kept telling me that Paul would die too if I fucked this up, so I played ball."

Jackson's fury was building again. "Including dropping me into the lap of the Federales? I thought that was a nice touch, stitched me up big style."

"It was the only way I could save your life. They were going to take you out to sea and dump you overboard, I suggested dropping you at a hospital and tell them you were a criminal. At least then, they had you guarded. Paul was going call the Embassy and have you picked up, but you'd escaped, nice going there by the way."

Jackson nodded. "Well I want no arguments from you, I am going to kill them all, you're either with me or I drop you with the rest of your buddies right here and now."

"I'm with you," Danny said, "you know that. I always am, but if they find out I helped you they will still kill Sonia."

"She's safe Danny."

Jackson filled Danny in on the rescue and the firefight with Fallon. Danny sat with his mouth ajar the whole time, just staring into the distance.

"I need to get Hal in here and then we need all the information we can get. So that means hauling the other pieces of shit in here and go to work on them. This is where you choose your side mate."

They released Hal from his bonds and brought him into the kitchen, tied him to the radiator and gave him a hot drink, Hal was frozen to the bone. They then retrieved the rest of the team placing them in the garage. They were not getting the nice warm treatment that Hal was. Danny made rudimentary hoods for them both and sat them against the cold wall. Hawkins stirred first. The realisation of what had happened to him seemed to wash over him. He began a valiantly attempt to loosen his binds, but only succeeded in tightening them.

Jackson lifted him up with his weight supported by the wall and bent his legs. This stress position would test every muscle in his body.

"Stay there!" Jackson growled at him, "do not sit down, and do not move. If you drop you pay!"

Hawkins's breathing laboured under the gag and they could hear the wheezing of his nose as the effort to remain in that position started to take its toll.

Simpson stirred a few minutes later. They repeated the position with him, giving him the same warning.

They sat watching the two men shake with the effort of maintaining the position, Hawkins's legs were shaking badly and he began to sink back towards the floor. Jackson scooped up a piece of rubber hosing from the workbench and gave Hawkins several hits with just a hint of venom, before replacing him in the position. Simpson was next to try to alleviate the pressure by dropping. He too got the same treatment. They kept this up for an hour, before eventually taking Hawkins's hood off.

Jackson squatted down so he was level with the sniper's face.

"You feel like answering my questions yet or do you fancy another hour if this? I got all day, doubt if you do!"

Hawkins glared at him defiantly and mumbled some form of "go to hell" through his gag. Jackson replaced the hood and gave him four swipes with the hose, this time a fraction harder than the last.

Next up was Simpson, he gave the same answer as Hawkins, but Jackson noted that it was not as confident a response. He would be the one to break.

Another hour had passed and the rain had subsided. They took turns watching the men while the other sat with Hal. By now, they had untied Hal and he was sleeping. When Jackson returned to the garage, Danny was just taking Simpsons hood off. Hawkins was still in position.

"All yours Jax, I think this one seems to want to talk"

Jackson lowered himself onto a small pot and sat facing Simpson whilst drawing the KA-Bar from its scabbard.

"Right mate, we're going to remove the gag, if you shout out or say anything at all until I tell you, I will make sure your screams will be real, we understand each other?"

Simpson nodded wearily, so Danny untied the gag and Simpson gasped for breath.

"Now," Jackson continued, "where are the rest of the guys?"

Simpson panted. "They have gone to the drop point to keep the airstrip secure."

"Which airstrip would that be?" Danny asked.

"The one in Dryden isn't it?" Jackson asked looking at Simpson, whose face looked white with shock.

"Oh yes I know where that is, and I know when the drop is, only thing I need from you is who will be there and how many bodies on the ground?"

Simpson palled at the hopelessness of his position. "Milton, Taylor and Marco are heading security. Me and him…" Simpson pointed at Hawkins, "we were going to set up range obs to secure our Exfil. Martinez is personally dropping this one, as it's bigger than usual, so he will have Ramon and his own security in the plane. Rourke will be there to take the shipment to his warehouse."

Jackson looked at Danny, who realised that Simpson had made a mistake.

"You said Rourke?" Danny said. "Don't you mean Yorke?" Simpson shrugged tiredly. "Rourke, Yorke. Some guy call him whatever you want, I've been more than co-operative I think, don't you?"

Danny stood up and pulled Jackson to one side. "Who's Rourke?"

Jackson moved close to Danny's ear and spoke softly. "Rourke is the CIA department head that all of Sonia's Intel has been filtered to. Yorke owns Trident Holdings, the freight company they are using as the distribution hub. Yorke and Rourke is the same person. That is why they were onto Sonia so quick, and that is why they brought your buddy Milton and his boys on board to keep you in line. You've been played mate, and they dragged me into it."

He let that sink in for a few minutes, watching Danny's face change from confusion, to deep burning anger.

"We need to take them all down, that means everyone, but we have a small problem!"

Jackson told Danny about the FBI and his promise to Joanne.

"We need to find a way to give her what she wants, but get what we want too, it is thinking cap time mate.

Chapter 13

Choose sides

They returned to the house leaving Simpson and Hawkins tied together to the stovepipe. They were going nowhere fast. When they returned to the kitchen, Hal was at the stove, He had made a rough stew from whatever was in the refrigerator. Jackson and Danny looked at each other and smiled. Hal turned to see their expressions.

"Hey I'm with you guys. You have been straight with me, so I'll be straight with you. They threatened my son. I got no loyalty to guys like that."

Jackson gave Hal a gentle pat on his back. "We will make sure your son is safe from them, but I need you to play along with them, be our eyes and ears on the inside. Feed us with as much Intel as you can, then we will take them all down. You will be in the clear because you helped us, I will guarantee that!"

"Just make sure my Shaun is safe, he's all I got."

They ate and while Hal was busy clearing up, they began to formulate their plan. Firstly, they had to get protection for Hal's son.

Jackson could solve that one with phone call. He called Joanne and gave her Shaun's details, being careful not to tell her what they had planned. He told her he had to get Shaun safe so he could free Danny. It was a 'white lie', but the longer he could keep her at bay the better chance they had to succeed.

Once he and Danny were happy with what they needed to do, they returned to the kitchen, where Hal was sitting at the table. They sat opposite him; both men had serious looks on their faces.

"OK Hal," Jackson said, "this is the deal. The FBI are heading over to scoop Shaun up and hide him. Once I have the nod that he's safe we then move to the next phase."

Hal looked at Jackson with teary eyes. Jackson could see the pain in them. This was a good guy who was in a hole, well not anymore.

"Once we know Shaun's safe we need you to play your part," Jackson continued, "we will tie you up in here. We are going to make it so you can get loose, once you do get loose I need you to call Milton and tell him you've escaped but the rest of his team are missing. Once he brings you in, you will communicate using an email system we have devised. Milton can't track it and will keep you safe. But for now, play along as the disgruntled hostage who now has an axe to grind with us".

While Danny gave Hal instructions on the email set up, Jackson went up to his room. He needed to get some people in play and check on Sonia and Cat.

After a shower and a shave, he felt more human. He called Sonia, giving the password once she answered. She told him they were safe and had taken Cat and Benito to a place she used to hang out in when she was on vacation. Even Danny did not know where that was.

He called Joanne again and confirmed the Shaun was indeed safe and in protective custody. He told her about the drop, leaving out the location, claiming he would get her more information as he got it. He could tell she was not buying it, but he had her over a barrel and it felt good.

Next up he dialled a number from memory and let it ring, he just hoped the person would talk to him. After five rings, a gravelled voice answered.

"DS Forster"

"Dave." Jackson said, "it's Jax."

"Jackie? Jesus mate thought you'd topped yourself, been trying to get hold of you for days."

David Forster was a Detective Sergeant who worked as Jackson's partner for five years. He was from Bermondsey, South East London and was a fanatical Millwall F.C. fan. He was a short man, only five feet eight, but powerful. He had a rugby player's physique and the hardness to match. He was the one person that Jackson would think twice about locking horns with, but he was straight. He did his level best to keep Jackson on the force, even threatening to punch out anyone who spoke against him. In the end, he was powerless to stop proceedings going the way they did.

"Listen Dave, I need your help. I don't have much time, but I'll explain everything to you when I can. I need two favours off you, but you have to keep this very much on the quiet mate."

"Hey, anything you need mate, you know me, if I can, I will!"

"I have sent an envelope to your house. It will have an El Paso postal mark. I want you to-"

"El Paso?" Dave interrupted, "why are you in Mexico?"

"El Paso's in America you doughnut!"

Dave was a good copper, but often very obtuse.

"Never mind that shit. I need you to keep the envelope safe, do not open it, but if anything happens to me, I want you to send it to a Chris Tanner from The Guardian newspaper. Can you do that for me?"

"Of course I can Jax. You in some sorta trouble mate?"

Jackson chuckled. "You know me. I came here to forget my troubles, and inherited a whole new set."

He could hear Dave snigger.

"Yes Jackie, that's just you. What is the other favour? You said you had two?"

"The other is; I need you to use your contacts in Research, and get you the number for a Frank Chambers. He is the senior investigator for Interpol. Tell him I have information regarding a certain James Fallon, he'll know who you mean. Give him my number and tell him if he doesn't want the FBI stealing his collar, then he'd better talk to me now! You got that mate?"

"Sure mate, I got it. You sure you can't tell me what this is all about? Maybe I could help?" Dave sounded curious, but a little desperate.

"You not got enough shit going on there without coming here and getting mine?"

He would love to have Dave on this. His ability to be a battering ram would certainly help with Taylor.

"Bored outta me nut here mate. Chief Super's got us all filling in more forms than ever. Can't just nick someone now, gotta do mind studies and method statements. Doin' me nut in mate!"

Jackson thought a moment. "Do these favours for me, and I'll touch base with you later, yeah?"

"Definitely mate. I'll let you know when I get anything!"

"I really appreciate this mate," Jackson said, "a lot of people are going to owe us a big debt once this is over. Take care mate and be careful too. I don't know how high this goes, but normal protocols don't apply here. Just you, me and Frank in the loop for now."

"You got it Jax, Speak soon mate." With that, he hung up.

Jackson returned to the kitchen. They tied Hal to the radiator loosely. If he used friction, he could loosen the ropes with little fuss, and would attain the relevant rope burn to make it look convincing. Leaving the light on, they returned to where the van was and backed it up the driveway. After bundling the two captives into the back and securing them to the bulkhead, they loaded the rest of Danny's safe and headed out.

They needed a place to regroup and lose any surveillance that the FBI may have put on the area. They headed north up highway 15 towards L.A. then swung right across the 10 towards Phoenix.

The San Bernardino Forest gave way to the Joshua Tree National Park. Jackson began humming the tune for 'Where The Streets Have No Name' by U2, from their 'Joshua Tree' album. Danny joined in and before long, they were singing along together. The hills and desert vista became clearer as the sky lightened and the rains left in their wake. Jackson could feel the grip of purpose take hold of him. This was the endgame, and it was now into its crucial part.

They trundled through Mesa Verde and into Phoenix. The city took the tan colour of the desert and blended its buildings into it. The heat was beginning to rise and the traffic was mercifully light. They booked into the Best Western next to the airport. Jackson told Danny to drive the van into the Airport and lose it in the long stay parking lot. He would tell Joanne where to find it later.

Danny returned with a black Jeep Cherokee he had rented for the week, using his security ID to avoid the DMV checks. They ate in the nearby BBQ restaurant and sat with two large coffees. Danny looked tired; he was staring into space, lost in his own thoughts.

"Penny for them."

Danny looked up and smiled wearily. "I've let them play me Jax, they've used me and it's almost cost me the three people I love. How could I have been so blind?"

Jackson put his hand on Danny's. "Listen mate, we've all trusted the wrong people and it's cost us. The secret is not to make the same mistake twice. We have to be ruthless here, no prisoners. It's shooting to kill and taking our chances with the FBI later."

He fixed Danny with a serious gaze. "You have to be one hundred percent on board here mate, or we are fucked, you hear me?"

Danny nodded weakly, he could see he was not completely comfortable with conducting operations on home soil, but this was no longer a case of doing the right thing, this was war. Danny drifted off into his own thoughts again. Jackson decided to leave it, let him work his own demons out in his head. He needed him focussed, not conflicted. Jackson's phone punctured the silence with its shrill tone. Jackson studied the number. He did not recognise it. He clicked to answer but said nothing, just listened.

"Hello? Is that Mr Shaw?"

It was an English accent, slight Birmingham twang softened by years of working with various different accents.

Jackson just said. "Go on."

"Mr Shaw, this is Frank Chambers. I received a message from a DS Forster, stating that I should get in touch with you regarding a certain Mr Fallon. Is this true, or was I misinformed?"

Jackson felt a surge of adrenaline coursing through him. Was this a trap or was this progress. He decided to tread carefully.

"Mr Chambers," he decided to play it cagey, "you were investigating Mr Fallon as part of a wider investigation. Can you you confirm the details of that investigation?"

There was a long pause. Jackson thought at first the man had hung up, but when he looked at the phone screen, it showed the connection was still ongoing.

"Well Mr Shaw, I'm sure you are aware that I cannot divulge the details of my investigation over the phone. I am assuming you want details to prove that I am who I say I am?"

"That's right!"

"You are interested in Mr Fallon, but who else is?"

"Well Mr Shaw, I can't go into specifics, but Special Agent Phillips is my U.S. contact and is currently linking him with an investigation of her own. I am really not at liberty to expand on that I'm afraid Mr Shaw, but I assure you, I am most definitely on the side of justice. So unless you have something to tell me, then this conversation's over."

Jackson figured he had to trust someone eventually. "I can place Fallon at the scene of a pending drug drop on U.S. soil. I have the location and I have the time and date."

There was another long pause before Chambers responded.

"Okay, you have my attention. Go on!"

"I need assurances first. I need to protect people who may get hurt if this goes wrong. I need to know that you will protect them from retribution."

"I can assure you Mr Shaw, anyone who assists us in the capture of a highly dangerous terrorist will be extended the full support of Interpol and Her Majesty's Government."

Jackson could feel a large portion of the weight that he had been dragging around was lifting.

"Okay you have a deal, but for now I will tell you what I told Agent Phillips."

He proceeded to tell the whole story, from Sonia's discovery, her kidnapping, the involvement of the CIA and Milton and Fallon. When he finished there was silence for a long period as Forster processed the information.

"I think we should meet. This is a matter I am unwilling to discuss further on an unsecure line. You pick the place you feel most comfortable and I can be there tomorrow."

"I'll be in touch on this number. Stay by your phone." Jackson said before hanging up.

Jackson saved the incoming number as 'C' for Chambers. When he looked up Danny was staring at him quizzically.

"What was all that about?"

Jackson filled Danny in on Chambers's involvement with Joanne and his investigation into Fallon. He asked Danny to come up with a meeting place.

Danny sat thinking for a while and finally said. "There's a place outside Tucson. I went there when I was providing security for a tech mogul's visit. Nice coffee house with plenty of places to put our surveillance in, in case this guy's not who he says he is."

Jackson nodded. "That will be perfect."

Danny gave him the address and Jackson picked up his phone and typed a text message;

9136 E Valencia Rd, Tucson, AZ 85747

13.30 Tomorrow

Any funny business and we are in the wind.

Jackson pressed send and sat looking at the screen. They had just exposed themselves; he hoped his instincts were better than last time. His phone beeped, snapping him out of his thoughts. He looked at the screen;

I will be there.

The text contained nothing else. Jackson felt the weight of danger return. They needed to make arrangements. They needed to recon the area and put in their own counter surveillance measures.

They drove down to Tucson and pulled up next to a five-shop block. The coffee house was in the centre of the block. It was a modern looking place with pink rendering giving it a quintessential Spanish look. There was a Thai restaurant to its left and cleaners to its right. Its carpark was open and large. Across the road was a vast area of desert land filled with tall scrubs and undulating mounds.

They drove around the area to gauge the potential entry points. The streets were quiet. The occasional dog walker dragged their unwilling canine companions along the hot, broken pavements. The smell of food mixed with diesel from the nearby truck stop wafted in the air. They could see rows of big rigs parked with pattern and precision along the dirt hard standing. A thick layer of dust began to gather on a number of the cabs. They had clearly been there a while.

Jackson got out and wandered around the truck stop. Most of the vehicles were parked at ninety degrees to the coffee house, offering little to no cover. However, one rig was nestled into a slight layby parallel to the front of the shop. The trailer had a footplate on its side that moved when Jackson tested it with his foot. The rig had a large dark grey-skirted side kept in place by ratchet clasps. Jackson moved around the rig so that he was directly behind it and out of sight of the shop. After a few tugs on the clasp, he managed to loosen enough to lift a small section to peer inside. The trailer was empty.

Squeezing himself through the skirting, he managed to get into the trailer and stand up. There was a decent amount of light inside its dank interior to keep Jackson's claustrophobia at bay, thanks to several shafts of light pouring from various size holes in the tarpaulin. Jackson moved up to one such hole that was almost at eye level and peered out. It commanded a perfect view of the coffee shop carpark and front window. This would be ideal for an observation station.

Jackson squeezed back out and replaced the clasps. He would have to open them further to get all of Danny's six feet three inches through the gap. He returned to the car and told Danny what he wanted him to do. Danny nodded his agreement. He would be the backup. They just had to hope that the rig was still there tomorrow.

They checked into a hotel on the other side of the Highway and waited. This was the hardest part of this kind of situation. They were men of action, never happier than when the training kicks in and they go to work. The build-up just added to the tension. The sun was fading and night came calling. They slept until 3 am. Once they woke, they checked their equipment and headed back, pulling the Cherokee off into the desert area, stowing it behind a large area of scrub. Time to see if Chambers really was whom he said, he was.

Chapter 14

Phase One

Having squeezed Danny into the trailer with the M4 and the optics, Jackson returned to the Jeep and parked up in the carpark adjacent to the coffee shop. This gave him a perfect view of the shop front and the access to the carpark in front. From this vantage point, they could see every angle and viewpoint. If this Chambers was anywhere near as good as he sounded, then he would be bound to set up a similar precautionary perimeter. If this were a trap, he would soon know about it.

The morning dew burned away as the searing sun rose in all its majestic glory. The heat began to rise and Jackson began to perspire badly. He kept himself busy checking the Sig Sauer 9mm he took from Simpson. He removed the clip, emptied the rounds out and then reloaded them; testing the spring to make sure it had the right amount of tension. He pulled the slider back until it locked and checked down the chamber to make sure there were no blockages. Once he was satisfied that the weapon was in good condition, he reloaded the clip and re racked the slider, bringing a round into the chamber. He slid the slide back a fraction to check the round sat correctly.

Something caught Jackson subconscious attention. The garbage bins to the side of the Thai restaurant were now in a different position from last night, re-arranged into a triangle, a perfect vantage point to hide within; Jackson needed to check this out.

"Danny. You awake in there mate?" he said into his throat mike.

"Aye I'm here mate, everything okay there?"

"Not sure mate, think we may have early visitors. Can you see the bins from there mate."

"Wait one!"

There was a short pause then he returned on the net. "Yeah mate I got what you are looking at. Could be someone in there, but can't be sure. You wanna abort?"

Jackson gave it some thought. They could abort and rearrange but time was running out. The drop was in two days and they had a lot to do before then.

"No mate. I am going to neutralise the potential threat. Just cover my six and keep it peeled for other interested parties."

Danny gave him two clicks in response.

Jackson slipped out of the Jeep and made his way across the carpark to the short hedge that bordered it. He circled slowly, keeping his eyes roaming for others. As he circled around behind the garbage bins, he saw a black sedan nestled between a waste cardboard cage and a glass bottle-recycling hub. This had to be the advance team's ride.

He made his way around in a wide arc so be was hidden from view by the hub. Crouching low, he made it to the back of the car. It was a Ford Taurus. Its black and chrome trims gave it a mean look. He tried to look into the car, but the tinted windows made it impossible to make out if anyone was in the back. He changed his angle to get a look at the drivers mirror when he caught sight of movement to his left. He span around and came face to face with a solid looking man holding a Glock 17 at him.

As Jackson stood up, the rear door of the Taurus opened.

"Get in Mr Shaw." A voice he recognised.

He peered into the car. Sitting in the rear seat was an elegant looking black man, dressed in an impeccable black suit with a dark purple shirt with matching tie. This guy looked like he was going to a gala, he thought. Sitting in the front passenger seat and the owner of the voice was Special Agent Joanne Phillips.

"Get in." She repeated.

Jackson got into the car next to the man and closed the door keeping his hand on the butt of the Sig. Joanne turned in her seat to face him, her eyes drifted down to his hidden hand.

"Relax Jackson. If we wanted you in cuffs, you would be."

She gave him an open palm gesture to show him she had nothing hidden.

"Jackson, may I introduce Frank Chambers."

Chambers nodded his greeting and offered his hand to Jackson. They shook firmly. It was a good grip. His hands had the look of a man who had gotten them dirty the hard way, but was now the one who delegated; he clearly worked his way up. He had a gold signet ring with a red eagle motif.

"Mr Shaw, I apologise for all the cloak and dagger routine, but when Agent Phillips told me about you and your involvement, I have been very keen to meet you. She said you would seek me out, and here you are."

Jackson gave Joanne a hurt look. She just shrugged.

"We haven't let you out of our sight since you arrived in the U.S. Jackson. I read your jacket when we did the background checks on Mr Hughes and his known associates, so once you popped up at LAX we had you under surveillance."

The look on Jackson's face must have been priceless. She gave him a superior smirk, cocking her head to the side.

"I'm assuming Mr Hughes is listening?" she said pointing to the throat mike.

Jackson nodded. "Yes he is and if anything goes down, he has instructions to come in all guns blazing!"

Joanne rolled her eyes. "No need to be so dramatic Mr Shaw, after all in our own unique way, we are all on the same side here. You just facilitated in an operation that would have been very hard to negotiate politically. Therefore, we aided you where we could. But this is where things get serious."

She gestured to Chambers. "Mr Chambers? Your show."

Chambers leaned forward to look Jackson full in the face.

"What do you know about the operation you have been involved in disrupting?

Jackson shrugged. "The way I see it the Martinez family have been smuggling drugs into the U.S. via a contact in Texas. The customs problem circumvented by someone high up in a government position and distributed via a legitimate haulage company. Everything peachy until Sonia discovered a link between the CIA and Martinez. Now the CIA guy is getting twitchy and Martinez is getting scared, after all if he doesn't help quash the leak, he gets burned too, deniability to the highest bidder."

Chambers nodded in resignation. "I do have to admit, we have a situation that is equally dangerous to both the United Kingdom and our Cousins over here. The current drug problem is rising and dragging the terrorist networks with it. We have it on good authority that the finances raised from this particular drugs operation, are funding terrorist activities in the UK. So you can appreciate our interest in both angles."

Jackson could see that Chambers was angling at something, but he was not going to play into his hands that easily.

"So what do you want from me Frank?"

Jackson saw Chambers frown at the use of his first name, but fuck him. They needed him, so he had the upper hand.

"Well Mr Shaw," Chambers said tiredly, "What we would obviously like is the information you acquired, but I am guessing that that's not going to be forthcoming?"

Jackson merely raised his eyebrows, you got that right mate, he thought. "

So where does that leave us then Frank?"

Chambers flinched again, but maintained his composure.

"Well, if we can't control you, then we might as well use you. You clearly have a plan in mind, so we will offer support so long as we get what we want. Do we have an accord Mr Shaw?"

Jackson nodded. "Okay well what I need is to be able to protect the innocent victims in all of this. There are a few bad people out there, who will be looking to use them to get to us. I need to keep them safe, as well as giving them a safe future. If you can guarantee that and immunity from prosecution for myself and Danny, then I will play ball."

Chambers looked at Joanne who merely nodded slightly.

"You have a deal, Mr Shaw, but I want something from you. Call it an act of faith. We are giving you a free hand here. I need to know it's going to be advantageous to our cause."

Jackson pulled out his phone and scrolled to the images. He sent all four to Joanne's mobile phone, which beeped immediately. Joanne took her phone out and gazes at the imagery that popped up. With each swipe of her finger, her eyes widened and her face reddened. She looked up at Jackson. Her face was ashen and there was a hint of a tear there, being double-crossed hurts.

She gave her phone to Chambers, who showed an equal amount of surprise.

"We've known for some time that there was one or two bad apples in the Agency," Chambers said, "but we never suspected him, are you sure this information is genuine?"

Joanne snapped angrily. "I will vouch for the integrity of my source."

"Yeah, I will too." Jackson added.

Chamber raised his hands in mock surrender. "Okay, okay, I get it. So you said you had other evidence Mr Shaw?"

Jackson nodded. "Yes I have a bunch of files on an SD card, which I will get for you once I get the assurances I asked for."

He looked at them both in turn and added. "And I want them in writing first."

Chambers looked at Joanne, and they shared a look. Chambers sighed wearily. "Okay, Mr Shaw, I will get onto it immediately."

Jackson could feel a strange dread when he saw the look between the two agents; he was not going to get screwed over again.

"I will warn you both; I have taken steps to ensure not only my safety, but that of the people I just mentioned. If you play ball, then the copies I made of the whole sorry affair go to you, Special Agent Phillips. If you screw me, the files go straight to the press."

Joanne was about to erupt, the redness in her face screaming, but Chambers merely lifted a calming hand. "We can assure you Mr Shaw, neither of us want to 'screw you', as you so eloquently put it, everything you have asked for will be honoured. I have no doubts about your resourcefulness and tenacity."

He looked at Joanne who nodded her agreement. "So we are all on the same side, how do we play this?"

Joanne nodded at Jackson, "My experience recently has told me that Jackson seems to be very competent at getting the job done," she turned to Jackson, "So what did you have in mind?"

Jackson grinned at her. "Kill them all."

"Very subtle Mr Shaw." Joanne said sarcastically.

Jackson shrugged. "You asked. Listen, you want Martinez taken down, yes?"

They nodded.

"Well the best way is to hit them at the drop. I know that all parties will attend. You can nail your poison pill, and break up a drug network that has been operating with impunity for a long time."

Chambers leaned forward. "I need your assurance that you will keep Mr Rourke alive. We need to know how deep or high this goes. The rest are yours to do what you will with."

He smiled at Jackson. He could not tell if it did not have just a little hint of mischief in it.

Joanne jumped straight in. "I am not comfortable in sanctioning a hit squad on U.S. soil. That is the CIA's way, not the Bureau's. My bosses will never sign off on it, arrests yes, but all out warfare?"

Jackson looked at her in dismay. "After all we have done so far, and you still doubt that we can make this work?"

"This isn't a case of making it work, Jackson," she said tersely. "it's a case of legalities. If we snatch Rourke in an illegal bust, involving a foreign agency and two civilians, Rourke will walk. He will pool his buddies together and claim he was working to bring a drugs cartel down. Either that, or if it goes higher, he will be whacked before he ever testified. I want them all, and I want them in prison, not a box."

Jackson could see her point. "Look, Joanne," he said, knowing using her first name would annoy her, "if you are that bothered about the legalities of what we are going to do, then make it official. Go to your boss and spin it any way you can, but get my mate and me onto the battlefield and let us do what we do best. No offence to your people, they are good, but we are better. We will get you all the proof you need to bust his ass. But you are either in all the way, or you sit back and let us gift wrap this fucker for you."

She looked pale; the weight of what he was asking her to do did not sit well with her. "Can you assure me that we will get what we want?"

"Absolutely," Jackson said confidently. "with the evidence I have already and the evidence I will get for you, there will be no doubt that your guy is dirty and conducting an illegal operation. Give me logistical support and I will deliver your man."

She looked unconvinced.

"Either that, or jump on board and claim I went mad and started shooting up the place, but that's going to make meeting my demands tough and your position tricky. I mean CIA operating on U.S. soil and the FBI operating on foreign soil. Surely that would be severely damaging to both agencies."

Joanne frowned at this. "Doesn't seem like I have a choice do I?"

"No you don't," Jackson added, "But I guarantee you, you will come out of this well, I won't burn you."

He turned to Chambers. "Unfortunately for you, if I get Fallon in my sights then I am going to kill him. The only way you get him alive, is if I get him afterwards."

Chambers chuckled to himself. "I can live with that, Mr Shaw."

Joanne sighed. "Okay, what you want from us to make this work?"

Jackson thought about how he was going to achieve this.

"I need your team, but I need you out of the way. If you are there then you are complicit. I promise that they will be support only, well except one."

Joanne looked quizzically at him.

"Max," he said, "I'd like Max to help us on the field when it goes noisy."

"Why Max? I thought you didn't like him?"

"Not at all. He showed balls and initiative in coming to help us get away from the compound. I need a reliable guy to grip Rourke and hold him while we deal with the others. You got anyone better in mind and then I'm all ears."

Chambers looked troubled. "What is my role in all of this? You specifically asked for me. There must have been a reason."

Jackson looked at him. "I need you to arrange protection for my family back in the UK. If I know Fallon, then I am sure he has already put the wheels in motion to snatch them and use them as a bargaining chip. I want to get them safe without alerting him that I am coming for him."

"What makes you think he will even be at the drop? I mean he knows you know about him, and he knows that you have Miss Hughes back. Surely he will know he is blown?"

Jackson shook his head. "Fallon knows nothing. He was bluffing to get me to get the SD card. He will be there, because he needs me to get it, otherwise he will be running scared both in the UK and here. Besides which, his ego has taken a huge hit. He will want revenge for that."

Chambers nodded in agreement. "Consider it done, but I want him first, do I make myself clear?"

Jackson shrugged. "Okay, but I am going to kill him, rest assured."

Jackson laid his plan out to them, he knew it was risky giving away so much information, but he needed help. He could not defeat Milton and his crew as well as a drug smuggler's small army. He needed to be confident that he would get the job done. If anyone escaped, the results could be catastrophic.

Joanne left the car and made a phone call.

Chambers turned to Jackson once they were alone. "I understand your loyalty to your friend Mr Shaw, but this seems to be becoming very personal to you. Do you mind if I ask why?"

"Not at all," Jackson said, "When I was about 16, Jamie Clark, my best friend at school got into a bad crowd. He started with the weed, and then progressed to harder recreational drugs. In the end, what was once a promising footballer became a dark shell that no one could reach, eventually found in a local woods hanging from a tree. Drugs have killed so many gifted people Frank, so if that's my war, then I am more than willing to die stopping it."

Chambers gave him an approving look. "That's a good motivation."

Jackson nodded before adding. "And they hurt my friends, so that puts them firmly on my shit list!"

Joanne returned a few minutes later.

She looked tired. "My boss has just chewed my ass off. He said to drop this in the lap of the Director General and back away or it would be more than just my career that suffered. He was saying that if we screw this up, I would be sharing a cell with Rourke. Therefore, I have just put my neck on the executioner's block for you so I am coming too. You had better be as good as you say you are."

Chapter 14

Phase Two

Jackson returned to Danny, leaving the two agents to their arrangements. He filled Danny in on the plan. Danny looked a little sceptical.

"Can you trust them, Jax?"

"No probably not, but what choice do we have? If we do not drop them now, we will be forever looking over our shoulders. That means all of us. Joanne could have burned me twice now, but she's been straight up with me."

"And Chambers?"

"Chambers is a dark horse. I cannot work out whether he is shifty or just a little deep. I guess we will find out. But whatever he is, Fallon is not leaving that drop alive."

They returned to the Jeep and headed off towards Dryden. Danny drove while Jackson studied online maps of the area. There were plenty of places to conceal themselves, but Milton was a pro. He would know that, and would have his own perimeter in place. Jackson would have to out-think him.

Jackson opened the email and checked the drafts. Hal must have been discovered because a new draft had been entered, he opened it and read:-

J

Milton has stepped up security. He's drafted in his buddies from the hunting club he goes to. Means you got another six assholes to deal with.

He has them watching the roads in and out of the airfield. They will see you before you get within a mile of the place.

I'm not sure if he bought my story, but he seems OK with me for now.

Will let you know if I hear anything else.

H

Jackson clicked off and relayed the developments to Danny.

"How are we going to get to them?"

Jackson had already thought about this. "We will have to go in cross country; we need eyes on the area. We need Karl and his drone."

"What about Marco? His drone is better than ours; he will see us coming a mile away."

"I had thought of that," Jackson added, "Joanne is going to supply us with a frequency jammer. They use it to scramble signals within a five-block radius. Apparently, they use it on raids to stop the perps from messaging each other about their approach. We will attach it to Karl's drone. As soon as it enters the area, it will fill the signal with white noise. They won't be able to make anything out. It will give us enough time to get into position and prepare."

"That's impressive mate," Danny said. "but won't that mean we can't see them too?"

Good point, Jackson thought. "We can get Karl to turn if off occasionally so we can get eyes on. We know where to look, they don't."

Danny did not look convinced, but did not labour the point. As they approached Sanderson, Jackson got Danny to pull off and head up the back road. The gravel and stone track asked a lot of the tyres, especially on the incline, but the Jeep handled it well. They came up behind the motel and parked out of sight. Danny and Jackson got out and circled around the motel in opposite directions, meeting back at the front.

Jackson fished around the hanging planter and recovered the keys. He opened the room and they entered, guns drawn. The room was undisturbed. They stashed the weapons and equipment and headed out the back to where Jackson had stashed his bag.

Approaching in daylight was risky, but time was drifting away. They only had just over 24 hours until the plane was touching down. They needed to be in place before dawn broke tomorrow morning, Jackson thought.

They drew their handguns and spread out. Jackson directed Danny to the high ground, while Jackson cautiously approached the small hut. Jackson looked up towards Danny who gave him the universal 'OK' symbol. Keeping low, Jackson made his way to the window and peered inside. The hut was empty. He tried the door, this time it opened without protest.

Jackson squeezed into the hut and looked around. It was a basic technician's storage area. There were toolboxes, spare valves and pipes. Several manuals and report books lined a rickety looking wooden shelf. A small table and chairs nestled into the far corner. On the table were a thermos flask and an upturned cup. Jackson unscrewed the flask lid and the steam instantly wove its wispy dance into the air. The coffee was fresh. Someone was here.

He backed out of the hut and made his way to the corner opposite the tower. Danny was behind him. He waved at him, pointing at the tower. Using his index and middle finger to point at his eyes and then to the tower, he told Danny to recce the far side.

Danny worked his way around the small hill and emerged at the other side. Danny gave Jackson a poor impression of a telephone to his ear and the same signal to his eyes.

A few seconds later, Jackson's phone vibrated lightly.

He looked at the message;-

There's a guy on the platform.
Looks like a worker not a threat.
But he's milling around a large pipe matrix leading to a box.

Jackson gave Danny a thumbs up and replied;-
Keep any eye on him.
I'll make my way up to him.
If he looks armed buzz my phone.

Danny returned the thumbs up, so Jackson hurried to the ladder and began to climb. Climbing a ladder with a handgun was tricky, but he did not want to get to the top without a weapon in hand. When he was almost head height, he paused and listened. He could hear the man singing to himself and tapping on metal with some form of metal object.

Jackson eased himself onto the platform and edged around slowly. As he emerged from the cover of the bend, the man stood up and turned to look at him. He was a short stocky fellow, with tight curly greying hair protruding from an orange hard hat with a logo of a double 'T' over two waved lines. He had a yellow Hi-Vis jacket on sporting the same logo with the words 'Texas Treatments Inc.' beneath. His shirt was bulging under the strain of the man's stomach, which hung over his black cargo pants like an avalanche.

"You can't be up here man!" he shouted, "you gotta go back down, Can't be up here buddy!"

He looked down at Jackson's hand and the weapon. He put his hands up nervously. "Hey man, don't shoot. I don't want no trouble."

Jackson moved closer raising the Sig.

"Back up away from the pipes."

The man shuffled backwards until his legs touched the pipes, he then tentatively stepped over them so he was free from obstruction.

Jackson lowered the weapon slightly. "Put your hands down mate, I'm not here to hurt you, but I need you to do as you are told or I will shoot you, you understand me?"

The man nodded vigorously. "Sure thing buddy, anything you want, just don't shoot me. I just service the bleeders."

Jackson pointed to a spot against the water tower bulkhead. "Sit there and don't give me any problems. I don't want to hurt you, but I will if I have to."

The man sat down keeping his eyes down and his hands firmly to his sides.

Jackson signalled to Danny to join them and once he was there coving the frightened man, he checked the pressure gauge housing box, the splinter was still where he had left it. They retrieved the bag and they ushered the frightened technician down and into the hut, where they removed his wallet and tied him, leaving him enough room to move his arms. They found a bottle of water and placed it in his hand. Jackson opened the man's wallet.

According to his driving licence, the man's name was Bert Cranston and he was 62 years old. He lived in Beacon Hill, San Antonio.

Jackson showed Bert the licence. "Listen, Bert. You sit tight and I will send someone to release you when we have done what we need to do. The FBI are on their way and will take you to safety. For now the safest place for you is right here."

Jackson waved the licence at him. "Don't make me come looking for you. You understand?"

Bert nodded furiously. "Sure thing, I don't want to get involved."

Jackson patted Bert firmly on the shoulder. "Good man, Bert.....good man."

They left Bert there and returned to the room. The light was beginning to fade. They had a lot to prepare before Joanne's team descended.

Jackson pulled his phone and dialled Dave's number.

"Watchya Jackie, did the Interpol guy get in touch?"

"Yeah mate, he did cheers. Listen, I need your help."

Dave's voice raised an octave as the excitement rose. "You want me to come over? I could get the next -"

"No mate." Jackson interrupted, "I need you to do something from there, can you help me."

"Of course I can." The disappointment dropping his voice back down. "What do you need?"

Jackson knew Dave would have been handy here, but he was also the only man he trusted in the UK, which made him priceless.

"I need you to find Sarah and Ellie. Take them to yours, I don't care what you tell them, but stress that this is for their own safety. Do you still have that revolver we snatched from that hoodie in Peckham?"

Dave chuckled. "Sure do mate, still got his pepper spray too."

"Great. I need you to guard them for a few days, until I can get sorted here. Don't let them out of your sight."

"You got it mate." Dave said excitedly.

"Oh, and Dave?"

"Yes mate?"

Jackson put a little venom in his voice. "Tell no one about this. I mean it Dave, no one!"

"You can count on me Jax."

Jackson hung up.

Jackson called Sonia next. She told him everything was good there but Cat and Benito were getting restless. He told her to stay put a little while longer, but if they had not heard from either him or Danny in the next 24 hours to write his number down, ditch the phone and move on to somewhere else. He did not let Danny make the call; he needed the big man focussed.

Next job was to call Joanne. He told her what he needed Karl to do and she said they would be with them in a couple of hours.

He hung up and returned to where Danny was studying a satellite image of the airstrip and its surrounding area. There were four large inclines to the south and west of the strip. All had relatively decent amount of foliage and were close enough to use as a sniper nest and observation post. They just needed to find out which ones Milton would use. His snipers were out of action, but now they knew the hunting club guys were on the team too, Jackson figured Milton would have at least two of them in elevated positions.

A dirt track left the highway about five miles from the airstrip, and meandered parallel with a dry riverbed. Both snaked around the south of the airstrip and led off to the east about 1200 metres from the hills. They could use the Jeep to enter the riverbed and approach the hills behind the embankment. It would get them close. They could then approach on foot.

Jackson doubted the hunters would be aware, but he could not assume so. He needed Karl to recce both vantage points closest to the river. If they could take out both hills, Mitch, Andy, Mike and Pete could provide cover for Danny and Max to get close to the landing site. The bushed areas would give good cover, but would mean covering open ground, dangerous, even at night.

They heard the vehicles pull into the parking lot and drew their weapons. Danny turned the light off and they waited either side of the door. Jackson slightly parted the thin mustard colour curtain and let out a sigh of relief. It was Joanne's team, but surprisingly enough joined by Joanne ·herself.

Jackson opened the door as Danny turned the light back on. Joanne just coldly blanked him as she walked past into the room.

"Bit dramatic aren't we Mr Shaw?" She whispered under breath as she passed him.

She walked in and extended her hand to Danny with a smile. "Mr Hughes, Special Agent Phillips, lovely to meet you at last." She said shaking Danny's hand lightly.

Jackson smirked and shook his head. I am not going to bite, he thought to himself.

Max, Ruth and Phelps entered the room wheeling a set of black and silver flight cases.

"Okay gentlemen," she said in her usual authoritarian manner, "what have we got?"

Jackson ran them through his idea and the plan he wanted to put in motion. Karl fiddled with his glasses as Jackson laid out the signal mask idea. When he had finished, Karl stood thinking.

"Problem?" Jackson asked when he saw the look on Karl's face.

Karl rubbed his chin. "The sig mash I can do. The trouble with lifting and dropping it is that you run the risk of shorting it out." Jackson looked blankly at him. He gave Karl a look that said 'well and?' Karl rolled his eyes, clearly irked that he was probably, with the exception of Phelps, the only smart one in the room.

"Once the signal mash power spikes it will be like an IR splash the size of two city blocks. If they had any scanners it would show up like a spotlight."

Jackson saw the potential problem. If that happened before the drugs landed, then they would abort and scatter and it would be game over. If it happened while they were unloading, again they would scatter. They needed to close the noose before that happened, which meant they would have to use speed as well as stealth, tricky at the best of times.

Jackson stood for a few moments thinking. He needed a way to mask their approach. What would get Marco to send his drone far off in the opposite direction, while keeping any potential observers occupied? They would need a diversion.

He turned to Joanne, who was helping Ruth set up their communications equipment on the small table.

"Do you have any contacts in the local Sheriff's department here?"

She looked up and pondered for a second. "I know the Deputy Sheriff in Sheffield, why what are you thinking?"

Jackson returned to the map, tracing a line from Dryden to Sheffield.

"That's perfect," he said, pointing to a dirt road running parallel with the highway, "can you get him there? I need him to slowly drive up that road and park up with his lights on, about a mile out from the airstrip at 03.00."

Joanne looked concerned. "If these guys are watching the area, they will see him. I can't put a fellow officer in danger, Jax. He's not trained to deal with men like these."

She had a point. It was asking a lot of a hick town deputy. He needed a way to keep the guy safe.

He turned to Pete, who was on the sniper roster in the team.

"Hey, Pete?"

Pete was a compact man. Shorter than Jackson but looked very similar in appearance. He had a wiry frame and sinewy arms, showing the natural strength the man clearly possessed.

Pete looked up from the map, "Yeah what you need man?"

Jackson moved his finger to a space about 800 metres from the spot he had indicated for the deputy to park.

"You reckon you can cover the deputy from that position? Take out anyone who approaches him?"

Pete nodded and smiled. "Sure can buddy."

Pete turned to Joanne. "I'll need the night sight scope, but should be able to take out anyone who comes close. But I need authorisation to engage Ma'am."

Joanne looked pensive, but nodded her agreement. "Okay Pete, but I want team two standing by to intercept if they come at him en masse."

Jackson nodded. "Just keep them out of sight. We don't want to spook these guys."

Joanne nodded and sent Pete and the standby team off to Sheffield, while she phoned the Deputy Sheriff to inform him of the situation. Jackson just hoped the guy could hold his nerve.

The light was almost gone when they set off. About 5 miles out from the airstrip, was the dirt road they needed. They pulled onto it and parked up. Karl and Phelps set up their station and prepared the drone while the rest continued. The road, littered with potholes and small rocks, brutally bounced the vehicles. They drove using night vision goggles to avoid their lights giving their approach away, but that slowed them to a crawl as the drivers navigated the uneven terrain.

They crossed a small bridge and pulled off onto the dry riverbed. The bed was gauntlet of boulders and scrub formations. The going was slow but kept their noise to a minimum. After what seemed an eternity, they came upon the fissure in the rocks. This was what Jackson needed to see. The convoy stopped and did a comms check.

"Ok guys," Jackson said over the network, "We wait here. Karl I need you to send the drone up the two inclines we discussed. I need to know what's up there."

"You got it, Jax." Karl replied.

Jackson checked his email. There was a new entry from Hal. It read:-

J

We are about to get set up here.

Marco is setting his drone up from a farmhouse to the east of the strip

I think they want me to stay here.

If so I will take him out when it goes down.

That's the good news.

Unfortunately there's bad news too.

Martinez is bringing a bigger plane this time. Not more product, but more men.

Seems you have spooked him and he wants lots of protection.

Can't tell you anything more, sorry.

Good luck

H

Jackson debated on telling Joanne about this development, but he figured she's freak out, so he kept it to himself. It would not change things anyway. It just meant more targets.

"The rest of us will de-bus here

"Max you are with Danny and me. We are going through the gap. Joanne? Your team know what to do?"

Joanne replied sharply. "Of course we do."

She clearly did not like not being in charge.

"Jax? This is Karl. I got your position applying signal mash in 5. Wait out."

"Copy that, we are standing by."

"Ok guys," he said turning to Joanne and her team, "Get your teams into position and we will co-ordinate the approach once you are in position."

Joanne winced at being ordered, but snapped back into operation mode. "Okay people, let's move."

Chapter 15

Outnumbered

They left Jackson, Max and Danny, alongside the three snipers. The men huddled together.

"Okay fellas, this is the deal. I have good news and bad news. The good news is I have just had a message from Hal, he says Marco is holed up at a farmhouse on the east side. He says he will take Marco out when the place lights up, so that will take their eyes in the sky out and means Karl can relax."

Danny put his hand on Jackson's shoulder. "And the bad news?"

"The bad news is, we may have a lot more X-Rays to deal with. Hal says Martinez is bringing a bigger plane and with it more protection."

Jackson looked at the three snipers. "Unfortunately, this means we may need you to break ranks and engage them."

The three men looked at each other and nodded. "We are with you, Jax." Mitch said.

"I got a Daughter in her sophomore year," Andy added, "I don't want these animals poisoning her with their filth. So whatever it takes pal."

Jackson gave them a thumbs up. "Thanks guys. Means a lot."

"Jax, this is Karl. Got a sit rep for you."

"Go ahead Karl."

"Okay, well we got a clear summit on mount one, but two assholes on mount two. One is facing the strip, the other facing your direction. Advise moving as I don't know what kit they have."

Jackson thought for a moment. "Thanks Karl. Hang back and observe."

"Roger that." Karl replied.

Jackson returned his gaze to the men. "Okay fellas. Mitch and Andy, I need you two up there." He said pointing to their left.

"Danny? I need you and Max to head through the fissure, and hold at the edge. Mike, you are with me up this one." He pointed at the right hand slope.

They bumped fists and split up. Jackson led Mike around the slope to where it was at its steepest. He could see Mike look up and sag. He obviously did not like the climb.

"Stay here out of sight. I'll deal with those two," he said pointing up the slope, "I'll let you know when it's safe to come up the easy way."

Mike seemed happy with that idea. Jackson had to laugh to himself; these snipers were good from a distance, but wholly unreliable at close quarters.

He handed his rifle to Mike and began to make his way up. The going was steep and the pathways were narrow. The crumbling rock formations made for unstable handholds, but Jackson pressed on. The acid in his muscles screaming as he hauled himself up the almost vertical areas. Occasionally he found a natural ledge on which to rest his arms. He found a shallower pathway about halfway up, but it would take him around the hill and closer to the men at the top's line of sight. He passed up on the temptation and continued to haul himself.

About 60 feet from the top, the face became flat and smooth. Jackson had to traverse sideways, until he found a path to the top. His first foothold was strong, his second not so strong. As soon as he put his weight on it to lift himself to the next hand hold, the cropping split, sending his foot sideways, jarring his left hand from its grip. He slid downwards until he finally managed to get some purchase on the rock face.

Gasping for breath, he held himself in check, listening out for any sound that someone was coming to investigate the noise. His limbs began to shake, as the strain if remaining motionless became more unbearable.

"Jax?" Karl's voice burst through his earpiece. "You are clear to proceed. Either the guys didn't hear you or they are asleep. They haven't moved for quite a while. You may have the drop on them, out."

Jackson pressed on, invigorated by this revelation. He made the apex of the overhang quickly and slid his frame onto the flatter top. Regulating his breathing and opening his mouth to reduce the sound in his head, he scanned the area. There were two small clumps of trees, and randomly scattered dry bushes. The top looked remarkable flat so he gathered that the men were in one or both tree formations.

"The assholes are in the trees closest to you Jax," Karl said obviously seeing his indecision.

Jackson gave Karl a double squelch and moved to the edge of the trees, keeping low as he crept.

Carefully placing one foot down slowly, he eased into the small wood. After each step, he stopped and checked the area. Twenty feet in and he froze. The undergrowth in front of him had been disturbed. He followed the flattened foliage slowly. Sure enough, there was a boot, and then a leg of a man lying prone facing towards the riverbed. Jackson moved closer, wincing every time a twig made its protest at the excess weight, but the man still did not move. He could hear his heavy breathing clearly. He was asleep.

Jackson drew his KA-Bar and stood over the slumbering sniper. In one movement, he dropped his knee onto the man's back, while clamping his left hand over the startled man's mouth, sliding the knife under his neck and pressed it firmly against his throat. He leaned in close and whispered into the hunter's ear.

"Stay quiet or I'll open you up. Nod if you understand."

The man nodded slowly. Jackson withdrew the knife, sliding it back into its scabbard. With his right hand free, he delivered a vicious blow to the side of the man's head and he slumped unconsciously into the soil. Jackson took the man's boots off and tied his hands and feet with the laces. He then took his sock off and stuffed it into the man's mouth, one down.

Jackson stayed still and drew his Sig. After a minute, he slipped back into the trees and waited. If the guy's colleague was coming he'd be ready, but nobody came.

Jackson pressed on into the woods until he came across a similar patch of disturbed ground, only this time it was empty. He was torn. Had the guy returned to his friend to see what the noise was, or was he waiting for him to step into the killing ground. He decided to wait him out. Honing all of his senses, he scanned the area around him. He was about to return to the first man's position when something caught his eye. A small glint of metal between the leaves winked at him as it moved. It was a knife.

He did not want to kill these guys. After all, they may not even know why they were there, just going where the payday was. However, he was face to face with someone who clearly meant him harm. You have just lost your 'Get out of Jail Free' card, he thought to himself.

Jackson tried to envisage the man standing with the knife out in front of him about chest height, the standard stance of the untrained. He raised the Sig and fired two rounds. The first sailed harmlessly past its target, but the second hit home. The man let out a sharp breath and slumped forward clutching his chest.

Jackson was on him in a flash. Covering his mouth with his hand, he eased the man to the floor. Blood was seeping from the man's mouth and through Jackson's fingers as he struggled to breathe. His eyes were wide with shock and his body began to convulse. Jackson held him down until the tremors softened. The bullet had passed through the man's sternum and buried itself into one of his lungs. Jackson could hear the unmistakeable gurgle of a lung wall collapsing. He would be dead soon. After about a minute, the body became still. The air bubbles ceased and the man was dead.

Jackson got straight on the radio. "Mike? All clear to come up. Danny? You and Max are clear to make your way to the FOP. Mitch? You and Andy cover the front. Mike will cover our six, Copy?"

Everyone acknowledged. When Mike arrived, he was panting like a Cocker Spaniel.

"Out of shape are we mate?" Jackson said shaking his head sarcastically.

Mike laughed as he handed Jackson his rifle. "Fuck you, I'm a sniper not a grunt."

Suddenly over the radio, Karl's voice burst into life frantically. "Drone in the air! I repeat, drone in the air and it's heading your way, over?"

Jackson looked in the direction of the airstrip, but knew he would not see it. Marco was too good for that.

"Deploy signal mash Karl."

He checked his watch 02.30. The diversion would not be in place for another 30 minutes.

"ETA to our position, Karl?"

Jackson waited for a response, but none came.

"Karl, acknowledge."

The signal mash had done its job, but also meant their communications were down too. He took off down the hill as fast as he could. He needed to be in cover as soon as possible. He would soon know if anyone was looking in his direction.

He made the bottom and darted into an area of scrub, staying still to get his breathing under control. Rising up to peer across the open ground in front of them, he looked to where Danny and Max should be, he only saw Max.

"Danny you copy?" He whispered into the mic, again, no reply.

"Shit!" He cursed under his breath, "Stupid idea this was Jackson."

He took the NV Binoculars out and scanned the airstrip. He could see no movement. But then again he did not expect to. Milton and his team would not expose themselves until the aircraft was on approach, which was almost an hour away.

"Drone is returning to the airstrip. Sig Mash is down for now. I can't keep lifting it like this Jax, it's going to spike anytime soon. We will be lit up like a Christmas tree." Karl said with a touch of panic in his voice.

"Roger that. Keep your panties on. We will only need it one more time, then they will know we are here. But hopefully Hal will come through and we will have aerial control."

They stayed where they were for a further ten minutes. There was still no activity on the airstrip. He needed to know where people were.

"All teams sit rep?"

"Birdseye one and two have eyes on strip, no activity yet."

"Birdseye three in position, exit route clear."

"Team one in position."

"Team two in position awaiting decoy arrival, nothing yet."

"Max here, in position."

"Where's Danny? I thought I told you to stay together?" Jackson heard a laugh in his earpiece, then Danny's voice.

"Stop wetting yourself mate, I decided to give us a wider area of fire, you're like a nagging wife."

Jackson smiled, typical Danny. "Really professional Danny, remind me again how you were ever my commanding officer?"

"That's because the Head Shed liked me."

Jackson could hear him laughing as he continued, "You? You he hated. Sorry mate, Danny in position."

The low rumble of an approaching engine ruptured the jovial moment. On cue, the airstrip was illuminated. The small landing lights blinked into life and the meagre terminal building sprang to life. Jackson could see men taking up position either side of the northeast section of the 'X' shaped landing strip. Jackson switched to the thermal night sight. The heat signatures showed him that there were three men nearest the terminal and two loitering in the free space nearest the approach road.

"Team one; I need you to move forward to the southeast corner. One hundred metres and cover the rear of the strip. Team two; how's our distraction? Any sign of the Deputy yet?"

"He's on the highway three minutes out. We are six hundred metres to the north, shall we hold or move in?" said Perkins.

Jackson understood what Perkins was referring to, putting themselves between the strip and the deputy, meant that they could cover the road while protecting the Deputy. It was a sound tactical move.

"Roger that team two. Cover the waste ground behind the terminal."

Jackson started to crawl slowly towards the landing strip to get a better view of the tarmac.

"Danny? I need you and Max to close in, thirty metres and hold. I want all parties on the ground before we start recording."

"You got it Jax," Danny replied

"Max you set up with the camera?"

"Roger that," Max replied, "I am heading to-"

"Decoy's in position, Jax. He is lit up and engine is running. We are standing by." Perkins interrupted.

"Okay guys, stay sharp. We don't know how many are on board or where the other snipers are. Stay frosty. Karl as soon as Marco takes the bait, get your eyes on those ridges. We need to keep those snipers busy."

"Copy that." Karl replied.

Jackson was now only 40 feet from the side of the tarmac. Through his binoculars, he could make out Milton and Taylor, leaning against his Land Rover. Suddenly his attention snapped to the terminal. The door had swung open and three men emerged. The first man through the door was carrying a Heckler & Koch G3 rifle. Behind him emerged Fallon, barking orders to the men stood to at the edges of the tarmac. Once Fallon had cleared the the doorframe, the third man stepped out, it was Rourke.

"You getting this Max?".

"That's an affirmative, Jax, I'll keep rolling."

Jackson could hear the plane getting closer; it would not be long before the area lit up by the planes landing lights. This was the biggest danger, shadows and movement enhanced by the dancing lights as they swept over them like a searchlight.

"Drone in the air, Jax. Heading northeast, he's taking the bait."

"Okay Karl. Get our bird in the air. I need their positions on the ridge."

Karl gave Jackson two squelches in reply.

Suddenly two of the guards began moving in the direction of the Deputy.

"Team two? Be advised, two X-Rays foxtrot in your direction. Do not engage unless they threaten contact."

Perkins replied. "Copy that."

"Jax?" said Karl, "we got two snipers on either ridge. Both are facing the strip. They are covering Danny's position and Team one's, over."

Jackson figured they would. Those were the positions most at risk from breach.

"Okay, Birdseye one and two? When the plane comes over, you will have about a minute to acquire and take out the threat."

"Roger that." Mitch replied.

Suddenly Joanne broke through the net. "May I remind you that this is an unsanctioned hit. We have no authority to kill U.S. citizens."

Jackson could feel his temper rising.

"Would you rather they shot up your team. Try fucking explaining that one to your boss. I have tactical command, or I walk and you can read about it in the tabloids."

Jackson knew he had her over a barrel.

"Okay," she said reluctantly, "But this had better go down right."

The sky was becoming lighter as the plane drew closer. Jackson slid down into the scrub. The front landing lights cast an eerie shadow across the sandy floor. The scrubs shadows looked like dancing Geishas. Slowly rising and falling as the light passed over them.

"Jax? This is team two the two guys have taken up positions in front of decoy. Looks like they are covering, not engaging, over."

That was good news.

"Roger that," Jackson replied, "makes sense, no point in spooking the Deputy and him radio it in. Stay alert because the drone is up there."

Quickly, the deep whine of jet engines filled the air, as its airspeed reduced for landing. The two ridges were lit up so brightly that it was almost daylight. The Gulfstream G700 swept over them gracefully. There was very little headwind, so the pilot set it down gently and trundled towards the waiting men.

"Jax? This is Birdseye one. Targets are down, you are clear to proceed."

"Great work guys

"All teams, as soon as they unload, and make the transaction we move in. Karl I will need the Sig Mash one more time on my mark, over?"

Karl replied. "Copy that."

Once the Gulfstream had rolled to a halt, the door opened and dropped to reveal a set of steps. Three armed men descended first. They all carried AK-47 assault rifles, Ramon and two other men followed them. The armed men took up positions to the rear of the plane. Ramon signalled to the door, and Martinez emerged. He was a thickset man with black slicked back hair. His thick moustache almost stretched from ear to ear. He wore black trousers; a black waistcoat over a light shirt, kept in place by a tan double shoulder holster. His Nickel-plated Browning M1911 .45 calibre handguns glinted in the lights of the terminal. Four other guards emerged. The odds were becoming longer every second.

Martinez and Ramon approached Fallon, and they embraced. Then they shook hands with Rourke and Milton. They talked for a short while, before the men returned to plane. Milton and Fallon left the three men and moved to the rear of the terminal. After a few seconds, the sound of a truck rumbling to life drifted over to Jackson. A 7.5 tonne wagon pulled out from behind the building and reversed up to the Gulfstream.

"Okay guys, its ShowTime. As soon as the transaction goes down, we go in."

The adrenaline was coursing through him now. On the tarmac, the cargo hold opened and the men began unloading the packs by hand. They formed a human chain of four men. Pack after pack slowly filled the wagon.

"You getting this, Max?" Jackson asked.

"Clear as day Jax, we got 'em."

"Okay we need the money going to Rourke, and then we can nail the coffin shut. All teams stand by. Birdseye one focus on the guards still carrying weapons."

"Roger that." Mitch replied.

"Team two, close in of the two covering the Deputy," Jackson said, "I don't want them opening up on him, Take them as soon as it goes noisy."

"Copy that." Perkins replied.

The loading was continuing feverishly. Ramon disappeared into the Gulfstream, and returned with a case. It was the size of a travel suitcase and was obviously heavy; the way Ramon hefted it.

"Okay guys here we go, stand by."

Ramon lifted the the handle once he had cleared the steps, and wheeled the case towards Martinez, who took it and wheeled it over to where Rourke and Fallon were standing. He stopped the case at Rourke's feet. Rourke lifted it up and onto the bonnet of the Land Rover. He unzipped it and parted the flap. The case was filled to the brim with bundles of cash. Jackson could see Rourke tapping the bricks of cash, taking a brief count. He seemed to be happy with the transaction, he offered his hand to Martinez, and they shook. This was the final act of an illegal transaction. They had them all bang to rights.

Jackson filled the airwaves, "All teams. Stand by….Stand by….Go!"

Chapter 16

The Bust

Jackson was up and running towards the tarmac, his rifle brought to bear. He could see Danny to his left; he had kept up with him. Max was a few yards behind, but was up and running too. Jackson smiled. The kid was a team player after all. They hit the tarmac together as Joanne and her team hit the side of the terminal.

"EVERYONE ON THE FLOOR!" Jackson screamed at the startled men, who froze on the spot.

Rourke and Fallon dived behind the Range Rover while Martinez and Ramon made for the wagon. The air erupted in gunfire. Jackson dropped to one knee as rounds came at him from the side of the tarmac. The men loading had dropped their loads and were trying to bring their weapons around. Jackson opened fire, two of the men dropped as the rounds stitched across their chests.

There was a small firefighting station filled with sand to his right, he manged to get behind it and survey the scene. Danny had engaged Martinez and Ramon. They traded rounds. Max had the guards to the left of the tarmac pinned down, while Joanne and her team had the terminal under fire. Milton and Taylor would no doubt be in there.

Jackson needed to cover the ground to the Gulfstream to squeeze them into the middle of the airstrip. He threw a smoke grenade that popped with a light 'crump'. White smoke drifted in front of the guards and Fallon. Jackson took advantage of the cover and ran. He let a few rounds go as he ran, to keep their heads down. He made the wheels of the

Gulfstream and crouched down. The gunfight had intensified.

Jackson put rounds into the tail of the wagon. Fallon had pushed the two guards with him out and forced them to charge at Jackson. Jackson dropped one, but as he was lining up the second, a round caught him in the left shoulder and spun him around. The pain seared through him like a hot knife. A second round caught him flush in the back and threw him forward onto his face. The vest had done its job, or he would be dead.

He flipped onto his back as the guard bore down on him, ready to finish the job. The man raised his AK-47 ready to deliver the final act of Jackson's life. He never got the chance to pull the trigger. His head erupted from the side, as the high velocity round ripped through his temple, the force throwing him sideways. Jackson reminded himself to buy those guys a drink.

Instantly he was back up. His shoulder ached intensely, but he was back in the game. He looked over the large tyre and saw Fallon running towards the terminal. In a flash Jackson was up and in pursuit, he was not letting this man escape again.

To his right he saw one of Joanne's team lying face down; the others pinned down next to a pile of rusted scrap. Jackson had to help. Fallon would have to wait. He darted left and made it to the side of the terminal building. He could hear slow deliberate rounds fired from the windows. They were professionals, and not aimlessly firing into the scrap. It had to be Milton and Taylor.

"Joanne, hold your team back, I'm going in after Milton!"

"Once I've distracted them, help Danny out with Martinez."

Jackson shimmied around so he was side on to the window. He took out his final smoke grenade and flashbang.

He threw the smoke grenade through the open window. As soon as the count to the 'pop' was up, he threw in the flashbang. He hoped the noise of the smoke grenade would mask the flashbang clattering into the room.

There was a 'crump' as the smoke grenade ignited. Three seconds later the room shook with a deafening 'bang' as the flashbang filled the dark room with blinding light. Jackson heard the screams over the echoing rumble; they must have had night vision goggles on. Jackson dived through the open window and into the room. The smoke had rendered vision down to two feet. He saw Milton lying on the floor, his hands covering his eyes.

Jackson launched himself at the stricken Lieutenant Colonel. As if sensing Jackson's attack, Milton lifted his legs and stopped Jackson's momentum in its tracks. Springing Jackson back, Milton was up and on his feet, knife drawn and swinging his body left and right. His eyesight must still be suffering. Jackson drew his KA-Bar and charged at Milton, lifting his left forearm up to protect his face. Milton swung back towards him as Jackson arrived. The blade sliced into his arm as Milton delivered a blow with his left into Jackson's temple. It was not the hardest blow he had ever felt, but expertly delivered and Jackson's vision starred.

Rocked back but undeterred, Jackson swung his blade in the direction of Milton's chest. Milton tried to dodge backwards to avoid the blade. The knife sliced across his chest, causing the cloth to open, exposing an eight-inch gash. Nasty, but would not stop him. Milton grabbed Jackson's vest strap, trying to pull him onto his knife. Jackson swivelled his body to his left, wrapping his arm around Milton's neck and twisting him backwards and down.

The momentum slammed them both to the floor. Jackson lost his grip on the KA-Bar and it clattered away. Milton tried to shake Jackson loose, while slashing wildly at his face. Jackson managed to catch Milton's arm and twist the knife out of his grip. Milton's strength was ebbing as the exertions were taking their toll on him. While he had Milton in a chokehold, Jackson moved his right hand to the side of Milton's head and applied as much force as he could sideways.

Milton thrashed wildly, trying to dislodge Jackson's grip. His fingernails digging into Jackson's face searching for his eyes. Jackson put all his strength into the squeeze. A sudden 'pop' and Milton went limp. The vertebrae in his neck had separated. He was dead.

Jackson's lungs screamed for air, the smoke filled breaths burning his throat. He pushed Milton off and looked around the room. Where was Taylor?

He got to his feet and recovered his knife and rifle; he needed to find out who was where.

"All teams, I need a situ-"

He never finished the word before he was slammed sideways with a hit like bull. He flew into a nearby glass cabinet. The doors exploded into shards of glass, slicing his face and neck. Jackson rolled over and tried to move sideways.

Taylor was on him in a flash raining blows down on him. Jackson tried to protect his face but was too slow. One blow caught him flush to his temple and he saw the speckled lights of concussion fill his vision. Jackson tried to roll his body, but Taylor's bulk was immense. He threw punches of his own. But couldn't get the leverage and his blows merely landed on Taylors midriff, the padding absorbing much of the power.

Taylor batted his hands away and managed to get a hand around his throat. This man is strong, Jackson thought to himself. His windpipe constricting as Taylor squeezed. Jackson could feel his strength waning as the air deprivation began to take hold of him. He was losing. He was going to die.

Jackson's limbs felt heavy. Taylor's manic grin glared down at him.

"Thought you were good motherfucker!"

"Time to die asshole!"

He could feel himself passing out, the room was growing darker, and he had no fight left.

Suddenly Taylor released his grip and fell forward. Jackson felt warm liquid pouring over his neck. As he regained some of his senses, he saw that Taylor had a huge exit wound in his forehead and was spewing blood all over him. He tried to lift the dead man, but his strength had not fully returned. He tried to wriggle himself free. Suddenly Taylor was off him. He looked up and saw the smiling figure of Max, holding a Nickel-plated Browning.

"Nick of time eh, buddy?" Max said grinning at him.

"Thank you Max, I was finished there." He rasped as he slowly got to his feet. "How are we doing out there?"

Max rubbed his chin then jiggled the Browning. "Martinez is in custody. His men are all down. Phillips is-"

"Fallon?" Jackson interrupted.

Max shook his head sadly. "He got away."

Jackson could see a little shame in his face.

"He got to the Range Rover and managed to get clear."

Jackson felt his strength returning as the anger took over him.

"For fuck's sake."

He slammed the butt of his rifle into the remaining glass cabinet.

"It gets worse. Rourke and the other fella are with him too."

"Ramon?" Jackson asked, barely able to contain his rage.

Max nodded slowly.

They exited the terminal. Seeing the blood down his front, Danny rushed over to him. "You OK mate? You hurt?"

Jackson put his hand out to stop his friend from fussing over him. "I'm thanks to Max here, saved my life mate. Taylor had me down and out. Big fella capped him before I checked out."

Danny took Max's hand and shook it vigorously. "I can't thank you enough mate. This big lump is the closest thing I have to a brother. Any time you need my help I am there."

The two men held their grip a moment before a mutual nod. Danny patched Jackson's shoulder, which was not as bad as it had felt. The strap of his vest had taken the brunt of the impact. The round had not travelled far and Danny could easily remove it. He would need stitches, but he would live for now.

Jackson marched over the where Joanne had Martinez and two of his guards on their knees, cuffed.

"What's the score with Fallon? How the fuck did he slip through your team?"

Joanne looked shocked at this sudden rebuke and her face reddened.

"I don't think I like your tone Mr Shaw."

"I don't give a shit Joanne. You know who Fallon is and what he's capable of and you let him waltz right through you."

"They didn't waltz through. I have three men dead and Perkins missing. I'd say they blasted their way through, don't you?"

Jackson calmed, he knew what it was like to lose men in the field, but to top it off they had Perkins as a hostage. That changed the game somewhat.

"Have you checked the farmhouse?"

"Is Hal ok?"

Joanne shook her head and replied. "No, we were securing the area before moving onto the farmhouse. Andy says nobody has left, so they are still in there."

Jackson nodded. "Okay Danny and I will check the farmhouse."

He fixed Joanne with a hard stare. "Can you get Karl to recce Rourke's warehouse, you never know, they may still think it's secure."

Joanne nodded and was about to leave when Jackson grabbed her arm. "I'm sorry about your men," He said softly, "We will get Perkins back. Maybe put out a BOLO on the Range Rover, maybe we'll get lucky?"

Joanne smiled at him and walked off. He doubted that a 'Be On the Look Out' order would pay dividends, but it was worth a shot.

Jackson returned to Danny and Max. "I need to see if Hal is ok, you with me?"

Both men nodded and they headed off towards the farmhouse. Jackson had a dark feeling. His instincts were kicking in and he did not like what they were telling him.

They reached the farmhouse and took a side each. Jackson approached from the front, while Danny took left and Max right. The farmhouse was a rundown shack of a building. Its white washed exterior stained orange with sand and aviation fumes. Its wooden door was broken in three places and hanging on defiantly to the frame. It had two windows to the front downstairs and one upstairs in the centre. Jackson could see no movement as he approached it at a crouch. He made it to the wall and moved to the side of the window closest to him. He peered inside. It looked like a living room. The place was devoid of furniture, but it had a fireplace at the far right hand wall. Jackson tried the window gently. It was unlocked.

"I am going in front right window. Cover the exits and be ready to come in if I need you." He whispered into his mic.

He got two sets of squelches in return.

He slipped his KA-Bar into the gap he had created and softly prised the window up, until he could get his fingers between. Trying his best not to make a noise, he lifted the sash up. The wood complained and squeaked, but moved relatively easily. When he had it open enough, he slid his body through, and carefully stepped onto the floor.

The wooden floor creaked as he put his final weight onto it. Slowly he made his way towards the open door that led to the hallway. Every slow tentative step greeted with moaning wood. There was little light inside and he had left his NVG unit in the terminal. Jackson cursed his mistake.

He drew his mini Maglite and cupping his hand over the lens allowed the red glow to light his way. When he made it to the hallway, he had a choice to make. There was a staircase to his immediate left. The hallway led to an open door to the left, and another closed door at the bottom. The closed door showed a glow along its base. There was a light on. He could see a trail of blood on the floor; it spread from the door to the left and down the hall.

He made his way along the wall closest to the open door and peered inside. It looked like a small study. It was empty apart from a small writing desk. The chair that accompanied it was lying on its side. One leg had been broken off and the slats on the backrest smashed. Jackson allowed the beam out and scanned the room. Two empty bookcases where only other occupants of this room.

Jackson drew his SIG and moved to the front door, opening it slowly. Facing the end of the hallway, he stepped out backwards.

"Danny? Front door on me. Max stay put."

Danny emerged from the corner. "What we got?"

"Got a blood trail down the hall, I'm gonna check it out. Cover the stairs in case anyone comes down behind me."

Danny said. "Let me go, you cover this."

However, Jackson had already moved into the hall. Keeping the Maglite in his supporting hand, he used it as directional sight. He crept up to the door and moved to the side. Mercifully, the handle was an iron lever action, so he used the combined weight of the weapon and both hands to turn it slowly. The door gave way a fraction and Jackson became aware a familiar metallic smell, blood!

He counted to three in his head and burst through the door. A shocked Marco sat at a small dining table. He had blood all over his face and his bloodied hands had made a grab for his Glock. Frozen in shock he looked at Jackson.

Jackson snarled. "Move your hand away or I will slot you right here Scotty, palms flat on the table now!"

Marco complied and Jackson moved the Glock out of his reach.

"Is there anyone else here?"

Marco shook his head. He looked white and perspiring profusely.

"If you're lying, I am going make sure your last days are excruciating."

"I swear there's nobody here, just me!" Marco said hoarsely.

"Danny?" he whispered into his mic, "you check upstairs, Max? Make entry from your side. Clear your way to the kitchen."

Jackson looked at the trail of blood. It travelled along the floor and to another closed door to Jackson's left. "

Where's Hal?"

Marco's head lolled slightly. Jackson moved closer bringing the SIG to Marco's temple.

"I said where the fuck is Hal?"

Marco turned his head towards the closed door.

Danny shouted down. "All clear up here, Jax."

Max came into the kitchen from the rear door and stood facing the two men.

"All clear back there, Jax." he said slightly out of breath.

"Cover this Motherfucker. If he moves, kill him."

Max moved around so he was standing where Jackson was. Max scooped up the Glock and placed it in his strapping, keeping his own weapon pointed at Marco's face.

Jackson moved across the room to the door and cautiously opened it. Hal's lifeless eyes stared out into a black void, shocked look permanently frozen in time, his neck severed from ear to ear. His lifeblood formed a thick dark red ring around his lifeless form. In his shirt pocket was a folded piece of paper. His mouth formed a silent scream into which his mobile phone was protruding.

Jackson reached over and took the paper and the phone, waking it from its hibernation; he stared at the screen in horror. Hal had been about to type an email for him, and it had cost him his life. Jackson unfolded the paper, it was a note addressed to him:-

Jackie Boy.
The price of betrayal was high for Hal.
But the price you will pay will higher.
Be seeing you lad.
Jimmy

Jackson just stared at the note. What did he mean? He dialled Sonia's number. She answered and he gave her the password.

"Everything OK there?"

Sonia told him that they were fine, but Benito was beginning to get anxious being cooped up in a room. He told her to sit tight for just a little while longer. He did not want to spook her by mentioning Fallon's escape just yet.

Jackson returned to the kitchen, where Marco was sitting nervously staring at Hal's corpse. Jackson tied Marco's waist to his chair, before taking the seat next to him. He looked up at Danny and Max.

"Cover the front and rear, Scotty and I are going to have a little chat." He turned and gave Marco a sinister look.

"You can't torture him," Max said, the concern in his voice growing, "Phillips will freak!"

Jackson gave Max the same look. "Go get some air, or take a seat next to Hal!"

Danny put an arm around Max, shepherding him towards the door.

"You ain't going to win this one mate. Best leave him to it, trust me, and now is not the time to be 'By the Book'."

Jackson turned to Marco as the others departed. He slid out his KA-Bar and honing rod. He began slowly sharpening the edge, all the time looking into Marco's terrified eyes.

Marco was trembling. "I didn't kill him, I swear Jax."

Jackson looked back at the knife angrily. "Fallon?"

Marco nodded. "I tried to stop him, but they turned on me. Whupped my ass and Fallon shot me."

Jackson looked him over; he could not see any bullet wounds. Marco looked at him and then nodded down. Jackson looked under the table. Marco's knees had been shot out from behind, classic IRA punishment. 'Put you on sticks' they used to call it.

"Where have they gone?" he growled.

Marco looked afraid again.

"I can't tell you Jax. If they find out I have helped you then I am a dead man."

Jackson lifted the knife, bringing the blade close to Marco's right hand. "If you don't tell me what I want to know, then Fallon will be the last thing you have to worry about."

Marco was visibly shaking as Jackson unfurled his fingers, resting the blade against the knuckle of his right 'Pinkie'.

"Last chance mate." He said, fixing Marco with a smile that chilled him to the bone.

"I can't Jax, I swear."

Marco barely got the words out, when Jackson put his whole weight down onto Marco's little finger. The blade split the skin and then cartilage, as the finger separated from the rest of the hand. Marco let out a blood-curdling scream as the pain tore through him, sending his body into spasms.

"You have nine more, and then I start on your toes. Where have they gone?"

Marco hissed through clenched teeth. "I can't Jax. You can't do this to me; I'm an American citizen asshole!"

Jackson re sharpened the blade, and placed it onto the next finger. In one move, he took the finger off. Marco screamed even louder this time.

"I don't think you've got the stones to hold out eighteen more times. Last time, where are they?"

Marco's head lolled. Jackson thought the man was going to pass out. He moved onto his middle finger and applied a little pressure.

"Okay stop!" Marco gasped. "Please stop, I'll tell you."

Jackson pressed a little harder. "I'm listening." He snarled menacingly.

"Fallon has a freighter moored in Port Arthur. They are heading there. If they reach the port, then they are in the wind."

"Where are they headed?"

Marco was struggling with the pain and the blood loss. "Ireland…I heard Fallon say he was going home."

"What's the name of the freighter?"

Jackson pressed the blade into Marco's bone. Marco screamed again, the tears were streaming down his face now.

"I don't know, Jax. I swear. They never mentioned a name; just that it was Port Arthur. Please stop. I've told you everything I know."

Jackson rose and patted Marco on the shoulder.

"I know you have mate. Just sit tight. I'll get you a medic."

He left Marco slumped in his chair. He called Danny and Max to him and relayed what Marco had said.

"Are we going after them?" Danny asked.

Jackson nodded. "Of course we are, but they have a huge head start."

He turned to Max who was looking across to the rest of his unit, clearly uncomfortable with what had just gone down in the farmhouse. "Do you think your boss could get us there quickly? Helicopter maybe?"

Max snapped out of his trance. "I can ask," he thumbed towards the farmhouse, "what about him?"

Jackson shrugged. "Get him a medic. He'll live."

Chapter 17

The Pursuit

Joanne was furious when she learned of Marco's torture. She demanded that Jackson gave her the evidence now or he was going to jail. This time Jackson knew he had no more cards to play. He gave her his phone and directed her to the encrypted file. Finding out that Jackson had the evidence all the time just compounded her fury.

"Tell me why I don't bust your ass right now? You've been playing us for suckers all along, so you can wage your own personal war."

She threw her hands in the air in exasperation.

"And I go along with it. I should have known you weren't who you said you were."

Jackson put his hands up in mock surrender. "I needed to keep the innocent parties safe. Let us not forget that Sonia was only in danger, because you put her there. She wasn't trained for this kind of clandestine operation and you know it."

Joanne went to answer, but Jackson cut her off. "Not to mention using a British National to conduct an operation without the British Embassy's knowledge or approval. Shall I go on? Now all the while we are standing here bitching like a couple of school kids, Rourke and Fallon are getting away. For all we know with Perkins as a hostage. Why don't we put away our differences and get her back. We can resume the finger pointing later."

Danny pulled up an online satellite image of Port Arthur. There were several areas where a large vessel could moor. The nearby yacht club was too small to house anything resembling a freighter, but the East basin was perfect, as was the Sabine pass. The East basin led to the Sabine Lake and then through the Sabine Pass.

They decided to head for the Sabine Pass. That was the one point that the vessel had to pass through, and their best chance of intercepting.

Joanne pointed at the Coast Guard building on the map. "I will get Frank to pull some strings and get authority to detain the freighter if it manages to leave port."

Jackson's impatience was growing. "Can you get me there before they arrive?"

Joanne rolled her eyes at him, but turned away and made a call. Jackson and Danny looked at the area they were covering. It would be like finding a needle in a haystack if they did not know which ship was the right one.

"This is going to be tricky mate." Danny said as if reading Jackson's mind. "How are we going to know which ship to stakeout?"

Jackson scratched his head, puzzled by this too. He turned to Ruth. "I don't suppose the Harbour Master has a record of the destinations of departing vessels?"

Ruth shook her head. "No they don't. They only have records of arrivals and their journeys origin. Anything leaving only has to declare its cargo and manifest not its destination. That's the problem of the Harbour Master where it's going."

Almost at the same time, Max and Jackson looked at each other. They both had the same thought.

"We need to find out what ship is arriving in Ireland from Port Arthur." Max.

Jackson nodded his agreement. "It's our best shot at this."

When Joanne returned, she looked flustered. Jackson gave her a minute to collect her composure.

"Well? How did it go?" He asked softly. She needed keeping calm right now.

"Well, we have two Huey's coming in from the 16th Airforce base in San Antonio, ETA 30 minutes. Frank is sending his team to the Coast Guard headquarters and trying to shut down the port quietly. We don't want to spook them early."

Jackson saw a problem with this already. "If we tell the Coast Guard too much, they will take over the operation and will fuck it up. We need surprise on our side for this."

"Jax is right Ma'am," Max added, "from what we've seen so far, this Fallon guy is seriously switched on. He's going to smell a trap a mile away. I think we need to co-ordinate with them under a lesser investigation."

He filled Joanne in on his theory.

Jackson nodded his approval. "Spot on Max. Get Frank to tell the Harbour Masters, and the Coast Guard to check for the crew's insurance and permits, that way they can get on board and recce only. Tell them to stand down until we get there. I will make some calls; see if I can get my guy to find out what ship is scheduled to port."

He left them to organise their teams and walked over to the scrap pile. There were local police and FBI crime scene agents, taking prints and photographing all the evidence. He passed one agent who looked like he was in charge. He was a thin man, even with the long coat, which swamped his slight frame. His red hair made his skin look pasty and grey. He had a beard that looked unkempt and misshapen. Jackson approached him and extended his hand.

"Jackson Shaw," he introduced himself, "Are you in charge of the evidence?"

"Special Agent Potts," he said. His voice was nasally and droll, which gave him a natural condescension.

"Was there a case logged?"

He could see Potts was about to tell him that he could not discuss the scene without authority, definitely a company man. He put his best pathetic face on.

"Special Agent Phillips asked me to find out, only I don't know who to ask."

Potts gave him a superior smirk. Jackson disliked him instantly. Sanctimonious prick, he thought to himself.

"Tell Special Agent Phillips, that there was no case logged in the evidence docket, and no mention of it in any inventory."

Jackson waved his thanks and walked away. Once he was out of earshot from the people milling around, he dialled Dave's number. He answered after four rings.

"Hi mate, how's it going there, bud?" Dave said cheerily.

"It's been full on mate. Are the girls ok?"

Jackson realised that he had not even thought about them throughout this. He felt an inner guilt. He had put them in harm's way and did not even try to explain things to them.

"Yeah they are fine, but I have to tell you, Sarah's not happy. She was supposed to be going to Scotland for a break and has had to cancel. I don't think she swallowed my story. I told her a case you had worked on might put them under pressure from the defence attorneys. But she keeps grilling me on the case."

"I will talk to her, but I need you to do me another favour." Jackson replied. "I need you to use your contacts and find out if there's a freighter, or any ship for that matter, arriving in Ireland from Port Arthur, Texas. Reckon you can do that?"

Dave replied enthusiastically. "Of course mate. I know a girl who works for Customs Clearance in Dublin. I'll see what I can find out."

"I will need it quickly mate, and look into Chambers, something's off with him."

"I'll get straight on it mate,"

"Thanks Dave," Jackson said softly, "put Sarah on and I will tell her the truth."

He could hear Dave's hand muffling the mouthpiece. After a few moments, Sarah's voice flooded into Jackson's ears.

"What's going on Jax?" Her stern voice cut through any hope of niceties.

"Dave's bullshit attempt was pathetic. I want to know why, Ellie and me are stuck in this pokey little flat with your mate? And don't tell me it's a case. You've been sacked for months."

"I resigned, remember?" He corrected her. They had rowed over this so many times, it was becoming a case of every time they spoke she goaded him with it.

"Whatever!" she snapped. "Tell me the truth, or so help me God, I'll take Ellie out of here and you can go to hell!"

Jackson sighed; he knew he was not going to win this one. He told her everything. He figured he had lost them anyway, so nothing good was going to come from lying. When he had finished, there was a long silence.

"My God, Jax."

Jackson could hear the tremors in her voice.

"Do you think this Fallon guy is coming after us?"

"I don't know Sarah,"

He was not lying, but deep down he knew that Fallon would use them to get to him.

"I think it's possible. So I need you to stay with Dave until I can stop him. Can you do that for me? I can't do what I need to here, if I am worrying about you two."

Sarah's voice softened. "Oh Jax, be careful. They are obviously dangerous people. Let the Americans deal with them. Come home."

"I can't Sarah. Danny needs me to stop these guys, Cathy and Sonia are in the firing line too. It has to stop here."

"I know," she said softly, "I just don't want anything bad to happen to you."

"My insurance would take care of you both."

Sarah sighed. "I don't want money Jackson. I want my husband back, alive preferably."

Jackson felt his heart soar. Then he remembered everything that happened before, the way their relationship deteriorated. The way he had become more and more shut off from their lives as each case took their toll on him mentally. Then he remembered the way she tore into him when he refused to seek help. Could they put all of this behind them?

In addition, what would he do about Catalina? He would have to leave her here. He knew it would never be any more than it was, but he felt a responsibility to her and Benito.

"I can't guarantee that Sarah, I have to do this. There are a lot of people relying on me. But I will be safer knowing that you and Ellie are safe. So please, stay with Dave, just for a few days more."

Sarah signed in resignation. "Okay we will stay, but I want to hear from you regularly. You know our numbers. That is non-negotiable Jackson, and you know I mean it."

Jackson agreed and ended the call. He was not sure if he would hear her voice again, or see their faces, but he now felt better, even though there was a feeling washing over him. It was the same feeling he had, in Milton's company. It was betrayal.

Jackson returned to the group, they had acquired a larger satellite image of Port Arthur on a laptop. Danny looked up from it when he saw Jackson arrive.

"Good timing Shaw!"

His tone reminded him of when Danny was his C.O. He had an officer's tone, firm but fair. It was all business with him back then. Jackson gave him a mock salute, ensuring he annoyed him by its sloppy execution.

Danny shook his head and grinned. "Still a slacker, soldier. Still a slacker."

Jackson pushed into the huddle. "What we got?"

Joanne was the first to speak. "Frank wants to use his Interpol Authority to manage the operation. He says he can use us as the entry team, but his men will have command."

Jackson looked at her quizzically. "And you just agreed to that?"

Joanne looked taken aback by his candour. "I had no choice Mr Shaw," she said wearily, "He has the full backing of the Bureau and the Chief of Staff. If we want to be involved, then it is his show. Take it or leave it."

Jackson held his hands up in surrender. The dark feeling was getting stronger.

"We are to rendezvous with his team at the Coast Guard and await instructions. Hopefully by then we will have an idea which ship is the target."

Jackson was going to tell her about his phone call to Dave, but something was bugging him about this development. He decided to keep that one to himself for now. The 'whup whup' of the approaching helicopters broke their attention, and they filed out to gather their equipment.

The choppers touched down. Jackson counted three Hueys and an AH-64D Apache gunship. One of the Hueys had a team of eight men inside. All of them fully dressed in black tactical uniforms and fully armed. Jackson looked at Joanne, again with a questioning expression.

"What the hell is this?" He asked.

Joanne shrugged. "Compliments of the Chief of Staff. May I introduce you to Seal Team Six."

Joanne looked almost proud as she pronounced each word with a dramatic pause. Jackson looked over his shoulder to where Danny was standing, who proceeded to imitate a man masturbating while mouthing the word 'wankers' grinning afterwards as Jackson nodded his agreement.

"Bit over the top don't you think, Joanne?" he said, giving her an unimpressed look. "It's not as if we are storming a small fortress or taking on a small army are we?"

Joanne rolled her eyes at him. "What if Rourke has more teams like Milton's? Do you think we can take them on? Even with the mighty Mr Shaw leading the line."

She added the sarcasm with a little venom. Jackson raised an eyebrow. That was a good one, even for her.

"I get your point." He conceded. He turned back to Danny, who merely shrugged and resumed checking his weapons.

One man jumped off the Huey and approached the group. He was a solid man. About the same height as Jackson, but looked muscular. He was in his late forties and had an air of authority about his manner.

"Which one of you is Special Agent Phillips?" He asked, looking around the group. Jackson could tell he already knew, but liked to do things in a proficient military manner.

Joanne stepped forward and offered her hand. "I am Special Agent Phillips, Los Angeles FBI."

He shook her hand firmly, "Master Chief William Dawson, U.S. Navy, Seal Team Six, Ma'am."

He had probably rehearsed that line repeatedly in the mirror, the moment he was awarded the stripes, it was polished and precise.

"I was instructed to assist in the apprehension of a known terrorist and potentially an ex-military team. Is that correct Ma'am?"

Joanne nodded. "Yes, Master Chief," she said, trying to match his manner. "We are assisting in a joint U.S. and International operation, involving the FBI, Interpol and now it seems, the U.S. Navy."

Dawson gave her a knowing nod. "Yes Ma'am. I was lead to believe that Interpol has tactical command. May I speak with whoever is in charge of this operation?"

Joanne shook her head. "Sadly Senior Agent Chambers isn't here, although he has left instructions to rendezvous at the Coast Guard station at Sabine Pass."

"Very good, Ma'am. I will brief the team. As soon as you and your team are ready, we can get going."

He gave her a firm salute, about turned and marched back towards his team.

"Very anal." Jackson quipped.

Joanne gave him a disapproving look. "We can't all be as laid back as you are Mr Shaw. Some of us have jobs to do."

Jackson scowled at her, she was not even qualified to be on this op, let alone have any say in how it goes down, but he let it slide. His focus was on Fallon. He was the one Jackson wanted. The others were just a mere distraction, although he had come up with an idea that might help a few people out in the process. He figured he was owed a break, even if he had to steal it.

"Have you had any joy with the port authorities?"

She shook her head. "Frank is handling the surveillance. He is going to put teams on all four docks, so they will not slip through the net. Besides, it is an eight-hour drive to the docks from here, so we have plenty of time to be in place before they appear. Don't forget they don't know that we know where they are going. They will stick to the speed limits; maybe even take a back road route, which will be even longer. They won't want to get pulled over by Highway Patrol for gunning it, will they?"

Jackson agreed, it would make sense to keep off the highway and skirt their way to their destination.

He just could not shake the feeling that there were elements in play here that they were unaware. There was no way a man like Fallon had gotten this far in his criminal career without a number of contingency plans. The secret was to try to think as he does. If he were Fallon, how would he make his escape? Would he just want to flee, or would he have designs on that huge suitcase stuffed with cash. If Jackson were a betting man, he would stake it on the latter, which made Rourke and Ramon loose ends for sure.

He drew fresh ammunition and grenades and took on some liquids. He did not realise how much the smoke grenade and a good throttling would parch him so badly. Once he was satiated, he moved next to Danny ushering him away from the others.

"I don't like this one bit, mate." He said once they were out of range.

"What's up Jax?"

"Do you not think this is all just a little convenient?"

Danny looked blankly at him. He could see the wheels turning in Danny's head. "I don't follow mate, what's on your mind?"

Jackson pulled him closer. "I have got the same feeling I had when Milton turned up. Everything just seemed too good to be true, and we both know how that turned out."

Danny looked troubled. "You don't think Joanne's playing for the other side do you, mate?"

Jackson shook his head. "No. She's on the level. She could have burned us both several times so far. I saw the look on her face, when she saw Rourke. You cannot fake that level of betrayal. No, I am sure she is straight, but this Chambers fella? He's a bit too cloak and dagger for my liking. I don't trust him, and I'm uncomfortable with him dictating how this goes down."

"So how do we play this?"

"Well," Jackson said quietly, "I think we need to find out where this Fallon is ourselves. We can slip away from the group. I have Dave on the case; he's checking ports in Ireland for the ships tag. Once he lets me know, we can get on board. We can slot Fallon, relieve them of their case and leave the arrests to them."

Danny looked shocked. "Are you serious? They will throw both our asses in jail if they even think we've nicked the cash mate."

Jackson just smiled at him. "They don't know about it. I asked the crime scene guy about it. He didn't have a clue."

"What about Joanne and the others?"

"They were on the other side of the Gulfstream mate. The only other people who could have seen that case, were Max and the the two guys on the hill. However, Mitch and Andy were scoping the terminal and me. The only problem we have is Max. He filmed the exchange and -."

"Well there you go then," Danny interrupted, "game over. Once he submits the camera for evidence, they are going to know that there was a case full of cash. Then the fingers will point at the two Limeys who are nowhere to be seen."

Jackson laughed, and put a hand on the big man's shoulder. "Without any evidence to say we took it, who's to say it was even on the ship in the first place? They could have stashed it on the way. Unlikely, but reasonable doubt my friend," he winked. "reasonable doubt."

They loaded their equipment into the choppers and within minutes, lifted off the tarmac and into the air. The pursuit began.

Chapter 18

The Ruse

They landed at the Coast Guard station five hours later. Jackson slept all the way. He had a philosophy of sleep when you can, because you never know when you will get another chance. Even the stop to refuel had not broken his slumber. They disembarked and met by three men. Two looked like regular seamen, and they began helping unload the Hueys. The third man came over to Joanne and extended his hand in greeting.

As they shook, he introduced himself confidently. "Chief Petty Officer Wilson, United States Coast Guard, Sabine Pass."

"Special Agent Joanne Phillips," She replied, "FBI."

"We have been expecting you. Senior Agent Chambers has instructed us to assist you with a surveillance operation. Our docks are at your disposal. Can you tell us what this is all about, Ma'am? Unfortunately Senior Agent Chambers was less than forthwith with any details."

Joanne lied. "We are assisting in an investigation into illegal workers slipping into the U.S. through these docks. Unfortunately that is all I can tell you I'm afraid, Chief Petty Officer Wilson."

"Brandon." He replied.

"Excuse me?"

Joanne looked at him puzzled. He looked at her and gave her his all-American smile.

"Please you can just call me Brandon."

He was still smiling at her. "And what can I call you?"

Jackson watched Joanne cringe and coldly stare at the man. "You can call me Special Agent Phillips. We thank you for your assistance, but will only require access to secure areas of the docks and your records of vessels in and out in the last fourteen days, Chief Petty Officer Wilson."

Then she spun on her heels and marched back to her team.

Jackson saw the man visibly shrink before his eyes. He almost felt sorry for the man.

"Brandon?" he said, offering his hand. Wilson's smile returned. Jackson wanted to put the man at ease.

"Jackson." He said warmly, then in a sarcastic whisper, he added, "She's all warmth and light isn't she?"

He tried his own American smile.

Wilson nodded and shrugged. "That's a distinctive accent you got there, buddy?"

Jackson smiled warmly and nodded. "Sure is, North-East England.

"No shit!" Wilson exclaimed. "My Sister moved there about twenty years ago. She was an under graduate at Newcastle University. I visited her a few times."

He gave him soft elbow nudge. "Cold, but the beer was good."

Jackson nodded. "Yeah lots of pubs to choose from."

Wilson smiled and gave him a thumbs up.

Jackson left Wilson organising his records and returned to Danny, who stood just staring over at the docks in the distance.

"What's up Bruv?" Jackson asked, breaking Danny from his trance.

Danny turned to look at him. "I'm not comfortable about deceiving them," He said pointing his thumb at Joanne and her team, "I think we are underestimating the shit she could bring down on us if we get caught, Jax."

Jackson put a hand on Danny's shoulder. "Hey mate, we won't get caught. All we are doing is getting some reward for helping the U.S. Government crack a drug trafficking racket, involving a senior intelligence official."

He looked at him sternly. "Don't forget, it was these muppets that put your little girl in danger in the first place. She probably has no job at the Embassy to go back to and you will most certainly have to move after this. So why should you do all this and end up empty handed?"

Danny seemed to be weighing up Jackson's words.

"You know what? You're right, mate. They have royally screwed me and my family, not to mention using you too."

He looked almost angry now. "You know what? Fuck 'em. Let's do this, let's get paid."

Jackson patted him on the back. "That's the spirit mate, partners all the way."

They fist pumped each other and returned to the team. Joanne was in the middle of briefing the team, she turned as Danny and Jackson joined them.

"Nice of you to join us,"

"As I was just saying. This is an Interpol operation, we are to deploy where Senior Agent Chambers tells us. Seal Team will perform any on board breaches. We will set up surveillance and document all evidence for criminal proceedings."

She turned to Jackson and Danny, fixing them with a hard look. "That means no 'Gung-Ho' storming of the ship by unauthorised personnel. Is that clear you two?"

Jackson shrugged and raised a hand in acknowledgement.

"Whatever you say Joanne, this is your operation." He said shaking his head.

Joanne frowned at the use of her first name, and the look on Jackson's face. "Do you have something you want to get off your chest Mr Shaw?"

Jackson put his hand up again. "No."

"Good," Joanne continued, "as I was saying I-"

"Actually I do." Jackson interrupted. "How are you going to build a case against these men, if Interpol take control? They will ship Fallon off to Broadmoor Prison, coz he is a fruitcake. Ramon? He'll probably get sent to a Mexican Jail and Rourke will be dealt with off the books, to avoid any embarrassment to the CIA. Do you not think this is all just a little bit convenient? I mean who pays for the death, suffering and financial misery that these fuckers have inflicted on your people? Are you not just a little concerned that all is not what it seems to be here?"

Joanne rolled her eyes at him. "I haven't got time for your conspiracy theories. Not everything is a cover-up?"

Jackson gave her a menacing look. "And two days ago you thought Rourke was on your side."

Joanne went pale. He could see her processing that thought. He would love to see her fall flat on her face on this one, but one thing stopped him completely digging into her. He actually liked her. She was one of the only people he had met throughout this charade that was actually on the level.

"Jackson's got a point Ma'am." Max added. "You saw how prepared they were at the airstrip. What do you think about Martinez suddenly deciding to bring more men."

Max was on a roll now. "And what about Fallon at the compound? He had his escape all nicely set up. They have been a step ahead at every turn, Ma'am."

Joanne looked around the team. "Do we all share the same opinion?"

Greeted with a unanimous yes, she put her hand on her forehead and let out a long breath, the strain showing in her face when she emerged.

"How to I sell this theory to my Assistant Director? They require full updates, I just don't have time to-"

"Jesus Christ Joanne!" Jackson cut in. "Executive orders are issued by people who do not have a gun pointed at them. You are a good Agent and a good leader. Make a judgement. You are in charge here. It's your investigation, not that pompous prick from Interpol. It's time to shine girl."

"So what do you propose?"

"Well, I think we have to follow most of Frank's instructions, or it's going to spook him. Let Danny and me freelance. We will slip away and check out the ship and the 'so-called' Interpol team. That way you can say we were acting on our own and without your authorisation. Ruth can hook us up some comms, and Karl can get us some way of live feed directly to you. We keep our findings to ourselves and act as they come to us. You play your part for Frank and we will get you your evidence. If I'm wrong and Frank is Kosher, then you have lost nothing. You can publically bollock us if it helps."

Joanne seemed to brighten up. "You are taking a big risk."

"We are taking a bigger risk by letting Frank play this out."

"You stay in contact at all times and you keep them alive."

She fixed Jackson with a serious stare. "Dead suspects are no good to me Jackson. I need to see how deep this goes."

Jackson nodded. "Okay Rourke and Ramon will be in one piece. I can't say the same for Fallon."

Joanne conceded that one, stating that Fallon was not her concern right now. Jackson needed Dave now. He needed his friend to come through.

Ruth set them up with two scrambled radio sets. They were not as good as throat mics but would be more secure. They agreed on a code to punch in and then scramble the input. Karl set up a head camera on each man, activated by a push of a button. They would have to hide them when they were in contact with any Interpol or Seal Team members.

Jackson pulled Danny to one side. "I want you to take the rear on this one mate."

Danny shook his head in annoyance. "No way mate! I'm not letting you take all the risks."

Jackson shook the big man by his shoulders. "Look mate, you have to live here long after I've buggered off. If this goes sideways, just go. Get Cath and Sonia and head for the hills. Put as much distance between you and this lot as you can. The SD card is with my mate Dave. He knows what to do. There are instructions to get in touch with you, and use the card as leverage for you and your family. They can't touch you without opening up a can of worms in the media."

Danny began to tear up. "I don't know what to say Jax. You did all this for me? I could never repay you."

Jackson gripped him again. "Yes you can. You can get Catalina and Benito safe and make sure they stay that way. That is your commitment to me. Call it compensation for being a 'Dick' in the first place."

Danny put a huge hand on Jackson's shoulder. "You have my word. I will adopt them if I have to."

Jackson laughed, "It might come to that mate. I will remind you that you said that."

Max tapped Jackson on the shoulder indicating towards Joanne.

"She wants to see you buddy."

Jackson left them there and walked up to Joanne. "You wanted me?"

She looked at him for a moment. Her face softened and she smiled warmly at him. She was an attractive woman when she was not scowling all the time, he thought.

"I don't want you taking unnecessary risks out there Jax." Jackson was shocked. She had never been this personal with him before.

"I am good at what I do Joanne."

"I know you are Jackson, I have witnessed that first hand. If this all works out, would you consider working with us in the future?"

"Are you offering me a job?" He joked.

"I suppose I am." She said, a little embarrassed by her little showing of emotion.

Jackson gave her a light kiss on her cheek. "If I'm still alive after all this, then ask me again."

He left her staring at him. He could feel her unwavering gaze on him as he walked away. He planned to be enjoying sunny climates with the money he was about to relieve Rourke of, and a marriage to patch up. His phone rang and he checked the display, it was Dave.

"Hi Dave, what you got for me?"

"I talked to my contact and she says there is a ship scheduled to dock in Galway from Port Arthur in 32 days' time. Its manifest declares its cargo as machine parts. Crew of 25 only, chartered by a Trident Holdings Ltd."

"That's the one Dave. You got a name for the ship and where it's currently located?"

"I sure do mate. The ship named as 'Juno Star' is currently at KCS Dock in Port Arthur. She is due to set sail 22.00 hours local time."

Jackson checked his watch. It was already 13.20. He figured Fallon would lay low until it was dark, then make entry to the ship at the last moment. He would not want to sit exposed for any length of time. They could make entry to the ship just before it was due to set sail and hit Fallon when he was safely aboard.

"That's great Dave. What about the other thing?"

"Just a minute."

There was a long silence; Jackson could hear Dave rustling papers in the background.

"Ah yes," he continued, "here it is. Frank Chambers. Special Agent, Foreign Investigator, Interpol, Manchester."

Jackson sighed impatiently. "I know all of that mate, you not got anything else?"

"Jeez you're still impatient I see. Well what you may not know is….that he was fired six months ago and is currently wanted by his own people in connection with a terrorist investigation. The man is not Interpol Jax. I don't know what scam he's pulling there, but his creds are fake. If I was a suspicious man, and I am, then I'd say he was more than likely working for or with Fallon."

Jackson felt his blood run cold. He knew he should never have trusted him. He cursed himself for allowing Chambers to see the images. He thought back to the moment in the car. Chambers' reaction to one of the images was one of alarm.

"Thanks Dave, I owe you a big steak when I get home. Look after my girls and I'll call you later?"

He disconnected and opened his image gallery, scrolling until he reached Sonia's images. He went through them one at a time, looking for something that would cause Chambers to pause. Was it Milton? Or Rourke? Jackson did not think so. He stopped on the image of the table. He traced the figures of Martinez, Rourke and Milton, then Fallon, Taylor, and another man. He looked closer at the image.

That was when he saw it. Again, his blood went cold, then hot as the anger raged through him like molten lava, the ring. He had seen the same ring on Chambers' finger in the car. Chambers had been protecting the operation from within. He had gotten Hal killed and he was helping Fallon escape.

Just then, Danny came up beside him. Seeing Jackson's face, he looked concerned.

"What's up mate?"

Jackson told Danny about the conversation with Dave, and the revelation of Chambers. Danny's face clouded as he processed the information that Jackson had just laid upon him.

"He almost got everyone I love killed Jax."

"This fucker is not walking out of this alive."

Jackson looked up at him and they locked eyes. The steel between them was cold and vengeful.

"No," Jackson hissed. "No he's not."

"What are we going to tell Phillips?"

Jackson thought for a while. If they told Joanne now, she would go into 'Bureau mode' and have the operation pulled. She would bring in agents to secure the area, and by the time she was in a position to move on Chambers, the lot of them would be gone. They needed Chambers there to catch him in the same net.

"We keep schtum mate. We need Chambers to think his plan to infiltrate the FBI is working."

He gave Danny a serious look. "But it's you and me now mate. We need to grip Fallon and Chambers together and bury them both. Joanne can have Rourke and Ramon. I don't give a fuck about those two, but I want Fallon. He's going to pay for Sonia and Hal."

They drew a night scope and NVG goggles, along with H&K MP5SD submachine guns. They would be better in close quarters areas of a ship. Joanne had set up her command station inside the Coast Guard mess hall. Jackson could see her pacing back and forwards with a head set on. She looked intense, her scowl had returned, and whomever she was talking to, were clearly giving her orders. Jackson entered the room once she had finished her conversation.

"What's the score boss?"

Joanne looked stressed. "Chambers has identified the ship. He has ordered the Seal Team to make ready for hard entry and containment. He wants us to take up positions in reserve on the exits to the docks. We can arrest Rourke once he has Fallon in custody."

Jackson studied her face. He could see the division in her eyes, torn between obeying orders, and going with her gut feeling. Should he tell her about Chambers yet or not? If he did, he would kiss goodbye to getting his hands on Fallon, and dishing out his own justice on him and Chambers. However, if he did not, and Chambers manages to get his allies away, then her career as a field agent would be over. She would be operating a safe house in Nova Scotia by the end of the week. He was warming to this woman.

"Do we know the name of the ship?"

Joanne shook her head wearily. "He says he will confirm once we are in position. We are to RV there in an hour. He has put Dawson in charge of the operation. He has tactical command now."

Jackson rubbed his chin. He could see the ruse forming in his head. How would he do it if he were Chambers? Answer was, exactly the same way Chambers was doing it.

"So he wants us out of sight and manning the roadblocks?" He said sarcastically.

Joanne smiled at him. "Yeah, you could say that."

"I'm not buying it Joanne. I don't trust him, and I don't think he's giving you all the information."

"What can I do, Jax?" She asked. She looked tired and it was clearly taking its toll on her.

"Do you trust me?"

"What?...erm'…well yes I guess?"

"No, not you guess. I am asking you seriously. Do…you…trust…me?"

"Yes Jackson, I do. Despite your lack of respect for authority, and your less than conventional methods, you have always been straight with me."

Jackson smiled. "Then trust me now. Chambers is dirty. I wouldn't trust his operation. Danny and I think we know what ship Ramon is planning to escape on, but trust me; I don't think you will find Rourke or Fallon on board."

Joanne frowned. "What are you not telling me Jackson?"

"You say I should trust you? Then show me something. Give me something. Anything, Jax!"

"Okay, okay! I believe that all of this is a ruse." Joanne looked perplexed. "A ruse?" She asked.

Jackson nodded. "Yes. I think he is giving us a target to hit, while our primary targets slip away."

"Go on? I'm listening."

Jackson ignored the condescension and continued.

"Well, it was all too convenient that Marco told us the exact port they were heading to, not to mention the fact that Chambers was so well informed."

He let that sink in a moment.

"I mean, I had only just found out that they were planning to leave by ship. Chambers had a senior Seal Team not only en-route, but also briefed."

Again, he let those words hit home.

"The way I see it, we have been playing this guy's plan to the letter. We have gone where he has pushed us. If you trust me to make this right, then you are going to have to put the FBI handbook in the trash and follow my instructions to the letter. Are you willing to do that?"

Joanne looked deflated. This was going against everything she trained for and the oath she took when she was sworn in.

"Okay Jackson. Tell me everything."

Jackson laid out Dave's findings, leaving nothing out. When he had finished, Joanne looked as though she was going to throw up. She sat slowly on a hard mess chair. Her hands were visibly shaking, and Jackson could see tears welling in her eyes. She looked as though the world was about to collapse on her head. She sat for a minute just staring at the far wall. The vacant look of a person whose career was imploding and she had no control of its demise.

When she had finally collected her thoughts, she looked back at Jackson. She smiled at his compassionate look.

"So what do we do?" She asked quietly. The emotion was still raw in her voice.

Jackson put a hand on hers and looked deep into her eyes.

"I need to get Chambers somewhere I can see him. He is going to be suspicious if I ask to meet him. Therefore, I am going to need to use you as bait. I cannot promise that he will be alone, but I will promise you that he will not hurt you in any way. I will be right there waiting for the right moment."

The tears began to roll down her cheeks. He had not seen her look vulnerable like this. He leaned forward. She seemed to sense his intentions, but instead of pulling away in horror, she leaned in too. They kissed softly. The tenderness was evident. He held her hands and she pulled them to her.

"Okay, let's make this happen."

Chapter 19

Exposed

Jackson and Danny worked their way across the Sabine Lake in the RHIB they had borrowed from Brandon. Joanne had reluctantly used Brandon's ego to persuade him that dinner was a good trade for use of the Rigid Hull Inflatable Boat. They moored at a local Yachting Club and made their way along Ellison Parkway. They passed the Gulfgate Bridge and came to clearing.

Scattered around the clearing were holiday trailers and a few cabins. The lake was a popular destination for groups of young people to party. They had rented a trailer that overlooked the docks and the East Basin. From this vantage point, they could set up cameras and communications.

Moored on its own was the 'Juno Star'. It was a medium sized transport ship. Its white superstructure sat at the rear of a red hull. The front area had several containers already loaded. Leading from its side was the gangway structure. Although they could not see the actual gangway, they could see the platform that lead to it. Unless their targets climbed up the frame, they would see them pass along the platform. They had a good view of both approach roads as well as the floating fuel platform. Nothing would get on or off the ship without them seeing.

Danny took first watch, while Jackson set up their communications. Karl and Phelps were going to be joining them later to add aerial support as well as Max to assist the extraction of the prisoners once secured. The rest of Joanne's team, including Joanne herself were at Dawson's disposal in menial roles. Jackson had told Joanne to play along and purposely told her nothing of their plan of attack.

If she did not know she could not hold her responsible, or worse still give the plan away.

After an hour, there had been little activity. Various crewmembers milled around the deck making the ship ready to sail. Jackson heard a car pull up outside. He drew his pistol and stood side on to the door. He peeked through the window. It was Karl and Phelps. Jackson helped set up the drone and a range amplified listening device, from here they would be able listen in for any clues. Their targets may already be on board, but Jackson doubted it. He reckoned they would arrive in the next hour or so, but he still had his doubts that they would even show.

The light was fading, so Jackson and Danny prepared their equipment. They would use breathing apparatus to approach the refuelling platform from the water. It would keep them on the blind side of anyone from the dock. Next up to arrive was Max. They greeted and Jackson pulled him to one side.

"What's going on over there?" He asked pointing his thumb across the water.

"They got our teams scattered around the docks, covering exits from one loading area."

Jackson looked out towards the shipyard. He could not see much from here, but there were two large vessels moored there.

"Have you got a name yet?"

Max just shrugged his shoulders. "Dawson and Chambers do, but we are out of the loop Jax. They sent Phillips away when she tried to get involved. They are definitely freezing us out."

Danny looked up from his scope. "You think they are even going to show mate?"

Jackson shrugged. "I'm not going to hold my breath mate, but until we get any solid Intel, this is the best lead we have."

The next hour went by without anything interesting of note. Jackson and Danny had switched places. The others were getting food down their necks while they could. Jackson rubbed his tired eyes.

This was the boring part of observations. It reminded him of an Operation he and Danny were on in Iraq. They were assisting British Special Forces in locating and mapping long-range Scud Missile Launch sites west of Mosul. They were protecting the flank of an SAS observation team. They had set up a perimeter around the Exfil site. They had sat for hours looking at barren desert land. Boredom and tiredness began to play tricks with the eyes after a while.

Jackson had remained in the same position for a number of hours, when he saw a shape emerge from a small crag in the hills. He was sure that there were no enemy troops in the area, but his eyes told him differently. He had relayed his sighting to his C.O. who had told him to stop buggering about and keep watching.

He had lost the shape so had discarded it as tiredness, until the location lit up with gunfire. It had been an Iraqi patrol point spotter he had seen. They had let them sneak up to within 300 yards of their position. Had his C.O. listened to him, they could have been prepared. Three of his troop lost their lives in the firefight that ensued. He made sure he never doubted his eyes again.

A movement to the right of the gangway platform caught his eye. A door had opened. The light sparkled in the looming dusk. Jackson switched the scope and focussed on the door. Two men emerged; one was carrying a small holdall. He was shorter than the second man was and carried a lot more weight. He wore dark overalls, which were bursting at the midriff. His slicked back black hair complimented the thick bushy moustache that nestled below his large bulbous nose.

The second man was taller and although he had his back to Jackson, he had a younger appearance. He too was dressed in overalls and had a white rolled woollen hat pulled tight to his head. The two men stood chatting for a short while, Jackson was about to move back to the ship, when the man turned towards the platform. Jackson's heart rate increased when he saw the man for the first time. There was no mistaking his face. It was Ramon.

Jackson followed the men to the platform. Ramon took the holdall from the smaller man and ascended the stairs; then greeted by a crewmember and they disappeared behind the hull. Jackson assumed they had boarded the ship.

"That's Ramon in play guys."

Maybe his theory was wrong. Maybe they were planning to escape this way.

"What about the others?" Danny said.

"Nothing yet,"

Jackson looked at his watch it was 20.35.

"We need to get ready. They may rush on and leave early. Max? I need you to take over here. We will be out of contact while we are under, but I will touch base when we are at the fuelling platform."

"OK, boss."

Jackson was beginning to respect this man. Despite their fractious introduction, he had become a very dependable and surprisingly loyal guy. Jackson put all of his equipment into a waterproof seal bag and attached it to his back. They would have no tactical vests because they needed buoyancy.

The light had finally given way to the thick blanket of night, and the clouds overhead threatened to unload their watery cargo any minute. Jackson secured his weapons and stepped into his breathing apparatus. Danny did the same and within a few minutes, they were ready to go. They made their way down to the anti-wash wall that separated the shore from the busy shipping lane. It was all-quiet for now, but would get busier soon. They dropped into the water and fixed their bearings. The current was steady, but would increase the further in they went.

They had decided to aim for a point 400 metres to the right of the docks. Danny reckoned that the current would take several degrees off their bearing without them noticing, so to aim ahead made sense. The water was dark and murky, but they managed to make the centre relatively close to the surface. The current pulled them sideways as Danny had predicted, but was gentler that expected. When they reached the centre, they descended twenty feet and pressed on. Only the feint glow of their wrist compasses gave them any perception of distance.

Suddenly the platform edge loomed into their vision. They reached it and waited, there was no sense in breaking the surface just yet. If anyone had seen any water disturbance, they would have watched for a while to see if anything surfaced. After a few minutes, Jackson slowly raised his head and broke the surface. They need not have worried about the water disturbance. The rain that had been threatening to fall had done so, and in torrents.

Jackson eased himself up and onto the footplate and shuffled behind the tanks of fuel. Danny joined him a few seconds later. The rhythmic metallic drumming of raindrops on the corrugated metal shelter, keeping the pipe mechanisms dry, made an almighty din; it would certainly mask any noise they made. He took his radio out of the seal bag and entered the 8-digit code.

He depressed the paddle. "Base, this is welcome party. You read me ok?"

"Read you loud and clear Jax. " Phelps said in return.

"Karl I need eyes on the deck. I know it's raining, but need an access point so we can make entry."

"Two minutes Jax. Will let you know when I have visual." Karl replied.

Jackson gave two squelches to acknowledge. They stowed their breathing apparatus in a gap under the fuel tanks. They checked their weapons were clear of obstructions and removed three items from Danny's bag. One was a length of ultra-strong thin climbing cord. Next out, was a folding hook. Danny pulled out the collapsible claws and locked them tight. It had a die-tapped recess at its base, allowing it to screw onto the final item out of the bag. It was an extendable pole. Jackson screwed the hook onto the end and pulled a few feet of pole out.

"Jax?" Karl interrupted their work.

"Go ahead Karl."

"I have your position. There is an automatic anchor engine housing about fifty feet from your twelve o'clock. There are three containers at the front, which will provide cover from the superstructure. There is an access hatch about five metres from the last of the three containers. By my schematics, that access hatch leads to the Forecastle and then the centre container. There should be a walkway from there to centre of the superstructure, via the engine room access doors."

"That's great Karl. Any sign of our other passengers?"

"Negative. They may already be aboard. Other than that, I'd say you've got Ramon only on there and no one else."

"Roger that."

He turned to Danny. "What do you think?"

Danny looked pensive. "We're here mate. Why not snatch Ramon. Drag his ass off the boat and if his mates don't show, we torture his ass until he gives up their plan. It's that or we pack up and go home."

Danny was right he knew that. One target might be useful, but no target was unproductive.

"Let's go for it. We will grip Ramon, and then wait out as long as possible. If no one shows, we pull him off the ship and go from there. Martinez might trade for his son's life."

They agreed their plan and prepared to make entry.

"Karl, I need you to keep eyes on the deck. We are making entry now."

"You're all clear, you can make entry now."

Jackson gave him two clicks and fitted the earpiece to the radio. He would need both hands from now on.

Danny lifted the hook and they moved below the anchor chain. Jackson attached the climbing cord to the ring of the hook and fed it through his fingers as Danny slowly extended the pole. As each section reached its maximum length, two small footholds sprang out to stop the pole simply sliding back down.

Using the cord to help stabilise the pole, they hoisted it up. The claws slipped through the chain housing. They had a rubber compound covering the metal parts, to absorb any noise. Danny tugged on the pole to test the grip. Once he was happy that it was secure, he wrapped his body around it as an anchor, and signalled to Jackson to begin his climb.

Jackson took hold of the highest footholds he could reach and pulled his body up. Once he had a secure foothold, he used the cord to take the strain off the pole, which in turn, took the strain off Danny. Using his weight to keep the pole steady he began climbing. The thumping rain made the foot pegs slippery, even his rubber soles were losing traction. He needed to scale the side quickly. The pole was beginning to sway a fraction as he neared the top; the shortening distance from cord to pole was negating its usefulness.

Finally, Jackson managed to hook a hand onto the top chain link and transfer his weight onto the chain. The loops of the chain were enormous and could easily support his weight. However, the rain and grease had made them treacherous. Jackson lifted himself over the gunwale, and onto the deck. He tethered the hook and the cord to the housing and gave Danny the OK to begin his ascent. With the top secure, Danny was able to make faster progress up the pole.

They hunkered down behind the motor housing and waited, the rain had masked their entry and nobody had come to investigate. They removed their weapons and made their way towards the containers. The deck was deserted. Apart from one man who was gathering strapping to tether their loose cargo elsewhere on the ship. Jackson and Danny covered both sides of the vessel.

Once they were happy that they were unobserved, they made their way to the hatch. Jackson undid the clasps and gently opened the hatch. He pushed his head through the opening and checked there were no crewmembers lurking. Confident that it was clear, they descended down the ladder and into the bowels of the ship.

The dull orange lighting gave the hold a claustrophobic feel. Jackson was beginning to feel his anxiety building. The air seemed hotter than normal, and not much of it. The forecastle was a machinery storage area and the lower part that they were in had a small living quarters. By the looks of the rooms, they had not housed crewmembers for a long time. The musty smell made the air thick and oily.

They came to a sealed door with a porthole window top and centre. Jackson peered through it. On the other side of the door was a large storage area. There were pallets and pallets of shrink-wrapped boxes stacking all the way to the top. Two forklift aisles created between the towers for access. A few crewmembers were huddled around a small desk at the far end of the area.

Jackson softly opened the door and they both slipped out, immediately darting to their right and out of sight of the huddle of men. They took an aisle each and made their way down towards the far end of the hold. They encountered nobody and were soon at the edge of the pallets. Jackson signalled to Danny to hold there and observe. He gave him a thumbs up in acknowledgment.

They held station for what seemed like an eternity. Eventually the huddle broke up. Whatever the meeting was about, it had ran its course. The men headed towards the forecastle leaving the door to the engine room area clear. They slipped around and formed up next to the last pallet. Jackson peered around and back towards the forecastle. The men were dragging metal securing rods from the forecastle. The high-pitched shriek of metal on metal pierced their ears like a hot poker. They used the noise cover to head through the door to a low-lit corridor.

There were several doors along its length. Each one housed various elements of the vessels propulsion from prop housing to an engineer's office and workshop. All aspects of rooms culminating in the final engine room at the far end. Three quarters of the way along the corridor was a stairway opening that would lead into the superstructure itself.

Jackson and Danny ignored the engineer's rooms. Ramon would never allow himself to be imprisoned in such squalor. They climbed the stairs slowly. Danny aimed his weapon to the rear to cover anyone coming up behind them, while Jackson covered the front. The metal stairs were solid, and their rubber soles made very little noise as they climbed. When Jackson's eye line was almost level with the first landing, he drew his weapon up, gently rising above the metal horizon. In front of him stretched a long corridor. Several doors ran along either side, leading to another stairwell at the far end. The doors were all open and brightly lit rooms illuminated the corridor. It was empty.

Jackson quickly made his way to the first set of doors; quickly joined by Danny, who was still covering their rear. Jackson kept his back pressed against the left hand wall and leaned sideways to look into the right hand room. It contained twelve bunks all neatly made and squared away, and a menial relaxing area. This crew were efficient.

Danny moved to the right hand wall and repeated Jackson's technique, while Jackson took over the rear cover. Danny indicated that it was clear, and they made their way along to the next set of doors. They were showers and the ships head. They checked inside that they were clear before emerging back into the corridor.

The next door was the mess hall. Jackson peered into the expansive dining area. There were long metal tables in three lines. Each table had nine placings. At the far wall was a long serving station, which meant the final door would be the galley. Just as they were about to proceed along towards the stairwell, a man emerged from the galley. He was an older man, in his mid-sixties, by Jackson's reckoning. Dressed in whites, he had to be the ships cook.

The man froze when he saw the armed men. Jackson put his finger to his lips and beckoned the man towards him. He complied. Jackson tied him with plastic handcuffs and led him to the sleeping quarters, tethering him to one of the bunk frames.

"Stay here and keep quiet, or I will put you down. Do you understand?"

The man nodded vigorously. He understood.

They edged slowly down the corridor when Jackson felt a slow rumbling vibration through his back as he hugged the wall. He looked at Danny who had felt it too. They both mouthed the same thing to each other in unison, 'Engines on!'

This was a bad turn of events. It narrowed the timing of their operation. The engines would take about fifteen minutes to reach optimum temperature, so departure could be as little as twenty minutes away. This had become a race against time.

Chapter 20

Duped

Jackson reached the stairs first and they repeated the process. Jackson climbed up first covering the front, while Danny remained guarding the corridor below. Jackson reached the next level. This was the officer's deck. He was convinced they would find Ramon and the others if they were aboard.

The corridor was a lot plusher. The carpet was clean and bright red and the walls had been freshly painted white. It was very sterile looking, but neat. Instantly a shadow emerged from one of the rooms and Jackson made himself as small as he could. A figure emerged from the doorway. The man wore white uniform and black shoes, pristinely polished. He was tall and lean and carried himself with an air of authority as we walked. This had to be the Captain he thought.

The Captain turned and looked back into the room he had just vacated. "We just have the final checks to do. We will have you under way in twenty minutes Mr Martinez."

The Captain headed up the corridor and climbed the stairs at the far end.

Jackson's adrenaline levels rose. His quarry was within touching distance. He drew level with the door and switched to his P226 9mm, fitted with a suppressor, but would still make a noise. A suppressor does exactly that. It suppresses the escaping gasses and suppresses the retort. However, the working parts still make one hell of a noise in a quiet space.

Jackson counted to three in his head and spun through the doorway, weapon at the ready. He came face to face with a startled Ramon Martinez. Jackson looked around the room. It was the officer's mess. There was a decent sized dark mahogany table in the centre, with seating for six diners. Around the outer extremities of the mess were sideboards sporting drinks and reading material, as well as a serving area.

Ramon jumped to his feet and was about to shout, when Jackson pulled the hammer back with a sinister 'click'. Ramon slowly returned to his seated position.

"Where are the others?" Jackson snarled..

Ramon looked as though he was going to pass out.

"They're not here, Senor."

The memories of how close he came to losing a finger were clearly fresh in his mind.

"Where are they?"

"They went North, Senor. I was supposed to be going back to Colombia. They were going north. I don't know where, I swear, Senor."

"On your feet Ramon!"

Ramon stood and Jackson handcuffed him. Using a cloth serviette from the sideboard, he gagged the Colombian and shepherded him towards the door. Shoving him into the corridor and down towards the stairs.

A voice startled him. "Can I help you?"

Jackson spun around and saw a young man holding a tray with sandwiches and a teapot. He was only in his late teens. The acne marks still red and angry on his freckled face. A mop of red hair and this face gave the lad a very young appearance. He was thin and short.

Gripping Ramon's collar, Jackson signalled for the lad to come closer.

"Why don't you join us?" He said pointing his weapon at him. The frightened lad shuffled forward, still holding his tray.

"Down!"

He herded them down the stairs to where Danny was waiting.

"Where did this one come from?"

Jackson grinned. "I picked up a stray, you know how it is."

"What's your name, son?" Danny asked.

"Aaron, sir."

His voice was high-pitched and not quite broken yet.

"Well Aaron," Danny continued, "do as we say and you will not be harmed. Fuck us about? Then we will go to town on your ass. You got it?"

Aaron was visibly shaking. "Y-Y-Yes sir."

They guided Aaron onto the same room as the cook, secured them just far enough apart to stop them freeing each other. Using the pillowcases, they gagged the two men but made sure they were comfortable.

Danny squatted in front of the two men. "Be good boys and stay quiet. One of your colleagues will find you soon. We only want him." He said indicating Ramon.

"Believe me, if you knew the pain and misery he and his pops have caused ordinary folk like you, then you would be thanking us for removing this stain."

They left the men and made their way back through the accommodation level.

At the stairs, they paused to listen. The engines whined loudly. Departure was imminent.

"Jax?" Karl burst into their earpieces.

"Go ahead Karl." Jackson replied.

"The gangplank tower has started up. Looks like you will be moving soon. Get ya' asses off or you are going for a holiday."

"Roger that, on our way."

Jackson shoved Ramon. "Vamos!"

They picked up the pace and hurried down the stairs and back through the engineering level. As they exited the final opening into the hold, the men were back at the table. They looked up in unison and began to fan out. Jackson pushed Ramon to the side and raised his weapon. Danny followed.

"Okay fellas," Jackson said, "everyone into the forecastle."

Nobody moved. Jackson fired once into the table, scattering the papers all over the floor.

The men backed up and threw their hands in the air.

"Move guys," Jackson added, "I won't tell you all again."

The men turned and headed to the forecastle hatch, hands stretched firmly towards the roof. When they were through the hatch, Danny closed it behind them and secured the seals. They handcuffed the men together and secured them to the bulkhead.

"Okay guys," Jackson said. "This is the end of the scary part. We are heading out of here. If we see anyone following us or attempting to signal anyone, then they will get slotted. We all clear on this?"

They all nodded as one.

Danny climbed the ladder and exited onto the deck. Jackson shoved Ramon towards the ladder. Realising that he could not get the man up the ladder without releasing him, Jackson took a length of light rope, using his knife; he cut the rope in two. He made a rudimentary noose with one half, and secured it around Ramon's neck. The other half, he tied the noose to his belt. If Ramon tried to jump, he would snap his neck. If he tried to fight, Jackson could simply yank him off the ladder and his neck would snap.

Ramon sagged as his escape ideas went up in smoke. The ship's horn erupted; it had the bass boom of a Rhino about to charge. They were leaving. Jackson shoved Ramon up the ladder and through the hatch. Danny gripped him as soon as he emerged and then helped Jackson to his feet.

"We have to go mate." Danny urged pointing out at the dock. The ship was slowly raising its gangplank and the anchor was up.

Jackson shouted over the engines. "No time for the pole mate. Over the side when we are clear."

Danny nodded.

The ship began to crawl slowly backwards. The bow was beginning to turn away from the dock. Jackson hauled Ramon up and onto the gunwale. Danny came up next to him. Suddenly a shrill whistle ruptured the engines monotony, followed by a loud klaxon. The tethered men had been discovered.

"Get in there Danny!"

Danny secured his rifle and launched himself off the side into the dark water below. When he surfaced and was stable, Jackson shoved Ramon off. He wind-milled all the way down, plunging ungracefully into the surf. Danny immediately gripped him and began side swimming towards the refuelling platform.

Jackson secured his own weapon and followed over the side, just as he heard shouts from behind him. He hit the water hard. It had been a long time since he had jumped into water from any height, and had forgotten to control his descent. Once he had regained his bearings, he followed Danny. As he looked up, he could see men at the gunwale pointing down in their direction.

He hauled himself out of the water and joined Danny and Ramon behind the pump housing. They spent a few seconds regaining control of their their breathing.

"Karl this is Jax."

"Go ahead Jax."

"Tell Max to get his ass here with a boat. We have a package to deliver."

"Roger that."

Max had brought the RHIB from the mooring when he had arrived, it would not take long to cross the short body of water. Jackson scanned the area. Something caught his eye, lights. Flashing lights to be specific and they were heading in their direction. Coast Guard, he thought. He pointed out in their direction and shook Danny, who followed his finger.

"We're about to have company. I guess their operation wasn't as successful as ours."

Danny looked nervously at Jackson. "If they catch us with this prick, they are going to know that we knew it was bullshit."

Jackson nodded. Danny had a good point there.

"Karl. ETA on Max. We are about to have some uncomfortable questions to answer."

"Two minutes out Jax, sit tight."

OK for him to say, he thought, but we are about to be arrested. As if reading his mind, a small pinprick of light twinkled to his left. It was Max. He drifted up to the platform and they quickly jumped aboard. As soon as the last boot hit the rubber, Max turned the throttle and they slipped away from the platform.

Keeping the revs down so as not to create too much of a swell, they headed up towards a liquid gas factory. They could hide in the stathes until the Coast Guard were satisfied that they were not still there.

A tanker emerged behind them; the wake began to throw them against the wooden supports. They could not stay there.

"Max, get us out of here."

Max looked from the dock to the tanker and back. He turned the boat towards the tanker passing along its port side. Jackson gave him a puzzled look. Max just raised a hand and mouthed, 'trust me'.

They passed the stern and began to turn. Max steered them down the starboard side until they were halfway down the tanker's starboard flank. Jackson looked at Max, as the genius of his idea sank in. He grinned like a Cheshire Cat and Max grinned back. Jackson slapped him on the shoulder.

"Genius son, pure genius."

They matched the tanker's speed as they passed the dock. Once they were far enough out from the scene of the abduction, Max gunned it. Skirting around the tanker's bow and headed back towards the Yacht marina.

Karl met them at the dock and they bundled Ramon into the SUV and back to the cabin. They tied Ramon to a chair while Max reported to Joanne. Jackson and Danny changed clothes and they all met up at the kitchen table. Jackson positioned Ramon in the centre of the room facing the table, still gagged and sweating profusely. He looked like a condemned man awaiting execution.

Jackson ungagged him and turned his own chair around so that he was leaning with his arms crossed over the back. He had his chin resting on his arms. He just stared at Ramon intensely, but said nothing. Ramon began to fidget nervously in his chair.

"This is the score Ramon," Jackson said menacingly, "there will be no phoney waterboarding, like you enjoyed with Milton. This is the real deal. I am going to ask you some questions and you are going to answer truthfully and without hesitation."

Jackson drew his KA-Bar and continued. "I have a sure-fire way of detecting bullshit, so I'd advise you to get straight to it, or this is going to feel like the longest twenty-four hours of your life mate. Do you understand me?"

Ramon began to shake physically, but nodded weakly.

"Good, so let's get straight down to it. Where is Rourke and Fallon, and what have they done with the woman?"

Ramon looked puzzled. Jackson rose and stood behind him, leaning down so that his mouth was at Ramon's ear.

"Sorry maybe you couldn't hear me. I said, where is Rourke and Fallon, and what have they done with the woman?"

Ramon began breathing heavily. "I don't know Senor, I swear."

"Not good enough Ramon." Jackson growled, resting the blade into the crook of Ramon's left ear.

"I know he sent you to the docks, and I know he told you to wait for him there. Why did you split up and where did he tell you he was going?"

"He said I had to wait for him and Mr Fallon and they would be back once they had secured Mr Yorke's wife."

Jackson looked up at Max, who shrugged and left the room. "What wife, Ramon?"

"I don't know her name Senor, I swear. I was supposed to stay there and they would get me back to Colombia with Mr Fallon."

Ramon began looking very nervous. Jackson could see that he had panicked when he mentioned the wife. He obviously had not intended to let that slip.

"They never told me where they were going Senor."

Jackson put a little extra pressure on the ear and slowly ran the blade along the flesh, causing Ramon to flinch. Jackson dug a fraction deeper and broke the skin slightly. Ramon cried out in pain.

"Now why don't I believe you Ramon? How about you try again?"

Ramon tried moving his head away from the knife, so Jackson gripped his head with his arm and this time sliced the right ear. Ramon emitted a blood-curdling scream shaking his head in a vain attempt to shake Jackson loose. It did not work. Jackson leaned onto him slicing deeper into the gristle part of the ear.

"Where have they gone Ramon? I know you are full of shit. There's no way you would wait there that long and they not show. You knew it was just you, which means you also know where they were heading. Not south, because why not take you into Mexico with them? You would have been the perfect cover, so no, not south. Not east either because that was the direction you were heading anyway."

Jackson dug into Ramon's ear deeper. The Colombian's crying was becoming almost hysterical by now.

"So it's either west back to L.A. or north."

He felt Ramon tense up when he said north.

"Ah so north it is." He said triumphantly.

"They will kill my family, Senor."

Jackson moved the blade to Ramon's hand, gripping it with all the strength he could muster. Flattening the fingers out into a fan shape, he rested the blade onto the knuckle of Ramon's left 'Pinkie'. He lifted the knife and with full venom, plunged the tip of the blade through the back of Ramon's hand and into the table below. Ramon screamed again. Jackson grabbed the crying man's hair, dragging his head back so he could look into his face.

"Where are they? Last chance Ramon!"

"N-N-New York. They were going to New York. Please, I have told you everything I know. Please stop."

Jackson let go of him, and his head lolled forward as he passed out.

Jackson looked up at Karl. "You can give this piece of shit to Phillips now. I'm done with him."

He suddenly realised that they were all staring at him dumfounded. Danny shook his head slowly.

"Jesus Jax, remind me not to cross you again mate." He said slowly, looking at the knife still sticking out of Ramon's hand.

Jackson looked down, suddenly realising the brutality he had inflicted. Stoically, he pulled the knife out, wiped it on Ramon's shoulder, then returned it to its sheath and said with a little malice in his low tone. "Indeed."

Jackson left the cabin and took in some fresh air. He knew he had gone too far again, and Joanne was going to freak when she saw the state he had left Ramon in, but he did not care. His mission was to kill Fallon. Everything else was mere window dressing. He thought about the look on Joanne's face being pretty much the same look that his Chief Superintendent had had right before he suspended him.

Jackson smiled. "Not changed at all have you Jackson?" He whispered to himself with a slight chuckle.

His thoughts interrupted by the return of Max; he looked very sheepishly at Jackson.

He gave Max a puzzled look. "Developments?"

Max nodded almost embarrassed. "I don't know how we missed it Jax, it turns out that Yorke has a wife. Her name is Samantha and get this," he said paused, "she's a Brit like you Jax."

Jackson thanked Max and pulled his phone out. He dialled Dave's number. Dave answered and he asked him to check out Samantha Yorke. He wanted her background, family, address and maiden name. He asked about Sarah and Ellie and got the same answer as last time. They were OK, but getting ratty at being cooped up in the flat. Jackson thanked him and rang off. He did not have time to deal with Sarah just now.

They bundled Ramon onto the boat in the Yacht Marina and Max took him back to the Coast Guard station. Danny pulled him to one side.

"What's the plan then mate?"

Jackson patted Danny on the shoulder. "We take them in New York. This fucker is not disappearing again."

Jackson's phone began to ring.

Jackson checked the caller ID. "What you got, Dave?"

"Well Jax, you are never going to believe this. Samantha Yorke was originally Samantha Edwards, she was-."

Jackson impatiently barged in. "That's over-fucking-whelming Dave. Is that it?"

"Hold yer horses Jax," Dave replied. The irritation was evident in his voice. "I cross referenced Samantha Edwards with UK records and came up blank. So I checked the U.S. register and the only Samantha Edwards from the UK was a petition to change name in 2008, from, and get this, Freya Fallon."

He let that linger for a moment. "I got an address as well. Dundalk, County Louth in Ireland. Yep you guessed it, she's Fallon's sister."

Jackson stood in a trance for a few moments. "Do we know what she looks like?"

"Sorry mate, but I can tell you that she is booked into the Warwick hotel in Manhattan. She booked two rooms for three guests for the next three nights. Her credit card lit up like a beacon when we ran her details. She has been spending money as if it is free. My guess is that they are having a little family reunion in the 'Big Apple' my friend."

"Dave you are a diamond. See if you can get a recent picture of her and send it to my phone."

He was about to hang up, but added. "Oh and Dave? Keep my girls safe mate."

Jackson turned to Danny and grinned. Danny gave him a quizzical look.

"What gives? You look like you have just won the Lottery."

Jackson shook Danny's shoulder. "Better than that mate. We are going to New York. Got a 'Paddy' to bury.

Chapter 21

Big Apple

Jackson briefed Joanne on his revelations. She was horrified that Chambers had been systematically thwarting their attempts to bring Fallon down, while shielding Rourke and his wife from investigation.

The bogus raid had unsurprisingly turned up nothing more than an illegal people smuggling racket. Thirty illegal immigrants detained, and due for deportation back to Nigeria. Chambers had left the scene and his whereabouts was so far unknown.

Jackson laid his plan out to Joanne, who reluctantly agreed to support. He and Danny caught a flight out to JFK the following day. Using his Western Union account, he booked a room for three nights at the Warwick Hotel.

The Warwick sat four blocks from Central Park. Its dark marble and gold entrance with the illuminated hotel name emblazoned on the marble floor, gave it an air of extravagance higher than the room rate depicted.

The dark oak and cream reception was inviting, but efficient looking. They checked in and were give room 402. The elevator was manned by a smartly dressed elderly gentleman, his silver hair matching his dark grey cap and pristine uniform. His gold buttons polished to a perfect shine. This man took pride in his work, Jackson thought warmly.

The room was spacious and grand. It was camel and sage in colour scheme. The large windows gave it an airy feel, with huge twin beds. They dumped their bags and stowed their weapons under the beds and taking only their handguns with them, left the room.

They rode the elevator back down and nestled into the bar area. The bar was dark and moody, with just enough light to see, but dim enough to give a tranquil ambiance. They chose a seat near large Yucca plant. From here, they had a perfect view of reception and the elevators, while remaining relatively hidden.

They ordered two beers and nursed them for the best part of an hour. Business executives and holidaymakers made up the bulk of the human traffic through the large lobby. The heavyset door attendant was constantly opening the door to cars and cabs, ceremoniously tipping his cap to every arrival.

Jackson scanned the faces as they passed by; his eyes were dry and his head hurt. He had not realised just how tired he was until he sat still for a long period, desperately fighting the urge to drift off to sleep, but feeling his eyelids getting incredibly heavy.

"Hope you aren't sleeping there mate?" Danny said, making Jackson jump.

He had not noticed Danny get up and stand behind him. He must have dropped off.

"No I was awake."

Danny put a hand on Jackson's shoulder softly. "Why don't you go get an hour or so. I can hold the fort here."

Jackson shook his head defiantly. "No, I want to be here when they emerge, we might have to react quickly and I don't want you stuck here on your own. I will be ok mate, maybe get me a coffee?"

Danny squeezed his friends shoulder and walked off towards the bar.

Jackson rubbed his eyes again and sat up straight, making himself as uncomfortable as he could. He felt for his Sig Sauer, the relief he felt having his weapon at hand calmed him. As he was scanning the reception area again, a flash of silver hair caught his eye, and then it was gone. He craned his neck to get a wider view but could not pick the hair out again.

Danny returned with two hot black coffees, but stopped before placing them on the table in front of him. He was transfixed on a spot behind the Yucca plant. Jackson followed his gaze and had to lift himself up and stretch around to see. Sure enough, there he was, Fallon. The adrenaline began to course through his body like an electric pulse. He was no longer tired; he was now completely wired.

Fallon was joined by Rourke, and the two men left by the front entrance. Jackson was up and after them in a flash, Danny rushing to keep up.

"Cool it mate. Let's keep our distance; we don't want to spook them. We need as much information as we can get. Don't forget they still have Perkins somewhere, she could still be alive."

Jackson nodded and dropped his pace a fraction. At the junction of West 54th Street and 6th Avenue, they turned right and headed towards Central Park. Fallon and Yorke performed no counter surveillance techniques; their demeanour seemed relaxed and calm. Jackson and Danny kept a good hundred-yard gap between them, trying to be as casual as they could.

They suddenly crossed and the Junction of 57th and 6th, entering a Starbucks. Jackson stopped at a street vendor and bought two black 'I Love NY' baseball caps and two sets on wraparound sunglasses. They looked more like tourists now. They bought a couple of chilli dogs and loitered with the rest of the pavement diners. The meat was spicy and the chilli sweet. Jackson had not noticed his hunger until just then. He wolfed his down in four bites and bought another.

Fallon and Yorke emerged holding paper cups and pretzels. They turned left and continued towards Central Park. Jackson and Danny followed, maintaining their hundred-yard gap.

"Do you think they are meeting Chambers?"

Jackson thought about it for a moment." They could be mate."

"Or they might be organising their escape. I guess we'll find out soon enough."

They followed the men over West 59th and into Central Park. The Park was a hive of activity. Small stalls sold food of various nationalities. Street mimes silently acted out their imaginations, while buskers fought for airtime. The river of people began to thicken as the inevitable bottleneck began to herd them together. Jackson was struggling to keep Fallon in sight. Thankfully, at six feet and three inches, Danny was a giant compared to ninety percent of the people in front of them, unfortunately, that made him stand out too.

Down the tree lined cycle way of Centre Drive, they walked at a casual pace. Past waffle stands and Playmates arch. Suddenly as the walkway bent to the right, they skipped left at the bend's apex. Jackson and Danny moved into the surrounding trees as the people thinned out, to almost nothing. Fallon and Yorke stopped at the Shakespeare Statue and sat on a long bench seat facing the green island. Jackson leaned against the tree out of direct sight. Danny moved to the opposite side and did the same. Both men pretended to be texting.

Fallon and Yorke were locked in a heavy, heated discussion. Jackson could not hear what the men were saying, but the arms movements and mannerisms told Jackson that this was less than friendly. Jackson's phone vibrated, he had an incoming text message from Joanne. It read:-

Where are you? We are in New York now. We have
surveillance on the hotel and at JFK security. You can stand
down, we have this!!

Jackson kept an eye on his targets while he replied.

We have eyes on Fallon and Rourke. They look like they are
waiting for someone.
Will intercept them when they complete their meeting.

J

Still the heated debate between Fallon and Yorke raged on. Jackson's phone buzzed again.

DO NOT, I REPEAT, DO NOT INTERCEPT!!
Please remember that they still have one of my agents. Her
safety is my no.1 priority. If anything happens to her, I will
hold you responsible.

Jackson wanted to tell her to fuck off, but she did have a point.

His attention turned to the bench again. The row had stopped and they were both standing up. A man was approaching them from the left. He was a short overweight man, balding badly. He wore a navy blue tracksuit and black trainers. The men shook and 'Tracksuit' sat. He unzipped his tracksuit top and produced a thick brown envelope. Fallon took it and examined its contents. From Jackson's vantage point, it looked like it was full of passports. He looked over at Danny, who was recording the meeting on his phone. 'Nice one Danny.' He thought to himself.

The contents were clearly satisfactory, because Fallon produced an even thicker envelope. Tracksuit opened it and fanned through a large bundle of notes. Payment for services rendered. Tracksuit then got up and hurried away without even a backwards glance. Fallon patted Yorke on the back;

the two men stood and headed back the way they had come. Keeping out of sight, until they had passed, Jackson and Danny fell in behind them and continued to follow. They headed back to the hotel and went inside.

Jackson quickened his pace and came to the lobby just as Fallon stepped onto the empty elevator. He stood watching the floor indicator as it rose past two and three. It did not stop. It passed four and five. It stopped on six. Jackson waited. Would it go up, or down? After what seemed like an eternity, the elevator began to descend, all the way back to the lobby. Jackson and Danny moved into cover, just in case Fallon had decided to come back down. The elevator doors opened and a large man with a black ill-fitting suit stepped off. Floor six. Now which room?

Jackson messaged Joanne with the information they had gained. She told them to keep eyes on the lobby and she was on her way. When she arrived, they had returned to the bar, only this time they sat at the opposite side, so they could see the elevators. She ordered coffee and sat next to Jackson, facing the elevators.

"Okay guys, where are we at?" She asked, slightly out of breath.

"Sixth floor, as I said in my text, we don't know which room. There are fourteen rooms on our floor. I'm assuming the same goes for the sixth floor too."

Joanne looked at him and nodded. "I could use my creds and request the floor, but if the concierge has been paid off, then we will show our hand. Up to now, they don't know we know about New York. I have sent a fake memo to my department, saying that we think they've crossed into Mexico, and we want permission to pursue. It will be denied of course, but if Rourke is still monitoring the chatter, then he will relax a little."

Jackson nodded his approval.

"So what do we do? Lift them when they leave? They will probably hail a cab, or have a driver come and get them; we don't know what names they are travelling under, or where they are headed."

Joanne fixed him with a serious look. "We don't want to engage in a firefight here. I say we tail them from here and grip them at the airport. We can control the collateral damage better outside."

"Fallon will spot a tail in New York traffic." Jackson said.

Joanne thought for a moment. "We can sequester a yellow cab. Nobody notices a yellow in New York, they are everywhere."

Jackson liked that idea. "Get two," he said, "that way we can alternate numbers. You'd be amazed how the mind recognises things subconsciously."

They agreed and Joanne left to organise the surveillance.

When Joanne had left, Jackson turned to Danny. "You know that the tail won't work, I don't care what she says."

Danny nodded. "So what do you have in mind?"

"We take them in their room, that way we can control the situation."

"How are we going to find out what room they are in? Like you said, if Joanne flashes her creds, we might scare them off."

Jackson stared off into the distance. His friend was quite right; they had no way of getting that information without showing their hand.

Lost in his thoughts, Jackson studied the lobby. People came and went. It was a hive of activity. The constant cacophony of voices had a hypnotic effect on him. A loud clatter broke him from his trance. The service elevator had opened and a small Korean girl exited with her trolley, she was a hotel cleaner. It was as if a light switched on in Jackson's head.

"I've got it." He said.

Danny looked up quizzically. "What have you got?"

Jackson pointed to the cleaner. "They are the worst paid staff here, relying on tips, yes?"

Danny nodded.

"Well, Fallon is not gonna want a maid poking around in his room, especially if he has Perkins in there."

Danny frowned at it him. "I don't get where this is going mate?"

Jackson rolled his eyes in frustration. "It's simple. He is going to have a 'Do Not Disturb' sign on the door. We go up check how many rooms have the sign out, which should narrow the rooms down."

Danny nodded. "That's genius mate, but suppose he hasn't?"

Jackson had considered this. "Well we will just have to take our chances. But I will bet my balls on being right."

"Okay so we find out which rooms have the signs on the doors, we still won't know which one is his, unless he's the only one."

Jackson knew Danny had a point. It was a risky plan. One that Joanne would never endorse. "Stay put," Jackson said. "Keep an eye on the elevators, if they come down text me."

Jackson got up and headed over to the stairs. By the time he reached the sixth floor he was sweating and out of breath. He made a mental promise to get back into the gym when all this was over. If he was still alive, that is.

He checked his weapon was ready and softly pushed the door open. He emerged to left of the three elevators on this floor, two for the guests, and one service elevator for the hotel staff. To his right were three rooms, all had no signs on their handles.

Jackson moved left slowly scanning the doors as he crept along, one hand on the butt of his Sig Sauer. The long corridor, painted in a pale burgundy with dark mahogany wooden panels, had three doors both sides and one at the end, none of which had signs on. Jackson felt his heart sink. Back to square one at this rate, he thought. The red-carpeted corridor turned right revealing another four doors. The two at the end had the tell-tale 'Do Not Disturb' signs hanging from their handles. They had to be in one of these rooms.

Jackson retreated to the stairs and took his phone out, just as it buzzed. It was Danny:-

The 2 muppets are on the move. Get down here!!

Jackson tore down the stairs. He halted halfway between floors two and one. At the junction of the dogleg, was a maintenance cupboard, and its door was ajar. Hanging up were three sets of coveralls and a tool belt. Jackson used the screwdriver to loosen the door hasp. He returned the screwdriver and continued down to the lobby.

Slowly opening the door a fraction, he could see Rourke standing talking to the Receptionist. Fallon was outside, clearly waiting for him. Jackson made it to the bar where Danny was lurking behind the entrance.

"They came down just as you went in mate."

They stood watching and Rourke flashed the concierge his credentials and handed him a piece of paper. They talked for a few moments, before Rourke turned and headed out after Fallon.

"You follow them." Jackson said. "I'll get a look at that paper and check the room. We might get Perkins out before they get back. Then we can take them out when they get back."

Danny nodded and headed out after the two men, again they turned right.

Once they were out of sight, Jackson strolled over to the concierge. He was on the phone and signalled for Jackson to wait.

Jackson browsed the rack of brochures offering the sights of New York, from theatre trips to access to the Empire State Building. Jackson edged closer to the reception back desk. The piece of paper sat on the desk next to the phone. Jackson casually craned his neck to get a better look.

On the paper, torn from the desk pad that all the rooms had displayed along with room service menus and laundry request forms, was a hand-written message, it read:-

Room 613
Private Car
JFK Terminal 5
07/03/2018 12.45
3 Passengers

Jackson's heart rate rose rapidly. He now knew the room. All he had to do was get in and get Perkins safe. He went back to the elevators and rode the car up to the second floor. He left the car, entered the stairwell, pulled his phone out and dialled Dave's number. After five rings, Dave answered.

"Hi Jax, how's it going?"

"Nightmare mate, pure nightmare. Listen mate, I need another favour."

"I need you to get me that picture of Rourke's wife soon. I have to assume she will be armed. Don't want to get slotted by her because I was careless. Can you do that ASAP mate?"

"You got it mate." Dave said and hung up.

Jackson then dialled Danny's number.

"Sit-Rep mate."

Danny sounded slightly out of breath. "They have gone back to the statue."

"Same meeting?"

"Yeah, same guy, same hand-over I suspect." Danny replied. "You think they are about to split up?"

Jackson told him about the note.

"That's International Departures mate." Danny said. "They are skipping the country. I'd hazard a guess that Fallon's going home."

"Makes sense, mate. Text me when they head back."

Jackson headed down to the maintenance cupboard. This time he tried the door but found it locked. Jackson took his KA-Bar out and wedged it between the lock and the hasp. The loose hasp gave way easily and Jackson opened the door with little effort.

Jackson climbed into one of the sets of coveralls. They felt a little loose on him, but would just have to do. He took the tool belt and found a baseball cap emblazoned with the hotels motif. Jackson moved the Sig so he could access it through the pocket gap and slid the KA-Bar behind the screwdrivers. He returned to the elevators and rode up to the sixth floor. He checked his phone. The message from Danny was there, they were heading back, and he did not have long.

Jackson exited the elevator, just as an elderly couple approached.

"Excuse me son?" said the man. He was a small man, stooped over by the curvature of his frail frame. He was elegantly dressed in a light blue suit with a cream shirt and blue tie.

"We need the faucet in our bathroom looking at. Could you look at it for me?"

Jackson gave him a warm smile. "You need to report it to reception, then I will get straight on it sir."

Jackson nodded to the couple as the doors closed.

He followed the corridor to the end. Room 613 was the right hand door at the end of the corridor. The door at the very end was 614. Jackson knocked gently on 614 and waited. There was no answer, so he knocked again. When no answer came, he drew his knife. Using the blade to prise the jamb back, he popped the door open.

Drawing the Sig, he entered the room, closing the door gently. The room was empty. Jackson checked the bathroom and the wardrobes. The room had no occupants recently. The bed made, and the ornate swan towel sculpture proudly awaited the glee of the next inhabitant.

Jackson stood to the side of the door, opening it a fraction, so he could see 613 clearly. After a few moments he heard the elevator declare it had arrived and the metallic dragging of the doors opening. The men's voices grew louder as the approached. Jackson's phone vibrated. Danny had messaged him. They were heading up and Danny was following.

He heard Fallon speak as they rounded the corner. "Good night at the bar and then tomorrow we are home free."

The two men stopped outside 613 and Fallon inserted the key card. As the door clicked, Fallon opened it and was about to step in, when Jackson burst from his hiding place. He kicked Rourke square in the back sending him sprawling face down onto the floor.

Pressing the Sig against Fallon's head, he shoved him forward.

"Inside." He growled, sliding the .357 Magnum from Fallon's waistband.

Fallon raised his hands and stepping deep into the room. Shoving Fallon onto the chair next to the door, he dragged Rourke by his collar and shoved him against the wall next to Fallon.

"Where is she?"

Rourke's breathing began to get frantic as his eyes darted from Jackson to the bathroom.

Jackson's phone buzzed again. It would have to wait, he did not have enough hands. Jackson edged towards the bathroom door just as it opened. Standing in the doorway was Perkins. She looked wet as though she had just showered and dressed. She looked shocked.

"Jackson," she said. "How did you find us?"

Jackson handed her the Magnum. "Watch those two." He said, pulling his phone out.

He had two messages. First, one was from Danny. He was taking the stairs. The second one was from Dave. A picture message entitled Freya Fallon. Jackson looked at it in horror as the cold steel pressed firmly into the back of his head. The picture was Perkins. Fallon took Jackson's Sig Sauer just as Danny appeared in the doorway.

"No!" Jackson yelled, but it was too late.

Fallon's weapon barked twice, hitting Danny centre mass, throwing him back into the corridor. Jackson lunged forward but a vicious blow to the back of his neck sent his world black.

Chapter 22

Enlightened.

When Jackson came to, he was no longer in the room. He was in the middle of an inspection pit and tied to a wooden straight-backed chair. He was in a garage. Wrapped around his knees were two sets of copper wires leading off into a large unit. Jackson felt himself drifting again, when a venomous slap snapped him back into consciousness.

"Wakey wakey, Jackie Boy," said Fallon, in his usual jovial tone. "Comfy are we?"

Jackson just glared at him. The pain in the back of his head felt like a jackhammer pounding in his skull. Then the memory flooded back to him, Danny. Was he alive or dead? Had anyone tailed them here or was he on his own? He had to assume that it was the latter. Fallon moved closer so that his face was level with Jackson's own. Jackson could smell the sour mix of coffee and whiskey. He vainly attempted to head-butt the Irishman but came up just short.

"Still got a lot of fight left in ye."

"Let me loose Fallon. Just you and me. We'll see who has the most fight left then."

Fallon's smirk returned as he moved towards the unit. "I bet you'd love to kill me with you bare hands eh Jackie boy?"

"Fuck you Fallon."

Fallon shrugged his shoulders and flipped a switch on the unit.

Jackson's muscles contracted violently as the current ran through his body. Convulsing as each wave of electricity seared his blood. Then it stopped. Jackson slumped forward gasping for breath as Fallon returned in front of him. Calmly lifted Jackson's chin and looked him straight in the eye.

"How did you find us Jackie? Do the Feds know where we are?"

Jackson spat into Fallon's face. "Fuck you. You are a dead man. I'm going to peel that smug fucking grin off your dead face."

Fallon straightened up. "Okay Jackie boy, have it your way."

He returned to the unit and flipped the switch. Jackson cried out as the lactic acid tore through his muscles, cramping every sinew tight. He closed his eyes trying to fight the pain. He began to shake and his knuckles whitened as he gripped the armrests tightly. Then it stopped again and Jackson could feel his consciousness fading.

Just as he was about to pass out, he was hit with a wall of ice-cold water, snapping him back into life. Jackson opened his eyes to see Perkins standing holding a bucket.

"You bitch," he growled, "we came to save you. Danny died saving you, you piece of shit."

Perkins shrugged. "You should have stayed away. Nobody invited you. Poked your nose into business that had nothing to do with you. That's what you get."

"Enough of this shit." Fallon shouted. His irritation was evident. "Tell me what I want to know or you'll be begging me to put a bullet in your head."

Rourke ran into the room. "We're gonna have company."

Fallon looked puzzled and angry at the same time. He glared at Jackson. "How are they finding me? Are you transmitting?"

Jackson smiled at him. Fallon swung a heavy fist at his head. It connected to his cheekbone with a frightening amount of power. Jackson began to see lights as his face began to go numb with the impact.

"Get him in the van. We go with plan B

Rourke removed the wires and tipped Jackson back and dragging him backwards. He and Perkins hoisted Jackson into the back of a small panel van. Inside the van sat the suitcase.

The doors closed and the engine fired into life. The van sped away. The driver was erratic and lost control of the van frequently. Every turn sent Jackson skidding across the van's wooden floor, crashing into the wheel arch. Jackson got the sliding under control, aiming the legs of the chair at the solid arches. Lifting his legs at the last minute caused the wooden leg to splinter and snap, releasing his right leg.

Struggling to pull his body upright, another aggressive turn sent him crashing backwards against the van wall, loosening the backrest. Jackson folded his body as tightly as he could. The wood protested, but eventually succumbed to the pressure and snapped. Jackson freed himself from his restraints and grabbed one of the chair legs. It had split to form a lethal looking spike.

Between the cab and back of the van was a thin cloth divider. Jackson pressed against it, running his fingers along until he found the driver's seat. Aiming slightly to the right of the seat, he plunged the spike through the cloth. It found its mark. A loud scream erupted from the cab as the van careened sideways and flipped on its side.

The impact took the breath out of Jackson as he launched against the van side. The back door burst open on impact and Jackson could see that they were sliding along the road.

Jackson grabbed the case and squeezed through the buckled opening. He was up and running as soon as he stopped sliding. Behind him, he heard the doors kicked open as the three kidnappers climbed out of the van. They must have spotted him with the case. Gunfire erupted behind him. He heard a round whiz past him and impact on the wall close to his head. He looked around him as he ran.

The brick wall to his right gave way to a chain link fence with a small gate. He kicked at the gate as he reached it, his momentum snapping open the basic clasp. In front of Jackson was a ramp leading down into a railway siding. There were rows and rows of dormant rolling stock.

Jackson darted behind the first carriage as the rounds began to rain down at him showering fragments of metal over him. He climbed under a carriage and nestled into a walkway between two carriages. He opened his mouth to hear clearly. He could make out the sound of feet on gravel; the sound was slow and deliberate. They would have split up and would be traversing the rows searching. Jackson would have given anything for a weapon right now.

The footsteps behind his position grew louder, whoever was coming, had chosen the right row and were bearing down on him. He hefted the suitcase up to chest height and held it close. It was not an idea weapon, but it was the best he had to work with. The sound became clearer as the pursuer bore down on his position. Jackson saw a shadow appear in front of him and then a hand. He thrust himself forward, using the case as a shield.

He ploughed straight into the body of the assailant. It was Perkins. Her slight frame was no match for the combined weight of Jackson and the case. The impact sent her sprawling into the gravel and spilling her weapon to the side. With amazing dexterity, she was up on her feet and squaring up to Jackson, her combat blade glistening in the sun. Jackson charged at her, but she sidestepped him with the gracefulness of a ballerina.

"I thought you were a bad-ass." She goaded. "Come on big boy, show me what ya' got."

Jackson charged again, this time he managed to grab her clothing and spun her around, but not before the blade sliced into his hip.

Using all his weight as a counter to her motion, he dropped onto his back and tucking his foot into her side, flipped her over headfirst. As soon as she made impact with the floor, he swung his legs around her arm, pinning it in a straight elbow lock.

Jackson wrestled the knife from her grip as she bucked and weaved, desperately trying to loosen his grip. Jackson could see that she was scrabbling to reach the Sig Sauer.

Dragging her arm towards him, he rolled over her and made a grab for the weapon, immediately regretting his decision. Perkins grabbed the 9mm and swung it towards Jackson's head.

With just seconds to spare, Jackson buried the combat knife deep into her chest, shock frozen on her face as she dropped the weapon and instinctively clutched her chest. Jackson looked into her eyes as the life ebbed out of them, leaning down to her ear.

"That's for Danny, bitch." He whispered.

"NO!" came a cry from behind him as he stood up.

Jackson spun round to see Rourke standing transfixed on the body of his dead wife. Rage filled his expression as he raised his Beretta at Jackson. Jackson grabbed the Sig and the case then dived under the carriage as the rounds smacked the metalwork. Jackson rolled out the other side just as Rourke reached Perkins's lifeless form.

Jackson heard voices from the other side of the stock.

"Freeze Rourke!" The voice belonged to Max.

Jackson wedged the case into the carriage's axel. Stooping down to see below the carriage, Jackson could see Rourke on his knees, then lying with his hands on his head. He turned to look at Jackson. The hatred burned into him as a knee landed on his back. Max cuffed him and dragged him back up as Jackson emerged from the siding.

Joanne and Mitch joined them out of breath. Jackson looked at her.

"Fallon?" he asked.

Joanne shook her head. "I'm sorry Jax, we gave chase but lost him in the tunnel. He won't get far, we have the airports on standby with orders to run all passports for facial recognition. He won't get out of here."

Jackson's face reddened. "He isn't going to the airport Joanne." His irritation was impossible to disguise.

"He picked this area for a reason, he will have a plan."

Joanne dialled a number and walked away with Mitch, leaving Jackson and Max alone with Rourke. Jackson turned to Rourke and punched him heavily in the stomach, sending the CIA man flying on his back. Rourke couched violently as he struggled to regain his breath.

"Where is he going Rourke? You know something and you are going to tell me, or so help me God, I am going to snap your spine." Jackson dragged him to his feet.

"You killed my wife." Rourke said defiantly. "I'm not telling you shit."

Jackson drew his knife and was about to lunge at him when

"Jackson. Back off."

"Fuck you Joanne. This motherfucker helped kill Danny and he is behind every bad thing that has happened to me since I've been here. He's going to tell –"

"Danny's alive, Jax." Joanne interrupted.

Jackson looked shocked, but elated at the same time.

"What are you talking about? I saw him take two in the chest before I was hit from behind."

Joanne put a hand on his shoulder, guiding Jackson away from Rourke as Max dragged him away.

"He's in surgery Jax. It's touch and go but he is alive. Don't worry about Rourke, he will talk. Right now Danny needs you with him."

Jackson calmed as Joanne kneeled next to Perkins.

"I can't believe we never saw the leak in our own team."

Joanne looked up at Jackson. "She seemed like a dedicated agent."

Jackson gave her a weak smile. "They were a step ahead of us all the way. There was no way Rourke could know what we were planning without help. We kept this operation from everyone but our team. Even Chambers didn't know our time frame."

Joanne nodded. "Speaking of Chambers, we have information that he's fled to Germany. He landed in Berlin this morning. We have our sources scouring the country for him."

Jackson had forgotten all about him. "He knows a lot about me. He could still be a problem."

Joanne stood and looked serious, handing Jackson his phone back. "Leave him to us. We will find them both. Max will take you to the hospital when you have composed yourself."

Jackson walked down the row of carriages and returned to the other side where he had stashed the case. He retrieved it and headed back up towards the fence.

Spotting a telecom junction box, he wedged the case behind it. It was a snug fit but it would be out of sight. To add to the camouflage, Jackson piled random garbage over it. Happy that it was unlikely to be found anytime soon, he tagged the GPS co-ordinates into his phone and walked up through the gate and up to the SUV that Max had waiting for him.

The adrenaline was beginning to ebb away and he could feel the pain in his hip. Max handed him a Medi-kit and he covered the wound with a small cotton pad and tape.

Max parked outside Mount Sinai Hospital in Queens. Max led him through a maze of corridors until they reached a bank of elevators. They stepped out into the emergency surgery department. Max flashed his creds to the nurse at the reception desk as Jackson took his phone out and dialled Sonia's number.

"Where are you?" Jackson asked when Sonia answered.

"I lost her Jax."

"What do you mean, you lost her?"

"I went out for food. When I got back, Catalina and Benito had gone. I searched everywhere but there was no sign."

Jackson told Sonia about Danny. Once she had calmed down, she told Jackson that she had made her way to Kansas City, where she had lost Catalina. Jackson told her to make her way to Kansas City Airport. They would find Catalina later.

He booked Sonia a flight to La Guardia that evening and arranged with Joanne to have her collected and brought to the hospital. Max returned and told him that Danny was still in surgery. They had removed one bullet from his lung, but the other slug had nestled between the Aorta and the Right Ventricle, making removal tricky. They would let them know when they knew more.

Jackson called Joanne again. This time he asked her to put a BOLO out on Catalina and Benito. He told her about Kansas City and her fear of police. She promised to do what she could. She told him that they think Fallon might have left the country by ship, but she could not be entirely sure.

She thought he had taken the money with him as it was not in the wreckage of the van, and Rourke had specifically said that he had put the case there himself. Jackson chuckled to himself, picturing Fallon empty handed, but also annoyed that they had lost him yet again.

Next, he called Dave, who told him that they would keep an eye out for Fallon returning to the UK. He spoke to Sarah, telling her about Danny. She insisted on coming over to join him in his vigil, but he talked her out of it, reminding her that she may still be a target, and the safest place for them both right now was with Dave.

The hours passed slowly. Jackson spent the time pacing the hallways and the canteen. He was onto his fifteenth coffee, and feeling drained. The nurse at the reception desk had noticed the blood on Jackson's hip and she cleaned and stapled the wound.

After another hour, the door to the operating theatres opened and a tall man in green scrubs emerged and approached them. Jackson rushed over to him.

"How is he?"

The surgeon gave him a calming smile. "He's out of surgery. We managed to remove the bullet, but there has been a significant amount of tissue damage. He has lost a lot of blood and we will have to monitor him. The rupture in the Ventricle was extensive, but thankfully the Aorta is intact."

"But he is going to live, isn't he?"

"The next twenty-four to forty-eight hours are going to crucial, but we are confident he will pull through. He will need a period of convalescence and physiotherapy. Once he regains consciousness, we will let you know."

Jackson felt his temper rise again. "He will make a full recovery won't he? I mean he's not going to be a vegetable is he?"

The Surgeon lifted a calming hand. "I'm afraid that is all I can tell you for now. As soon as I know anything, I will let you know."

He turned about face and walked back through the doors.

More hours passed. Jackson had dozed off, woken only by the sound of heels clacking on the hard floor next to him. He groggily looked up to see Joanne standing over him. After checking on his welfare again, she asked Jackson to follow her to the canteen.

They ordered coffee and sat by the window. It was dark outside but the sky had the dark blue hue of the pending sunrise. Jackson looked at the clock on the wall; it told him that it was 4 am.

"I know you are worried, but I need to know what happened. You were supposed to maintain surveillance and wait for us; not go charging in yourself."

Jackson could feel his blood boiling. "You saying this is my fault?"

Joanne held her hand up. "No I am not; I just need to know why we had a firefight in a top New York Hotel without approval. Don't forget, I'm going out on a limb for you here. My boss wants you locked up or sent back to the UK, so help me out here."

Jackson told her about the note and how he found out the room number, he told her about the rescue attempt and the eventual discovery of Perkins identity, emphasising the fact that the embarrassment of the infiltration of a known terrorist's sibling into the Bureau would be damaging.

Joanne put her head in her hands, the stress showing. "This is a mess."

"You stopped a massive conspiracy and a significant drug operation. Surely that counts as a success?"

Joanne smiled wearily and touched his hand. "You are sweet, but you don't know how things work over here. There will be an investigation. At best I get to keep my job and avoid charges of negligence."

Jackson smiled at her softly. "It will work out, I have confidence that, once they realise just how deep this goes, that they cannot hide behind the book. They will have to step from behind it and back their senior agent. If they can you, they will have me to deal with."

Joanne chuckled. "God help them."

"By the way," Jackson said, "how the hell did you find me at the garage?"

Joanne grinned mischievously. "We low-jacked the phone you brought with you. I wasn't going to lose track of you a third time."

Jackson smiled and squeezed her hand. "Thank you. You probably saved my life. They were going to kill me."

Max appeared and told them that the surgeon was back. They rushed into the ward just as Sonia came running in, throwing her arms around Jackson as she sobbed.

Jackson turned to the surgeon. "This is Miss Hughes, Mr Hughes's daughter."

The surgeon held his hand out to her. "Charles Wentworth, Miss Hughes."

"Your father is stable. The bleeding seems to have stopped, and is responding well to the medication. He is being moved to a private room, where we will monitor him."

"Can I see him?"

Charles shook his head. "I'm afraid that's not possible at this moment. Once we have him stabilised in his room we will let you know and you can see him. Please be patient just a while longer, and please don't worry. He is in the best of hands."

Joanne stepped up to the surgeon and handed him her business card.

"I am Special Agent Joanne Phillips. The bureau will be taking care of the medical bill, so anything he needs, he gets?"

Charles nodded to her. "Of course, Special Agent Phillips, he will receive the very best care." He nodded to each of them in turn and returned to the surgery.

Jackson turned to Joanne and gave her a light kiss on her cheek.

"Thank you. He means the world to me."

She gave him a soft nod and turned to Max. "Max you come with me. We have an Irishman to track down."

Max said, "Ma'am."
They both left the room.

Chapter 23

Revenge is sweet.

Jackson spent the next two days between the hotel and Danny's bedside. He had hired a car, and returned to the railyard and retrieved the case. While he did not count it to the penny, he estimated that it contained around Ten million dollars in U.S. currency. He stashed the bundles of cash into the ceiling of his hotel room and disposed of the case into the Hudson before returning to the hospital.

Danny's room was compact and filled with every monitor imaginable. The constant beeping of the heart monitor made for a tense soundtrack. The hospital allowed Sonia to use a room in the hospital to sleep. She had spent the whole time by her father's side and looked exhausted.

Jackson put a hand on her shoulder, breaking her from her vigil.

"Why don't you go and get some sleep. I will take the next shift. I promise I'll come and get you if there are any developments."

Sonia stood slowly. She reluctantly headed for the door.

Jackson called after her. "Have you heard from your Mum?"

Sonia nodded. "Yeah she should be arriving today. It was the first flight she could get."

She left the room and Danny took her place next to his friend.

Jackson sat for an hour holding Danny's hand. His mind was racing. This was his fault. If he had not been so cock sure of himself, he might have seen the danger. He cursed his impetuousness. He should have handled this alone. His hatred for Fallon had made him careless, and it almost cost him the only true friend he had in the world. He would make sure that Danny wanted for nothing. He owed him more than that. He owed him revenge.

When Sonia returned a couple of hours later, Jackson left her and called Joanne. They had a tip off that Chambers had surfaced in Dusseldorf, but his exact whereabouts were as of yet unknown. Fallon had vanished completely, but border controls at all the major U.S. and European ports were all on high alert, and Interpol were tracking all movements from the States.

Jackson returned to his hotel and managed a couple of hours sleep. His body ached and his head throbbed. There was a sense of doom washing over him. He needed his friend to recover for him to function properly, now he was merely freewheeling. His sleep ended with a loud knock on the door.

Jackson drew his weapon and checked the spy hole. It was Joanne. He let her in but when she turned to him, she had a troubled expression.

"What's up?"

"Sit down."

Jackson sat in the desk chair. "Is Danny OK?"

Joanne nodded. "Yes, Mr Hughes is doing well."

"So what's with the dramatic entrance?"

Joanne stared intensely at him. "Fallon has surfaced."

"Where?"

"England." She added.

"South East England to be exact. CCTV picked him up at South Bermondsey Station, but lost him shortly afterwards"

Jackson heart raced and his eyes widened as the realisation of what she was telling him. "What? What are you telling me?"

Joanne looked at him intensely. "We think he's after your family. You have to warn them before he catches up to them."

Jackson snatched up his phone and dialled Dave's number. It rang and rang, but no answer. He dialled it again, still no answer. Panic was beginning to set in.

"I need to get home now

Joanne stood and headed towards the door. "I will get us a flight. Compose yourself and meet me downstairs when you are ready."

Jackson's head was spinning. He dialled Dave's number again, as before it rang on. He packed his Sig and spare rounds. Everything else could wait. He locked up and headed down the stairs, taking them three at a time. By the time he had reached the lobby, Joanne and Max were waiting by reception.

"The hotel will keep your room on, but we do have to hurry."

"I have pulled some strings and we have three diplomatic seats on tonight's flight to Heathrow. I have arranged a diplomatic pouch to be sent with us".

She pointed at Jackson's bulging waistband.

"I will have that weapon please."

They got into a waiting car and Jackson handed over his Sig and spare magazines. He felt naked and very vulnerable without a weapon.

Joanne saw his troubled look.

"It's the only way we can get them into the country in such short notice. Don't worry, I promise you will get them back when we get there."

Jackson tried Dave's phone again, still no answer.

"I will arrange with Chief Superintendent Charlton to track down your family and ex colleague. He will inform us when they have been located."

This was no comfort to Jackson. He knew how much Charlton despised him. Would he really make every effort to find them? Probably wasn't worth the paperwork to him.

Rushed through security and taken to the priority lounge. They boarded into the first class section. Jackson spent the entire flight in deep thought. While they were in the air, there was no contact with Dave or anyone for that matter. Jackson's frustration was building. He could not sleep or think about anything else. They touched down and rushed off into the diplomatic arrivals hub.

They travelled as an FBI delegation party, and were subject to very little scrutiny as the delegate from the U.S. Embassy welcomed them and escorted them out into a side exit area and shepherded into two large black Range Rovers. Joanne handed him back his weapon.

Jackson tried Dave's number, while Joanne called Charlton for an update. Jackson still had no luck. Jackson heard Joanne demand to speak to the Home Secretary. As predicted, Charlton was dragging his feet. When she had hung up, she turned to him.

"I have the Home Secretary calling me back, but I fear we won't be waiting for back up?"

Jackson scowled. "Fuck that. Just get me to his flat."

He gave her the address and she instructed the driver to make speed.

Dave's flat was part of large complex, split over three floors and four entrances, servicing six apartments each. They were large and well maintained and clean. Dave was a massive Millwall FC fan, and this apartment was only a short stroll from 'The Den', Millwall FC's home ground.

As they pulled up into the numbered carpark, Jackson noticed that Dave's black and red Ford Focus ST was still in its allotted space. Joanne handed him his weapon and he threw the door open, not waiting to close it, he bolted to the second entrance from the right.

Taking the stairs three at a time, Jackson scaled the six flights easily. He stopped in horror as he came face to face with Dave's front door. The lock had been prised open and shards of wood and metal lay scattered.

Max and Joanne finally caught up with him. Weapon drawn, he eased the door gently and entered the gloomy hallway. There were four doorways in front of him. To his immediate left was the kitchen. It was small, but functional, with all the modern appliances a single man would collect. It was empty. Next door was the main bedroom to the right.

Jackson eased the door open. The curtains were drawn and the room was dark. Only the glow from behind him cast any light. Dave was a minimalist kind of guy, he preferred space over possessions. The bedroom was also empty. The next door was also on the right. That was also a bedroom, a lot smaller than the master, but still sizeable. This room had all the hallmarks of female occupants. Hairbrushes, make up, scattered clothes and the faint aroma of perfume. This room was also empty.

Last door on the left was the lounge. Jackson stood to the side to let Max cover the other side of the room. He turned the handle gently and the door moved silently. The same unmistakeable metallic smell hit him, blood. Jackson signalled a count of three with his fingers. On three, they all burst into the room weapons at the ready. The sight that greeted them was straight out of a horror movie.

Tied to a dining chair sat Dave. He was naked. His throat, severed so deeply that only his spinal cord attached his head to the rest of his body. The Hyoid bone severed, causing the head to loll backwards. Nails pinned Dave's hands to his knees. Everything coated in a thick congealing blood shroud. The smell of blood mixed with faeces made them gag, it was overpowering. Jackson looked at the others. They stood transfixed to the macabre vision.

Joanne left to call it in as Jackson and Max checked the body out for any clues. When Max moved to the front of the corpse, he gasped in horror. Jackson joined him and saw what had made Max gasp. Dave's testicles were missing from their intended location.

Instead, someone had stuffed them into Dave's mouth, frozen into a scream. Jackson looked away, trying to block out the savagery he was witnessing. Jackson checked the rest of the room and it was empty but something caught his eye. It was the mirror.

The large mirror that occupied three quarters of the far wall had something in the bottom left corner, written in pink lipstick, Ellie's pink lipstick. Jackson moved closer to read it.

Eye for an Eye Jackie.

The tears welled in Jackson's eyes. His mind raced with different scenarios, all of which were too horrible to contemplate. Below the mirror was a small black and chrome glass table. On the table was a glass bowl with smokes glass pebbles. Next to that was Dave's mobile phone wrapped in a piece of lined paper.

Max handed him a pair of latex gloves and he squeezed his large hands into them before picking the phone up. He unravelled the paper and opened it up. Written in the same pink lipstick were the words, 'Photo Gallery'

Jackson woke the phone from its standby mode and found the photo gallery. There were only two pictures available. Jackson opened the first image.

Standing in front of the mirror was Sarah, gagged and looking dishevelled, her pink blouse, torn down to reveal her cleavage. Her eyes darkened by heavily mascara-laden tears. Fallon's face protruded from her right shoulder. His ghoulish grin completed the sinister picture.

The next picture was a copy of the first, with one exception. This time Sarah was holding a piece of paper and the image flipped. Jackson struggled to read the scrawl, but eventually deciphered it.

Plas Road Allotments Holyhead
Midnight Come alone or they are dead.
F

Jackson sent the image to his phone and shut it down. Joanne returned and told them that Special Branch were taking over the scene and they were to leave the scene as they found it. Jackson put Dave's phone in his pocket and left the room. The rage was eating away at him now. He was going to kill this man, but not until he made him pay for everything.

They waited outside the apartment until officers arrived. Jackson recognised two Scene Of Crime Officers from his time with CID. They nodded to him as they passed.

Joanne pulled the lead officer to one side and briefed him on the scene he was about to enter. Jackson could see the man visible turn white at the mere thought of what lay behind the door.

"The police want to interview us all when SOCO are finished here."

Jackson pulled her to one side. "I can't stay. Fallon has my girls."

Joanne looked puzzled. "How do you know that?"

Jackson told her about the phone and the images, alongside the message.

"Well the police will mobilise when they see the phone. Let them handle this Jackson."

Jackson pulled the phone out of his pocket and covertly showed her.

Joanne's eyes widened. "You took evidence from a crime scene. Are you insane?"

"I can't let the police swarm all over this like a ham-fisted child. They will get them killed for sure. I need to do this myself. He wants me and me alone, so he'll get me."

"I'm coming with you then."

Jackson shook his head. "You can't. If they think you fled the scene, they will scour every CCTV camera for you. They don't know my involvement. I need you to head Charlton off, hopefully I will get to him before they suss I was here."

Joanne nodded eventually.

"I will need one of the cars though."

Joanne followed him down the stairs to the parked Range Rovers. She signalled for one of the drivers to get out and took the keys from him.

"This is U.S. property. Try to bring it back in one piece."

She handed him the keys. She also gave him a hands free earpiece for his phone and a small disc about the size of a quarter.

"This has a GPS tracker inside. If it looks like he is getting the better of you, or he is going to get away, put this on him and we will be able to track him."

Jackson leaned forward and gave Joanne a light kiss on the lips. Joanne's hand gently touched his face.

"Thank you."

Joanne smiled at him warmly. "Just come back to me alive. I need you."

Jackson smiled. She was beginning to get under his skin, but he had to push all that from his mind. Fallon was his prey, and he would stop at nothing to get his girls back and bury the bastard.

Jackson fired up the Range Rover and with a small wave headed off toward Old Kent Road and the M40. Traffic was remarkably light for the time of day and he reached the M40 in a decent fifty minutes. Once on the M40 he could put his foot down. He stuck to 80 mph because he did not want to get pulled over by a traffic cop, they tended to let a slight speed slide if you drove sensibly. He wanted to get there long before time, to recce the area before playing his hand.

He checked his weapon was loaded correctly and the two spare magazines were full.

In the glove compartment, he found a plain black baseball cap and a pair of tinted driving glasses. He synchronised Dave's phone to the car's on-board computer and scrolled through the contacts. Nothing jumped out at him. He had hoped that Fallon would have put his number in there to taunt him. He scrolled past and then stopped.

Next, he checked the call lists. Dave had called very few people in the last three days. Jackson saw Sarah's number and his own. There were calls to a Chinese take-away and a local Dominos, other than that it, nothing. He checked the incoming calls. There were six missed calls, all from Jackson himself and two from Sarah. Then he stopped as two untagged numbers sat nestled between.

According to the phone's log, they called Dave yesterday around midday and two. Jackson called Joanne giving her the numbers. He was hopeful that they could get a fix on them if they called anyone before he got there. They can at least ping the mast used to connect them.

Jackson reached Junction 20 and turned off onto the M56. After ten minutes, his phone rang. Joanne told him that they had a basic location on both numbers. The first number connected half an hour ago in the Croydon area. Jackson discarded that one. The other number connected six minutes ago from a mast in Trearddur Bay.

"That must be him."

She agreed to have the phone traced and would keep him posted if it moves.

The M56 gave way to the North Wales Expressway and over the Pont Britannia Bridge. Jackson's phone rang it was Joanne.

"He's on the move." She said, straight down to business.

"Which way?"

"He popped up on our screen just outside Holyhead heading north."

Jackson accelerated along the A55 into Holyhead. He could only be a short distance behind him. He passed through Holyhead, passed an ASDA, and a McDonalds. At the Kingsland roundabout, he took Kingsland road towards the west of town. The allotments were only a quarter of a mile away.

He turned off before Plas Road and ran parallel with it, until he reached a cemetery. Across the road from the cemetery was a disused factory. Jackson reversed the car into the gateway and got out.

He dialled Joanne's number as he walked into the cemetery. Joanne told him that they had his position and Fallon was still a mile out. Jackson circled north and approached from the left of the allotments, hurrying past row upon row of headstones in various degrees of weathering. The cemetery was vast and he was out of breath by the time he reached the far wall. He scaled it and dropped down into a small wooded area, keeping Joanne in his ear as he crossed the low scrubbed field to the back of the allotments, taking care stay out of sight from the house nestled in a small copse.

"Fallon is at the allotments." Joanne said, breaking the silence.

"Okay, got it."

Now was the time for complete concentration. Any mistakes now would have serious consequences for Sarah and Ellie. He wanted Fallon dead, but not at any cost. He switched his phone off. Joanne did not need to be privy to what he was about to do. The less she knew the better. He was about to commit murder. He did not want her to be an accomplice.

The allotment wall was about six feet high and topped with three lines of basic barbed wire. Jackson found a dozen discarded bags of cuttings and used those to hoist himself level with the top. Using his Jacket to counter the barbs, he swung a leg over and cleared the barbed wire. The looming sunset was beginning to rob him of the natural light. Thankfully, he had emerged behind a tall row of Runner Beans.

Jackson drew his Sig and checked the chamber to make sure the round was sitting correctly. Scanning the area through the intertwined branches of the beans, Jackson saw that the plots were nearly all deserted. He pushed out from his cover and crossed a patch of strawberries. He reached a small shed, but it was locked and in complete darkness. He straddled to his right, checking every structure as he made his way towards the main access road that dissected the two halves of the plots. Halfway up the dirt road, Jackson could see a Toyota Hilux parked side on, blocking the road from the main gate. Fallon had barricaded himself in, he thought to himself.

Keeping low, Jackson continued to circle right, keeping the Hilux in sight. A light caught his eye about thirty yards in front of him to the left. Three sheds in a row all had their lights on, the dull glow making the outside area appear darker. With darkness descending upon him quickly, he needed to check out the rest of the allotment. It took him fifteen agonising minutes to check the right half of the plots. They were all clear. Fallon had to be on the left hand side. He would have a good vantage point of the entrance and the surrounding sheds.

Jackson crossed the road quickly and took cover behind a greenhouse about ten yards from the sheds. As Jackson stretched his neck to get a view of the side, the glass in front of him erupted, scattering shards of green glass all over him. Jackson dived to his left as more rounds obliterated the greenhouse.

"That you Jackie Boy?"

"I swear you are tenacious, I'll give you that."

"You wanted me, Fallon? Well I'm here. Let the girls go and you can have me."

"You think I'm going to make it that easy for you? I think not laddie."

Jackson tried to crawl to the next shed, but the ground in front of him churned as the rounds hit so Jackson retreated.

Jackson moved to the other side of the greenhouse.

"Let's settle this properly. Let the women go, they aren't part of this."

"You should have thought of that before you killed my sister. Now you will know what it's like to lose those you love."

Jackson leaned out a fraction and a round thudded against the frame of the greenhouse. Jackson had enough time to see the small flash from the bed of the Hilux.

Jackson swung his hand around the corner and fired off three rounds in Fallon's direction. In a flash, he was up and sprinting left. Rounds smacked into the ground behind him, then stopped. Fallon's magazine was empty. Taking this opportunity, Jackson weaved across a cabbage patch and slid behind one of the lit sheds.

Lifting his head, he peered into the shed. Its small dull bulb gave little light, but enough to tell him that it was empty apart from an array of gardening tools and pots. A round flew into the side of the shed and buried itself three inches from Jackson's head.

Ducking back down, he crawled between the first and second sheds. The back of the Hilux was just visible from the corner.

"Sarah!" Jackson called out. "Ellie!"

More rounds created a hole in the side of the first shed and Jackson could see more of the Hilux's rear. Two more rounds found the hole but missed him by inches. Jackson returned fire, throwing himself down the side of the second shed. This one was more substantial than the first. Corrugated steel was the material of choice, offering Jackson more protection. Jackson called out again, still getting no response.

He lifted his head and peered through the window but ducked back down quickly as the window shattered as a bullet passed through. Diving backwards, he brought the Sig up to the aim as the door burst open and a figure emerged. Jackson let two rounds go.

The first missed its mark, but the second found home. The figure staggered backwards but did not fall. The figure let off three wild shots; one struck Jackson in the thigh. Pain seared through him as the round buried itself into the thick muscle.

Jackson fired again this time his aim was true. Three rounds landed square into the assailant's face, splitting it open like a ripe melon. The spray covered the broken window with blood and brain matter as the man dropped. Jackson crawled over him and into the shed. Now it was empty again.

The corrugated sheeting suddenly peppered with holes as Fallon switched to automatic, emptying the remainder of his clip into the structure. Once Fallon had stopped shooting, Jackson backed out of the shed.

He was about to stand when a round grazed his back. Instinctively he dropped away from the impact, seeing another man looming out of the tall trees. Jackson fired and emptied his clip at the target, dropping the man to his knees. Jackson jumped up and dived at the figure, ploughing into him shoulder first. Raining blows into the man's head as they hit the ground. The man did not move again, he was clearly dead.

Jackson pushed the dead man away and dragged his weary body towards the third shed. He was losing a lot of blood from his leg. Tearing his T-Shirt and shredding it, he made a makeshift bandage, covering the wound as best he could. The cold air on his chest brought him back to his senses.

"Are you dead yet?"

"Come and find out Fallon."

"No thanks Jackie, but if you stick your head out, I'll take away your pain."

"You don't know what pain is Fallon. But you will when I cut your balls off."

"Oh you liked that? I figured you'd appreciate the gesture."

Jackson lifted himself up and leaned against the third shed. Easing himself around to its side, he inserted a fresh magazine and returned the slider forward. More rounds hit the gap and forced him to move around the other way. As his face passed the window, he saw them. His jaw dropped and his eyes glazed.

Lying on the floor of the shed were Sarah and Ellie. Gagged and bound. Their lifeless eyes stared up at the roof. The wounds in their heads had ceased bleeding as death washed over them.

Jackson propped against the shell to stop himself from falling. Rage took over. The red mist filled his eyes and he rounded the corner firing wildly. All control had vanished and his feral instincts took over.

Fallon was climbing into the cab as the rounds twanged into the door. As he fired the big flatbed up, he pushed his

.357 through the smashed window and returned fire, hitting Jackson high up in his chest, sending him crashing backwards.

More rounds hit the Hilux from somewhere behind Jackson. Fallon put the truck into a skidded turn and sped through the allotment's exit. Once again, Fallon was gone.

Jackson's head was spinning. The faces of his daughter and wife flooded into his mind as his surroundings went dark. He looked up and saw Max bending down to him, and then he passed out.

Chapter 24

Say Goodbye

The light burned Jackson's blurred vision as he came to. Only the pain in his chest surpassed the pain in his head. He remembered being shot. He remembered falling. Then he remembered what happened before that.

The pain moved from his head to his heart. They were gone. Fallon had taken everything he ever cared about, ripped his heart out and pinned it to his chest. Anger welled up in him again, he tried to sit up but was halted. He was handcuffed to a hospital bed for the second time.

Looking around he spotted Joanne standing behind the door talking to someone out of sight. Locked in heated debate, she gesticulated wildly. As she turned, she looked straight at him, raising a hand before entering alone. Her worried, but warm smile returned as she looked at him.

"How are you feeling?" She asked, but then raised her hand in apology. "Sorry stupid question, forgive me."

"How long have I been out?"

"You were in intensive care for a few days. They moved you here yesterday."

Jackson raised his cuffed wrist and rattled the metal against the side of his bed. He did not have to say anything.

"Chief Superintendent Charlton wants to know why you were running around Anglesey with an illegal handgun, engaging in a firefight that claimed the lives of four people. He has requested you be detained until a full enquiry is made."

Jackson sat back exhausted.

"He's a prick. If he had done his job, my family would still be alive. The blood is on his hands. He might as well have held the gun himself."

Joanne put a hand on his shoulder to calm him down. "You can't stress yourself. The doctor says you need full rest. You have had a major injury and will be laid up for at least a week."

"A week?" he said angrily.

"I'm not staying in this shit-hole for a day. Get me out of here."

"I can't. This is their show. We are spectators remember."

"Fallon is out there free as a bird Joanne."

"I know that Jax, but my hands are tied. It's not as if I..."

She stopped mid-sentence and hurried out of the door. Jackson laid back. How could he have let this happen? He had lost his wife and child. He had lost a very good friend and almost lost his best friend. Two people who trusted him were missing. He pressed the morphine dispenser and a wave of warmth washed over him, like lying on a sunny beach as the warm surf washed slowly over his body. He lost consciousness again.

When he woke, Joanne was sitting in the chair to his right.

"Hey there sleepy head." She said softly when she saw him looking at her.

"Hey."

He tried to sit up again, only this time he was unobstructed. The handcuffs were gone. Jackson looked at his wrist and then at Joanne.

"What the hell?"

"The Home Secretary has allowed us to extradite you to the states, to face weapons charges. You are now in my custody and will return to the States once you are fit to travel. I have assured him that you are not a flight risk and pose no threat to the public. He agrees that your actions in Holyhead were self-defence and is willing to waiver the weapons charge."

Jackson looked amazed. He could not believe the lengths this woman has gone to to help him over the last few weeks, but the cloud in his head simply would not pass.

"I can't leave yet. Fallon is still out there and I have a wife and daughter to bury. I have to be there for them."

Joanne stood and sat on the bed beside him, putting a hand on his.

"I know. I have arranged the funeral to be in your native Newcastle and the bodies moved there immediately. As soon as the doctor has assessed you, he will release you into my custody."

"And Fallon?"

"Fallon is a ghost Jax. Every time we get close, he vanishes. He will surface, and when he does, we will have him. But until then, the further away from here you are, the safer you are."

Jackson was about to protest, when she pushed him back down onto the bed.

"Please trust me Jackson. You owe me that much. Danny is alive and needs you by his side. Concentrate on the living. Killing yourself chasing ghosts won't bring them back."

She stood leaned forward and kissed him on the forehead.

"I need you by my side too."

She left the room without looking back.

The doctor entered the room. He was a middle-aged man with a thick neck. The fat rolled over his blue shirt collar and his face reminded him of a St. Bernard. His mouth drooped at the sides and his hooded eyes shadowed by the strip lighting. His white coat barely stretched over his ample stomach.

He shuffled over and picked up the chart attached to the foot of Jackson's bed. When he looked up, he smiled. "Hi there Mr Shaw,"

His voice was deep and gravelled. He had a slight foreign accent, but Jackson just could not place it.

"I am Doctor Lejeune. I need to take some vitals and bloods, and then we can get you out of here. Your friend is very keen to discharge you, but I need to assess you first. Is that OK?"

Jackson lifted his hand. "Hey you're the boss doc."

They took his blood pressure. They took his blood. They took his temperature. They looked into his eyes and his ears. They made him pee in a jar. They flexed his joints and checked his dressings. After hours of prodding and pricking, Doctor Lejeune returned with a wheelchair.

"Right Mr Shaw, I think we are done. I am discharging you into Miss Phillips's care. Take these for the pain."

He handed Jackson a box of morphine tablets. "They are slow release so only one every evening before bed."

Jackson thanked him and between them, they managed to ease him into the wheelchair. He felt very naked in the standard issue hospital gown. He was even more aware as Joanne entered the room and immediately looked him up and down.

"Very fetching." She said smiling at his embarrassment. "I have your clothes, let's get you dressed."

Joanne removed his gown. Her gaze lingered on his body a fraction longer than a mere glance. Jackson looked at her as she handed him his underwear. He slipped on the boxers and lifted his arms as she pushed him into a fresh T-shirt. The musky smell of her perfume lingered and the feel of her hair on his face felt good.

He struggled into loose sweatpants and slippers. Once he was decent, she wheeled him to the door.

"Let's get outta here eh?"

They travelled by train to Newcastle Central Station. The doctor had refused to let him fly for at least twenty-four hours. A car met them outside the station and whisked them away to the Copthorne Hotel on Newcastle's famous Quayside. Jackson's room was spacious and had a lovely view of the River Tyne and its famous Tyne Bridge, but despite this being the place he grew up in, he did not feel at home.

The next forty-eight hours consisted of meetings with Sarah's sister Christine and her cousin. The funeral was to be a joint cremation at the Westgate Road Crematorium followed by a wake at the family's pub in the centre of the town. They tried to be sympathetic to his grief, but deep down Jackson knew that they secretly blamed him for everything. The animosity bubbled below the surface of the façade of solidarity.

The Funeral was a grey affair. The rain had arrived on cue and the wind had a bite that only northeast people knew well. Joanne stayed by Jackson's side throughout the whole proceedings, never straying further than three feet from him. Jackson saw people who he either had not seen for years, and those he had never met.

The service readings were simple and humanist. The music was a mixture of Sarah's love for Bon Jovi and Ellie's 'Girl Crush' Adele. Jackson could feel the dark clouds returning to his mind as the two coffins disappeared behind the curtains for the last time.

"I will kill him." He whispered to the two girls. "He will pay, if it takes me a lifetime. I promise you both that."

Joanne looked down at him. She must have heard it, because she gave his shoulder a light squeeze.

The wake was busy. People came and went. Jackson found the pain in his leg diminishing as the alcohol took effect. Sarah's sister made a point of distancing herself from him and he felt as uncomfortable as he could possibly be.

When the volume of people thinned out, Jackson noticed a tall figure standing at the bar. His thin stature and long 'beak-like' nose was unmistakeable from where he was standing.

Chief Superintendent Gordon Charlton was in full dress uniform and looked out of place amongst the civilians. Jackson's mood darkened and he dragged his battered frame over to him. Charlton cringed as he saw him approaching. Charlton extended his hand to Jackson.

"I am so sorry for your loss." His monotone voice held no emotion or sincerity.

Without hesitation, Jackson threw a venomous straight right, catching Charlton flush on his large nose, breaking it instantly. Charlton staggered backwards and slumped against the bar and down the wooden panelled wall behind him. Several glasses of various drinks followed him showering him with glass and alcohol.

"Fuck you Charlton. They are all dead because of you."

Joanne tried to pull him away, but he shrugged her off. He grabbed Charlton by his lapels and dragged him towards him, hitting him again with even more force. Charlton's face was a mask of blood and snot.

"Have you lost your mind Shaw?" Charlton said, desperately trying to breathe through the river of blood cascading down his throat.

"I had no authority to launch a major search operation. You of all people should know that Shaw. People have to be missing twenty-four hours before we can launch a search."

Jackson went to hit him again but instead merely pushed him back on his backside.

"If you weren't so full of yourself those people would be still alive. I am going to bury you Charlton. You won't wriggle your way out of this, I promise you."

Charlton's laboured breathing and his anger began to escalate into a guttural growl.

"I will have you arrested for this Shaw. You just assaulted a senior police officer in front of dozens of witnesses. You're finished."

Jackson lunged to grab Charlton again, but Joanne stepped between, leaning down to look at Charlton.

"I don't see it that way Chief Superintendent. I have informed the Home Secretary of your deliberate negligence in the deaths of Sarah and Ellie Shaw, not to mention the death of a fellow officer, specifically Detective Sergeant David Forster." Joanne said in a voice so cold it sent a chill through Jackson.

"Mr Home secretary agrees with me that your actions were criminal in their intent and you are to face charges of culpable manslaughter."

Joanne leaned closer to Charlton, who had paled significantly. "So you see Gordon. It's you who are finished."

She stood and guided Jackson through the gathered spectators, who had heard the whole episode.

The group parted and they passed through. Jackson turned his head and looked at Christine as they passed by. They locked eyes. Christine's look of hatred, replaced with warmth. They exchanged a knowing nod then a gentle hug.

"I am sorry Jax." Christine whispered. "I had no idea."

Jackson pulled away and looked into her eyes. "Take care of yourself Chris."

His look darkened and he fixed her with a steely stare. "They will pay." He added, before turning to look at Charlton, still on the floor. "They will all pay."

Turning to Joanne, who was still watching him intently, Jackson hooked an arm through hers.

"Let's go home." He said softly.

"Yours or mine?"

"You choose." He replied.

With that they pushed through the doors and into the cold light of day.

Chapter 25

The hunt

Jackson and Joanne returned to Los Angeles. The Deputy Director granted her special dispensation to fast track Jackson into her department as an overseas operative. He would never be officially on the FBI's books, but he had earned the badge and the powers of arrest.

Jackson spent two weeks in a medical facility. Physiotherapy and exercises were strenuous but effective. Jackson's strength returned and he began to feel better. Although he just couldn't shake the dark feelings that haunted his sleep.

Joanne moved him into a rented apartment in the city, to continue his convalescence. He used the next two weeks to increase his fitness. Joanne set up a network link to the FBI mainframe and allowed him to continue his search for Fallon and Catalina, provided he worked with her at the same time.

He had retrieved the cash from the hotel. He gave the bulk to Sonia to help Danny's rehabilitation, keeping $2 million for himself. Over $10 million would keep them comfortable and safe. He opened two Swiss bank accounts in Christine and Catalina's names and deposited $500,000 in each. If Catalina ever surfaced, she would be granted citizenship and a future.

They gave Danny and his family new identities within the WITSEC programme. Jackson promised to never see them again, but he was happy knowing that they still had their covert email system to keep in touch. He would keep that to himself. He just wasn't ready to give up the only family he had left.

Jackson stood at the window to his apartment. His thoughts drifted to his loss, as they always did when he was alone. The self-blame was just too hard to shake off.

A knock at the door broke him from his trance. He peered through the spyhole to see Joanne standing there.

Jackson let her in and immediately saw a troubled expression.

"What's wrong?"

Joanne stood staring into space.

"Joanne. What is it?"

"You were right?" She said, slowly sitting on the small grey sofa. The small living space was basically furnished. A TV and a small coffee table were the only items that distinguished this space from the bed and small kitchenette.

"Right about what?"

Joanne put her head in her hands. "There are more people involved in this than we thought."

"Do you have any names?"

Joanne shook her head. "Not yet, but Rourke has been released and has vanished."

Jackson's anger boiled over.

"Who the fuck released him?"

"The DA signed him over to the CIA in return for his testimony. He's been granted immunity Jax."

Jackson slammed his fist into the wall. "He's not fucking immune from me."

"You have to calm down. I will see what I can find out."

Jackson calmed slightly and sat next to her.

"What was on that disk Joanne?"

Joanne shook her head slowly. Jackson could see the conflict in her face. There was something she wasn't telling him, more bad news probably. Jackson had not pressed her on the subject since he gave her the file, but now there seems to be more to this whole situation.

"What was on the disk?" He asked again.

Joanne sighed deeply. "I can't tell you Jax."

Jackson was incensed. "Why the fuck not? That disk has caused me more pain than anything before."

"I am off the case Jax. I can't go anywhere near it. It's the Director's call. If I want to keep my job that is."

Jackson looked at her blankly.

"How high does this thing go?"

"High."

"How high?"

Joanne looked pale and exhausted. "Almost to the top. I'm afraid for our safety Jackson. This goes beyond where we thought.

"So they are covering this up?"

Joanne shrugged her shoulders. "Someone is."

"They can't get away with this. I busted my balls to bring this to you. Are you saying they already knew what was on it?"

Joanne began to sob uncontrollably. Jackson placed an arm around her shoulders and guided her into his chest. Her tears flowed like a torrent. This woman has been through hell and back.

"Listen to me. We can't let them get away with this."

Joanne looked up, her mascara had run all down her cheeks and she looked almost Gothic.

"There's nothing I can do. All my communications are monitored and all of my access privileges have been downgraded. I'm dead in the water."

Jackson looked at his computer and then back to Joanne.

"Can you get a copy of the inventory at the crime scene in London?"

Joanne looked puzzled.

"There's an envelope there from me somewhere in that flat. If I know Dave as I do, he would have hidden it safely. So if it isn't in the inventory, then he has stashed it somewhere inside the flat."

Joanne seemed to brighten.

"I will get on it."

Jackson nodded. "In the meantime, could I borrow Karl."

"I can't let you grill him. He knows nothing. He was not there when I opened the file."

Jackson frowned. "So you do know what is on it?"

Joanne dropped her head. "I only saw it briefly Jackson, you have to believe me. No sooner had I opened it, than Richard marched in and took my whole laptop away. I was out of the loop from that moment on. Then they told me to forget it and move on to the next assignment."

Jackson's anger rose again.

"I need Karl to get me into the mainframe. I can do the rest on my own."

Joanne stood up angrily. "Forget it Jax. I am not letting Karl do anything to jeopardize his career or worse."

"He just needs to show me how to get in. I will take the risks. I have nothing else to lose."

Joanne sat back down. "Okay, I will see what I can do. But know this. If you get caught, then I will personally bury you myself. You hear me mister?"

"I got it."

Joanne stood and left.

Jackson went to the store and bought another two Pay-As-You-Go phones. He opened his computer and opened the email and saved a message giving Danny the new numbers and the latest revelation.

He knew he should keep Danny as far away from this as possible, but Danny had almost paid for this with his life. He owed it to the big man to keep him informed, in case he had to run. He didn't trust the WITSEC program now that higher powers were involved. Caution was the key here. He had to make it look like they were out of the loop.

He closed the email down and sat staring at the screen, when a knock at his door broke his trance.

Karl stepped in when Jackson opened the door. Karl grinned at him.

"You need my assistance I hear."

Jackson patted him on the shoulder. "I sure do mate."

Jackson filled Karl in on his requirements. Karl just nodded and rubbed his hands. Jackson made coffee while Karl got to work. He heard lots of blowing of cheeks and cursing, but after a couple of hours and 3 coffees, he sat back triumphantly.

"All done Jax."

Jackson sat next to him.

"Okay go slowly, I am a novice here."

Karl smirked at him before cracking his knuckles and running Jackson through the programs and the security bypasses. Most of it might as well have been in Greek, but Jackson got the basics and the protocols he would have to follow to remain undetected.

Jackson got Karl to patch into the LAPD mainframe and set up an alert email. This would ping his phone whenever they got a hit on Fallon, Rourke or Catalina.

Next he got Karl to do the same with Interpol adding Chambers to the list. He also got Karl to direct him to all the information he could on Chambers and his personal life. There must be a link and he would find out what that was.

Jackson spent the next three days trawling through page after page of useless information. Interpol had files on both Chambers and the Fallon family. They connected them to two bombings and a host of unexplained disappearances.

Fallon was heavily into horse racing and owned half a share in a prize racehorse. Jackson figured Chambers owned the other half.

Interpol had wire taps and and surveillance on Chambers stretching back months. He made a promise to himself to kill this man too.

Jackson trawled through the wiretaps for clues. Mostly they were small telephone conversations between Chambers and various different people. The majority of them were inconsequential, but finally he came across one that pricked his attention.

The soundbite was only two minutes long, but Chambers mentioned to an unknown person, that he had secured communications and contact in Mexico. Chambers gave the man on the other end a name and a contact number. This was a breakthrough. He knew Interpol would no doubt investigate that number too. So he tagged the name and number into his flag.

He called Joanne and asked her to come over.

About an hour later Joanne came over. Jackson filled her in on what he had found. She was furious that he had coerced Karl into letting him spy on the very security she worked to protect. But he eventually convinced her that his intentions would in no way lead back to her or her department.

He handed Joanne one of the burners.

"I want to know everything you find out. I am going to look for Catalina, and I need credentials to be able to get results. I know I am asking a lot, but can you push them through."

"I don't think I can. My boss has agreed to let you work for us, but he is reluctant to let you loose on your own."

Jackson had to concede this. He wouldn't have let him either.

"Can you just try please? I need to find her before she ends up back in Mexico. If they get deported then they are dead and it's my fault."

Joanne looked at him warmly.

"We have arranged to be notified if she gets picked up. I really don't know what else you can do."

"I have to try at least. I need to know where she went once she left Sonia. It just doesn't make sense that she just ran away. She knew Sonia was her best chance to a life. Something must have happened to her."

Joanne nodded. "Okay I will push through some creds. They will only be temporary, but should get you into most police stations with little problem."

She turned to leave. "But know this. You start causing problems and I will revoke it and all the future plans and throw your ass in jail."

Jackson held a hand up and smiled. "You know me, I will be subtle."

She shook her head as she walked away.

"That's what I am afraid of."

Once Joanne returned with his temporary credentials, Jackson hired a car and drove to the Kansas City Police Headquarters on Minnesota Avenue, stopping overnight in Denver. It was a large red brick and concrete structure, facing a security bank. Probably the safest bank in the world Jackson thought. He walked into its lobby and approached the reception.

"Can I help you?" A uniformed woman asked. She was a solid looking black woman with hair tied back in a large bun. Her eyes were piercing and bright, but she had steel in her expression. Jackson would bet nobody messed with her. Efficient and tough, her nametag said Delores Patterson.

"Yes Ma'am." Jackson said, showing his credentials. "I am need to access CCTV archives for the area around the Holiday Inn off East 13th Street."

"Can I ask what this is in relation to?"

Jackson wasn't expecting any resistance, but he wasn't really up to speed with how things worked over here.

"I am investigating the disappearance of a witness."

Delores gave him a condescending look.

"What time scale are you after?"

"Three weeks ago. The whole week basically."

Delores told him to take a seat and someone would be down to assist him.

Jackson had expected a hive of activity, but very few people came or went. After an hour, a tall thin man approached him. He wasn't a uniformed officer; instead his ill-fitting brown jacket and trousers, paired with the tan shoes, made him look like an English teacher. He extended his hand as he approached and smiled. His brown teeth and odour gave away his smoking and coffee addictions.

"Lieutenant Dixon, Mr Shaw."

They shook.

"How can we help you? I've just got off the phone to the commissioner. He tells me that we have no knowledge of any witness being logged in the jurisdiction roster. Plus they have never heard of you either."

Jackson had to think quickly.

"I have just been assigned to this department. They asked me to look into their witness going missing. I think they were merely passing through when she absconded."

"I think this a test to see if I am any good at field work."

Jackson put on his most pathetic expression. The rookie, who has been given the run around to get him out of their hair.

Dixon smiled. He clearly got it.

"Let's take you over to the Control Centre and get you hooked up.

Jackson nodded his thanks and followed Dixon to his car. They drove for about ten minutes. Jackson was pleased to get out of the car. The smell of stale cigarettes made him gag. The Control Centre was part of a Municipal Office block, housing various civilian departments of law enforcement. Once they were safely inside the Centre, Jackson relayed his request to the receptionist. Dixon left him there promising to return when Jackson was done.

Jackson was escorted to a room with several computers in a row. It looked like a classroom. They all faced a large screen. Jackson sat at one of the terminals and waited.

After half an hour, the door opened and a short overweight man entered.

"Mr Shaw, I am Officer Maitland. I understand you need footage of the Downtown area. I have uploaded five blocks from your target areas. Unfortunately the footage is montaged together, so you will have to look at the big screen to see all the cameras simultaneously."

The large screen flickered to life and filled with dozens of images, all running together. Jackson saw the enormity of the task ahead.

"Can you tell me which camera is the one closest to the Holiday entrance?"

Maitland studied the codes and pointed to several squares to the bottom left of the big screen. Handing him a trackball remote to scroll the feeds, he left him to it.

Jackson pressed play and settled in for a long shift. Using the trackball to skip timeframes, he watched people fly past in a hurry, it was almost comical. Maitland returned with coffee and a stale sandwich from one of the Centre's vending machines.

Jackson scrolled forwards triple time. He doubted he would find anything. Another hour had passed when something caught his eye. He saw Sonia. She left the hotel alone and headed left. Jackson followed her until she vanished from one square and appeared into another one. She crossed four screens finally stopping at a shop and entered. After twenty minutes, she retraced her steps carrying two large grocery bags.

Jackson followed her into the hotel. A few minutes she reappeared. Her demeanor was now frantic, looking up and down the street, before returning back inside. Something was wrong.

Jackson returned the feed back to Sonia's first exit and concentrated on the hotel front. Five minutes after Sonia left, Catalina and Benito emerged with two men dressed in black. She was pulling him along. He was clearly unwilling to go. Jackson could see why. They were being marched out by the men and bundled into a large sedan. Jackson's blood went cold. Who were they? How did they know she was there?

Jackson paused at the image of the car and the two men. He checked several other angles. He found one that showed one of the men clearly. He zoomed in and left the room.

Finding Maitland in an office down the hall, he requested stills of the imagery he needed. The stills showed a man in his mid-forties. He was tall and broad. His short cropped black hair and sharp features clear in the shot.

The next shot was of the car. He caught a partial plate, it was a Texas plate.

BK1 H9

It was missing one or two digits, but it was a start.

Jackson downloaded the images to his phone and after thanking Maitland for his help and Dixon for his lift back to his car, he returned to L.A.

Jackson returned to his apartment the following day. He was exhausted, but invigorated by his progress. He called Joanne and arranged to meet her for lunch.

They met in Sam's Burger Bar. It was cheerful and plastic. He could tell Joanne was uncomfortable in these meagre surroundings.

Jackson relayed his findings in Kansas City. Joanne looked shocked.

"I don't get it. I thought you said Sonia was the only person who knew where they were."

Jackson frowned. "She was. Even I didn't know where she was."

"Did she call anyone?"

"She said she didn't. She paid cash for everything. Unless the hotel manager decided to check them out for using cash? But that means we have a bigger problem."

Joanne nodded. The gravity of what he was saying weighing her down.

"I will look into it."

Jackson's phone pinged. Jackson opened up the alert. They had a breakthrough.

"We have to go."

Jackson opened his laptop once they got back to his apartment. He fired through the security protocols and opened the alert. The file opened and a folder appeared. It contained a report from a wiretap entitled Phillipe and 3 wiretaps. The report mentioned the arrival of an Irishman and his subsequent transport into the U.S.

Jackson and Joanne looked at each other.

Jackson clicked onto the audio link. It fired up and they were treated to ten seconds worth of static before a voice hit the airwaves. It was Fallon.

"Frank my boy. Cheers for the taxi. I've posted my contacts to your device. The password is our horse. If you need to arrange anymore fundraising, then you can contact me from there."

Jackson opened another.

"Jimmy?"

"Frank, how are ye?"

"Concerned Jimmy."

"What's wrong?"

"Where's my money Jimmy?"

"It's on its way Frank. £200 k as agreed.

"Don't cross me Frank, don't forget, you would be in prison or worse if it wasn't for me."

"Frankie boy. Have I ever not kept me word?"

"Just so you know."

Jackson opened the last one.

"Jimmy."

"Yes?"

"Got my case, thanks."

"Didn't I say I would?"

"Yes well you can't blame me for being cautious."

"Indeed Frank, indeed. So what do you want?"

"I have a contact for you, to resume our little business venture. You interested?"

"I am always interested Frank. What you got?"

"I have a guy over in Colorado who wants to pick up where we left off. I think you know who we mean."

"Why you fiendish devil. Of course I do."

"Send me another £150 k and we are back in business."

"Okay I will have it sent to you."

"No, this time send it to me personally."

"You do know what I will do to you if you are crossing me Frank."

"I swear to you. This one is bigger than before. Ten times the profit."

"Sternstraße 67, 40479 Düsseldorf, Germany. I will give you the contact once it is there."

"Outstanding Frankie boy. Good to have you back son."

Jackson looked at Joanne.

"Guess I am going on my holidays."

Joanne was about to protest, but knew it was fruitless.

"I will arrange a contact to get you whatever you need. But please."

Jackson looked at her. "What?"

"I don't want to know what you did. As far as I am concerned, this is all on you."

Jackson guided her to the door.

"Just the way I like it."

Chapter 26

Six Weeks Later

Dusseldorf, Germany.

Frank Chambers exited the steel doors and emerged into the dark underground carpark. He shuffled past the tightly parked cars that had nestled together like suckling calves feeding from their mother. He came to a stop behind a silver Mercedes S-Class and popped the trunk, taking a large black leather briefcase from it. He opened it to reveal rows of bundled cash. Chambers stroked the cash with the gentle caress of love, before closing the lid and returning the trunk lid to its closed position.

Chambers stood for a moment and let out a content sigh. That was when Jackson emerged for the shadows, his Sig Sauer complete with suppressor aimed squarely at Chambers' forehead. Chambers' eyes widened in shock as his brain registered Jackson's face.

"Not pleased to see me Frank?" Jackson said. "I'm hurt."

"I had nothing to do with your family's deaths Jackson." Chambers said, his voice trembling with fear. "It was all Fallon. He is crazy. Please don't kill me." Chambers began to shake uncontrollably.

"Where is he Frank?"

"I don't know, I swear."

"You're lying, Frank; you know how I know you're lying?"

Chambers shook his head.

"I know you're lying, because we have been monitoring your emails and calls for the last month."

Jackson removed a black wallet and flipping it open. Chambers looked in horror as the letters appeared in front of him, FBI, Special International Counter Crime Division.

"That's right Frank. I have the weight of the United States of America behind me this time. I know you arranged his return to the U.S."

Jackson looked at the briefcase.

"I also know that is payment for serviced rendered. I need to know where he is Frank. I'm not fucking around here."

Chambers shuffled nervously. "I honestly don't know where he is Jackson. All I know is, he asked me to get him stateside and I arranged for him to return to Mexico and passage into the U.S. from there. After that I have no idea where he is."

Jackson eyed him suspiciously. He knew how easily Chambers had lied in the past. He was not going to make that mistake twice.

"You're lying again Frank."

Jackson moved closer. The barrel now only inches from Chambers' head.

"Now if you won't tell me where he is, I have to assume that you were in on everything Fallon has done. So last chance Chambers, where is Fallon?"

Chambers put the briefcase down and kicked it to Jackson.

Chambers voice crackled with fear as he struggled to contain the tears. "Here take it. It's all yours. Just let me go. I swear I'll disappear. You will never hear from me again. I will cut all ties with Fallon."

"Give me your phone too.".

Chambers looked nervously at him. "You can't do this Jackson. He won't believe it's me without the password. It won't do you any good."

"Give it to me and get on your knees Frank

Chambers pulled his phone out and handed it to Jackson. Slowly dropping to his knees, head bowed.

Jackson pocketed the phone and reached behind him, pulling out a yellow A4 manila envelope from his waistband. Jackson stared at the envelope for a brief second before handing it to Chambers.

"What's that?" Chambers asked, reluctant to take it.

"Just take it Frank."

Chambers took the envelope with a shaky hand, his eyes switching nervously between the envelope and the weapon in Jackson's hand.

"Open it Frank

Chambers pushed a fat finger into the gap and slid it along the flap, popping it open. He looked inside before removing its contents, three photographs and a folded piece of paper. Chambers looked at the pictures. He began to shake more violently as the realisation of who they were hit him. He looked up at Jackson who glared at him.

"Sarah was my wife. Ellie was my daughter and Dave was my friend. All killed by Fallon, who you are protecting with your password Frank."

Chambers looked down at the pictures.

"I'm sorry, but I can't betray him." He said, and then looked up at Jackson. A look of smug defiance washed over his face. "I guess the password and the trail dies with me if you shoot me."

Jackson steadied the Sig with both hands, concentrating his stare on Chambers' eyes.

"Open the note."

"What is this?" Chambers said, waving the paper like a fan.

"Just open it and you will see."

Chambers unfolded the paper, never taking his eyes off Jackson. After a few moments, he looked down at the words written on the paper. His eyes widened in horror as he stared at it. It read:

'Cantilever Child'

"Your racehorse right?"

"And your password."

Chambers looked up at him. The mask of terror etched into every feature of his face.

"No wait I-"

Chambers never finished his sentence. Jackson pulled the trigger once. The round tore through Chambers' forehead, erupting out of the back, sending blood and brain matter splattering over his Mercedes. Chambers rocked backwards, before slumping forward. On his knees head bowed as if in mock prayer. Chambers was dead.

Jackson holstered the Sig, before picking up the photographs and the note, putting them back into the envelope. He returned the envelope to his rear waistband before stooping and picking up the briefcase.

"Goodbye Frank." He said to the corpse kneeling in front of him.

"Oh yeah, and fuck you too."

Jackson walked calmly out of the parking area and up the ramp to the street, where a white taxi was waiting. He got into the back and placed the briefcase on his lap, rubbing his eyes. "One down, one to go." He whispered to himself.

"Where to?" The taxi driver asked in broken English.

"Airport mate," he replied. "No rush."

The driver started the engine, put the car in gear and drove Jackson off into the night, and onto his next hunt.

The End

Printed in Great Britain
by Amazon

81611722R00210